The Short Stories of Aphra Behn

Volume II

Aphra Behn was a prolific and well established writer but facts about her remain scant and difficult to confirm. What can safely be said though is that Aphra Behn is now regarded as a key English playwright and a major figure in Restoration theatre

Aphra was born into the rising tensions to the English Civil War. Obviously a time of much division and difficulty as the King and Parliament, and their respective forces, came ever closer to conflict.

There are claims she was a spy, that she travelled abroad, possibly as far as Surinam.

By 1664 her marriage was over (though by death or separation is not known but presumably the former as it occurred in the year of their marriage) and she now used Mrs Behn as her professional name.

Aphra now moved towards pursuing a more sustainable and substantial career and began work for the King's Company and the Duke's Company players as a scribe.

Previously her only writing had been poetry but now she would become a playwright. Her first, "The Forc'd Marriage", was staged in 1670, followed by "The Amorous Prince" (1671). After her third play, "The Dutch Lover", Aphra had a three year lull in her writing career. Again it is speculated that she went travelling again, possibly once again as a spy.

After this sojourn her writing moves towards comic works, which prove commercially more successful. Her most popular works included "The Rover" and "Love-Letters Between a Nobleman and His Sister" (1684–87).

With her growing reputation Aphra became friends with many of the most notable writers of the day. This is The Age of Dryden and his literary dominance.

From the mid 1680's Aphra's health began to decline. This was exacerbated by her continual state of debt and descent into poverty.

Aphra Behn died on April 16th 1689, and is buried in the East Cloister of Westminster Abbey. The inscription on her tombstone reads: "Here lies a Proof that Wit can never be Defence enough against Mortality." She was quoted as stating that she had led a "life dedicated to pleasure and poetry."

Index of Contents

The Unhappy Mistake; or, The Impious Vow Punish'd
Aphra Behn – A Short Biography
Aphra Behn – A Concise Bibliography

THE HISTORY OF THE NUN; OR, THE FAIR VOW-BREAKER

THE HISTORY OF THE NUN; OR, THE FAIR VOW-BREAKER

INTRODUCTION

In the Epistle Dedicatory to Antony Hammond, Esq., of Somersham-Place, prefacing that pathetic tragedy, The Fatal Marriage; or, The Innocent Adultery [1] (4to, 1694), Southerne writes: 'I took the Hint of the Tragical part of this Play from a Novel of Mrs. Behn's, call'd The Fair Vow-Breaker; you will forgive me for calling it a Hint, when you find I have little more than borrow'd the Question, how far such a Distress was to be carry'd, upon the Misfortune of a Woman's having innocently two Husbands, at the same time'.

In the many collected editions of Mrs. Behn's popular novels and histories, from the first, published under the auspices of Gildon in 1696, to the ninth (2 vols, 12mo, London, 1751), there appears, however, no such novel as The Fair Vow-Breaker, but on the other hand all contain The Nun; or, the Perjur'd Beauty. For over two hundred years then, critics, theatrical historians, bibliographers alike have laid down that The Fair Vow-Breaker is merely another title for The Nun; or, The Perjur'd Beauty, and that it is to this romance we must look for the source of Southerne's tragedy. The slight dissimilarity of name was truly of no great account. On the title-page of another novel we have The Fair Jilt; or, The History of Prince Tarquin and Miranda; on the half-title of the same The Fair Hypocrite; or, The Amours of Prince Tarquin and Miranda (12mo, 1688). And so Thomas Evans in the preface to his edition of Southerne (3 vols, 1774), writing the dramatist's life, says: 'the plot by the author's confession is taken from a novel of Mrs. Behn's called The Nun; or, The Fair Vow-Breaker'. All the modern writers have duly, but wrongly, accepted this; and Miss Charlotte E. Morgan in her monograph, The English Novel till 1749, informs us in more than one place that The Fair Vow-Breaker (12mo, 1689) was the name of the edition princeps of The Nun; or, The Perjur'd Beauty.

A crux, however, was soon apparent. Upon investigation it is obvious that the plot of The Fatal Marriage; or, The Innocent Adultery has simply nothing in common with The Nun; or, The Perjur'd Beauty. Mrs. Behn's Ardelia is a mere coquette who through her trifling with three different men is responsible for five deaths: her lovers', Elvira's, and her own. Isabella, Southerne's heroine, on the other hand, falls a sad victim to the machinations of Carlos, her wicked brother-in-law. She is virtuous and constant; Ardelia is a jade capable of heartless treachery. Both novel and play end tragically it is true, but from entirely different motives and in a dissimilar manner. There is no likeness between them.

Whence then did Southerne derive his plot, and what exactly did he mean by the statement that he owed 'the Hint of the Tragical part' of his drama to a novel of Mrs. Behn's?

Professor Paul Hamelius of Liège set out to solve the difficulty, and in a scholarly article (Modern Language Review, July, 1909), he marshals the facts and seeks a solution. 'Among her [Mrs. Behn's] collected novels'[2] he writes 'there is one entitled The Nun; or, The Perjur'd Beauty and Mr. Gosse has kindly informed me that the story is identical with The Nun; or, The Fair Vow-Breaker which appears in the editio princeps of 1689 (inaccessible to me).' Unfortunately he can find no analogy and is obliged to draw attention to other sources. He points to The Virgin Captive, the fifth story in Roger L'Estrange's The Spanish Decameron (1687). Again: there is the famous legend of the lovers of Teruel as dramatized in 1638 by Juan Perez de Montalvan, Los Amantes de Teruel. An earlier comedia exists on the same subject written by A. Rey de Artieda, 1581, and yet another play by Tirso de Molina, 1635, based on Artieda. Hamelius was obviously not satisfied with his researches, and with a half-suggestion that Southerne may have merely intended to pay a compliment to his 'literary friend Mrs. Behn,' his conclusion is that 'the question is naturally still open whether Southerne was not drawing from some more immediate source, possibly even from some lost version of the story by Mrs. Behn herself.'

In the course of my preparing the present edition of Mrs. Behn's complete works, Mr. Gosse, adding yet another to innumerable kindnesses and encouragements, entrusted me with a little volume[3] from his private library: The History of the Nun; or, The Fair Vow-Breaker (12mo, 1689, Licensed 22 October, 1688), and I soon found this to be the immediate source of Southerne's tragedy, a totally different novel from The Nun; or, The Perjur'd Beauty, and one, moreover, which has never till now been included in any edition of Mrs. Behn's works or, indeed, reprinted in any form. It were superfluous to compare novel and tragedy detail by detail. Many striking, many minor points are the same in each. In several instances the nomenclature has been preserved. The chief divergence is, of course, the main catastrophe. Mrs. Behn's execution could ill have been represented on the boards, and Southerne's heroine, the victim of villainies and intrigue, is, it must be confessed, an infinitely more pathetic figure than guilty Isabella in the romance.

The story of a man returning after long absence and finding his spouse (or betrothed) wedded to another, familiarized to the generality of modern readers by Tennyson's Enoch Arden, occurs in every shape and tongue. No. 69 of Les Cent Nouvelles Nouvelles is L'Honneste femme à Deux Maris.[4] A more famous exemplar we have in the Decameron, Day IV, Novella 8, whose rubric runs: 'Girolamo ama la Salvestra: va, costretto da' prieghi della madre, a Parigi: torna, e truovala maritata: entrale di nascoso in casa, e muorle allato; e portato in una chiesa, muore la Salvestra allata a lui.'

Scenes of the amusing underplot of The Fatal Marriage which contain some excellent comedy, Southerne took directly from The Night Walker; or, The Little Thief (printed as Fletcher's in 1640 and 'corrected by Shirley' in 1633 according to Herbert's license). The purgatorial farce may be traced to the Decameron, Day III, 8. 'Ferondo, mangiata certa polvere, è sotterrato per morto: e dall' abate, chi la moglie di lui si gode, tratto dalla sepoltura, è messo in prigione e fattogli credere, che egli è in purgatoro; e poi risuscitato . . .' It is the Feronde; ou, le Purgatoire of La Fontaine.

The Fatal Marriage; or, The Innocent Adultery long kept the stage.[5] On 2 December, 1757, Garrick's version, which omitting the comic relief weakens and considerably shortens the play, was produced at Drury Lane with himself as Biron and Mrs. Cibber as Isabella. The actual name of the tragedy, however, was not changed to Isabella till some years after. Mrs. Barry, the original Isabella, was acknowledged supreme in this tragedy, and our greatest actresses, Mrs. Porter, Mrs. Crawford, Miss Young, Mrs. Siddons, Miss O'Neill, have all triumphed in the rôle.

[Footnote 1: This has nothing to do with Scarron's novel, L' Innocent Adultère which translated was so popular in the 17th and 18th centuries. Bellmour carried it in his pocket when he went a-courting Laetitia, to the horror of old Fondlewife who discovered the tome, (The Old Batchelor, 1693), and Lydia Languish was partial to its perusal in 1775.]

[Footnote 2: Hamelius used the collected edition of 1705.]

[**Footnote 3**: It is interesting to note that the book originally belonged to Scott's friend and critic, Charles Kirkpatrick Sharpe.]

[**Footnote 4**: Reproduced by Celio Malespini Ducento Novelle, No. 9 (Venice, 4to, 1609, but probably written about thirty years before).]

[**Footnote 5**: A French prose translation of Southerne is to be found in Vol. VIII of Le Théâtre Anglois, Londres, 1746. It is entitled L'Adultère Innocent; but the comic underplot is very sketchily analyzed, scene by scene, and the whole is very mediocre withal.]

To the Most Illustrious Princess, The Dutchess of Mazarine.

Madam,

There are none of an Illustrious Quality, who have not been made, by some Poet or other, the Patronesses of his Distress'd Hero, or Unfortunate Damsel; and such Addresses are Tributes, due only to the most Elevated, where they have always been very well receiv'd, since they are the greatest Testimonies we can give, of our Esteem and Veneration.

Madam, when I survey'd the whole Toor of Ladies at Court, which was adorn'd by you, who appear'd there with a Grace and Majesty, peculiar to Your Great Self only, mix'd with an irresistible Air of Sweetness, Generosity, and Wit, I was impatient for an Opportunity, to tell Your Grace, how infinitely one of Your own Sex ador'd You, and that, among all the numerous Conquest, Your Grace has made over the Hearts of Men, Your Grace had not subdu'd a more entire Slave; I assure you, Madam, there is neither Compliment nor Poetry, in this humble Declaration, but a Truth, which has cost me a great deal of Inquietude, for that Fortune has not set me in such a Station, as might justifie my Pretence to the honour and satisfaction of being ever near Your Grace, to view eternally that lovely Person, and hear that surprizing Wit; what can be more grateful to a Heart, than so great, and so agreeable, an Entertainment? And how few Objects are there, that can render it so entire a Pleasure, as at once to hear you speak, and to look upon your Beauty? A Beauty that is heighten'd, if possible, with an air of Negligence, in Dress, wholly Charming, as if your Beauty disdain'd those little Arts of your Sex, whose Nicety alone is their greatest Charm, while yours, Madam, even without the Assistance of your exalted Birth, begets an Awe and Reverence in all that do approach you, and every one is proud, and pleas'd, in paying you Homage their several ways, according to their Capacities and Talents; mine, Madam, can only be exprest by my Pen, which would be infinitely honour'd, in being permitted to celebrate your great Name for ever, and perpetually to serve, where it has so great an inclination.

In the mean time, Madam, I presume to lay this little Trifle at your Feet; the Story is true, as it is on the Records of the Town, where it was transacted; and if my fair unfortunate VOW-BREAKER do not deserve the honour of your Graces Protection, at least, she will be found worthy of your Pity; which will be a sufficient Glory, both for her, and,

Madam,
Your Graces most humble, and most obedient Servant,
A. BEHN.

Of all the sins, incident to Human Nature, there is none, of which Heaven has took so particular, visible, and frequent Notice, and Revenge, as on that of Violated Vows, which never go unpunished; and the Cupids may boast what they will, for the encouragement of their Trade of Love, that Heaven never takes cognisance of Lovers broken Vows and Oaths, and that 'tis the only Perjury that escapes the Anger of the Gods; But I verily believe, if it were search'd into, we should find these frequent Perjuries, that pass in the World for so many Gallantries only, to be the occasion of so many unhappy Marriages, and the cause of all those Misfortunes, which are so frequent to the Nuptiall'd Pair. For not one of a Thousand, but, either on his side, or on hers, has been perjur'd, and broke Vows made to some fond believing Wretch, whom they have abandon'd and undone. What Man that does not boast of the Numbers he has thus ruin'd, and, who does not glory in the shameful Triumph? Nay, what Woman, almost, has not a pleasure in Deceiving, taught, perhaps, at first, by some dear false one, who had fatally instructed her Youth in an Art she ever after practis'd, in Revenge on all those she could be too hard for, and conquer at their own Weapons? For, without all dispute, Women are by Nature more Constant and Just, than Men, and did not their first Lovers teach them the trick of Change, they would be Doves, that would never quit their Mate, and, like Indian Wives, would leap alive into the Graves of their deceased Lovers, and be buried quick with 'em. But Customs of Countries change even Nature her self, and long Habit takes her place: The Women are taught, by the Lives of the Men, to live up to all their Vices, and are become almost as inconstant; and 'tis but Modesty that makes the difference, and, hardly, inclination; so deprav'd the nicest Appetites grow in time, by bad Examples.

But, as there are degrees of Vows, so there are degrees of Punishments for Vows, there are solemn Matrimonial Vows, such as contract and are the most effectual Marriage, and have the most reason to be so; there are a thousand Vows and Friendships, that pass between Man and Man, on a thousand Occasions; but there is another Vow, call'd a Sacred Vow, made to God only; and, by which, we oblige our selves eternally to serve him with all Chastity and Devotion: This Vow is only taken, and made, by those that enter into Holy Orders, and, of all broken Vows, these are those, that receive the most severe and notorious Revenges of God; and I am almost certain, there is not one Example to be produc'd in the World, where Perjuries of this nature have past unpunish'd, nay, that have not been persu'd with the greatest and most rigorous of Punishments. I could my self, of my own knowledge, give an hundred Examples of the fatal Consequences of the Violation of Sacred Vows; and who ever make it their business, and are curious in the search of such Misfortunes, shall find, as I say, that they never go unregarded.

The young Beauty therefore, who dedicates her self to Heaven, and weds her self for ever to the service of God, ought, first, very well to consider the Self-denial she is going to put upon her youth, her fickle faithless deceiving Youth, of one Opinion to day, and of another to morrow; like Flowers, which never remain in one state or fashion, but bud to day, and blow by insensible degrees, and decay as imperceptibly. The Resolution, we promise, and believe we shall maintain, is not in our power, and nothing is so deceitful as human Hearts.

I once was design'd an humble Votary in the House of Devotion, but fancying my self not endu'd with an obstinacy of Mind, great enough to secure me from the Efforts and Vanities of the World, I rather chose to deny my self that Content I could not certainly promise my self, than to languish (as I have seen some do) in a certain Affliction; tho' possibly, since, I have sufficiently bewailed that mistaken and inconsiderate Approbation and Preference of the false ungrateful World, (full of nothing but Nonsense, Noise, false Notions, and Contradiction) before the Innocence and Quiet of a Cloyster; nevertheless, I could wish, for the prevention of abundance of Mischiefs and Miseries, that Nunneries and Marriages were not to be enter'd into, 'till the Maid, so destin'd, were of a mature Age to make her own Choice; and that Parents would not make use of their justly assum'd Authority to compel their Children, neither to the one or the other; but since I cannot alter Custom, nor shall ever be allow'd to make new Laws, or rectify the old ones, I must leave the Young Nuns inclos'd to their best Endeavours, of making a Virtue of Necessity; and the young Wives, to make the best of a bad Market.

In Iper, a Town, not long since, in the Dominions of the King of Spain, and now in possession of the King of France, there liv'd a Man of Quality, of a considerable Fortune, call'd, Count Henrick de Vallary, who had a very beautiful Lady, by whom, he had one Daughter, call'd Isabella, whose Mother dying when she was about two years old to the unspeakable Grief of the Count, her Husband, he resolv'd never to partake of any Pleasure more, that this transitory World could court him with, but determin'd, with himself, to dedicate his Youth, and future Days, to Heaven, and to take upon him Holy Orders; and, without considering, that, possibly, the young Isabella, when she grew to Woman, might have Sentiments contrary to those that now possess him, he design'd she should also become a Nun; However, he was not so positive in that Resolution, as to put the matter wholly out of her Choice, but divided his Estate; one half he carried with him to the Monastery of Jesuits, of which number, he became one; and the other half, he gave with Isabella, to the Monastery, of which, his only Sister was Lady Abbess, of the Order of St. Augustine; but so he ordered the matter, that if, at the Age of Thirteen, Isabella had not a mind to take Orders, or that the Lady Abbess found her Inclination averse to a Monastick Life, she should have such a proportion of the Revenue, as should be fit to marry her to a Noble Man, and left it to the discretion of the Lady Abbess, who was a Lady of known Piety, and admirable strictness of Life, and so nearly related to Isabella, that there was no doubt made of her Integrity and Justice.

The little Isabella was carried immediately (in her Mourning for her dead Mother) into the Nunnery, and was receiv'd as a very diverting Companion by all the young Ladies, and, above all, by her Reverend Aunt, for she was come just to the Age of delighting her Parents; she was the prettiest forward Pratler in the World, and had a thousand little Charms to please, besides the young Beauties that were just budding in her little Angel Face: So that she soon became the dear lov'd Favourite of the whole House; and as she was an Entertainment to them all, so they made it their study to find all the Diversions they could for the pretty Isabella; and as she grew in Wit and Beauty every day, so they fail'd not to cultivate her Mind; and delicate Apprehension, in all that was advantageous to her Sex, and whatever Excellency any one abounded in, she was sure to communicate it to the young Isabella, if one could Dance, another Sing, another play on this Instrument, and another on that; if this spoke one Language, and that another; if she had Wit, and she Discretion, and a third, the finest Fashion and Manners; all joyn'd to compleat the Mind and Body of this beautiful young Girl; Who, being undiverted with the less noble, and less solid, Vanities of the World, took to these Virtues, and excell'd in all; and her Youth and Wit being apt for all Impressions, she soon became a greater Mistress of their Arts, than those who taught her; so that at the Age of eight or nine Years, she was thought fit to receive and entertain all the great Men and Ladies, and the Strangers of any Nation, at the Grate; and that with so admirable a Grace, so quick and piercing a Wit, and so delightful and sweet a Conversation, that she became the whole Discourse of the Town, and Strangers spread her Fame, as prodigious, throughout the Christian World; for Strangers came daily to hear her talk, and sing, and play, and to admire her Beauty; and Ladies brought their Children, to shame 'em into good Fashion and Manners, with looking on the lovely young Isabella.

The Lady Abbess, her Aunt, you may believe, was not a little proud of the Excellencies and Virtues of her fair Niece, and omitted nothing that might adorn her Mind; because, not only of the vastness of her Parts and Fame, and the Credit she would do her House, by residing there for ever; but also, being very loth to part with her considerable Fortune, which she must resign, if she returned into the World, she us'd all her Arts and Stratagems to make her become a Nun, to which all the fair Sisterhood contributed their Cunning, but it was altogether needless; her Inclination, the strictness of her Devotion, her early Prayers, and those continual, and innate Stedfastness, and Calm, she was Mistress of; her Ignorance of the World's Vanities, and those that uninclos'd young Ladies count Pleasures and Diversions, being all unknown to her, she thought there was no Joy out of a Nunnery, and no Satisfactions on the other side of a Grate.

The Lady Abbess, seeing, that of her self she yielded faster than she could expect; to discharge her Conscience to her Brother, who came frequently to visit his Darling Isabella, would very often discourse to her of the Pleasures of the World, telling her, how much happier she would think her self, to be the Wife of some gallant young Cavalier, and to have Coaches and Equipages; to see the World, to behold a thousand Rarities she had never seen, to live in Splendor, to eat high, and wear magnificent Clothes, to be bow'd to as she pass'd, and have a thousand Adorers, to see in time a pretty Offspring, the products of Love, that should talk, and look, and delight, as she did, the Heart of their Parents; but to all, her Father and the Lady Abbess could say of the World, and its Pleasures, Isabella brought a thousand Reasons and Arguments, so Pious, so Devout, that the Abbess was very well pleased, to find her (purposely weak) Propositions so well overthrown; and gives an account of her daily Discourses to her Brother, which were no less pleasing to him; and tho' Isabella went already dress'd as richly as her Quality deserv'd, yet her Father, to try the utmost that the World's Vanity could do, upon her young Heart, orders the most Glorious Clothes should be bought her, and that the Lady Abbess should suffer her to go abroad with those Ladies of Quality, that were her Relations, and her Mother's Acquaintance; that she should visit and go on the Toore, (that is, the Hide Park there) that she should see all that was diverting, to try, whether it were not for want of Temptation to Vanity, that made her leave the World, and love an inclos'd Life.

As the Count had commanded, all things were performed; and Isabella arriving at her Thirteenth Year of Age, and being pretty tall of Stature, with the finest Shape that Fancy can create, with all the Adornment of a perfect brown-hair'd Beauty, Eyes black and lovely, Complexion fair; to a Miracle, all her Features of the rarest proportion, the Mouth red, the Teeth white, and a thousand Graces in her Meen and Air; she came no sooner abroad, but she had a thousand Persons fighting for love of her; the Reputation her Wit had acquir'd, got her Adorers without seeing her, but when they saw her, they found themselves conquer'd and undone; all were glad she was come into the World, of whom they had heard so much, and all the Youth of the Town dress'd only for Isabella de Valerie, that rose like a new Star that Eclips'd all the rest, and which set the World a-gazing. Some hop'd, and some despair'd, but all lov'd, while Isabella regarded not their Eyes, their distant darling Looks of Love, and their signs of Adoration; she was civil and affable to all, but so reserv'd, that none durst tell her his Passion, or name that strange and abhorr'd thing, Love, to her; the Relations with whom she went abroad every day, were fein to force her out, and when she went, 'twas the motive of Civility, and not Satisfaction, that made her go; whatever she saw, she beheld with no admiration, and nothing created wonder in her, tho' never so strange and Novel. She survey'd all things with an indifference, that tho' it was not sullen, was far from Transport, so that her evenness of Mind was infinitely admir'd and prais'd. And now it was, that, young as she was, her Conduct and Discretion appear'd equal to her Wit and Beauty, and she encreas'd daily in Reputation, insomuch, that the Parents of abundance of young Noble Men, made it their business to endeavour to marry their Sons to so admirable and noble a Maid, and one, whose Virtues were the Discourse of all the World; the Father, the Lady Abbess, and those who had her abroad, were solicited to make an Alliance; for the Father, he would give no answer, but left it to the discretion of Isabella, who could not be persuaded to hear any thing of that nature; so that for a long time she refus'd her company to all those, who propos'd any thing of Marriage to her; she said, she had seen nothing in the World that was worth her Care, or the venturing the losing of Heaven for, and therefore was resolv'd to dedicate her self to that; that the more she saw of the World, the worse she lik'd it, and pity'd the Wretches that were condemn'd to it; that she had consider'd it, and found no one Inclination that forbad her immediate Entrance into a Religious Life; to which, her Father, after using all the Arguments he could, to make her take good heed of what she went about, to consider it well; and had urg'd all the Inconveniencies of Severe Life, Watchings, Midnight Risings in all Weathers and Seasons to Prayers, hard Lodging, course Diet, and homely Habit, with a thousand other things of Labour and Work us'd among the Nuns; and finding her still resolv'd and inflexible to all contrary persuasions, he consented, kiss'd her, and told her, She had argu'd according to the wish of his Soul, and that he never believ'd himself truly happy, till this moment that he was assur'd, she would become a Religious.

This News, to the Heart-breaking of a thousand Lovers, was spread all over the Town, and there was nothing but Songs of Complaint, and of her retiring, after she had shewn her self to the World, and vanquish'd so many Hearts; all Wits were at work on this Cruel Subject, and one begat another, as is usual in such Affairs. Amongst the number of these Lovers, there was a young Gentleman, Nobly born, his name was Villenoys, who was admirably made, and very handsom, had travell'd and accomplish'd himself, as much as was possible for one so young to do; he was about Eighteen, and was going to the Siege of Candia, in a very good Equipage, but, overtaken by his Fate, surpris'd in his way to Glory, he stopt at Ipers, so fell most passionately in love with this Maid of Immortal Fame; but being defeated in his hopes by this News, was the Man that made the softest Complaints to this fair Beauty, and whose violence of Passion oppress'd him to that degree, that he was the only Lover, who durst himself tell her, he was in love with her; he writ Billets so soft and tender, that she had, of all her Lovers, most compassion for Villenoys, and dain'd several times, in pity of him, to send him answers to his Letters, but they were such, as absolutely forbad him to love her; such as incited him to follow Glory, the Mistress that could noblest reward him; and that, for her part, her Prayers should always be, that he might be victorious, and the Darling of that Fortune he was going to court; and that she, for her part, had fix'd her Mind on Heaven, and no Earthly Thought should bring it down; but she should ever retain for him all Sisterly Respect, and begg'd, in her Solitudes, to hear, whether her Prayers had prov'd effectual or not, and if Fortune were so kind to him, as she should perpetually wish.

When Villenoys found she was resolv'd, he design'd to persue his Journy, but could not leave the Town, till he had seen the fatal Ceremony of Isabella's being made a Nun, which was every day expected; and while he stay'd, he could not forbear writing daily to her, but receiv'd no more Answers from her, she already accusing her self of having done too much, for a Maid in her Circumstances; but she confess'd, of all she had seen, she lik'd Villenoys the best; and if she ever could have lov'd, she believ'd it would have been Villenoys, for he had all the good Qualities, and grace, that could render him agreeable to the Fair; besides, that he was only Son to a very rich and noble Parent, and one that might very well presume to lay claim to a Maid of Isabella's Beauty and Fortune.

As the time approach'd, when he must eternally lose all hope, by Isabella's taking Orders, he found himself less able to bear the Efforts of that Despair it possess'd him with, he languished with the thought, so that it was visible to all his Friends, the decays it wrought on his Beauty and Gaiety: So that he fell at last into a Feaver; and 'twas the whole Discourse of the Town, That Villenoys was dying for the Fair Isabella; his Relations, being all of Quality, were extreamly afflicted at his Misfortune, and joyn'd their Interests yet, to dissuade this fair young Victoress from an act so cruel, as to inclose herself in a Nunnery, while the finest of all the youths of Quality was dying for her, and ask'd her, If it would not be more acceptable to Heaven to save a Life, and perhaps a Soul, than to go and expose her own to a thousand Tortures? They assur'd her, Villenoys was dying, and dying Adoring her; that nothing could save his Life, but her kind Eyes turn'd upon the fainting Lover; a Lover, that could breath nothing, but her Name in Sighs; and find satisfaction in nothing, but weeping and crying out, 'I dye for Isabella!' This Discourse fetch'd abundance of Tears from the fair Eyes of this tender Maid; but, at the same time, she besought them to believe, these Tears ought not to give them hope, she should ever yield to save his Life, by quitting her Resolution, of becoming a Nun; but, on the contrary, they were Tears, that only bewail'd her own Misfortune, in having been the occasion of the death of any Man, especially, a Man, who had so many Excellencies, as might have render'd him entirely Happy and Glorious for a long race of Years, had it not been his ill fortune to have seen her unlucky Face. She believ'd, it was for her Sins of Curiosity, and going beyond the Walls of the Monastery, to wander after the Vanities of the foolish World, that had occasion'd this Misfortune to the young Count of Villenoys, and she would put a severe Penance on her Body, for the Mischiefs her Eyes had done him; she fears she might, by something in her looks, have intic'd his Heart, for she own'd she saw him, with wonder at his Beauty, and much more she admir'd him, when she found the Beauties of his Mind; she confess'd, she had given him hope, by answering his Letters; and that when she found her Heart grow a little more than usually tender, when she thought on him, she believ'd it a Crime, that ought to be check'd by a Virtue, such as she pretended to profess, and hop'd she should ever carry to her Grave; and she desired his Relations to implore him, in her Name, to rest contented, in knowing he was the first, and should be the last, that should ever make an impression on her Heart; that what she had conceiv'd there, for him, should remain with her to her dying day, and that she besought him to live, that she might see, he both deserv'd this Esteem she had for him, and to repay it her, otherwise he would dye in her debt, and make her Life ever after reposeless.

This being all they could get from her, they return'd with Looks that told their Message; however, they render'd those soft things Isabella had said, in so moving a manner, as fail'd not to please, and while he remain'd in this condition, the Ceremonies were compleated, of making Isabella a Nun; which was a Secret to none but Villenoys, and from him it was carefully conceal'd, so that in a little time he recover'd his lost health, at least, so well, as to support the fatal News, and upon the first hearing it, he made ready his Equipage, and departed immediately for Candia; where he behav'd himself very gallantly, under the Command of the Duke De Beaufort, and, with him, return'd to France, after the loss of that noble City to the Turks.

In all the time of his absence, that he might the sooner establish his Repose, he forbore sending to the fair Cruel Nun, and she heard no more of Villenoys in above two years; so that giving her self wholly up to Devotion, there was never seen any one, who led so Austere and Pious a Life, as this young Votress; she was a Saint in the Chapel, and an Angel at the Grate: She there laid by all her severe Looks, and mortify'd Discourse, and being at perfect peace and tranquility within, she was outwardly all gay, sprightly, and entertaining, being satisfy'd, no Sights, no Freedoms, could give any temptations to worldly desires; she gave a loose to all that was modest, and that Virtue and Honour would permit, and was the most charming Conversation that ever was admir'd; and the whole World that pass'd through Iper; of Strangers, came directed and recommended to the lovely Isabella; I mean, those of Quality: But however Diverting she was at the Grate, she was most exemplary Devout in the Cloister, doing more

Penance, and imposing a more rigid Severity and Task on her self, than was requir'd, giving such rare Examples to all the Nuns that were less Devout, that her Life was a Proverb, and a President, and when they would express a very Holy Woman indeed, they would say, 'She was a very ISABELLA.'

There was in this Nunnery, a young Nun, call'd, Sister Katteriena, Daughter to the Grave Vanhenault, that is to say, an Earl, who liv'd about six Miles from the Town, in a noble Villa; this Sister Katteriena was not only a very beautiful Maid, but very witty, and had all the good qualities to make her be belov'd, and had most wonderfully gain'd upon the Heart of the fair Isabella, she was her Chamber-Fellow and Companion in all her Devotions and Diversions, so that where one was, there was the other, and they never went but together to the Grate, to the Garden, or to any place, whither their Affairs call'd either. This young Katteriena had a Brother, who lov'd her intirely, and came every day to see her, he was about twenty Years of Age, rather tall than middle Statur'd, his Hair and Eyes brown, but his Face exceeding beautiful, adorn'd with a thousand Graces, and the most nobly and exactly made, that 'twas possible for Nature to form; to the Fineness and Charms of his Person, he had an Air in his Meen and Dressing, so very agreeable, besides rich, that 'twas impossible to look on him, without wishing him happy, because he did so absolutely merit being so. His Wit and his Manner was so perfectly Obliging, a Goodness and Generosity so Sincere and Gallant, that it would even have aton'd for Ugliness. As he was eldest Son to so great a Father, he was kept at home, while the rest of his Brothers were employ'd in Wars abroad; this made him of a melancholy Temper, and fit for soft Impressions; he was very Bookish, and had the best Tutors that could be got, for Learning and Languages, and all that could compleat a Man; but was unus'd to Action, and of a temper Lazy, and given to Repose, so that his Father could hardly ever get him to use any Exercise, or so much as ride abroad, which he would call, Losing Time from his Studies: He car'd not for the Conversation of Men, because he lov'd not Debauch, as they usually did; so that for Exercise, more than any Design, he came on Horseback every day to Iper to the Monastery, and would sit at the Grate, entertaining his Sister the most part of the Afternoon, and, in the Evening, retire; he had often seen and convers'd with the lovely Isabella, and found from the first sight of her, he had more Esteem for her, than any other of her Sex: But as Love very rarely takes Birth without Hope; so he never believ'd that the Pleasure he took in beholding her, and in discoursing with her, was Love, because he regarded her, as a Thing consecrate to Heaven, and never so much as thought to wish, she were a Mortal fit for his Addresses; yet he found himself more and more fill'd with Reflections on her which was not usual with him; he found she grew upon his Memory, and oftner came there, than he us'd to do, that he lov'd his Studies less, and going to Iper more; and, that every time he went, he found a new Joy at his Heart that pleas'd him; he found, he could not get himself from the Grate, without Pain; nor part from the sight of that all-charming Object, without Sighs; and if, while he was there, any persons came to visit her, whose Quality she could not refuse the honour of her sight to, he would blush, and pant with uneasiness, especially, if they were handsom, and fit to make Impressions: And he would check this Uneasiness in himself, and ask his Heart, what it meant, by rising and beating in those Moments, and strive to assume an Indifference in vain, and depart dissatisfy'd, and out of humour.

On the other side, Isabella was not so Gay as she us'd to be, but, on the sudden, retir'd her self more from the Grate than she us'd to do, refus'd to receive Visits every day, and her Complexion grew a little pale and languid; she was observ'd not to sleep, or eat, as she us'd to do, nor exercise in those little Plays they made, and diverted themselves with, now and then; she was heard to sigh often, and it became the Discourse of the whole House, that she was much alter'd: The Lady Abbess, who lov'd her with a most tender Passion, was infinitely concern'd at this Change, and endeavour'd to find out the Cause, and 'twas generally believ'd, she was too Devout, for now she redoubled her Austerity; and in cold Winter Nights, of Frost and Snow, would be up at all Hours, and lying upon the cold Stones, before the Altar, prostrate at Prayers: So that she receiv'd Orders from the Lady Abbess, not to harass her self so very much, but to have a care of her Health, as well as her Soul; but she regarded not these Admonitions, tho' even persuaded daily by her Katteriena, whom she lov'd every day more and more.

But, one Night, when they were retir'd to their Chamber, amongst a thousand things that they spoke of, to pass away a tedious Evening, they talk'd of Pictures and Likenesses, and Katteriena told Isabella, that before she was a Nun, in her more happy days, she was so like her Brother Bernardo Henault, (who was the same that visited them every day) that she would, in Men's Clothes, undertake, she should not have known one from t'other, and fetching out his Picture, she had in a Dressing-Box, she threw it to Isabella, who, at the first sight of it, turns as pale as Ashes, and, being ready to swound, she bid her take it away, and could not, for her Soul, hide the sudden surprise the Picture brought: Katteriena had too much Wit, not to make a just Interpretation of this Change, and (as a Woman) was naturally curious to pry farther, tho' Discretion should have made her been silent, for Talking, in such cases, does but make the Wound rage the more; 'Why, my dear Sister, (said Katteriena) is the likeness of my Brother so offensive to you?' Isabella found by this, she had discover'd too much, and that Thought put her by all power of excusing it; she was confounded with Shame, and the more she strove to hide it, the more it disorder'd her; so that she (blushing extremely) hung down her Head, sigh'd, and confess'd all by her Looks. At last, after a considering Pause, she cry'd, 'My dearest Sister, I do confess, I was surpriz'd at the sight of Monsieur Henault, and much more than ever you have observ'd me to be at the sight of his Person, because there is scarce a day wherein I do not see that, and know beforehand I shall see him; I am prepar'd for the Encounter, and have lessen'd my Concern, or rather Confusion, by that time I come to the Grate, so much Mistress I am of my Passions, when they give me warning of their approach, and sure I can withstand the greatest assaults of Fate, if I can but foresee it; but if it surprize me, I find I am as feeble a Woman, as the most unresolv'd; you did not tell me, you had this Picture, nor say, you would shew me such a Picture; but when I least expect to see that Face, you shew it me, even in my Chamber.'

'Ah, my dear Sister! (reply'd Katteriena) I believe, that Paleness, and those Blushes, proceed from some other cause, than the Nicety of seeing the Picture of a Man in your Chamber':

'You have too much Wit, (reply'd Isabella) to be impos'd on by such an Excuse, if I were so silly to make it; but oh! my dear Sister! it was in my Thoughts to deceive you; could I have concealed my Pain and Sufferings, you should never have known them; but since I find it impossible, and that I am too sincere to make use of Fraud in any thing, 'tis fit I tell you, from what cause my change of Colour proceeds, and to own to you, I fear, 'tis Love, if ever therefore, oh gentle pitying Maid! thou wert a Lover? If ever thy tender Heart were touch'd with that Passion? Inform me, oh! inform me, of the nature of that cruel Disease, and how thou found'st a Cure?'

While she was speaking these words, she threw her Arms about the Neck of the fair Katteriena, and bath'd her Bosom (where she hid her Face) with a shower of Tears; Katteriena, embracing her with all the fondness of a dear Lover, told her, with a Sigh, that she could deny her nothing, and therefore confess'd to her, she had been a Lover, and that was the occasion of her being made a Nun, her Father finding out the Intrigue, which fatally happened to be with his own Page, a Youth of extraordinary Beauty. 'I was but Young, (said she) about Thirteen, and knew not what to call the new-known Pleasure that I felt; when e're I look'd upon the young Arnaldo, my Heart would heave, when e're he came in view, and my disorder'd Breath came doubly from my Bosom; a Shivering seiz'd me, and my Face grew wan; my Thought was at a stand, and Sense it self, for that short moment, lost its Faculties; But when he touch'd me, oh! no hunted Deer, tir'd with his flight, and just secur'd in Shades, pants with a nimbler motion than my Heart; at first, I thought the Youth had had some Magick Art, to make one faint and tremble at his touches; but he himself, when I accus'd his Cruelty, told me, he had no Art, but awful Passion, and vow'd that when I touch'd him, he was so; so trembling, so surprized, so charm'd, so pleas'd. When he was present, nothing could displease me, but when he parted from me; then 'twas rather a soft silent Grief, that eas'd itself by sighing, and by hoping, that some kind moment would restore my joy. When he was absent, nothing could divert me, howe're I strove, howe're I toyl'd for Mirth; no Smile, no Joy, dwelt in my Heart or Eyes; I could not feign, so very well I lov'd, impatient in his absence, I would count the tedious parting Hours, and pass them off like useless Visitants, whom we wish were gon; these are the Hours, where Life no business has, at least, a Lover's Life. But, oh! what Minutes seem'd the happy Hours, when on his Eyes I gaz'd, and he on mine, and half our Conversation lost in Sighs, Sighs, the soft moving Language of a Lover!'

'No more, no more, (reply'd Isabella, throwing her Arms again about the Neck of the transported Katteriena) thou blow'st my Flame by thy soft Words, and mak'st me know my Weakness, and my Shame: I love! I love! and feel those differing Passions!' Then pausing a moment, she proceeded, 'Yet so didst thou, but hast surmounted it. Now thou hast found the Nature of my Pain, oh! tell me thy saving Remedy?' 'Alas! (reply'd Katteriena) tho' there's but one Disease, there's many Remedies: They say, possession's one, but that to me seems a Riddle; Absence, they say, another, and that was mine; for Arnaldo having by chance lost one of my Billets, discover'd the Amour, and was sent to travel, and my self forc'd into this Monastery, where at last, Time convinc'd me, I had lov'd below my Quality, and that sham'd me into Holy Orders.' 'And is it a Disease, (reply'd Isabella) that People often recover?' 'Most frequently, (said Katteriena) and yet some dye of the Disease, but very rarely.' 'Nay then, (said Isabella) I fear, you will find me one of these Martyrs; for I have already oppos'd it with the most severe Devotion in the World: But all my Prayers are vain, your lovely Brother persues me into the greatest Solitude; he meets me at my very Midnight Devotions, and interrupts my Prayers; he gives me a thousand Thoughts, that ought not to enter into a Soul dedicated to Heaven; he ruins all the Glory I have achiev'd, even above my Sex, for Piety of Life, and the Observation of all Virtues. Oh Katteriena! he has a Power in his Eyes, that transcends all the World besides: And, to shew the weakness of Human Nature, and how vain all our Boastings are, he has done that in one fatal Hour, that the persuasions of all my Relations and Friends, Glory, Honour, Pleasure, and all that can tempt, could not perform in Years; I resisted all but Henault's Eyes, and they were Ordain'd to make me truly wretched; But yet with thy Assistance, and a Resolution to see him no more, and my perpetual Trust in Heaven, I may, perhaps, overcome this Tyrant of my Soul, who, I thought, had never enter'd into holy Houses, or mix'd his Devotions and Worship with the true Religion; but, oh! no Cells, no Cloysters, no Hermitages, are secur'd from his Efforts.'

This Discourse she ended with abundance of Tears, and it was resolv'd, since she was devoted for ever to a Holy Life, That it was best for her to make it as easy to her as was possible; in order to it, and the banishing this fond and useless Passion from her Heart, it was very necessary, she should see Henault no more: At first, Isabella was afraid, that, in refusing to see him, he might mistrust her Passion; but Katteriena who was both Pious and Discreet, and endeavour'd truly to cure her of so violent a Disease, which must, she knew, either end in her death or destruction, told her, She would take care of that matter, that it should not blemish her Honour; and so leaving her a while, after they had resolved on this, she left her in a thousand Confusions, she was now another Woman than what she had hitherto been; she was quite alter'd in every Sentiment, thought and Notion; she now repented, she had promis'd not to see Henault; she trembled and even fainted, for fear she should see him no more; she was not able to bear that thought, it made her rage within, like one possest, and all her Virtue could not calm her; yet since her word was past, and, as she was, she could not, without great Scandal, break it in that point, she resolv'd to dye a thousand Deaths, rather than not perform her Promise made to Katteriena; but 'tis not to be express'd what she endur'd; what Fits, Pains, and Convulsions, she sustain'd; and how much ado she had to dissemble to Dame Katteriena, who soon return'd to the afflicted Maid; the next day, about the time that Henault was to come, as he usually did, about two or three a Clock after Noon, 'tis impossible to express the uneasiness of Isabella; she ask'd, a thousand times, 'What, is not your Brother come?' When Dame Katteriena would reply, 'Why do you ask?' She would say, 'Because I would be sure not to see him': 'You need not fear, Madam, (reply'd Katteriena) for you shall keep your Chamber.' She need not have urg'd that, for Isabella was very ill without knowing it, and in a Feaver.

At last, one of the Nuns came up, and told Dame Katteriena, that her Brother was at the Grate, and she desired, he should be bid come about to the Private Grate above stairs, which he did, and she went to him, leaving Isabella even dead on the Bed, at the very name of Henault: But the more she conceal'd her Flame, the more violently it rag'd, which she strove in vain by Prayers, and those Recourses of Solitude to lessen; all this did but augment the Pain, and was Oyl to the Fire, so that she now could hope, that nothing but Death would put an end to her Griefs, and her Infamy. She was eternally thinking on him, how handsome his Face, how delicate every Feature, how charming his Air, how graceful his Meen, how soft and good his Disposition, and how witty and entertaining his Conversation. She now fancy'd, she was at the Grate, talking to him as she us'd to be, and blest those happy Hours she past then, and bewail'd her Misfortune, that she is no more destin'd to be so Happy, then gives a loose to Grief; Griefs, at which, no Mortals, but Despairing Lovers, can guess, or how tormenting they are; where the most easie Moments are, those, wherein one resolves to kill ones self, and the happiest Thought is Damnation; but from these Imaginations, she endeavours to fly, all frighted with horror; but, alas! whither would she fly, but to a Life more full of horror? She considers well, she cannot bear Despairing Love, and finds it impossible to cure her Despair; she cannot fly from the Thoughts of the Charming Henault, and 'tis impossible to quit 'em; and, at this rate, she found, Life could not long support it self, but would either reduce her to Madness, and so render her an hated Object of Scorn to the Censuring World, or force her Hand to commit a Murder upon her self. This she had found, this she had well consider'd, nor could her fervent and continual Prayers, her nightly Watchings, her Mortifications on the cold Marble in long Winter Season, and all her Acts of Devotion abate one spark of this shameful Feaver of Love, that was destroying her within. When she had rag'd and struggled with this unruly Passion, 'till she was quite tir'd and breathless, finding all her force in vain, she fill'd her fancy with a thousand charming Ideas of the lovely Henault, and, in that soft fit, had a mind to satisfy her panting Heart, and give it one Joy more, by beholding the Lord of its Desires, and the Author of its Pains: Pleas'd, yet trembling, at this Resolve, she rose from the Bed where she was laid, and softly advanc'd to the Stair-Case, from whence there open'd that Room where Dame Katteriena was, and where there was a private Grate, at which, she was entertaining her Brother; they were earnest in Discourse, and so loud, that Isabella could easily hear all they said, and the first words were from Katteriena, who, in a sort of Anger, cry'd, 'Urge me no more! My Virtue is too nice, to become an Advocate for a Passion, that can tend to nothing but your Ruin; for, suppose I should tell the fair Isabella, you dye for her, what can it avail you? What hope can any Man have, to move the Heart of a Virgin, so averse to Love? A Virgin, whose Modesty and Virtue is so very curious, it would fly the very word, Love, as some monstrous Witchcraft, or the foulest of Sins, who would loath me for bringing so lewd a Message, and banish you her Sight, as the Object of her Hate and Scorn; is it unknown to you, how many of the noblest Youths of Flanders have address'd themselves to her in vain, when yet she was in the World? Have you been ignorant, how the young Count de Villenoys languished, in vain, almost to Death for her? And, that no Persuasions, no Attractions in him, no wordly Advantages, or all his Pleadings, who had a Wit and Spirit capable of prevailing on any Heart, less severe and harsh, than hers? Do you not know, that all was lost on this insensible fair one, even when she was a proper Object for the Adoration of the Young and Amorous? And can you hope, now she has so entirely wedded her future days to Devotion, and given all to Heaven;

nay, lives a Life here more like a Saint, than a Woman; rather an Angel, than a mortal Creature? Do you imagin, with any Rhetorick you can deliver, now to turn the Heart, and whole Nature, of this Divine Maid, to consider your Earthly Passion? No, 'tis fondness, and an injury to her Virtue, to harbour such a Thought; quit it, quit it, my dear Brother! before it ruin your Repose.' 'Ah, Sister! (replied the dejected Henault) your Counsel comes too late, and your Reasons are of too feeble force, to rebate those Arrows, the Charming Isabella's Eyes have fix'd in my Heart and Soul; and I am undone, unless she know my Pain, which I shall dye, before I shall ever dare mention to her; but you, young Maids, have a thousand Familiarities together, can jest, and play, and say a thousand things between Railery and Earnest, that may first hint what you would deliver, and insinuate into each others Hearts a kind of Curiosity to know more; for naturally, (my dear Sister) Maids, are curious and vain; and however Divine the Mind of the fair Isabella may be, it bears the Tincture still of Mortal Woman.'

'Suppose this true, how could this Mortal part about her Advantage you, (said Katteriena) all that you can expect from this Discovery, (if she should be content to hear it, and to return you pity) would be, to make her wretched, like your self? What farther can you hope?' 'Oh! talk not, (replied Henault) of so much Happiness! I do not expect to be so blest, that she should pity me, or love to a degree of Inquietude; 'tis sufficient, for the ease of my Heart, that she know its Pains, and what it suffers for her; that she would give my Eyes leave to gaze upon her, and my Heart to vent a Sigh now and then; and, when I dare, to give me leave to speak, and tell her of my Passion; This, this, is all, my Sister.' And, at that word, the Tears glided down his Cheeks, and he declin'd his Eyes, and set a Look so charming, and so sad, that Isabella, whose Eyes were fix'd upon him, was a thousand times ready to throw her self into the Room, and to have made a Confession, how sensible she was of all she had heard and seen: But, with much ado, she contain'd and satisfy'd her self, with knowing, that she was ador'd by him whom she ador'd, and, with Prudence that is natural to her, she withdrew, and waited with patience the event of their Discourse. She impatiently long'd to know, how Katteriena would manage this Secret her Brother had given her, and was pleas'd, that the Friendship and Prudence of that Maid had conceal'd her Passion from her Brother; and now contented and joyful beyond imagination, to find her self belov'd, she knew she could dissemble her own Passion and make him the first Aggressor; the first that lov'd, or at least, that should seem to do so. This Thought restores her so great a part of her Peace of Mind, that she resolv'd to see him, and to dissemble with Katteriena so far, as to make her believe, she had subdu'd that Passion, she was really asham'd to own; she now, with her Woman's Skill, begins to practise an Art she never before understood, and has recourse to Cunning, and resolves to seem to reassume her former Repose: But hearing Katteriena approach, she laid her self again on her Bed, where she had left her, but compos'd her Face to more chearfulness, and put on a Resolution that indeed deceiv'd the Sister, who was extreamly pleased, she said, to see her look so well: When Isabella reply'd, 'Yes, I am another Woman now; I hope Heaven has heard, and granted, my long and humble Supplications, and driven from my Heart this tormenting God, that has so long disturb'd my purer Thoughts.' 'And are you sure, (said Dame Katteriena) that this wanton Deity is repell'd by the noble force of your Resolutions? Is he never to return?' 'No, (replied Isabella) never to my Heart.' 'Yes, (said Katteriena) if you should see the lovely Murderer of your Repose, your Wound would bleed anew.' At this, Isabella smiling with a little Disdain, reply'd, 'Because you once to love, and Henault's Charms defenceless found me, ah! do you think I have no Fortitude? But so in Fondness lost, remiss in Virtue, that when I have resolv'd, (and see it necessary for my after-Quiet) to want the power of keeping that Resolution? No, scorn me, and despise me then, as lost to all the Glories of my Sex, and all that Nicety I've hitherto preserv'd.' There needed no more from a Maid of Isabella's Integrity and Reputation, to convince any one of the Sincerity of what she said, since, in the whole course of her Life, she never could be charg'd with an Untruth, or an Equivocation; and Katteriena assur'd her, she believ'd her, and was infinitely glad she had vanquish'd a Passion, that would have prov'd destructive to her Repose: Isabella reply'd, She had not altogether vanquish'd her Passion, she did not boast of so absolute a power over her soft Nature, but had resolv'd things great, and Time would work the Cure; that she hop'd, Katteriena would make such Excuses to her Brother, for her not appearing at the Grate so gay and entertaining as she us'd, and, by a little absence, she should retrieve the Liberty she had lost: But she desir'd, such Excuses might be made for her, that young Henault might not perceive the Reason. At the naming him, she had much ado not to shew some Concern extraordinary, and Katteriena assur'd her, She had now a very good Excuse to keep from the Grate, when he was at it; 'For, (said she) now you have resolv'd, I may tell you, he is dying for you, raving in Love, and has this day made me promise to him, to give you some account of his Passion, and to make you sensible of his Languishment: I had not told you this, (reply'd Katteriena) but that I believe you fortify'd with brave Resolution and Virtue, and that this knowledge will rather put you more upon your Guard, than you were before.' While she spoke, she fixed her Eyes on Isabella, to see what alteration it would make in her Heart and Looks; but the Master-piece of this young Maid's Art was shewn in this minute, for she commanded her self so well, that her very Looks dissembled and shew'd no concern at a Relation, that made her Soul dance with Joy; but it was, what she was prepar'd for, or else I question her Fortitude. But, with a Calmness, which absolutely subdu'd Katteriena, she reply'd, 'I am almost glad he has confess'd a Passion for me, and you shall confess to him, you told me of it, and that I absent my self from the Grate, on purpose to avoid the sight of a Man, who durst love me, and confess it; and I assure you, my dear Sister! (continued she, dissembling) You could not have advanc'd my Cure by a more effectual way, than telling me of his Presumption.' At that word, Katteriena joyfully related to her all that had pass'd between young Henault and her self, and how he implor'd her Aid in this Amour; at the end of which Relation, Isabella smil'd, and carelesly reply'd, 'I pity him': And so going to their Devotion, they had no more Discourse of the Lover.

In the mean time, young Henault was a little satisfy'd, to know, his Sister would discover his Passion to the lovely Isabella; and though he dreaded the return, he was pleas'd that she should know, she had a Lover that ador'd her, though even without hope; for though the thought of possessing Isabella, was the most ravishing that could be; yet he had a dread upon him, when he thought of it, for he could not hope to accomplish that, without Sacrilege; and he was a young Man, very Devout, and even bigotted in Religion; and would often question and debate within himself, that, if it were possible, he should come to be belov'd by this Fair Creature, and that it were possible for her, to grant all that Youth in Love could require, whether he should receive the Blessing offer'd? And though he ador'd the Maid, whether he should not abhor the Nun in his Embraces? 'Twas an undetermin'd Thought, that chill'd his Fire as often as it approach'd; but he had too many that rekindled it again with the greater Flame and Ardor.

His impatience to know, what Success Katteriena had, with the Relation she was to make to Isabella in his behalf, brought him early to Iper the next day. He came again to the private Grate, where his Sister receiving him, and finding him, with a sad and dejected Look, expect what she had to say; she told him, That Look well became the News she had for him, it being such, as ought to make him, both Griev'd, and Penitent; for, to obey him, she had so absolutely displeas'd Isabella, that she was resolv'd never to believe her her Friend more, 'Or to see you, (said she) therefore, as you have made me commit a Crime against my Conscience, against my Order, against my Friendship, and against my Honour, you ought to do some brave thing; take some noble Resolution, worthy of your Courage, to redeem all; for your Repose, I promis'd, I would let Isabella know you lov'd, and, for the mitigation of my Crime, you ought to let me tell her, you have surmounted your Passion, as the last Remedy of Life and Fame.'

At these her last words, the Tears gush'd from his Eyes, and he was able only, a good while, to sigh; at last, cry'd, 'What! see her no more! see the Charming Isabella no more!' And then vented the Grief of his Soul in so passionate a manner, as his Sister had all the Compassion imaginable for him, but thought it great Sin and Indiscretion to cherish his Flame: So that, after a while, having heard her Counsel, he reply'd, 'And is this all, my Sister, you will do to save a Brother?' 'All! (reply'd she) I would not be the occasion of making a NUN violate her Vow, to save a Brother's Life, no, nor my own; assure your self of this, and take it as my last Resolution: Therefore, if you will be content with the Friendship of this young Lady, and so behave your self, that we may find no longer the Lover in the Friend, we shall reassume our former Conversation, and live with you, as we ought; otherwise, your Presence will continually banish her from the Grate, and, in time, make both her you love, and your self, a Town Discourse.'

Much more to this purpose she said, to dissuade him, and bid him retire, and keep himself from thence, till he could resolve to visit them without a Crime; and she protested, if he did not do this, and master his foolish Passion, she would let her Father understand his Conduct, who was a Man of temper so very precise, that should he believe, his Son should have a thought of Love to a Virgin vow'd to Heaven, he would abandon him to Shame, and eternal Poverty, by disinheriting him of all he could: Therefore, she said, he ought to lay all this to his Heart, and weigh it with his unheedy Passion. While the Sister talk'd thus wisely, Henault was not without his Thoughts, but consider'd as she spoke, but did not consider in the right place; he was not considering, how to please a Father, and save an Estate, but how to manage the matter so, to establish himself, as he was before with Isabella; for he imagin'd, since already she knew his Passion, and that if after that she would be prevail'd with to see him, he might, some lucky Minute or other, have the pleasure of speaking for himself, at least, he should again see and talk to her, which was a joyful Thought in the midst of so many dreadful ones: And, as if he had known what pass'd in Isabella's Heart, he, by a strange sympathy, took the same measures to deceive Katteriena, a well-meaning young Lady, and easily impos'd on from her own Innocence, he resolv'd to dissemble Patience, since he must have that Virtue, and own'd, his Sister's Reasons were just, and ought to be persu'd; that she had argu'd him into half his Peace, and that he would endeavour to recover the rest; that Youth ought to be pardon'd a thousand Failings, and Years would reduce him to a condition of laughing at his Follies of Youth, but that grave Direction was not yet arriv'd: And so desiring, she would pray for his Conversion, and that she would recommend him to the Devotions of the Fair Isabella, he took his leave, and came no more to the Nunnery in ten Days; in all which time, none but Impatient Lovers can guess, what Pain and Languishments Isabella suffer'd, not knowing the Cause of his Absence, nor daring to enquire; but she bore it out so admirably, that Dame Katteriena never so much as suspected she had any Thoughts of that nature that perplex'd her, and now believ'd indeed she had conquer'd all her Uneasiness: And one day, when Isabella and she were alone together, she ask'd that fair Dissembler, if she did not admire at the Conduct and Resolution of her Brother? 'Why!' (reply'd Isabella unconcernedly, while her Heart was fainting within, for fear of ill News:) With that, Katteriena told her the last Discourse she had with her Brother, and how at last she had persuaded him (for her sake) to quit his Passion; and that he had promis'd, he would endeavour to surmount it; and that, that was the reason he was absent now, and they were to see him no more, till he had made a Conquest over himself. You may assure your self, this News was not so welcom to Isabella, as Katteriena imagin'd; yet still she dissembled, with a force, beyond what the most cunning Practitioner could have shewn, and carry'd her self before People, as if no Pressures had lain upon her Heart; but when alone retir'd, in order to her Devotion, she would vent her Griefs in the most deplorable manner, that a distress'd distracted Maid could do, and which, in spite of all her severe Penances, she found no abatement of.

At last Henault came again to the Monastery, and, with a Look as gay as he could possibly assume, he saw his Sister, and told her, He had gain'd an absolute Victory over his Heart; and desir'd, he might see Isabella, only to convince, both her, and Katteriena, that he was no longer a Lover of that fair Creature, that had so lately charm'd him; that he had set Five thousand Pounds a Year, against a fruitless Passion, and found the solid Gold much the heavier in the Scale: And he smil'd, and talk'd the whole Day of indifferent things, with his Sister, and ask'd no more for Isabella; nor did Isabella look, or ask, after him, but in her Heart. Two Months pass'd in this Indifference, till it was taken notice of, that Sister Isabella came not to the Grate, when Henault was there, as she us'd to do; this being spoken to Dame Katteriena, she told it to Isabella, and said, 'The NUNS would believe, there was some Cause for her Absence, if she did not appear again': That if she could trust her Heart, she was sure she could trust her Brother, for he thought no more of her, she was confident; this, in lieu of pleasing, was a Dagger to the Heart of Isabella, who thought it time to retrieve the flying Lover, and therefore told Katteriena, She would the next Day entertain at the Low Grate, as she was wont to do, and accordingly, as soon as any People of Quality came, she appear'd there, where she had not been two Minutes, but she saw the lovely Henault, and it was well for both, that People were in the Room, they had else both sufficiently discover'd their Inclinations, or rather their not to be conceal'd Passions; after the General Conversation was over, by the going away of the Gentlemen that were at the Grate, Katteriena being employ'd elsewhere, Isabella was at last left alone with Henault; but who can guess the Confusion of these two Lovers, who wish'd, yet fear'd, to know each others Thoughts? She trembling with a dismal Apprehension, that he lov'd no more; and he almost dying with fear, she should Reproach or Upbraid him with his Presumption; so that both being possess'd with equal Sentiments of Love, Fear, and Shame, they both stood fix'd with dejected Looks and Hearts, that heav'd with stifled Sighs. At last, Isabella, the softer and tender-hearted of the two, tho' not the most a Lover perhaps, not being able to contain her Love any longer within the bounds of Dissimulation or Discretion, being by Nature innocent, burst out into Tears, and all fainting with pressing Thoughts within, she fell languishly into a Chair that stood there, while the distracted Henault, who could not come to her Assistance, and finding Marks of Love, rather than Anger or Disdain, in that Confusion of Isabella's, throwing himself on his Knees at the Grate, implor'd her to behold him, to hear him, and to pardon him, who dy'd every moment for her, and who ador'd her with a violent Ardor; but yet, with such an one, as should (tho' he perish'd with it) be conformable to her Commands; and as he spoke, the Tears stream'd down his dying Eyes, that beheld her with all the tender Regard that ever Lover was capable of; she recover'd a little, and turn'd her too beautiful Face to him, and pierc'd him with a Look, that darted a thousand Joys and Flames into his Heart, with Eyes, that told him her Heart was burning and dying for him; for which Assurances, he made Ten thousand Asseverations of his never-dying Passion, and expressing as many Raptures and Excesses of Joy, to find her Eyes and Looks confess, he was not odious to her, and that the knowledge he was her Lover, did not make her hate him: In fine, he spoke so many things all soft and moving, and so well convinc'd her of his Passion, that she at last was compell'd by a mighty force, absolutely irresistible, to speak.

'Sir, (said she) perhaps you will wonder, where I, a Maid, brought up in the simplicity of Virtue, should learn the Confidence, not only to hear of Love from you, but to confess I am sensible of the most violent of its Pain my self; and I wonder, and am amazed at my own Daring, that I should have the Courage, rather to speak, than dye, and bury it in silence; but such is my Fate. Hurried by an unknown Force, which I have endeavoured always, in vain, to resist, I am compell'd to tell you, I love you, and have done so from the first moment I saw you; and you are the only Man born to give me Life or Death, to make me Happy or Blest; perhaps, had I not been confin'd, and, as it were, utterly forbid by my Vow, as well as my Modesty, to tell you this, I should not have been so miserable to have fallen thus low, as to have confess'd my Shame; but our Opportunities of Speaking are so few, and Letters so impossible to be sent without discovery, that perhaps this is the only time I shall ever have to speak with you alone.' And, at that word the Tears flow'd abundantly from her Eyes, and gave Henault leave to speak. 'Ah Madam! (said he) do not, as soon as you have rais'd me to the greatest Happiness in the World, throw me with one word beneath your Scorn, much easier 'tis to dye, and know I am lov'd, than never, never, hope to hear that blessed sound again from that beautiful Mouth: Ah, Madam! rather let me make use of this one opportunity our happy Luck has given us, and contrive how we may for ever see, and speak, to each other; let us assure one another, there are a thousand ways to escape a place so rigid, as denies us that Happiness; and denies the fairest Maid in the World, the privilege of her Creation, and the end to which she was form'd so Angelical.' And seeing Isabella was going to speak, lest she should say something, that might dissuade from an Attempt so dangerous and wicked, he persu'd to tell her, it might be indeed the last moment Heaven would give 'em, and besought her to answer him what he implor'd, whether she would fly with him from the Monastery? At this Word, she grew pale, and started, as at some dreadful Sound, and cry'd, 'Hah! what is't you say? Is it possible, you should propose a thing so wicked? And can it enter into your Imagination, because I have so far forget my Virtue, and my Vow, to become a Lover, I should therefore fall to so wretched a degree of Infamy and Reprobation? No, name it to me no more, if you would see me; and if it be as you say, a Pleasure to be belov'd by me; for I will sooner dye, than yield to what . . . Alas! I but too well approve!' These last words, she spoke with a fainting Tone, and the Tears fell anew from her fair soft Eyes. 'If it be so,' said he, (with a Voice so languishing, it could scarce be heard) 'If it be so, and that you are resolv'd to try, if my Love be eternal without Hope, without expectation of any other Joy, than seeing and adoring you through the Grate; I am, and must, and will be contented, and you shall see, I can prefer the Sighing to these cold Irons, that separate us, before all the Possessions of the rest of the World; that I chuse rather to lead my Life here, at this cruel Distance from you, for ever, than before the Embrace of all the Fair; and you shall see, how pleas'd I will be, to languish here; but as you see me decay, (for surely so I shall) do not triumph o're my languid Looks, and laugh at my Pale and meager Face; but, Pitying, say, How easily I might have preserv'd that Face, those Eyes, and all that Youth and Vigour, now no more, from this total Ruine I now behold it in, and love your Slave that dyes, and will be daily and visibly dying, as long as my Eyes can gaze on that fair Object, and my Soul be fed and kept alive with her Charming Wit and Conversation; if Love can live on such Airy Food, (tho' rich in it self, yet unfit, alone, to sustain Life) it shall be for ever dedicated to the lovely ISABELLA: But, oh! that time cannot be long! Fate will not lend her Slave many days, who loves too violently, to be satisfy'd to enjoy the fair Object of his Desires, no otherwise than at a Grate.'

He ceas'd speaking, for Sighs and Tears stopt his Voice, and he begg'd the liberty to sit down; and his Looks being quite alter'd, ISABELLA found her self touch'd to the very Soul, with a concern the most tender, that ever yielding Maid was oppress'd with: She had no power to suffer him to Languish, while she by one soft word could restore him, and being about to say a thousand things that would have been agreeable to him, she saw herself approach'd by some of the Nuns, and only had time to say, 'If you love me, live and hope.' The rest of the Nuns began to ask Henault of News, for he always brought them all that was Novel in the Town, and they were glad still of his Visits, above all other, for they heard, how all Amours and Intrigues pass'd in the World, by this young Cavalier. These last words of Isabella's were a Cordial to his Soul, and he, from that, and to conceal the present Affair, endeavour'd to assume all the Gaity he could, and told 'em all he could either remember, or invent, to please 'em, tho' he wish'd them a great way off at that time.

Thus they pass'd the day, till it was a decent hour for him to quit the Grate, and for them to draw the Curtain; all that Night did Isabella dedicate to Love, she went to Bed, with a Resolution, to think over all she had to do, and to consider, how she should manage this great Affair of her Life: I have already said, she had try'd all that was possible in Human Strength to perform, in the design of quitting a Passion so injurious to her Honour and Virtue, and found no means possible to accomplish it: She had try'd Fasting long, Praying fervently, rigid Penances and Pains, severe Disciplines, all the Mortification, almost to the destruction of Life it self, to conquer the unruly Flame; but still it burnt and rag'd but the more; so, at last, she was forc'd to permit that to conquer her, she could not conquer, and submitted to her Fate, as a thing destin'd her by Heaven it self; and after all this opposition, she fancy'd it was resisting even

Divine Providence, to struggle any longer with her Heart; and this being her real Belief, she the more patiently gave way to all the Thoughts that pleas'd her.

As soon as she was laid, without discoursing (as she us'd to do) to Katteriena, after they were in Bed, she pretended to be sleepy, and turning from her, setled her self to profound Thinking, and was resolv'd to conclude the Matter, between her Heart, and her Vow of Devotion, that Night, and she, having no more to determine, might end the Affair accordingly, the first opportunity she should have to speak to Henault, which was, to fly, and marry him; or, to remain for ever fix'd to her Vow of Chastity. This was the Debate; she brings Reason on both sides: Against the first, she sets the Shame of a Violated Vow, and considers, where she shall shew her Face after such an Action; to the Vow, she argues, that she was born in Sin, and could not live without it; that she was Human, and no Angel, and that, possibly, that Sin might be as soon forgiven, as another; that since all her devout Endeavours could not defend her from the Cause, Heaven ought to execute the Effect; that as to shewing her Face, so she saw that of Henault always turned (Charming as it was) towards her with love; what had she to do with the World, or car'd to behold any other?

Some times, she thought, it would be more Brave and Pious to dye, than to break her Vow; but she soon answer'd that, as false Arguing, for Self-Murder was the worst of Sins, and in the Deadly Number. She could, after such an Action, live to repent, and, of two Evils, she ought to chuse the least; she dreads to think, since she had so great a Reputation for Virtue and Piety, both in the Monastery, and in the World, what they both would say, when she should commit an Action so contrary to both these, she posest; but, after a whole Night's Debate, Love was strongest, and gain'd the Victory. She never went about to think, how she should escape, because she knew it would be easy, the keeping of the Key of the Monastery, [was] often intrusted in her keeping, and was, by turns, in the hands of many more, whose Virtue and Discretion was Infallible, and out of Doubt; besides, her Aunt being the Lady Abbess, she had greater privilege than the rest; so that she had no more to do, she thought, than to acquaint Henault with her Design, as soon as she should get an opportunity. Which was not quickly; but, in the mean time, Isabella's Father dy'd, which put some little stop to our Lover's Happiness, and gave her a short time of Grief; but Love, who, while he is new and young, can do us Miracles, soon wip'd her Eyes, and chas'd away all Sorrows from her Heart, and grew every day more and more impatient, to put her new Design in Execution, being every day more resolv'd. Her Father's Death had remov'd one Obstacle, and secur'd her from his Reproaches; and now she only wants Opportunity, first, to acquaint Henault, and then to fly.

She waited not long, all things concurring to her desire; for Katteriena falling sick, she had the good luck, as she call'd it then, to entertain Henault at the Grate oftentimes alone; the first moment she did so, she entertain'd him with the good News, and told him, She had at last vanquish'd her Heart in favour of him, and loving him above all things, Honour, her Vow or Reputation, had resolv'd to abandon her self wholly to him, to give her self up to love and serve him, and that she had no other Consideration in the World; but Henault, instead of returning her an Answer, all Joy and Satisfaction, held down his Eyes, and Sighing, with a dejected Look, he cry'd, 'Ah, Madam! Pity a Man so wretched and undone, as not to be sensible of this Blessing as I ought.' She grew pale at this Reply, and trembling, expected he would proceed: ''Tis not (continued he) that I want Love, tenderest Passion, and all the desire Youth and Love can inspire; But, Oh, Madam! when I consider, (for raving mad in Love as I am for your sake, I do consider) that if I should take you from this Repose, Nobly Born and Educated, as you are; and, for that Act, should find a rigid Father deprive me of all that ought to support you, and afford your Birth, Beauty, and Merits, their due, what would you say? How would you Reproach me?' He sighing, expected her Answer, when Blushes overspreading her Face, she reply'd, in a Tone all haughty and angry, 'Ah,

Henault! Am I then refus'd, after having abandon'd all things for you? Is it thus, you reward my Sacrific'd Honour, Vows, and Virtue? Cannot you hazard the loss of Fortune to possess Isabella, who loses all for you!' Then bursting into Tears, at her misfortune of Loving, she suffer'd him to say, 'Oh, Charming fair one! how industrious is your Cruelty, to find out new Torments for an Heart, already press'd down with the Severities of Love? Is it possible, you can make so unhappy a Construction of the tenderest part of my Passion? And can you imagin it want of Love in me, to consider, how I shall preserve and merit the vast Blessing Heaven has given me? Is my Care a Crime? And would not the most deserving Beauty of the World hate me, if I should, to preserve my Life, and satisfy the Passion of my fond Heart, reduce her to the Extremities of Want and Misery? And is there any thing, in what I have said, but what you ought to take for the greatest Respect and tenderness!' 'Alas! (reply'd Isabella sighing) young as I am, all unskilful in Love I find, but what I feel, that Discretion is no part of it; and Consideration, inconsistent with the Nobler Passion, who will subsist of its own Nature, and Love unmixed with any other Sentiment? And 'tis not pure, if it be otherwise: I know, had I mix'd Discretion with mine, my Love must have been less, I never thought of living, but my Love; and, if I consider'd at all, it was, that Grandure and Magnificence were useless Trifles to Lovers, wholly needless and troublesom. I thought of living in some loanly Cottage, far from the noise of crowded busie Cities, to walk with thee in Groves, and silent Shades, where I might hear no Voice but thine; and when we had been tir'd, to sit us done by some cool murmuring Rivulet, and be to each a World, my Monarch thou, and I thy Sovereign Queen, while Wreaths of Flowers shall crown our happy Heads, some fragrant Bank our Throne, and Heaven our Canopy: Thus we might laugh at Fortune, and the Proud, despise the duller World, who place their Joys in mighty Shew and Equipage. Alas! my Nature could not bear it, I am unus'd to Wordly Vanities, and would boast of nothing but my Henault; no Riches, but his Love; no Grandure, but his Presence.' She ended speaking, with Tears, and he reply'd, 'Now, now, I find, my Isabella loves indeed, when she's content to abandon the World for my sake; Oh! thou hast named the only happy Life that suits my quiet Nature, to be retir'd, has always been my Joy! But to be so with thee! Oh! thou hast charm'd me with a Thought so dear, as has for ever banish'd all my Care, but how to receive thy Goodness! Please think no more what my angry Parent may do, when he shall hear, how I have dispos'd of my self against his Will and Pleasure, but trust to Love and Providence; no more! be gone all Thoughts, but those of Isabella!'

As soon as he had made an end of expressing his Joy, he fell to consulting how, and when, she should escape; and since it was uncertain, when she should be offer'd the Key, for she would not ask for it, she resolv'd to give him notice, either by word of Mouth, or a bit of Paper she would write in, and give him through the Grate the first opportunity; and, parting for that time, they both resolv'd to get up what was possible for their Support, till Time should reconcile Affairs and Friends, and to wait the happy hour.

Isabella's dead Mother had left Jewels, of the value of 2000l. to her Daughter, at her Decease, which Jewels were in the possession, now, of the Lady Abbess, and were upon Sale, to be added to the Revenue of the Monastery; and as Isabella was the most Prudent of her Sex, at least, had hitherto been so esteem'd, she was intrusted with all that was in possession of the Lady Abbess, and 'twas not difficult to make her self Mistress of all her own Jewels; as also, some 3 or 400l. in Gold, that was hoarded up in her Ladyship's Cabinet, against any Accidents that might arrive to the Monastery; these Isabella also made her own, and put up with the Jewels; and having acquainted Henault, with the Day and Hour of her Escape, he got together what he could, and waiting for her, with his Coach, one Night, when no body was awake but her self, when rising softly, as she us'd to do, in the Night, to her Devotion, she stole so dexterously out of the Monastery, as no body knew any thing of it; she carry'd away the Keys with her, after having lock'd all the Doors, for she was intrusted often with all. She found Henault waiting in his Coach, and trusted none but an honest Coachman that lov'd him; he receiv'd her with all the Transports of a truly ravish'd Lover, and she was infinitely charm'd with the new Pleasure of his Embraces and Kisses.

They drove out of Town immediately, and because she durst not be seen in that Habit, (for it had been immediate Death for both) they drove into a Thicket some three Miles from the Town, where Henault having brought her some of his younger Sister's Clothes, he made her put off her Habit, and put on those; and, rending the other, they hid them in a Sand-pit, covered over with Broom, and went that Night forty Miles from Iper, to a little Town upon the River Rhine, where, changing their Names, they were forthwith married, and took a House in a Country Village, a Farm, where they resolv'd to live retir'd, by the name of Beroone, and drove a Farming Trade; however, not forgetting to set Friends and Engines at work, to get their Pardon, as Criminals, first, that had trangress'd the Law; and, next, as disobedient Persons, who had done contrary to the Will and Desire of their Parents: Isabella writ to her Aunt the most moving Letters in the World, so did Henault to his Father; but she was a long time, before she could gain so much as an answer from her Aunt, and Henault was so unhappy, as never to gain one from his Father; who no sooner heard the News that was spread over all the Town and Country, that young Henault was fled with the so fam'd Isabella, a Nun, and singular for Devotion and Piety of Life, but he immediately setled his Estate on his younger Son, cutting Henault off with all his Birthright, which was 5000l. a Year. This News, you may believe, was not very pleasing to the young Man, who tho' in possession of the loveliest Virgin, and now Wife, that ever Man was bless'd with; yet when he reflected, he should have children by her, and these and she should come to want, (he having been magnificently Educated, and impatient of scanty Fortune) he laid it to Heart, and it gave him a thousand Uneasinesses in the midst of unspeakable Joys; and the more be strove to hide his Sentiments from Isabella, the more tormenting it was within; he durst not name it to her, so insuperable a Grief it would cause in her, to hear him complain; and tho' she could live hardly, as being bred to a devout and severe Life, he could not, but must let the Man of Quality shew it self; even in the disguise of an humbler Farmer: Besides all this, he found nothing of his Industry thrive, his Cattel still dy'd in the midst of those that were in full Vigour and Health of other Peoples; his Crops of Wheat and Barly, and other Grain, tho' manag'd by able and knowing Husbandmen, were all, either Mildew'd, or Blasted, or some Misfortune still arriv'd to him; his Coach-Horses would fight and kill one another, his Barns sometimes be fir'd; so that it became a Proverb all over the Country, if any ill Luck had arriv'd to any body, they would say, 'They had Monsieur BEROONE'S Luck.' All these Reflections did but add to his Melancholy, and he grew at last to be in some want, insomuch, that Isabella, who had by her frequent Letters, and submissive Supplications, to her Aunt, (who lov'd her tenderly) obtain'd her Pardon, and her Blessing; she now press'd her for some Money, and besought her to consider, how great a Fortune she had brought to the Monastery, and implor'd, she would allow her some Sallary out of it, for she had been marry'd two Years, and most of what she had was exhausted. The Aunt, who found, that what was done, could not be undone, did, from time to time, supply her so, as one might have liv'd very decently on that very Revenue; but that would not satisfy the great Heart of Henault. He was now about three and twenty Years old, and Isabella about eighteen, too young, and too lovely a Pair, to begin their Misfortunes so soon; they were both the most Just and Pious in the World; they were Examples of Goodness, and Eminent for Holy Living, and for perfect Loving, and yet nothing thriv'd they undertook; they had no Children, and all their Joy was in each other; at last, one good Fortune arriv'd to them, by the Solicitations of the Lady Abbess, and the Bishop, who was her near Kinsman, they got a Pardon for Isabella's quitting the Monastery, and marrying, so that she might now return to her own Country again. Henault having also his Pardon, they immediately quit the place, where they had remain'd for two Years, and came again into Flanders, hoping, the change of place might afford 'em better Luck.

Henault then began again to solicit his Cruel Father, but nothing would do, he refus'd to see him, or to receive any Letters from him; but, at last, he prevail'd so far with him, as that he sent a Kinsman to him, to assure him, if he would leave his Wife, and go into the French Campagn, he would Equip him as well as his Quality requir'd, and that, according as he behav'd himself, he should gain his Favour; but if he liv'd Idly at home, giving up his Youth and Glory to lazy Love, he would have no more to say to him, but race him out of his Heart, and out of his Memory.

He had setled himself in a very pretty House, furnished with what was fitting for the Reception of any Body of Quality that would live a private Life, and they found all the Respect that their Merits deserv'd from all the World, every body entirely loving and endeavouring to serve them; and Isabella so perfectly had the Ascendent over her Aunt's Heart, that she procur'd from her all that she could desire, and much more than she could expect. She was perpetually progging and saving all that she could, to enrich and advance her, and, at last, pardoning and forgiving Henault, lov'd him as her own Child; so that all things look'd with a better Face than before, and never was so dear and fond a Couple seen, as Henault and Isabella; but, at last, she prov'd with Child, and the Aunt, who might reasonably believe, so young a Couple would have a great many Children, and foreseeing there was no Provision likely to be made them, unless he pleas'd his Father, for if the Aunt should chance to dye, all their Hope was gone; she therefore daily solicited him to obey his Father, and go to the Camp; and that having atchiev'd Fame and Renown, he would return a Favourite to his Father, and Comfort to his Wife: After she had solicited in vain, for he was not able to endure the thought of leaving Isabella, melancholy as he was with his ill Fortune; the Bishop, kinsman to Isabella, took him to task, and urg'd his Youth and Birth, and that he ought not to wast both without Action, when all the World was employ'd; and, that since his Father had so great a desire he should go into a Campagn, either to serve the Venetian against the Turks, or into the French Service, which he lik'd best; he besought him to think of it; and since he had satisfy'd his Love, he should and ought to satisfy his Duty, it being absolutely necessary for the wiping off the Stain of his Sacrilege, and to gain him the favour of Heaven, which, he found, had hitherto been averse to all he had undertaken: In fine, all his Friends, and all who lov'd him, joyn'd in this Design, and all thought it convenient, nor was he insensible of the Advantage it might bring him; but Love, which every day grew fonder and fonder in his Heart, oppos'd all their Reasonings, tho' he saw all the Brave Youth of the Age preparing to go, either to one Army, or the other.

At last, he lets Isabella know, what Propositions he had made him, both by his Father, and his Relations; at the very first Motion, she almost fainted in his Arms, while he was speaking, and it possess'd her with so intire a Grief, that she miscarry'd, to the insupportable Torment of her tender Husband and Lover, so that, to re-establish her Repose, he was forc'd to promise not to go; however, she consider'd all their Circumstances, and weigh'd the Advantages that might redound both to his Honour and Fortune, by it; and, in a matter of a Month's time, with the Persuasions and Reasons of her Friends, she suffer'd him to resolve upon going, her self determining to retire to the Monastery, till the time of his Return; but when she nam'd the Monastery, he grew pale and disorder'd, and obliged her to promise him, not to enter into it any more, for fear they should never suffer her to come forth again; so that he resolv'd not to depart, till she had made a Vow to him, never to go again within the Walls of a Religious House, which had already been so fatal to them. She promis'd, and he believ'd.

Henault, at last, overcame his Heart, which pleaded so for his Stay, and sent his Father word, he was ready to obey him, and to carry the first Efforts of his Arms against the common Foes of Christendom, the Turks; his Father was very well pleas'd at this, and sent him Two thousand Crowns, his Horses and Furniture sutable to his Quality, and a Man to wait on him; so that it was not long e're he got himself in order to be gone, after a dismal parting.

He made what hast he could to the French Army, then under the Command of the Monsignior, the Duke of Beaufort, then at Candia, and put himself a Voluntier under his Conduct; in which Station was Villenoys, who, you have already heard, was so passionate a Lover of Isabella, who no sooner heard of Henault's being arriv'd, and that he was Husband to Isabella, but he was impatient to learn, by what strange Adventure he came to gain her, even from her Vow'd Retreat, when he, with all his Courtship, could not be so happy, tho' she was then free in the World, and Unvow'd to Heaven.

As soon as he sent his Name to Henault, he was sent for up, for Henault had heard of Villenoys, and that he had been a Lover of Isabella; they receiv'd one another with all the endearing Civility imaginable for the aforesaid Reason, and for that he was his Country-man, tho' unknown to him, Villenoys being gone to the Army, just as Henault came from the Jesuits College. A great deal of Endearment pass'd between them, and they became, from that moment, like two sworn Brothers, and he receiv'd the whole Relation from Henault, of his Amour.

It was not long before the Siege began anew, for he arriv'd at the beginning of the Spring, and, as soon as he came, almost, they fell to Action; and it happen'd upon a day, that a Party of some Four hundred Men resolv'd to sally out upon the Enemy, as, when ever they could, they did; but as it is not my business to relate the History of the War, being wholly unacquainted with the Terms of Battels, I shall only say, That these Men were led by Villenoys, and that Henault would accompany him in this Sally, and that they acted very Noble, and great Things, worthy of a Memory in the History of that Siege; but this day, particularly, they had an occasion to shew their Valour, which they did very much to their Glory; but, venturing too far, they were ambush'd, in the persuit of the Party of the Enemies, and being surrounded, Villenoys had the unhappiness to see his gallant Friend fall, fighting and dealing of Wounds around him, even as he descended to the Earth, for he fell from his Horse at the same moment that he kill'd a Turk; and Villenoys could neither assist him, nor had he the satisfaction to be able to rescue his dead Body from under the Horses, but, with much ado, escaping with his own Life, got away, in spite of all that follow'd him, and recover'd the Town, before they could overtake him: He passionately bewail'd the Loss of this brave young Man, and offer'd any Recompence to those, that would have ventur'd to have search'd for his dead Body among the Slain; but it was not fit to hazard the Living, for unnecessary Services to the Dead; and tho' he had a great mind to have Interr'd him, he rested content with what he wish'd to pay his Friends Memory, tho' he could not: So that all the Service now he could do him, was, to write to Isabella, to whom he had not writ, tho' commanded by her so to do, in three Years before, which was never since she took Orders. He gave her an Account of the Death of her Husband, and how Gloriously he fell fighting for the Holy Cross, and how much Honour he had won, if it had been his Fate to have outliv'd that great, but unfortunate, Day, where, with 400 Men, they had kill'd 1500 of the Enemy. The General Beaufort himself had so great a Respect and Esteem for this young Man, and knowing him to be of Quality, that he did him the honour to bemoan him, and to send a Condoling Letter to Isabella, how much worth her Esteem he dy'd, and that he had Eterniz'd his Memory with the last Gasp of his Life.

When this News arriv'd, it may be easily imagin'd, what Impressions, or rather Ruins, it made in the Heart of this fair Mourner; the Letters came by his Man, who saw him fall in Battel, and came off with those few that escap'd with Villenoys; he brought back what Money he had, a few Jewels, with Isabella's Picture that he carry'd with him and had left in his Chamber in the Fort at Candia, for fear of breaking it in Action. And now Isabella's Sorrow grew to the Extremity, she thought, she could not suffer more than she did by his Absence, but she now found a Grief more killing; she hung her Chamber with Black, and liv'd without the Light of Day: Only Wax Lights, that let her behold the Picture of this Charming Man, before which she sacrific'd Floods of Tears. He had now been absent about ten Months, and she had learnt just to live without him, but Hope preserv'd her then; but now she had nothing, for which to wish to live. She, for about two Months after the News arriv'd, liv'd without seeing any Creature but a young Maid, that was her Woman; but extream Importunity oblig'd her to give way to the Visits of her Friends, who endeavour'd to restore her Melancholy Soul to its wonted Easiness; for, however it was oppress'd within, by Henault's Absence, she bore it off with a modest Chearfulness; but now she found, that Fortitude and Virtue fail'd her, when she was assur'd, he was no more: She continu'd thus Mourning, and thus inclos'd, the space of a whole Year, never suffering the Visit of any Man, but of a near Relation; so that she acquir'd a Reputation, such as never any young Beauty had, for she was now but Nineteen, and her Face and Shape more excellent than ever; she daily increas'd in Beauty, which, joyn'd to her Exemplary Piety, Charity, and all other excellent Qualities, gain'd her a wonderous Fame, and begat an Awe and Reverence in all that heard of her, and there was no Man of any Quality, that did not Adore her. After her Year was up, she went to the Churches, but would never be seen any where else abroad, but that was enough to procure her a thousand Lovers; and some, who had the boldness to send her Letters, which, if she receiv'd, she gave no Answer to, and many she sent back unread and unseal'd: So that she would encourage none, tho' their Quality was far beyond what she could hope; but she was resolv'd to marry no more, however her Fortune might require it.

It happen'd, that, about this time, Candia being unfortunately taken by the Turks, all the brave Men that escap'd the Sword, return'd, among them, Villenoys, who no sooner arriv'd, but he sent to let Isabella know of it, and to beg the Honour of waiting on her; desirous to learn what Fate befel her dear Lord, she suffer'd him to visit her, where he found her, in her Mourning, a thousand times more Fair, (at least, he fancy'd so) than ever she appear'd to be; so that if he lov'd her before, he now ador'd her; if he burnt then, he rages now; but the awful Sadness, and soft Languishment of her Eyes, hinder'd him from the presumption of speaking of his Passion to her, tho' it would have been no new thing; and his first Visit was spent in the Relation of every Circumstance of Henault's Death; and, at his going away, he begg'd leave to visit her sometimes, and she gave him permission: He lost no time, but made use of the Liberty she had given him; and when his Sister, who was a great Companion of Isabella's, went to see her, he would still wait on her; so that, either with his own Visits, and those of his Sister's, he saw Isabella every day, and had the good luck to see, he diverted her, by giving her Relations of Transactions of the Siege, and the Customs and Manners of the Turks: All he said, was with so good a Grace, that he render'd every thing agreeable; he was, besides, very Beautiful, well made, of Quality and Fortune, and fit to inspire Love.

He made his Visits so often, and so long, that, at last, he took the Courage to speak of his Passion, which, at first, Isabella would by no means hear of, but, by degrees, she yielded more and more to listen to his tender Discourse; and he liv'd thus with her two Years, before he could gain any more upon her Heart, than to suffer him to speak of Love to her; but that, which subdu'd her quite was, That her Aunt, the Lady Abbess, dy'd, and with her, all the Hopes and Fortune of Isabella, so that she was left with only a Charming Face and Meen, a Virtue, and a Discretion above her Sex, to make her Fortune within the World; into a Religious House, she was resolv'd not to go, because her Heart deceiv'd her once, and she durst not trust it again, whatever it promis'd.

The death of this Lady made her look more favourably on Villenoys; but yet, she was resolv'd to try his Love to the utmost, and keep him off, as long as 'twas possible she could subsist, and 'twas for Interest she married again, tho' she lik'd the Person very well; and since she was forc'd to submit her self to be a second time a Wife, she thought, she could live better with Villenoys, than any other, since for him she ever had a great Esteem; and fancy'd the Hand of Heaven had pointed out her Destiny, which she could not avoid, without a Crime.

So that when she was again importun'd by her impatient Lover, she told him, She had made a Vow to remain three Years, at least, before she would marry again, after the Death of the best of Men and Husbands, and him who had the Fruits of her early Heart; and, notwithstanding all the Solicitations of Villenoys, she would not consent to marry him, till her Vow of Widowhood was expir'd.

He took her promise, which he urg'd her to give him, and to shew the height of his Passion in his obedience; he condescends to stay her appointed time, tho' he saw her every day, and all his Friends and Relations made her Visits upon this new account, and there was nothing talk'd on, but this design'd Wedding, which, when the time was expir'd, was perform'd accordingly with great Pomp and Magnificence, for Villenoys had no Parents to hinder his Design; or if he had, the Reputation and Virtue of this Lady would have subdu'd them.

The Marriage was celebrated in this House, where she liv'd ever since her Return from Germany, from the time she got her Pardon; and when Villenoys was preparing all things in a more magnificent Order at his Villa, some ten Miles from the City, she was very melancholy, and would often say, She had been us'd to such profound Retreat, and to live without the fatigue of Noise and Equipage, that, she fear'd, she should never endure that Grandeur, which was proper for his Quality; and tho' the House, in the Country, was the most beautifully Situated in all Flanders, she was afraid of a numerous Train, and kept him, for the most part, in this pretty City Mansion, which he Adorn'd and Enlarg'd, as much as she would give him leave; so that there wanted nothing, to make this House fit to receive the People of the greatest Quality, little as it was: But all the Servants and Footmen, all but one Valet, and the Maid, were lodg'd abroad, for Isabella, not much us'd to the sight of Men about her, suffer'd them as seldom as possible, to come in her Presence, so that she liv'd more like a Nun still, than a Lady of the World; and very rarely any Maids came about her, but Maria, who had always permission to come, when ever she pleas'd, unless forbidden.

As Villenoys had the most tender and violent Passion for his Wife, in the World, he suffer'd her to be pleas'd at any rate, and to live in what Method she best lik'd, and was infinitely satisfy'd with the Austerity and manner of her Conduct, since in his Arms, and alone, with him, she wanted nothing that could Charm; so that she was esteemed the fairest and best of Wives, and he the most happy of all Mankind. When she would go abroad, she had her Coaches Rich and Gay, and her Livery ready to attend her in all the Splendour imaginable; and he was always buying one rich Jewel, or Necklace, or some great Rarity or other, that might please her; so that there was nothing her Soul could desire, which it had not, except the Assurance of Eternal Happiness, which she labour'd incessantly to gain. She had no Discontent, but because she was not bless'd with a Child; but she submits to the pleasure of Heaven, and endeavour'd, by her good Works, and her Charity, to make the Poor her Children, and was ever doing Acts of Virtue, to make the Proverb good, That more are the Children of the Barren, than the Fruitful Woman. She liv'd in this Tranquility, belov'd by all, for the space of five Years, and Time (and perpetual Obligations from Villenoys, who was the most indulgent and indearing Man in the World) had almost worn out of her Heart the Thought of Henault, or if she remember'd him, it was in her Prayers, or sometimes with a short sigh, and no more, tho' it was a great while, before she could subdue her Heart to that Calmness; but she was prudent, and wisely bent all her Endeavours to please, oblige, and caress, the deserving Living, and to strive all she could, to forget the unhappy Dead, since it could not but redound to the disturbance of her Repose, to think of him; so that she had now transferr'd all that Tenderness she had for him, to Villenoys.

Villenoys, of all Diversions, lov'd Hunting, and kept, at his Country House, a very famous Pack of Dogs, which he us'd to lend, sometimes, to a young Lord, who was his dear Friend, and his Neighbour in the Country, who would often take them, and be out two or three days together, where he heard of Game, and oftentimes Villenoys and he would be a whole Week at a time exercising in this Sport, for there was no Game near at hand. This young Lord had sent him a Letter, to invite him fifteen Miles farther than his own Villa, to hunt, and appointed to meet him at his Country House, in order to go in search of this promis'd Game; So that Villenoys got about a Week's Provision, of what Necessaries he thought he should want in that time; and taking only his Valet, who lov'd the Sport, he left Isabella for a Week to her Devotion, and her other innocent Diversions of fine Work, at which she was Excellent, and left the Town to go meet this young Challenger.

When Villenoys was at any time out, it was the custom of Isabella to retire to her Chamber, and to receive no Visits, not even the Ladies, so absolutely she devoted her self to her Husband: All the first day she pass'd over in this manner, and Evening being come, she order'd her Supper to be brought to her Chamber, and, because it was Washing-day the next day, she order'd all her Maids to go very early to Bed, that they might be up betimes, and to leave only Maria to attend her; which was accordingly done. This Maria was a young Maid, that was very discreet, and, of all things in the World, lov'd her Lady, whom she had liv'd with, ever since she came from the Monastery.

When all were in Bed, and the little light Supper just carry'd up to the Lady, and only, as I said, Maria attending, some body knock'd at the Gate, it being about Nine of the Clock at Night; so Maria snatching up a Candle, went to the Gate, to see who it might be; when she open'd the Door, she found a Man in a very odd Habit, and a worse Countenance, and asking, Who he would speak with? He told her, Her Lady: My Lady (reply'd Maria) does not use to receive Visits at this hour; Pray, what is your Business? He reply'd, That which I will deliver only to your Lady, and that she may give me Admittance, pray, deliver her this Ring: And pulling off a small Ring, with Isabella's Name and Hair in it, he gave it Maria, who, shutting the Gate upon him, went in with the Ring; as soon as Isabella saw it, she was ready to swound on the Chair where she sate, and cry'd, Where had you this? Maria reply'd, An old rusty Fellow at the Gate gave it me, and desired, it might be his Pasport to you; I ask'd his Name, but he said, You knew him not, but he had great News to tell you. Isabella reply'd, (almost swounding again) Oh, Maria! I am ruin'd. The Maid, all this while, knew not what she meant, nor, that that was a Ring given to Henault by her Mistress, but endeavouring to recover her, only ask'd her, What she should say to the old Messenger? Isabella bid her bring him up to her, (she had scarce Life to utter these last words) and before she was well recover'd, Maria enter'd with the Man; and Isabella making a Sign to her, to depart the Room, she was left alone with him.

Henault (for it was he) stood trembling and speechless before her, giving her leisure to take a strict Survey of him; at first finding no Feature nor Part of Henault about him, her Fears began to lessen, and she hop'd, it was not he, as her first Apprehensions had suggested; when he (with the Tears of Joy standing in his Eyes, and not daring suddenly to approach her, for fear of encreasing that Disorder he saw in her pale Face) began to speak to her, and cry'd, Fair Creature! is there no Remains of your Henault left in this Face of mine, all o'regrown with Hair? Nothing in these Eyes, sunk with eight Years Absence from you, and Sorrows? Nothing in this Shape, bow'd with Labour and Griefs, that can inform you? I was once that happy Man you lov'd! At these words, Tears stop'd his Speech, and Isabella kept them Company, for yet she wanted Words. Shame and Confusion fill'd her Soul, and she was not able to lift her Eyes up, to consider the Face of him, whose Voice she knew so perfectly well. In one moment, she run over a thousand Thoughts. She finds, by his Return, she is not only expos'd to all the Shame imaginable; to all the Upbraiding, on his part, when he shall know she is marry'd to another; but all the Fury and Rage of Villenoys, and the Scorn of the Town, who will look on her as an Adulteress: She sees Henault poor, and knew, she must fall from all the Glory and Tranquility she had for five happy Years triumph'd in; in which time, she had known no Sorrow, or Care, tho' she had endur'd a thousand with Henault. She dyes, to think, however, that he should know, she had been so lightly in Love with him, to marry again; and she dyes, to think, that Villenoys must see her again in the Arms of Henault; besides, she could not recal her Love, for Love, like Reputation, once fled, never returns more. 'Tis impossible to love, and cease to love, (and love another) and yet return again to the first Passion, tho' the Person have all the Charms, or a thousand times more than it had, when it first conquer'd. This Mistery in Love, it may be, is not generally known, but nothing is more certain. One may a while suffer the Flame to languish, but there may be a reviving Spark in the Ashes, rak'd up, that may burn anew; but when 'tis quite extinguish'd, it never returns or rekindles.

'Twas so with the Heart of Isabella; had she believ'd, Henault had been living, she had lov'd to the last moment of their Lives; but, alas! the Dead are soon forgotten, and she now lov'd only Villenoys.

After they had both thus silently wept, with very different sentiments, she thought 'twas time to speak; and dissembling as well as she could, she caress'd him in her Arms, and told him, She could not express her Surprize and Joy for his Arrival. If she did not Embrace him heartily, or speak so Passionately as she us'd to do, he fancy'd it her Confusion, and his being in a condition not so fit to receive Embraces from her; and evaded them as much as 'twas possible for him to do, in respect to her, till he had dress'd his Face, and put himself in order; but the Supper being just brought up, when he knock'd, she order'd him to sit down and Eat, and he desir'd her not to let Maria know who he was, to see how long it would be, before she knew him or would call him to mind. But Isabella commanded Maria, to make up a Bed in such a Chamber, without disturbing her Fellows, and dismiss'd her from waiting at Table. The Maid admir'd, what strange, good, and joyful News, this Man had brought her Mistress, that he was so Treated, and alone with her, which never any Man had yet been; but she never imagin'd the Truth, and knew her Lady's Prudence too well, to question her Conduct. While they were at Supper, Isabella oblig'd him to tell her, How he came to be reported Dead; of which, she receiv'd Letters, both from Monsieur Villenoys, and the Duke of Beaufort, and by his Man the News, who saw him Dead? He told her, That, after the Fight, of which, first, he gave her an account, he being left among the Dead, when the Enemy came to Plunder and strip 'em, they found, he had Life in him, and appearing as an Eminent Person, they thought it better Booty to save me, (continu'd he) and get my Ransom, than to strip me, and bury me among the Dead; so they bore me off to a Tent, and recover'd me to Life; and, after that, I was recover'd of my Wounds, and sold, by the Soldier that had taken me, to a Spahee, who kept me a Slave, setting a great Ransom on me, such as I was not able to pay. I writ several times, to give you, and my Father, an account of my Misery, but receiv'd no Answer, and endur'd seven Years of Dreadful Slavery: When I found, at last, an opportunity to make my Escape, and from that time, resolv'd, never to cut the Hair of this Beard, till I should either see my dearest Isabella again, or hear some News of her. All that I fear'd, was, That she was Dead; and, at that word, he fetch'd a deep Sigh; and viewing all things so infinitely more Magnificent than he had left 'em, or, believ'd, she could afford; and, that she was far more Beautiful in Person, and Rich in Dress, than when he left her: He had a thousand Torments of Jealousie that seiz'd him, of which, he durst not make any mention, but rather chose to wait a little, and see, whether she had lost her Virtue: He desir'd, he might send for a Barber, to put his Face in some handsomer Order, and more fit for the Happiness 'twas that Night to receive; but she told him, No Dress, no Disguise, could render him more Dear and Acceptable to her, and that to morrow was time enough, and that his Travels had render'd him more fit for Repose, than Dressing. So that after a little while, they had talk'd over all they had a mind to say, all that was very indearing on his side, and as much Concern as she could force, on hers; she conducted him to his Chamber, which was very rich, and which gave him a very great addition of Jealousie: However, he suffer'd her to help him to Bed, which she seem'd to do, with all the tenderness in the World; and when she had seen him laid, she said, She would go to her Prayers, and come to him as soon as she had done, which being before her usual Custom, it was not a wonder to him she stay'd long, and he, being extreamly tir'd with his Journy, fell asleep. 'Tis true, Isabella essay'd to Pray, but alas! it was in vain, she was distracted with a thousand Thoughts what to do, which the more she thought, the more it distracted her; she was a thousand times about to end her Life, and, at one stroke, rid her self of the Infamy, that, she saw, must inevitably fall upon her; but Nature was frail, and the Tempter strong: And after a thousand Convulsions, even worse than Death it self, she resolv'd upon the Murder of Henault, as the only means of removing all the obstacles to her future Happiness; she resolv'd on this, but after she had done so, she was seiz'd with so great Horror, that she imagin'd, if she perform'd it, she should run Mad; and yet, if she did not, she should be also Frantick, with the Shames and Miseries that would befal her; and believing the Murder the least Evil, since she could never live with him, she fix'd her Heart on that; and causing her self to be put immediately to Bed, in her own Bed, she made Maria go to hers, and when all was still, she softly rose, and taking a Candle with her, only in her Night-Gown and Slippers, she goes to the Bed of the Unfortunate Henault, with a Penknife in her hand; but considering, she knew not how to conceal the Blood, should she cut his Throat, she resolves to Strangle him, or Smother him with a Pillow; that last thought was no sooner borne, but put in Execution; and, as he soundly slept, she smother'd him without any Noise, or so much as his Strugling: But when she had done this dreadful Deed, and saw the dead Corps of her once-lov'd Lord, lye Smiling (as it were) upon her, she fell into a Swound with the Horror of the Deed, and it had been well for her she had there dy'd; but she reviv'd again, and awaken'd to more and new Horrors, she flyes all frighted from the Chamber, and fancies, the Phantom of her dead Lord persues her; she runs from Room to Room, and starts and stares, as if she saw him continually before her. Now all that was ever Soft and Dear to her, with him, comes into her Heart, and, she finds, he conquers anew, being Dead, who could not gain her Pity, while Living.

While she was thus flying from her Guilt, in vain, she hears one knock with Authority at the Door: She is now more affrighted, if possible, and knows not whither to fly for Refuge; she fancies, they are already the Officers of Justice, and that Ten thousand Tortures and Wrecks are fastening on her, to make her confess the horrid Murder; the knocking increases, and so loud, that the Laundry Maids believing it to be the Woman that us'd to call them up, and help them to Wash, rose, and, opening the Door, let in Villenoys; who having been at his Country Villa, and finding there a Footman, instead of his Friend, who waited to tell him, His Master was fallen sick of the Small Pox, and could not wait on him, he took Horse, and came back to his lovely Isabella; but running up, as he us'd to do, to her Chamber, he found her not, and seeing a Light in another Room, he went in, but found Isabella flying from him, out at another Door, with all the speed she could, he admires at this Action, and the more, because his Maid told him Her Lady had been a Bed a good while; he grows a little Jealous, and persues her, but still she flies; at last he caught her in his Arms, where she fell into a swound, but quickly recovering, he set her down in a Chair, and, kneeling before her, implor'd to know what she ayl'd, and why she fled from him, who ador'd her? She only fix'd a ghastly Look upon him, and said, She was not well: 'Oh! (said he) put not me off with such poor Excuses, Isabella never fled from me, when Ill, but came to my Arms, and to my Bosom, to find a Cure; therefore, tell me, what's the matter?' At that, she fell a weeping in a most violent manner, and cry'd, She was for ever undone: He, being mov'd with Love and Compassion, conjur'd her to tell what she ayl'd: 'Ah! (said she) thou and I, and all of us, are undone!' At this, he lost all Patience and rav'd, and cry'd, Tell me, and tell me immediately, what's the matter? When she saw his Face pale, and his Eyes fierce, she fell on her knees, and cry'd, 'Oh! you can never Pardon me, if I should tell you, and yet, alas! I am innocent of Ill, by all that's good, I am.' But her Conscience accusing her at that word, she was silent. If thou art Innocent, said Villenoys, taking her up in his Arms, and kissing her wet Face, 'By all that's Good, I Pardon thee, what ever thou hast done.' 'Alas! (said she) Oh! but I dare not name it, 'till you swear.' 'By all that's Sacred, (reply'd he) and by whatever Oath you can oblige me to; by my inviolable Love to thee, and by thy own dear Self, I swear, whate're it be, I do forgive thee; I know, thou art too good to commit a Sin I may not with Honour, pardon.'

With this, and hearten'd by his Caresses, she told him, That Henault was return'd; and repeating to him his Escape, she said, She had put him to Bed, and when he expected her to come, she fell on her Knees at the Bedside, and confess'd, She was married to Villenoys; at that word (said she) he fetch'd a deep Sigh or two, and presently after, with a very little struggling, dy'd; and, yonder, he lyes still in the Bed. After this, she wept so abundantly, that all Villenoys could do, could hardly calm her Spirits; but after, consulting what they should do in this Affair, Villenoys ask'd her, Who of the House saw him? She said, Only Maria, who knew not who he was; so that, resolving to save Isabella's Honour, which was the only Misfortune to come, Villenoys himself propos'd the carrying him out to the Bridge, and throwing him into the River, where the Stream would carry him down to the Sea, and lose him; or, if he were found, none could know him. So Villenoys took a Candle, and went and look'd on him, and found him altogether chang'd, that no Body would know who he was; he therefore put on his Clothes, which was not hard for him to do, for he was scarce yet cold, and comforting again Isabella, as well as he could, he went himself into the Stable, and fetched a Sack, such as they us'd for Oats, a new Sack, whereon stuck a great Needle, with a Pack-thread in it; this Sack he brings into the House, and shews to Isabella, telling her, He would put the Body in there, for the better convenience of carrying it on his Back. Isabella all this while said but little, but, fill'd with Thoughts all Black and Hellish, she ponder'd within, while the Fond and Passionate Villenoys was endeavouring to hide her Shame, and to make this an absolute Secret: She imagin'd, that could she live after a Deed so black, Villenoys would be eternal reproaching her, if not with his Tongue, at least with his Heart, and embolden'd by one Wickedness, she was the readier for another, and another of such a Nature, as has, in my Opinion, far less Excuse, than the first; but when Fate begins to afflict, she goes through stitch with her Black Work.

When Villenoys, who would, for the Safety of Isabella's Honour, be the sole Actor in the disposing of this Body; and since he was Young, Vigorous, and Strong, and able to bear it, would trust no one with the Secret, he having put up the Body, and ty'd it fast, set it on a Chair, turning his Back towards it, with the more conveniency to take it upon his Back, bidding Isabella give him the two Corners of the Sack in his Hands; telling her, They must do this last office for the Dead, more, in order to the securing their Honour and Tranquility hereafter, than for any other Reason, and bid her be of good Courage, till he came back, for it was not far to the Bridge, and it being the dead of the Night, he should pass well enough. When he had the Sack on his Back, and ready to go with it, she cry'd, Stay, my Dear, some of his Clothes hang out, which I will put in; and with that, taking the Pack-needle with the Thread, sew'd the Sack, with several strong Stitches, to the Collar of Villenoy's Coat, without his perceiving it, and bid him go now; and when you come to the Bridge, (said she) and that you are throwing him over the Rail, (which is not above Breast high) be sure you give him a good swing, least the Sack should hang on any thing at the side of the Bridge, and not fall into the Stream; I'le warrant you, (said Villenoys) I know how to secure his falling. And going his way with it, Love lent him Strength, and he soon arriv'd at the Bridge; where, turning his Back to the Rail, and heaving the Body over, he threw himself with all his force backward, the better to swing the Body into the River, whose weight (it being made fast to his Collar) pull'd Villenoys after it, and both the live and the dead Man falling into the River, which, being rapid at the Bridge, soon drown'd him, especially when so great a weight hung to his Neck; so that he dy'd, without considering what was the occasion of his Fate.

Isabella remain'd the most part of the Night sitting in her Chamber, without going to Bed, to see what would become of her Damnable Design; but when it was towards Morning, and she heard no News, she put herself into Bed, but not to find Repose or Rest there, for that she thought impossible, after so great a Barbarity as she had committed; No, (said she) it is but just I should for ever wake, who have, in one fatal Night, destroy'd two such Innocents. Oh! what Fate, what Destiny, is mine? Under what cursed Planet was I born, that Heaven it self could not divert my Ruine? It was not many Hours since I thought my self the most happy and blest of Women, and now am fallen to the Misery of one of the worst Fiends of Hell.

Such were her Thoughts, and such her Cryes, till the Light brought on new Matter for Grief; for, about Ten of the Clock, News was brought, that Two Men were found dead in the River, and that they were carry'd to the Town-Hall, to lye there, till they were own'd: Within an hour after, News was brought in, that one of these Unhappy Men was Villenoys; his Valet, who, all this while, imagin'd him in Bed with his Lady, ran to the Hall, to undeceive the People, for he knew, if his Lord were gone out, he should have been call'd to Dress him; but finding it, as 'twas reported, he fell a weeping, and wringing his Hands, in a most miserable manner, he ran home with the News; where, knocking at his Lady's Chamber Door, and finding it fast lock'd, he almost hop'd again, he was deceiv'd; but Isabella rising, and opening the Door, Maria first enter'd weeping, with the News, and then brought the Valet, to testify the fatal Truth of it. Isabella, tho' it were nothing but what she expected to hear, almost swounded in her Chair; nor did she feign it, but felt really all the Pangs of Killing Grief; and was so alter'd with her Night's Watching and Grieving, that this new Sorrow look'd very Natural in her. When she was recover'd, she asked a thousand Questions about him, and question'd the Possibility of it; for (said she) he went out this Morning early from me, and had no signs, in his Face, of any Grief or Discontent. Alas! (said the Valet) Madam, he is not his own Murderer, some one has done it in Revenge; and then told her, how he was found fasten'd to a Sack, with a dead strange Man ty'd up within it; and every body concludes, that they were both first murder'd, and then drawn to the River, and thrown both in. At the Relation of this Strange Man, she seem'd more amaz'd than before, and commanding the Valet to go to the Hall, and to take Order about the Coroner's sitting on the Body of Villenoys, and then to have it brought home: She called Maria to her, and, after bidding her shut the Door, she cry'd, Ah, Maria! I will tell thee what my Heart imagins; but first, (said she) run to the Chamber of the Stranger, and see, if he be still in Bed, which I fear he is not; she did so, and brought word, he was gone; then (said she) my Forebodings are true. When I was in Bed last night, with Villenoys (and at that word, she sigh'd as if her Heart-Strings had broken) I told him, I had lodg'd a Stranger in my House, who was by, when my first Lord and Husband fell in Battel; and that, after the Fight, finding him yet alive, he spoke to him, and gave him that Ring you brought me last Night; and conjur'd him, if ever his Fortune should bring him to Flanders, to see me, and give me that Ring, and tell me (with that, she wept, and could scarce speak) a thousand tender and endearing things, and then dy'd in his Arms. For my dear Henault's sake (said she) I us'd him nobly, and dismiss'd you that Night, because I was asham'd to have any Witness of the Griefs I paid his Memory: All this I told to Villenoys whom I found disorder'd; and, after a sleepless Night, I fancy he got up, and took this poor Man, and has occasion'd his Death: At that, she wept anew, and Maria, to whom, all that her Mistress said, was Gospel, verily believ'd it so, without examining Reason; and Isabella conjuring her, since none of the House knew of the old Man's being there, (for Old he appear'd to be) that she would let it for ever be a Secret, and, to this she bound her by an Oath; so that none knowing Henault, altho' his Body was expos'd there for three Days to Publick View: When the Coroner had Set on the Bodies, he found, they had been first Murder'd some way or other, and then afterwards tack'd together, and thrown into the River, they brought the Body of Villenoys home to his House, where, it being laid on a Table, all the House infinitely bewail'd it; and Isabella did nothing but swound away, almost as fast as she recover'd Life; however, she would, to compleat her Misery, be led to see this dreadful Victim of her

Cruelty, and, coming near the Table, the Body, whose Eyes were before close shut, now open'd themselves wide, and fix'd them upon Isabella, who, giving a great Schreek, fell down in a swound, and the Eyes clos'd again; they had much ado to bring her to Life, but, at last, they did so, and led her back to her Bed, where she remain'd a good while. Different Opinions and Discourses were made, concerning the opening of the Eyes of the Dead Man, and viewing Isabella; but she was a Woman of so admirable a Life and Conversation, of so undoubted a Piety and Sanctity of Living, that not the least Conjecture could be made, of her having a hand in it, besides the improbability of it; yet the whole thing was a Mystery, which, they thought, they ought to look into: But a few Days after, the Body of Villenoys being interr'd in a most magnificent manner, and, by Will all he had, was long since setled on Isabella, the World, instead of Suspecting her, Ador'd her the more, and every Body of Quality was already hoping to be next, tho' the fair Mourner still kept her Bed, and Languish'd daily.

It happen'd, not long after this, there came to the Town a French Gentleman, who was taken at the Siege of Candia, and was Fellow-Slave with Henault, for seven Years, in Turky, and who had escap'd with Henault, and came as far as Liege with him, where, having some Business and Acquaintance with a Merchant, he stay'd some time; but when he parted with Henault, he ask'd him, Where he should find him in Flanders? Henault gave him a Note, with his Name, and Place of Abode, if his Wife were alive; if not, to enquire at his Sister's, or his Father's. This French Man came at last, to the very House of Isabella, enquiring for this Man, and receiv'd a strange Answer, and was laugh'd at; He found, that was the House, and that the Lady; and enquiring about the Town, and speaking of Henault's Return, describing the Man, it was quickly discover'd, to be the same that was in the Sack: He had his Friend taken up (for he was buried) and found him the same, and, causing a Barber to Trim him, when his bushy Beard was off, a great many People remember'd him; and the French Man affirming, he went to his own Home, all Isabella's Family, and her self, were cited before the Magistrate of Justice, where, as soon as she was accus'd, she confess'd the whole Matter of Fact, and, without any Disorder, deliver'd her self in the Hands of Justice, as the Murderess of two Husbands (both belov'd) in one Night: The whole World stood amaz'd at this; who knew her Life a Holy and Charitable Life, and how dearly and well she had liv'd with her Husbands, and every one bewail'd her Misfortune, and she alone was the only Person, that was not afflicted for her self; she was Try'd, and Condemn'd to lose her Head; which Sentence, she joyfully receiv'd, and said, Heaven, and her Judges, were too Merciful to her, and that her Sins had deserv'd much more.

While she was in Prison, she was always at Prayers, and very Chearful and Easie, distributing all she had amongst, and for the Use of, the Poor of the Town, especially to the Poor Widows; exhorting daily, the Young, and the Fair, that came perpetually to visit her, never to break a Vow: for that was first the Ruine of her, and she never since prosper'd, do whatever other good Deeds she could. When the day of Execution came, she appear'd on the Scaffold all in Mourning, but with a Meen so very Majestick and Charming, and a Face so surprizing Fair, where no Languishment or Fear appear'd, but all Chearful as a Bride, that she set all Hearts a flaming, even in that mortifying Minute of Preparation for Death: She made a Speech of half an Hour long, so Eloquent, so admirable a warning to the Vow-Breakers, that it was as amazing to hear her, as it was to behold her.

After she had done with the help of Maria, she put off her Mourning Vail, and, without any thing over her Face, she kneel'd down, and the Executioner, at one Blow, sever'd her Beautiful Head from her Delicate Body, being then in her Seven and Twentieth Year. She was generally Lamented, and Honourably Bury'd.

The Dutchess of Mazarine. Hortense Mancini, niece of the great Cardinal, was born at Rome in 1646. Her beauty and wit were such that Charles II (whilst in exile) and other princes of royal blood sought her hand. She married, however, 28 February, 1661, Armand-Charles de la Meilleraye, said to be 'the richest subject in Europe'. The union was unhappy, and in 1666 she demanded a judicial separation. Fearful, however, lest this should be refused, she fled from Paris 13 June, 1668, and, after several years of wandering, in 1675 came to London at the invitation of Charles II, who assigned her a pension. Her gallantries, her friendship with Saint-Evremond, her lavish patronage of the fine arts and literature are well known. She died at her Chelsea house in the summer of 1699. Her end is said to have been hastened by intemperance. Evelyn dubs her 'the famous beauty and errant lady.'

THE NUN: or, The Perjur'd Beauty

A TRUE NOVEL

Don Henrique was a Person of great Birth, of a great Estate, of a Bravery equal to either, of a most generous Education, but of more Passion than Reason: He was besides of an opener and freer Temper than generally his Countrymen are (I mean, the Spaniards) and always engag'd in some Love-Intrigue or other.

One Night as he was retreating from one of those Engagements, Don Sebastian, whose Sister he had abus'd with a Promise of Marriage, set upon him at the Corner of a Street, in Madrid, and by the Help of three of his Friends, design'd to have dispatch'd him on a doubtful Embassy to the Almighty Monarch: But he receiv'd their first Instructions with better Address than they expected, and dismiss'd his Envoy first, killing one of Don Sebastian's Friends. Which so enrag'd the injur'd Brother, that his Strength and Resolution seem'd to be redoubled, and so animated his two surviving Companions, that (doubtless) they had gain'd a dishonourable Victory, had not Don Antonio accidentally come in to the Rescue; who after a short Dispute, kill'd one of the two who attack'd him only; whilst Don Henrique, with the greatest Difficulty, defended his Life, for some Moments, against Sebastian, whose Rage depriv'd him of Strength, and gave his Adversary the unwish'd Advantage of his seeming Death, tho' not without bequeathing some bloody Legacies to Don Henrique. Antonio had receiv'd but one slight Wound in the left Arm, and his surviving Antagonist none; who however thought it not adviseable to begin a fresh Dispute against two, of whose Courage he had but too fatal a Proof, tho' one of 'em was sufficiently disabled. The Conquerors, on the other Side, politickly retreated, and quitting the Field to the Conquer'd, left the Living to bury the Dead, if he could, or thought convenient.

As they were marching off, Don Antonio, who all this while knew not whose Life he had so happily preserv'd, told his Companion in Arms, that he thought it indispensibly necessary that he should quarter with him that Night, for his further Preservation. To which he prudently consented, and went, with no little Uneasiness, to his Lodgings; where he surpriz'd Antonio with the Sight of his dearest Friend. For they had certainly the nearest Sympathy in all their Thoughts, that ever made two brave Men unhappy: And, undoubtedly, nothing but Death, or more fatal Love, could have divided them. However, at present, they were united and secure.

In the mean time, Don Sebastian's Friend was just going to call Help to carry off the Bodies, as the ----came by; who seeing three Men lie dead, seiz'd the fourth; who as he was about to justify himself, by discovering one of the Authors of so much Blood-shed, was interrupted by a Groan from his supposed dead Friend Don Sebastian; whom, after a brief Account of some Part of the Matter, and the Knowledge of his Quality, they took up, and carried to his House; where, within a few Days, he was recovered past the Fear of Death. All this While Henrique and Antonio durst not appear, so much as by Night; nor could be found, tho' diligent and daily Search was made after the first; but upon Don Sebastian's Recovery, the Search ceasing, they took the Advantage of the Night, and, in Disguise, retreated to Seville. 'Twas there they thought themselves most secure, where indeed they were in the greatest Danger; for tho' (haply) they might there have escap'd the murderous Attempt of Don Sebastian, and his Friends, yet they could not there avoid the malicious Influence of their Stars.

This City gave Birth to Antonio, and to the Cause of his greatest Misfortunes, as well as of his Death. Dona Ardelia was born there, a Miracle of Beauty and Falshood. 'Twas more than a Year since Don Antonio had first seen and loved her. For 'twas impossible any Man should do one without the other. He had had the unkind Opportunity of speaking and conveying a Billet to her at Church; and to his greater Misfortune, the next Time he found her there, he met with too Kind a Return both from her Eyes and from her Hand, which privately slipt a Paper into his; in which he found abundantly more than he expected, directing him in that, how he should proceed, in order to carry her off from her Father with the least Danger he could look for in such an Attempt; since it would have been vain and fruitless to have asked her of her Father, because their Families had been at Enmity for several Years; tho' Antonio was as well descended as she, and had as ample a Fortune; nor was his Person, according to his Sex, any way inferior to her's; and certainly, the Beauties of his Mind were more excellent, especially if it be an Excellence to be constant.

He had made several Attempts to take Possession of her; but all prov'd ineffectual; however, he had the good Fortune not to be known, tho' once or twice he narrowly escap'd with Life, bearing off his Wounds with Difficulty. (Alas, that the Wounds of Love should cause those of Hate!) Upon which she was strictly confin'd to one Room, whose only Window was towards the Garden, and that too was grated with Iron; and, once a Month, when she went to Church, she was constantly and carefully attended by her Father, and a Mother-in-Law, worse than a Duegna. Under this miserable Confinement Antonio understood she still continued, at his Return to Seville, with Don Henrique, whom he acquainted with his invincible Passion for her; lamenting the Severity of her present Circumstances, that admitted of no Prospect of Relief; which caus'd a generous Concern in Don Henrique, both for the Sufferings of his Friend, and of the Lady. He proposed several Ways to Don Antonio, for the Release of the fair Prisoner; but none of them was thought practicable, or at least likely to succeed. But Antonio, who (you may believe) was then more nearly engag'd, bethought himself of an Expedient that would undoubtedly reward their Endeavours. 'Twas, that Don Henrique, who was very well acquainted with Ardelia's Father, should make him a Visit, with Pretence of begging his Consent and Admission to make his Addresses to his Daughter; which, in all Probability, he could not refuse to Don Henrique's Quality and Estate; and then this Freedom of Access to her would give him the Opportunity of delivering the Lady to his Friend. This was thought so reasonable, that the very next Day it was put in Practice; and with so good Success, that Don Henrique was received by the Father of Ardelia with the greatest and most respectful Ceremony imaginable: And when he made the Proposal to him of marrying his Daughter, it was embraced with a visible Satisfaction and Joy in the Air of his Face. This their first Conversation ended with all imaginable Content on both Sides; Don Henrique being invited by the Father to Dinner the next Day, when Dona Ardelia was to be present; who, at that Time, was said to be indispos'd, (as 'tis very probable she was, with so close an Imprisonment.) Henrique returned to Antonio, and made him happy with the Account of his Reception; which could not but have terminated in the perfect Felicity of Antonio, had his Fate been just to the Merits of his Love. The Day and Hour came which brought Henrique, with a private Commission from his Friend, to Ardelia. He saw her; (ah! would he had only seen her veil'd!) and, with the first Opportunity, gave her the Letter, which held so much Love, and so much Truth, as ought to have preserved him in the Empire of her Heart. It contained, besides, a Discovery of his whole Design upon her Father, for the compleating of their Happiness; which nothing then could obstruct but her self. But Henrique had seen her; he had gaz'd, and swallowed all her Beauties at his Eyes. How greedily his Soul drank the strong Poison in! But yet his Honour and his Friendship were strong as ever, and bravely fought against the Usurper Love, and got a noble Victory; at least he thought and wish'd so. With this, and a short Answer to his Letter, Henrique return'd to the longing Antonio; who, receiving the Paper with the greatest Devotion, and kissing it with the greatest Zeal, open'd and read these Words to himself:

Don Antonio,

You have, at last, made Use of the best and only Expedient for my Enlargement; for which I thank you, since I know it is purely the Effect of your Love. Your Agent has a mighty Influence on my Father: And you may assure yourself, that as you have advis'd and desir'd me, he shall have no less on me, who am

Your's entirely,
And only your's,

ARDELIA.

Having respectfully and tenderly kiss'd the Name, he could not chuse but shew the Billet to his Friend; who reading that Part of it which concern'd himself, started and blush'd: Which Antonio observing, was curious to know the Cause of it. Henrique told him, That he was surpriz'd to find her express so little Love, after so long an Absence. To which his Friend reply'd for her, That, doubtless, she had not Time enough to attempt so great a Matter as a perfect Account of her Love; and added, that it was Confirmation enough to him of its Continuance, since she subscrib'd her self his entirely, and only his. How blind is Love! Don Henrique knew how to make it bear another Meaning; which, however, he had the Discretion to conceal. Antonio, who was as real in his Friendship, as constant in his Love, ask'd him what he thought of her Beauty? To which the other answer'd, that he thought it irresistable to any, but to a Soul preposses'd, and nobly fortify'd with a perfect Friendship: Such as is thine, my Henrique, (added Antonio;) yet as sincere and perfect as that is, I know you must, nay, I know you do love her. As I ought to do, (reply'd Henrique.) Yes, yes, (return'd his Friend) it must be so; otherwise the Sympathy which unites our Souls would be wanting, and consequently our Friendship were in a State of Imperfection. How industriously you would argue me into a Crime, that would tear and destroy the Foundation of the strongest Ties of Truth and Honour! (said Henrique.) But (he continu'd) I hope within a few Days, to put it out of my Power to be guilty of so great a Sacrilege. I can't determine (said Antonio) if I knew that you lov'd one another, whether I could easier part with my Friend, or my Mistress. Tho' what you say, is highly generous, (reply'd Henrique) yet give me Leave to urge, that it looks like a Trial of Friendship, and argues you inclinable to Jealousy: But, pardon me, I know it to be sincerely meant by you; and must therefore own, that 'tis the best, because 'tis the noblest Way of securing both your Friend and Mistress. I need not make use of any Arts to secure me of either, (reply'd Antonio) but expect to enjoy 'em both in a little Time.

Henrique, who was a little uneasy with a Discourse of this Nature, diverted it, by reflecting on what had pass'd at Madrid, between them two and Don Sebastian and his Friends; which caus'd Antonio to bethink himself of the Danger to which he expos'd his Friend, by appearing daily, tho' in Disguise: For, doubtless, Don Sebastian would pursue his Revenge to the utmost Extremity. These Thoughts put him upon desiring his Friend, for his own Sake, to hasten the Performance of his Attempt; and accordingly, each Day Don Henrique brought Antonio nearer the Hopes of Happiness, while he himself was hourly sinking into the lowest State of Misery. The last Night before the Day in which Antonio expected to be bless'd in her Love, Don Henrique had a long and fatal Conference with her about her Liberty. Being then with her alone in an Arbour of the Garden, which Privilege he had had for some Days; after a long Silence, and observing Don Henrique in much Disorder, by the Motion of his Eyes, which were sometimes stedfastly fix'd on the Ground, then lifted up to her or Heaven, (for he could see nothing more beautiful on Earth) she made use of the Privilege of her Sex, and began the Discourse first, to this Effect: Has any Thing happened, Sir, since our Retreat hither, to occasion that Disorder which is but too visible in your Face, and too dreadful in your continued Silence? Speak, I beseech you, Sir, and let me know if I have any Way unhappily contributed to it! No, Madam, (replyed he) my Friendship is now likely to be the only Cause of my greatest Misery; for To-morrow I must be guilty of an unpardonable Crime, in betraying the generous Confidence which your noble Father has plac'd in me: To-morrow (added he, with a piteous Sigh) I must deliver you into the Hands of one whom your Father hates even to Death, instead of doing myself the Honour of becoming his Son-in-law within a few Days more. But, I will consider and remind myself, that I give you into the Hands of my Friend; of my Friend, that loves you better than his Life, which he has often expos'd for your Sake; and what is more than all, to my Friend, whom you love more than any Consideration on Earth. And must this be done? (she ask'd.) Is it inevitable as Fate? Fix'd as the Laws of Nature, Madam, (reply'd he) don't you find the Necessity of it, Ardelia? (continued he, by Way of Question:) Does not your Love require it? Think, you are going to your dear Antonio, who alone can merit you, and whom only you can love. Were your last Words true (returned she) I should yet be unhappy in the Displeasure of a dear and tender Father, and infinitely more, in being the Cause of your Infidelity to him: No, Don Henrique (continued she) I could with greater Satisfaction return to my miserable Confinement, than by any Means disturb the Peace of your Mind, or occasion one Moment's Interruption of your Quiet. Would to Heaven you did not, (sigh'd he to himself.) Then addressing his Words more distinctly to her, cry'd he, Ah, cruel! ah, unjust Ardelia! these Words belong to none but Antonio; why then would you endeavour to persuade me, that I do, or even can merit the Tenderness of such an Expression? Have a Care! (pursued he) have a Care, Ardelia! your outward Beauties are too powerful to be resisted; even your Frowns have such a Sweetness that they attract the very Soul that is not strongly prepossessed with the noblest Friendship, and the highest Principles of Honour: Why then, alas! did you add such sweet and Charming Accents? Why, ah, Don Henrique! (she interrupted) why did you appear to me so charming in your Person, so great in your Friendship, and so illustrious in your Reputation? Why did my Father, ever since your first Visit, continually fill my Ears and Thoughts with noble Characters and glorious Ideas, which yet but imperfectly and faintly represent the inimitable Original! But (what is most severe and cruel) why, Don Henrique, why will you defeat my Father in his Ambition of your Alliance, and me of those glorious Hopes with which you had bless'd my Soul, by casting me away from you to Antonio! Ha! (cry'd he, starting) what said you, Madam? What did Ardelia say? That I had bless'd your Soul with Hopes! That I would cast you away to Antonio! Can they who safely arrive in their wish'd-for Port, be said to be shipwreck'd? Or, can an abject indigent Wretch make a King? These are more than Riddles, Madam; and I must not think to expound 'em. No, (said she) let it alone, Don Henrique; I'll ease you of that Trouble, and tell you plainly that I love you. Ah! (cry'd he) now all my Fears are come upon me! How! (ask'd she) were you afraid I should love you? Is my Love so dreadful then? Yes, when misplac'd (reply'd he;) but 'twas your Falshood that I fear'd: Your Love was what I would have sought with the utmost Hazard of my Life, nay, even of my future Happiness, I fear, had you not been engag'd: strongly oblig'd to love elsewhere, both by your own Choice and Vows, as well as by his dangerous Services, and matchless Constancy. For which (said she) I do not hate him, tho' his Father kill'd my Uncle: Nay, perhaps (continu'd she) I have a Friendship for him, but no more. No more, said you, Madam? (cry'd he;) but tell me, did you never love him? Indeed, I did, (reply'd she;) but the Sight of you has better instructed me, both in my Duty to my Father, and in causing my Passion for you, without whom I shall be eternally miserable. Ah, then pursue your honourable Proposal, and make my Father happy in my Marriage! It must not be (return'd Don Henrique) my Honour, my Friendship forbids it. No (she return'd) your Honour requires it; and if your Friendship opposes your Honour, it can have no sure and solid Foundation. Female Sophistry! (cry'd Henrique;) but you need no Art nor Artifice, Ardelia, to make me love you: Love you! (pursu'd he:) By that bright Sun, the Light and Heat of all the World, you are my only Light and Heat. Oh, Friendship! Sacred Friendship, now assist me! [Here for a Time he paus'd, and then afresh proceeded thus,] You told me, or my Ears deceiv'd me, that you lov'd me, Ardelia. I did, she reply'd; and that I do love you, is as true as that I told you so. 'Tis well; But would it were not so! Did ever Man receive a Blessing thus? Why, I could wish I did not love you, Ardelia! But that were impossible. At least unjust, (interrupted she.) Well then (he went on) to shew you that I do sincerely consult your particular Happiness, without any regard to my own, To-morrow I will give you to Don Antonio; and as a Proof of your Love to me, I expect your ready Consent to it. To let you see, Don Henrique, how perfectly and tenderly I love you, I will be sacrificed To-morrow to Don Antonio, and to your Quiet. Oh, strongest, dearest Obligation! cry'd Henrique: To-morrow then, as I have told your Father, I am to bring you to see the dearest Friend I have on Earth, who dares not appear within this City for some unhappy Reasons, and therefore cannot be present at our Nuptials; for which Cause, I could not but think it my Duty to one so nearly related to my Soul, to make him happy in the Sight of my beautiful Choice, e'er yet she be my Bride. I hope (said she) my loving Obedience may merit your Compassion; and that at last, e'er the Fire is lighted that must consume the Offering, I mean the Marriage-Tapers (alluding to the old Roman Ceremony) that you or some other pitying Angel, will snatch me from the Altar. Ah, no more, Ardelia! say no more (cry'd he) we must be cruel, to be just to our selves. [Here their Discourse ended, and they walked into the House, where they found the good old Gentleman and his Lady, with whom he stay'd till about an Hour after Supper, when he returned to his Friend with joyful News, but a sorrowful Heart.]

Antonio was all Rapture with the Thoughts of the approaching Day; which tho' it brought Don Henrique and his dear Ardelia to him, about five o'Clock in the Evening, yet at the same Time brought his last and greatest Misfortune. He saw her then at a She Relation's of his, above three Miles from Seville, which was the Place assigned for their fatal Interview. He saw her, I say; but ah! how strange! how altered from the dear, kind Ardelia she was when last he left her! 'Tis true, he flew to her with Arms expanded, and with so swift and eager a Motion, that she could not avoid, nor get loose from his Embrace, till he had kissed, and sighed, and dropt some Tears, which all the Strength of his Mind could not restrain; whether they were the Effects of Joy, or whether (which rather may be feared) they were the Heat-drops which preceded and threaten'd the Thunder and Tempest that should fall on his Head, I cannot positively say; yet all this she was then forced to endure, e'er she had Liberty to speak, or indeed to breathe. But as soon as she had freed herself from the loving Circle that should have been the dear and lov'd Confinement or Centre of a Faithful Heart, she began to dart whole Showers of Tortures on him from her Eyes; which that Mouth that he had just before so tenderly and sacredly kiss'd, seconded with whole Volleys of Deaths crammed in every Sentence, pointed with the keenest Affliction that ever pierc'd a Soul. Antonio, (she began) you have treated me now as if you were never like to see me more: and would to Heaven you were not! Ha! (cry'd he, starting and staring wildly on her;) What said you, Madam? What said you, my Ardelia? If you like the Repetition, take it? (reply'd she, unmoved) Would to Heaven you were never like to see me more! Good! very Good! (cry'd he, with a Sigh that threw him trembling into a Chair behind him, and gave her the Opportunity of proceeding thus:) Yet, Antonio, I must not have my Wish; I must continue with you, not out of Choice, but by Command, by the strictest and severest Obligation that ever bound Humanity; Don Henrique, your Friend, commands it; Don Henrique, the dearest Object of my Soul, enjoins it; Don Henrique, whose only Aversion I am, will have it so. Oh, do not wrong me, Madam! (cry'd Don Henrique.) Lead me, lead me a little more by the Light of your Discourse, I beseech you (said Don Antonio) that I may see your Meaning! for hitherto 'tis Darkness all to me. Attend therefore with your best Faculties (pursu'd Ardelia) and know, That I do most sincerely and most passionately love Don Henrique; and as a Proof of my Love to him, I have this Day consented to be delivered up to you by him; not for your Sake in the least, Antonio, but purely to sacrifice all the Quiet of my Life to his Satisfaction. And now, Sir (continued she, addressing her self to Don Henrique) now, Sir, if you can be so cruel, execute your own most dreadful Decree, and join our Hands, though our Hearts never can meet. All this to try me! It's too much, Ardelia (said Antonio:) And then turning to Don Henrique, he went on, Speak thou! if yet thou art not Apostate to our Friendship! Yet speak, however! Speak, though the Devil has been tampering with thee too! Thou art a Man, a Man of Honour once. And when I forfeit my just Title to that (interrupted Don Henrique) may I be made most miserable! May I lose the Blessings of thy Friendship! May I lose thee! Say on then, Henrique! (cry'd Antonio:) And I charge thee, by all the sacred Ties of Friendship, say, Is this a Trial of me? Is't Illusion, Sport, or shameful murderous Truth? Oh, my Soul burns within me, and I can bear no longer! Tell! Speak! Say on! [Here, with folded Arms, and Eyes fixed stedfastly on Henrique, he stood like a Statue, without Motion; unless sometimes, when his swelling Heart raised his over-charged Breast.] After a little Pause, and a hearty Sigh or two, Henrique began; Oh, Antonio! Oh my Friend! prepare thy self to hear yet more dreadful Accents! I am (pursu'd he) unhappily the greatest and most innocent Criminal that e'er till now offended: I love her, Antonio, I love Ardelia with a Passion strong and violent as thine! Oh! summon all that us'd to be more than Man about thee, to suffer to the End of my Discourse, which nothing but a Resolution like thine can bear! I know it by myself. Tho' there be Wounds, Horror, and Death in each Syllable (interrupted Antonio) yet prithee now go on, but with all Haste. I will, (returned Don Henrique) tho' I feel my own Words have the same cruel Effects on me. I say, again, my Soul loves Ardelia: And how can it be otherwise? Have we not both the self-same Appetites, the same Disgusts? How then could I avoid my Destiny, that has decreed that I should love and hate just as you do? Oh, hard Necessity! that obliged you to use me in the Recovery of this Lady! Alas, can you think that any Man of Sense or Passion could have seen, and not have lov'd her! Then how should I, whose Thoughts are Unisons to yours, evade those Charms that had prevail'd on you? And now, to let you know, 'tis no Illusion, no Sport, but serious and amazing woeful Truth, Ardelia best can tell you whom she loves. What I have already said, is true, by Heaven (cry'd she) 'tis you, Don Henrique, whom I only love, and who alone can give me Happiness: Ah, would you would! With you, Antonio, I must remain unhappy, wretched, cursed: Thou art my Hell; Don Henrique is my Heaven. And thou art mine, (returned he) which here I part with to my dearest Friend. Then taking her Hand, Pardon me, Antonio, (pursued he) that I thus take my last Farewel of all the Tastes of Bliss from your Ardelia, at this Moment. [At which Words he kiss'd her Hand, and gave it to Don Antonio; who received it, and gently pressed it close to his Heart, as if he would have her feel the Disorders she had caus'd there.] Be happy, Antonio, (cry'd Henrique:) Be very tender of her; To-morrow early I shall hope to see thee. Ardelia (pursued he) All Happiness and Joy surround thee! May'st thou ne'er want those Blessings thou can'st give Antonio! Farewel to both! (added he, going out.) Ah (cry'd she) Farewel to all Joys, Blessings, Happiness, if you forsake me. Yet do not go! Ah, cruel! (continu'd she, seeing him quit the Room) but you shall take my Soul with you. Here she swooned away in Don Antonio's Arms; who, though he was happy that he had her fast there, yet was obliged to call in his Cousin, and Ardelia's Attendants, e'er she could be perfectly recovered. In the mean while Don Henrique had not the Power to go out of Sight of the House, but wandred to and fro about it, distracted in his Soul; and not being able longer to refrain her Sight, her last Words still resounding in his Ears, he came again into the Room where he left her with Don Antonio, just as she revived, and called him, exclaiming on his Cruelty, in leaving her so soon. But when, turning her Eyes towards the Door, she saw him; Oh! with what eager Haste she flew to him! then clasped him round the Waist, obliging him, with all the tender Expressions that the Soul of a Lover, and a Woman's too, is capable of uttering, not to leave her in the Possession of Don Antonio. This so amaz'd her slighted Lover, that he knew not, at first, how to proceed in this tormenting Scene; but at last, summoning all his wonted Resolution, and Strength of Mind, he told her, He would put her out of his Power, if she would consent to retreat for some few Hours to a Nunnery that was not above half a Mile distant from thence, till he had discoursed his Friend, Don Henrique something more particularly than hitherto, about this Matter: To which she readily agreed, upon the Promise that Don Henrique made her, of seeing her with the first Opportunity. They waited on her then to the Convent, where she was kindly and respectfully received by the Lady Abbess; but it was not long before her Grief renewing with greater Violence, and more afflicting Circumstances, had obliged them to stay with her till it was almost dark, when they once more begged the Liberty of an Hour's Absence; and the better to palliate their Design, Henrique told her, that he would make use of her Father Don Richardo's Coach, in which they came to Don Antonio's, for so small a Time: which they did, leaving only Eleonora her Attendant with her, with out whom she had been at a Loss, among so many fair Strangers; Strangers, I mean, to her unhappy Circumstances: Whilst they were carry'd near a Mile farther, where, just as 'twas dark, they lighted from the Coach, Don Henrique, ordering the Servants not to stir thence till their Return from their private Walk, which was about a Furlong, in a Field that belong'd to the Convent. Here Don Antonio told Don Henrique, That he had not acted honourably; That he had betray'd him, and robb'd him at once both of a Friend and Mistress. To which t'other returned, That he understood his Meaning, when he proposed a particular Discourse about this Affair, which he now perceived must end in Blood: But you may remind your self (continued he) that I have kept my Promise in delivering her to you. Yes, (cry'd Antonio) after you had practis'd foully and basely on her. Not at all! (returned Henrique) It was her Fate that brought this Mischief on her; for I urged the Shame and Scandal of Inconstancy, but all in vain, to her. But don't you love her, Henrique? (the other ask'd.) Too well, and cannot live without her, though I fear I may feel the cursed Effects of the same Inconstancy: However, I had quitted her all to you, but you see how she resents it. And you shall see, Sir, (cry'd Antonio, drawing his Sword in a Rage) how I resent it. Here, without more Words, they fell to Action; to bloody Action. (Ah! how wretched are our Sex, in being the unhappy Occasion of so many fatal Mischiefs, even between the dearest Friends!) They fought on each Side with the greatest Animosity of Rivals, forgetting all the sacred Bonds of their former Friendship; till Don Antonio fell, and said, dying, 'Forgive me, Henrique! I was to blame; I could not live without her: I fear she will betray thy Life, which haste and preserve, for my sake. Let me not die all at once! Heaven pardon both of us! Farewel! Oh, haste! Farewel! (returned Don Henrique) Farewel, thou bravest, truest Friend! Farewel thou noblest Part of me! And Farewel all the Quiet of my Soul.' Then stooping, he kissed his Cheek; but, rising, he found he must retire in time, or else must perish through Loss of Blood, for he had received two or three dangerous Wounds, besides others of less Consequence: Wherefore he made all the convenient Haste he could to the Coach, into which, by the Help of the Footmen, he got, and order'd 'em to drive him directly to Don Richardo's with all imaginable Speed; where he arriv'd in little more than half an Hour's Time, and was received by Ardelia's Father with the greatest Confusion and Amazement that is expressible, seeing him return'd without his Daughter, and so desperately wounded. Before he thought it convenient to ask him any Question more than to enquire of his Daughter's Safety, to which he receiv'd a short but satisfactory Answer, Don Richardo sent for an eminent and able Surgeon, who probed and dress'd Don Henrique's Wounds, who was immediately put to Bed; not without some Despondency of his Recovery; but (thanks to his kind Stars, and kinder Constitution!) he rested pretty well for some Hours that Night, and early in the Morning, Ardelia's Father, who had scarce taken any Rest all that Night, came to visit him, as soon as he understood from the Servants who watched with him, that he was in a Condition to suffer a short Discourse; which, you may be sure, was to learn the Circumstances of the past Night's Adventure; of which Don Henrique gave him a perfect and pleasant Account, since he heard that Don Antonio, his mortal Enemy, was killed; the Assurance of whose Death was the more delightful to him, since, by this Relation, he found that Antonio was the Man, whom his Care of his Daughter had so often frustrated. Don Henrique had hardly made an End of his Narration, e'er a Servant came hastily to give Richardo Notice, that the Officers were come to search for his Son-in-Law that should have been; whom the Old Gentleman's wise Precaution had secured in a Room so unsuspected, that they might as reasonably have imagined the entire Walls of his House had a Door made of Stones, as that there should have been one to that close Apartment: He went therefore boldly to the Officers, and gave them all the Keys of his House, with free Liberty to examine every Room and Chamber; which they did, but to no Purpose; and Don Henrique lay there undiscover'd, till his Cure was perfected.

In the mean time Ardelia, who that fatal Night but too rightly guess'd that the Death of one or both her Lovers was the Cause that they did not return to their Promise, the next Day fell into a high Fever, in which her Father found her soon after he had clear'd himself of those who come to search for a Lover. The Assurance which her Father gave her of Henrique's Life, seemed a little to revive her; but the Severity of Antonio's Fate was no Way obliging to her, since she could not but retain the Memory of his Love and Constancy; which added to her Afflictions, and heightned her Distemper, insomuch that Richardo was constrain'd to leave her under the Care of the good Lady Abbess, and to the diligent Attendance of Eleonora, not daring to hazard her Life in a Removal to his own House. All their Care and Diligence was however ineffectual; for she languished even to the least Hope of Recovery, till immediately after the first Visit of Don Henrique, which was the first he made in a Month's Time, and that by Night incognito, with her Father, her Distemper visibly retreated each Day: Yet when at last she enjoy'd a perfect Health of Body, her Mind grew sick, and she plunged into a deep Melancholy; which made her entertain a positive Resolution of taking the Veil at the End of her Novitiate; which accordingly she did, notwithstanding all the Intreaties, Prayers, and Tears both of her Father and Lover. But she soon repented her Vow, and often wish'd that she might by any Means see and speak to Don Henrique, by whose Help she promised to her self a Deliverance out of her voluntary Imprisonment: Nor were his Wishes wanting to the same Effect, tho' he was forced to fly into Italy, to avoid the Prosecution of Antonio's Friends. Thither she pursu'd him; nor could he any way shun her, unless he could have left his Heart at a Distance from his Body: Which made him take a fatal Resolution of returning to Seville in Disguise, where he wander'd about the Convent every Night like a Ghost (for indeed his Soul was within, while his inanimate Trunk was without) till at last he found Means to convey a Letter to her, which both surprized and delighted her. The Messenger that brought it her was one of her Mother-in-Law's Maids, whom he had known before, and met accidentally one Night as he was going his Rounds, and she coming out from Ardelia; with her he prevail'd, and with Gold obliged her to Secrecy and Assistance: Which proved so successful, that he understood from Ardelia her strong Desire of Liberty, and the Continuance of her Passion for him, together with the Means and Time most convenient and likely to succeed for her Enlargement. The Time was the fourteenth Night following, at twelve o'Clock, which just compleated a Month since his Return thither; at which Time they both promised themselves the greatest Happiness on Earth. But you may observe the Justice of Heaven, in their Disappointment.

Don Sebastian, who still pursu'd him with a most implacable Hatred, had traced him even to Italy, and there narrowly missing him, posted after him to Toledo; so sure and secret was his Intelligence! As soon as he arriv'd, he went directly to the Convent where his Sister Elvira had been one of the Profess'd, ever since Don Henrique had forsaken her, and where Ardelia had taken her repented Vow. Elvira had all along conceal'd the Occasion of her coming thither from Ardelia; and tho' she was her only Confident, and knew the whole Story of her Misfortunes, and heard the Name of Don Henrique repeated a hundred Times a Day, whom still she lov'd most perfectly, yet never gave her beautiful Rival any Cause of Suspicion that she lov'd him, either by Words or Looks: Nay more, when she understood that Don Henrique came to the Convent with Ardelia and Antonio, and at other Times with her Father; yet she had so great a Command of her self, as to refrain seeing him, or to be seen by him; nor ever intended to have spoken or writ to him, had not her Brother Don Sebastian put her upon the cruel Necessity of doing the last; who coming to visit his Sister (as I have said before) found her with Dona Ardelia, whom he never remembred to have seen, nor who ever had seen him but twice, and that was about six Years before, when she was but ten Years of Age, when she fell passionately in Love with him, and continu'd her Passion till about the fourteenth Year of her Empire, when unfortunate Antonio first began his Court to her. Don Sebastian was really a very desirable Person, being at that time very beautiful, his Age not exceeding six and twenty, of a sweet Conversation, very brave, but revengeful and irreconcilable (like most of his Countrymen) and of an honourable Family. At the Sight of him Ardelia felt her former Passion renew; which proceeded and continued with such Violence, that it utterly defac'd the Ideas of Antonio and Henrique. (No Wonder that she who could resolve to forsake her God for Man, should quit one Lover for another.) In short, she then only wished that he might love her equally, and then she doubted not of contriving the Means of their Happiness betwixt 'em. She had her Wish, and more, if possible; for he lov'd her beyond the Thought of any other present or future Blessing, and fail'd not to let her know it, at the second Interview; when he receiv'd the greatest Pleasure he could have wish'd, next to the Joys of a Bridal Bed: For she confessed her Love to him, and presently put him upon thinking on the Means of her Escape; but not finding his Designs so likely to succeed, as those Measures she had sent to Don Henrique, she communicates the very same to Don Sebastian, and agreed with him to make use of them on that very Night, wherein she had obliged Don Henrique to attempt her Deliverance: The Hour indeed was different, being determined to be at eleven. Elvira, who was present at the Conference, took the Hint; and not being willing to disoblige a Brother who had so hazarded his Life in Vindication of her, either does not, or would not seem to oppose his Inclinations at that Time: However, when he retired with her to talk more particularly of his intended Revenge on Don Henrique, who he told her lay somewhere absconded in Toledo, and whom he had resolved, as he assured her, to sacrifice to her injur'd Honour, and his Resentments; she oppos'd that his vindictive Resolution with all the forcible Arguments in a virtuous and pious Lady's Capacity, but in vain: so that immediately upon his Retreat from the Convent, she took the Opportunity of writing to Don Henrique as follows, the fatal Hour not being then seven Nights distant.

Don Henrique,

My Brother is now in Town, in Pursuit of your Life; nay more, of your Mistress, who has consented to make her Escape from the Convent, at the same Place of it, and by the same Means on which she had agreed to give her self entirely to you, but the Hour is eleven. I know, Henrique, your Ardelia is dearer to you than your Life: But your Life, your dear Life, is more desired than any Thing in this World, by

Your injur'd and forsaken

ELVIRA.

This she delivered to Richardo's Servant, whom Henrique had gained that Night, as soon as she came to visit Ardelia, at her usual Hour, just as she went out of the Cloister.

Don Henrique was not a little surprized with this Billet; however, he could hardly resolve to forbear his accustom'd Visits to Ardelia, at first: But upon more mature Consideration, he only chose to converse with her by Letters, which still press'd her to be mindful of her Promise, and of the Hour, not taking notice of any Caution that he had received of her Treachery. To which she still return'd in Words that might assure him of her Constancy.

The dreadful Hour wanted not a Quarter of being perfect, when Don Henrique came; and having fixed his Rope-Ladder to that Part of the Garden-Wall, where he was expected, Ardelia, who had not stir'd from that very Place for a Quarter of an Hour before, prepar'd to ascend by it; which she did, as soon as his Servant had returned and fixed it on the inner-side of the Wall: On the Top of which, at a little Distance, she found another fasten'd, for her to descend on the out-side, whilst Don Henrique eagerly waited to receive her. She came at last, and flew into his Arms; which made Henrique cry out in a Rapture, Am I at last once more happy in having my Ardelia in my Possession! She, who knew his Voice, and now found she was betray'd, but knew not by whom, shriek'd out, I am ruined! help! help! Loose me, I charge you, Henrique! Loose me! At that very Moment, and at those very Words, came Sebastian, attended by only one Servant; and hearing Henrique reply, Not all the Powers of Hell shall snatch you from me, drawing his Sword, without one Word, made a furious Pass at him: But his Rage and Haste misguided his Arm, for his Sword went quite through Ardelia's Body, who only said, Ah, wretched Maid! and drop'd from Henrique's Arms, who then was obliged to quit her, to preserve his own Life, if possible: however he had not had so much Time as to draw, had not Sebastian been amazed at this dreadful Mistake of his Sword; but presently recollecting himself, he flew with redoubled Rage to attack Henrique; and his Servant had seconded him, had not Henrique's, who was now descended, otherwise diverted him. They fought with the greatest Animosity on both Sides, and with equal Advantage; for they both fell together: Ah, my Ardelia, I come to thee now! (Sebastian groan'd out,) 'Twas this unlucky Arm, which now embraces thee, that killed thee. Just Heaven! (she sigh'd out,) Oh, yet have Mercy! [Here they both dy'd.] Amen, (cry'd Henrique, dying) I want it most - Oh, Antonio! Oh, Elvira! Ah, there's the Weight that sinks me down. And yet I wish Forgiveness. Once more, sweet Heaven, have Mercy! He could not out-live that last Word; which was echo'd by Elvira, who all this while stood weeping, and calling out for Help, as she stood close to the Wall in the Garden.

This alarmed the Rest of the Sisters, who rising, caus'd the Bell to be rung out, as upon dangerous Occasions it used to be; which rais'd the Neighbourhood, who came time enough to remove the dead Bodies of the two Rivals, and of the late fallen Angel Ardelia. The injur'd and neglected Elvira, whose Piety designed quite contrary Effects, was immediately seiz'd with a violent Fever; which, as it was violent, did not last long: for she dy'd within four and twenty Hours, with all the happy Symptoms of a departing Saint.

THE LUCKY MISTAKE

TO GEORGE GREENVIEL, ESQ;

Sir,

At this Critical Juncture, I find the Authors will have need of a Protector, as well as the Nation, we having peculiar Laws and Liberties to be defended as well as that, but of how different a Nature, none but such Judges as you are fit to determine; whatever our Province be, I am sure it should be Wit, and you know what Ellevated Ben says, That none can judge of Wit but Wit. Let the Heroes toyl for Crowns and Kingdoms and with what pretences they please. Let the Slaves of State drudge on for false and empty Glories, troubling the repose of the World and ruining their own to gain uneasy Grandure, whilst you, oh! happyer Sir, great enough by your Birth, yet more Illustrious by your Wit, are capable of enjoying alone that true Felicity of Mind, which belongs to an absolutely Vertuous and Gallant Man, by that, and the lively Notions of Honour Imprinted in your Soul, you are above Ambition, and can Form Kings and Heroes, when 'ere your delicate Fancy shall put you upon the Poetical Creation.

You can make those Heroes Lovers too, and inspire 'em with a Language so Irresistable as may instruct the Fair, how easily you may Conquer when it comes to your turn, to plead for a Heart, nor is your delicate Wit the only Charm; your Person claims an equal share of Graces with those of your Mind, and both together are capable of rendering you Victorious, whereever you shall please to Address 'em, but your Vertue keeps you from those Ravages of Beauty, which so wholly imploy the hours of the Rest of the Gay and Young, whilst you have business more sollid, and more noble for yours.

I would not by this have the World imagine you are therefore exempt from the tenderness of Love, it rather seems you were on purpose form'd for that Soft Entertainment, such an Agreement there is between the Harmony of your Soul and your Person, and sure the Muses who have so divinely inspir'd you with Poetic Fires, have furnisht you with that Necessary Material (Love) to maintain it, and to make it burn with the more Ellevated Flame.

'Tis therefore, Sir, I expect you will the more easily Pardon the Dedicating to your idler hours (if any such you have) this little Amour, all that I shall say for it, is, that 'tis not Translation but an Original, that has more of realty than fiction, if I have not made it fuller of intreague, 'twas because I had a mind to keep close to the Truth.

I must own, Sir, the Obligations I have to you, deserves a greater testimony of my respect, than this little piece, too trivial to bear the honour of your Name, but my increasing Indisposition makes me fear I shall not have many opportunities of this Kind, and shou'd be loath to leave this ungrateful World, without acknowledging my Gratitude more signally than barely by word of Mouth, and without wishing you all the happiness your merit and admirable Vertues deserve and of assuring you how unfeignedly I am (and how Proud of being) Sir,

Your most obliged and most humble servant   A. Behn.

THE LUCKY MISTAKE: A NEW NOVEL.

The River Loyre has on its delightful Banks abundance of handsome, beautiful and rich Towns and Villages, to which the noble Stream adds no small Graces and Advantages, blessing their Fields with Plenty, and their Eyes with a thousand Diversions. In one of these happily situated Towns, called Orleans, where abundance of People of the best Quality and Condition reside, there was a rich Nobleman, now retir'd from the busy Court, where in his Youth he had been bred, weary'd with the Toils of Ceremony and Noise, to enjoy that perfect Tranquillity of Life, which is no where to be found but in Retreat, a faithful Friend, and a good Library; and, as the admirable Horace says, in a little House and a large Garden. Count Bellyaurd, for so was this Nobleman call'd, was of this Opinion; and the rather, because he had one only Son, called Rinaldo, now grown to the Age of fifteen, who having all the excellent Qualities and Graces of Youth by Nature, he would bring him up in all Virtues and noble Sciences, which he believ'd the Gaiety and Lustre of the Court might divert: he therefore in his Retirement spar'd no Cost to those that could instruct and accomplish him; and he had the best Tutors and Masters that could be purchased at Court: Bellyaurd making far less Account of Riches than of fine Parts. He found his Son capable of all Impressions, having a Wit suitable to his delicate Person, so that he was the sole Joy of his Life, and the Darling of his Eyes.

In the very next House, which join'd close to that of Bellyaurd's, there lived another Count, who had in his Youth been banished the Court of France for some Misunderstandings in some high Affairs wherein he was concern'd: his Name was De Pais, a Man of great Birth, but of no Fortune; or at least one not suitable to the Grandeur of his Original. And as it is most natural for great Souls to be most proud (if I may call a handsome Disdain by that vulgar Name) when they are most depress'd; so De Pais was more retir'd, more estrang'd from his Neighbours, and kept a greater Distance, than if he had enjoy'd all he had lost at Court; and took more Solemnity and State upon him, because he would not be subject to the Reproaches of the World, by making himself familiar with it: So that he rarely visited; and, contrary to the Custom of those in France, who are easy of Access, and free of Conversation, he kept his Family retir'd so close, that 'twas rare to see any of them; and when they went abroad, which was but seldom, they wanted nothing as to outward Appearance, that was fit for his Quality, and what was much above his Condition.

This old Count had two only Daughters, of exceeding Beauty, who gave the generous Father ten thousand Torments, as often as he beheld them, when he consider'd their extreme Beauty, their fine Wit, their Innocence, Modesty, and above all their Birth; and that he had not a Fortune to marry them according to their Quality; and below it, he had rather see them laid in their silent Graves, than consent to it: for he scorn'd the World should see him forced by his Poverty to commit an Action below his Dignity.

There lived in a neighbouring Town, a certain Nobleman, Friend to De Pais, call'd Count Vernole, a Man of about forty years of Age, of low Stature, Complexion very black and swarthy, lean, lame, extreme proud and haughty; extracted of a Descent from the Blood-Royal; not extremely brave, but very glorious: he had no very great Estate, but was in Election of a greater, and of an Addition of Honour from the King, his Father having done most worthy Services against the Hugonots, and by the high Favour of Cardinal Mazarine, was represented to his Majesty, as a Man related to the Crown, of great Name, but small Estate: so that there were now nothing but great Expectations and Preparations in the Family of Count Vernole to go to the Court, to which he daily hoped an Invitation or Command.

Vernole's Fortune being hitherto something a-kin to that of De Pais, there was a greater Correspondency between these two Gentlemen, than they had with any other Persons; they accounting themselves above the rest of the World, believed none so proper and fit for their Conversation, as that of each other: so that there was a very particular Intimacy between them. Whenever they went abroad, they clubb'd their Train, to make one great Show; and were always together, bemoaning each other's Fortune, and that from so high a Descent, as one from Monarchs by the Mother's side, and the other from Dukes of the Father's Side, they were reduc'd by Fate to the Degree of private Gentlemen. They would often consult how to manage Affairs most to Advantage, and often De Pais would ask Counsel of Vernole, how best he should dispose of his Daughters, which now were about their ninth Year the eldest, and eighth the youngest. Vernole had often seen those two Buds of Beauty, and already saw opening in Atlante's Face and Mind (for that was the Name of the eldest, and Charlot the youngest) a

Glory of Wit and Beauty, which could not but one Day display it self, with dazling Lustre, to the wondring World.

Vernole was a great Virtuoso, of a Humour nice, delicate, critical and opinionative: he had nothing of the French Mein in him, but all the Gravity of the Don. His ill-favour'd Person, and his low Estate, put him out of Humour with the World; and because that should not upbraid or reproach his Follies and Defects, he was sure to be beforehand with that, and to be always satirick upon it; and lov'd to live and act contrary to the Custom and Usage of all Mankind besides.

He was infinitely delighted to find a Man of his own Humour in De Pais, or at least a Man that would be persuaded to like his so well, to live up to it; and it was no little Joy and Satisfaction to him to find, that he kept his Daughters in that Severity, which was wholly agreeable to him, and so contrary to the Manner and Fashion of the French Quality; who allow all Freedoms, which to Vernole's rigid Nature, seem'd as so many Steps to Vice, and in his Opinion, the Ruiner of all Virtue and Honour in Womankind. De Pais was extremely glad his Conduct was so well interpreted, which was no other in him than a proud Frugality; who, because they could not appear in so much Gallantry as their Quality required, kept 'em retir'd, and unseen to all, but his particular Friends, of whom Vernole was the chief.

Vernole never appear'd before Atlante (which was seldom) but he assum'd a Gravity and Respect fit to have entertain'd a Maid of Twenty, or rather a Matron of much greater Years and Judgment. His Discourses were always of Matters of State or Philosophy; and sometimes when De Pais would (laughing) say, 'He might as well entertain Atlante with Greek and Hebrew,' he would reply gravely, 'You are mistaken, Sir, I find the Seeds of great and profound Matter in the Soul of this young Maid, which ought to be nourish'd now while she is young, and they will grow up to very great Perfection: I find Atlante capable of the noble Virtues of the Mind, and am infinitely mistaken in my Observations, and Art of Physiognomy, if Atlante be not born for greater Things than her Fortune does now Promise: She will be very considerable in the World, (believe me) and this will arrive to her perfectly from the Force of her Charms.' De Pais was extremely overjoy'd to hear such Good prophesied of Atlante, and from that Time set a sort of an Esteem upon her, which he did not on Charlot his younger; whom, by the Persuasions of Vernole, he resolv'd to put in a Monastery, that what he had might descend to Atlante: not but he confess'd Charlot had Beauty extremely attractive, and a Wit that promised much, when it should be cultivated by Years and Experience; and would shew it self with great Advantage and Lustre in a Monastery. All this pleased De Pais very well, who was easily persuaded, since he had not a Fortune to marry her well in the World.

As yet Vernole had never spoke to Atlante of Love, nor did his Gravity think it Prudence to discover his Heart to so young a Maid; he waited her more sensible Years, when he could hope to have some Return. And all he expected from this her tender Age, was by his daily Converse with her, and the Presents he made her suitable to her Years, to ingratiate himself insensibly into her Friendship and Esteem, since she was not yet capable of Love; but even in that he mistook his Aim, for every day he grew more and more disagreeable to Atlante, and would have been her absolute Aversion, had she known she had every Day entertained a Lover; but as she grew in Years and Sense, he seemed the more despicable in her Eyes as to his Person; yet as she had respect to his Parts and Qualities, she paid him all the Complaisance she could, and which was due to him, and so must be confess'd. Tho' he had a stiff Formality in all he said and did, yet he had Wit and Learning, and was a great Philosopher. As much of his Learning as Atlante was capable of attaining to, he made her Mistress of, and that was no small Portion; for all his Discourse was fine and easily comprehended, his Notions of Philosophy fit for Ladies; and he took greater Pains with Atlante, than any Master would have done with a Scholar: So that it was most certain, he added very great Accomplishment to her natural Wit: and the more, because she took a great Delight in Philosophy; which very often made her impatient of his Coming, especially when she had many Questions to ask him concerning it, and she would often receive him with a Pleasure in her Face, which he did not fail to interpret to his own Advantage, being very apt to flatter himself. Her Sister Charlot would often ask her, 'How she could give whole Afternoons to so disagreeable a Man. What is it (said she) that charms you so? his tawny Leather-Face, his extraordinary high Nose, his wide Mouth and Eye-brows, that hang low'ring over his Eyes, his lean Carcase, and his lame and halting Hips?' But Atlante would discreetly reply, 'If I must grant all you say of Count Vernole to be true, yet he has a Wit and Learning that will atone sufficiently for all those Faults you mention: A fine Soul is infinitely to be preferr'd to a fine Body; this decays, but that's eternal; and Age that ruins one, refines the other.' Tho' possibly Atlante thought as ill of the Count as her Sister, yet in Respect to him, she would not own it.

Atlante was now arriv'd to her thirteenth Year, when her Beauty, which every Day increas'd, became the Discourse of the whole Town, which had already gain'd her as many Lovers as had beheld her; for none saw her without languishing for her, or at least, but what were in very great Admiration of her. Every body talk'd of the young Atlante, and all the Noblemen, who had Sons (knowing the Smallness of her Fortune, and the Lustre of her Beauty) would send them, for fear of their being charm'd with her Beauty, either to some other part of the World, or exhorted them, by way of Precaution, to keep out of her Sight. Old Bellyaurd was one of those wise Parents; and timely Prevention, as he thought, of Rinaldo's falling in Love with Atlante, perhaps was the Occasion of his being so: He had before heard of Atlante, and of her Beauty, yet it had made no Impressions on his Heart; but his Father no sooner forbid him Loving, than he felt a new Desire tormenting him, of seeing this lovely and dangerous young Person: he wonders at his unaccountable Pain, which daily sollicits him within, to go where he may behold this Beauty; of whom he frames a thousand Ideas, all such as were most agreeable to him; but then upbraids his Fancy for not forming her half so delicate as she was; and longs yet more to see her, to know how near she approaches to the Picture he has drawn of her in his Mind: and tho' he knew she liv'd the next House to him, yet he knew also she was kept within like a vow'd Nun, or with the Severity of a Spaniard. And tho' he had a Chamber, which had a jutting Window, that look'd just upon the Door of Monsieur De Pais, and that he would watch many Hours at a time, in hope to see them go out, yet he could never get a Glimpse of her; yet he heard she often frequented the Church of our Lady. Thither then young Rinaldo resolv'd to go, and did so two or three Mornings; in which time, to his unspeakable Grief, he saw no Beauty appear that charm'd him; and yet he fancy'd that Atlante was there, and that he had seen her; that some one of those young Ladies that he saw in the Church was she, tho' he had no body to enquire of, and that she was not so fair as the World reported; for which he would often sigh, as if he had lost some great Expectation. However, he ceased not to frequent this Church, and one day saw a young Beauty, who at first glimpse made his Heart leap to his Mouth, and fall a trembling again into its wonted Place; for it immediately told him, that that young Maid was Atlante: she was with her Sister Charlot, who was very handsome, but not comparable to Atlante. He fix'd his Eyes upon her as she kneel'd at the Altar; he never moved from that charming Face as long as she remain'd there; he forgot all Devotion, but what he paid to her; he ador'd her, he burnt and languished already for her, and found he must possess Atlante or die. Often as he gaz'd upon her, he saw her fair Eyes lifted up towards his, where they often met; which she perceiving, would cast hers down into her Bosom, or on her Book, and blush as if she had done a Fault. Charlot perceiv'd all the Motions of Rinaldo, how he folded his Arms, how he sigh'd and gaz'd on her Sister; she took notice of his Clothes, his Garniture, and every particular of his Dress, as young Girls use to do; and seeing him so very handsome, and so much better dress'd than all the young Cavaliers that were in the Church, she was very much pleas'd with him; and could not forbear saying, in a low Voice, to Atlante, 'Look, look my Sister, what a pretty Monsieur yonder is! see how fine his Face is, how delicate his Hair, how gallant his Dress! and do but look how he gazes on you!' This would make Atlante blush anew, who durst not raise her Eyes for fear she should encounter his. While he had the Pleasure to imagine they were talking of him, and he saw in the pretty Face of Charlot, that what she said was not to his Disadvantage, and by the Blushes of Atlante, that she was not displeas'd with what was spoken to her; he perceiv'd the young one importunate with her; and Atlante jogging her with her Elbow, as much as to say, Hold your Peace: all this he made a kind Interpretation of, and was transported with Joy at the good Omens. He was willing to flatter his new Flame, and to compliment his young Desire with a little Hope; but the divine Ceremony ceasing, Atlante left the Church, and it being very fair Weather, she walk'd home. Rinaldo, who saw her going, felt all the Agonies of a Lover, who parts with all that can make him happy; and seeing only Atlante attended with her Sister, and a Footman following with their Books, he was a thousand times about to speak to 'em; but he no sooner advanc'd a step or two towards 'em to that purpose (for he followed them) but his Heart fail'd, and a certain Awe and Reverence, or rather the Fears and Tremblings of a Lover, prevented him: but when he consider'd, that possibly he might never have so favourable an Opportunity again, he resolv'd a-new, and called up so much Courage to his Heart, as to speak to Atlante; but before he did so, Charlot looking behind her, saw Rinaldo very near to 'em, and cry'd out with a Voice of Joy, 'Oh! Sister, Sister! look where the handsome Monsieur is, just behind us! sure he is some-body of Quality, for see he has two Footmen that follow him, in just such Liveries, and so rich as those of our Neighbour Monsieur Bellyaurd.' At this Atlante could not forbear, but before she was aware of it, turn'd her Head, and look'd on Rinaldo; which encourag'd him to advance, and putting off his Hat, which he clapt under his Arm, with a low Bow, said, 'Ladies, you are slenderly attended, and so many Accidents arrive to the Fair in the rude Streets, that I humbly implore you will permit me, whose Duty it is as a Neighbour, to wait on you to your Door.' 'Sir, (said Atlante blushing) we fear no Insolence, and need no Protector; or if we did, we should not be so rude to take you out of your way, to serve us.' 'Madam, (said he) my way lies yours. I live at the next Door, and am Son to Bellyaurd, your Neighbour. But, Madam, (added he) if I were to go all my Life out of the way, to do you Service, I should take it for the greatest Happiness that could arrive to me; but, Madam, sure a Man can never be out of his Way, who has the Honour of so charming Company.' Atlante made no reply to this, but blush'd and bow'd: But Charlot said, 'Nay, Sir, if you are our Neighbour, we will give you leave to conduct us home; but pray, Sir, how came you to know we are your Neighbours? for we never saw you before, to our knowledge.' 'My pretty Miss, (reply'd Rinaldo) I knew it from that transcendent Beauty that appear'd in your Faces, and fine Shapes; for I have heard, there was no Beauty in the World like that of Atlante's; and I no sooner saw her, but my Heart told me it was she.' 'Heart! (said Charlot laughing) why, do Hearts use to speak?' 'The most intelligible of any thing, (Rinaldo reply'd) when 'tis tenderly touch'd, when 'tis charm'd and transported.' At these Words he sigh'd, and Atlante, to his extreme Satisfaction, blush'd. 'Touch'd, charm'd, and transported, (said Charlot) what's that? And how do you do to have it be all these things? For I would give any thing in the World to have my Heart speak.' 'Oh! (said Rinaldo) your Heart is too young, it is not yet arrived to the Years of Speaking; about thirteen or fourteen, it may possibly be saying a thousand soft things to you; but it must be first inspir'd by some noble Object, whose Idea it must retain.' 'What (reply'd the pretty Prattler) I'll warrant I must be in Love?' 'Yes, (said Rinaldo) most passionately, or you will have but little Conversation with your Heart.' 'Oh! (reply'd she) I am afraid the Pleasure of such a Conversation, will not make me amends for the Pain that Love will give me.' 'That (said Rinaldo) is according as the Object is kind, and as you hope; if he love, and you hope, you will have double Pleasure: And in this, how great an Advantage have fair Ladies above us Men! 'Tis always impossible for you to love in vain, you have your Choice of a thousand Hearts, which you have subdu'd, and may not only chuse your Slaves, but be assur'd of 'em; without speaking, you are belov'd, it needs not cost you a Sigh or a Tear: But unhappy Man is often destin'd to give his Heart, where it is not regarded, to sigh, to weep, and languish, without any hope of Pity.' 'You speak so feelingly, Sir, (said Charlot) that I am afraid this is your Case.' 'Yes, Madam, (reply'd Rinaldo, sighing) I am that unhappy Man.' 'Indeed it is pity (said she.) Pray, how long have you been so?' 'Ever since I heard of the charming Atlante, (reply'd he, sighing again) I ador'd her Character; but now I have seen her, I die for her.' 'For me, Sir! (said Atlante, who had not yet spoke) this is the common Compliment of all the young Men, who pretend to be Lovers; and if one should pity all those Sighers, we should have but very little left for our selves.' 'I believe (said Rinaldo) there are none that tell you so, who do not mean as they say: Yet among all those Adorers, and those who say they will die for you, you will find none will be so good as their Words but Rinaldo.' 'Perhaps (said Atlante) of all those who tell me of Dying, there are none that tell me of it with so little Reason as Rinaldo, if that be your Name, Sir.' 'Madam, it is, (said he) and who am transported with an unspeakable Joy, to hear those last Words from your fair Mouth: and let me, Oh lovely Atlante! assure you, that what I have said, are not Words of course, but proceed from a Heart that has vow'd it self eternally yours, even before I had the Happiness to behold this divine Person; but now that my Eyes have made good all my Heart before imagin'd, and did but hope, I swear, I will die a thousand Deaths, rather than violate what I have said to you; that I adore you; that my Soul and all my Faculties, are charm'd with your Beauty and Innocence, and that my Life and Fortune, not inconsiderable, shall be laid at your Feet.' This he spoke with a Fervency of Passion, that left her no Doubt of what he had said; yet she blush'd for Shame, and was a little angry at her self, for suffering him to say so much to her, the very first time she saw him, and accused her self for giving him any Encouragement: And in this Confusion she replied, 'Sir, you have said too much to be believ'd; and I cannot imagine so short an Acquaintance can make so considerable an Impression; of which Confession I accuse my self much more than you, in that I did not only hearken to what you said, without forbidding you to entertain me at that rate, but for unheedily speaking something, that has encourag'd this Boldness; for so I must call it, in a Man so great a Stranger to me.' 'Madam (said he) if I have offended by the Suddenness of my presumptuous Discovery, I beseech you to consider my Reasons for it, the few Opportunities I am like to have, and the Impossibility of waiting on you, both from the Severity of your Father and mine; who, ere I saw you, warn'd me of my Fate, as if he foresaw I should fall in love, as soon as I should chance to see you; and for that Reason has kept me closer to my Studies, than hitherto I have been. And from that time I began to feel a Flame, which was kindled by Report alone, and the Description my Father gave of your wondrous and dangerous Beauty: Therefore, Madam, I have not suddenly told you of my Passion. I have been long your Lover, and have long languish'd without telling of my Pain; and you ought to pardon it now, since it is done with all the Respect and religious Awe, that 'tis possible for a Heart to deliver and unload it self in; therefore, Madam, if you have by chance uttered any thing, that I have taken Advantage or Hope from, I assure you 'tis so small, that you have no reason to repent it; but rather, if you would have me live, send me not from you, without a Confirmation of that little Hope. See, Madam, (said he, more earnestly and trembling) see we are almost arriv'd at our Homes, send me not to mine in a Despair that I cannot support with Life; but tell me, I shall be bless'd with your Sight, sometimes in your Balcony, which is very near to a jetting Window in our House, from whence I have sent many a longing Look towards yours, in hope to have seen my Soul's Tormentor.' 'I shall be very unwilling (said she) to enter into an Intrigue of Love or Friendship with a Man, whose Parents will be averse to my Happiness, and possibly mine as refractory, tho' they cannot but know such an Alliance would be very considerable, my Fortune not being suitable to yours: I tell you this, that you may withdraw in time from an Engagement, in which I find there will be a great many Obstacles.' 'Oh! Madam, (reply'd Rinaldo, sighing) if my Person be not disagreeable to you, you will have no occasion to fear the rest; 'tis that I dread, and that which is all my Fear.' He, sighing, beheld her with a languishing Look, that told her, he expected her Answer; when she reply'd, 'Sir, if that will be Satisfaction enough for you at this time, I do assure you, I have no Aversion for your Person, in which I find more to be valu'd, than in any I have yet seen; and if what you say be real, and proceed from a Heart truly affected, I find, in spite of me, you will oblige me to give you Hope.'

They were come so near their own Houses, that he had not time to return her any Answer; but with a low Bow he acknowledg'd her Bounty, and express'd the Joy her last Words had given him, by a Look that made her understand he was charm'd and pleas'd; and she bowing to him with an Air of Satisfaction in her Face, he was well assur'd, there was nothing to be seen so lovely as she then appear'd, and left her to go into her own House: but till she was out of sight, he had not power to stir, and then sighing, retired to his own Apartment, to think over all that had past between them. He found nothing but what gave him a thousand Joys, in all she had said; and he blest this happy Day, and wondred how his Stars came so kind, to make him in one hour at once see Atlante, and have the happiness to know from her Mouth, that he was not disagreeable to her: Yet with this Satisfaction, he had a thousand Thoughts mix'd which were tormenting, and those were the Fear of their Parents; he foresaw from what his Father had said to him already, that it would be difficult to draw him to a Consent of his Marriage with Atlante. These Joys and Fears were his Companions all the Night, in which he took but little Rest. Nor was Atlante without her Inquietudes: She found Rinaldo more in her Thoughts than she wish'd, and a sudden Change of Humour, that made her know something was the matter with her more than usual; she calls to mind Rinaldo's speaking of the Conversation with his Heart, and found hers would be tattling to her, if she would give way to it; and yet the more she strove to avoid it, the more it importun'd her, and in spight of all her Resistance, would tell her, that Rinaldo had a thousand Charms: It tells her, that he loves and adores her, and that she would be the most cruel of her Sex, should she not be sensible of his Passion. She finds a thousand Graces in his Person and Conversation, and as many Advantages in his Fortune, which was one of the most considerable in all those Parts; for his Estate exceeded that of the most Noble Men in Orleans, and she imagines she should be the most fortunate of all Womankind in such a Match. With these Thoughts she employ'd all the Hours of the Night; so that she lay so long in Bed the next Day, that Count Vernole, who had invited himself to Dinner, came before she had quitted her Chamber, and she was forc'd to say, she had not been well. He had brought her a very fine Book, newly come out, of delicate Philosophy, fit for the Study of Ladies. But he appear'd so disagreeable to that Heart, wholly taken up with a new and fine Object, that she could now hardly pay him that Civility she was wont to do; while on the other side that little State and Pride Atlante assum'd, made her appear the more charming to him: so that if Atlante had no mind to begin a new Lesson of Philosophy, while she fancied her Thoughts were much better employ'd, the Count every moment expressing his Tenderness and Passion, had as little an Inclination to instruct her, as she had to be instructed: Love had taught her a new Lesson, and he would fain teach her a new Lesson of Love, but fears it will be a diminishing his Gravity and Grandeur, to open the Secrets of his Heart to so young a Maid; he therefore thinks it more agreeable to his Quality and Years, being about Forty, to use her Father's Authority in this Affair, and that it was sufficient for him to declare himself to Monsieur De Pais, who he knew would be proud of the Honour he did him. Some time past, before he could be persuaded even to declare himself to her Father: he fancies the little Coldness and Pride he saw in Atlante's Face, which was not usual, proceeded from some Discovery of Passion, which his Eyes had made, or now and then a Sigh, that unawares broke forth; and accuses himself of a Levity below his Quality, and the Dignity of his Wit and Gravity; and therefore assumes a more rigid and formal Behaviour than he was wont, which rendred him yet more disagreeable than before; and 'twas with greater Pain than ever, she gave him that Respect which was due to his Quality.

Rinaldo, after a restless Night, was up very early in the Morning; and tho' he was not certain of seeing his adorable Atlante, he dress'd himself with all that Care, as if he had been to have waited on her, and got himself into the Window, that overlook'd Monsieur De Pais's Balcony, where he had not remain'd long, before he saw the pretty Charlot come into it, not with any design of seeing Rinaldo, but to look and gaze about her a little. Rinaldo saw her, and made her a very low Reverence, and found some disorder'd Joy on the sight of even Charlot, since she was Sister to Atlante. He call'd to her, (for the

Window was so near her, he could easily be heard by her) and told her, 'He was infinitely indebted to her Bounty, for giving him an Opportunity yesterday of falling on that Discourse, which had made him the happiest Man in the World': He said, 'If she had not by her agreeable Conversation encourag'd him, and drawn him from one Word to another, he should never have had the Confidence to have told Atlante, how much he ador'd her.' 'I am very glad, (replyed Charlot) that I was the Occasion of the Beginning of an Amour, which was displeasing to neither one nor the other; for I assure you for your Comfort, my Sister nothing but thinks on you: We lie together, and you have taught her already to sigh so, that I could not sleep for her.' At this his Face was cover'd over with a rising Joy, which his Heart could not contain: And after some Discourse, in which this innocent Girl discovered more than Atlante wish'd she should, he besought her to become his Advocate; and since she had no Brother, to give him leave to assume that Honour, and call her Sister. Thus, by degrees, he flatter'd her into a Consent of carrying a Letter from him to Atlante; which she, who believ'd all as innocent as her self, and being not forbid to do so, immediately consented to; when he took his Pen and Ink, that stood in the Window, with Paper, and wrote Atlante this following Letter:

RINALDO to ATLANTE.

If my Fate be so severe, as to deny me the Happiness of sighing out   my Pain and Passion daily at your Feet, if there be any Faith in the   Hope you were pleased to give me (as 'twere a Sin to doubt) Oh charming Atlante! suffer me not to languish, both without   beholding you, and without the Blessing of now and then a Billet, in   answer to those that shall daily assure you of my eternal Faith and   Vows; 'tis all I ask, till Fortune, and our Affairs, shall allow me   the unspeakable Satisfaction of claiming you: yet if your Charity   can sometimes afford me a sight of you, either from your Balcony in   the Evening, or at a Church in the Morning, it would save me from   that Despair and Torment, which must possess a Heart so unassur'd,   as that of

Your Eternal Adorer,

Rin. Bellyaurd.

He having writ and seal'd this, toss'd it into the Balcony to Charlot, having first look'd about to see if none perceiv'd them. She put it in her Bosom, and ran in to her Sister, whom by chance she found alone; Vernole having taken De Pais into the Garden, to discourse him concerning the sending Charlot to the Monastery, which Work he desir'd to see perform'd, before he declar'd his Intentions to Atlante: for among all his other good Qualities, he was very avaricious; and as fair as Atlante was, he thought she would be much fairer with the Addition of Charlot's Portion. This Affair of his with Monsieur De Pais, gave Charlot an opportunity of delivering her Letter to her Sister; who no sooner drew it from her Bosom, but Atlante's Face was covered over with Blushes: For she imagin'd from whence it came, and had a secret Joy in that Imagination, tho' she thought she must put on the Severity and Niceness of a Virgin, who would not be thought to have surrendered her Heart with so small an Assault, and the first too. So she demanded from whence Charlot had that Letter? Who replyed with Joy, 'From the fine young Gentleman, our Neighbour.' At which Atlante assum'd all the Gravity she could, to chide her Sister; who replied, 'Well, Sister, had you this day seen him, you would not have been angry to have receiv'd a Letter from him; he look'd so handsome, and was so richly dress'd, ten times finer than he was yesterday; and I promis'd him you should read it: therefore, pray let me keep my Word with him; and not only so, but carry him an Answer.' 'Well (said Atlante) to save your Credit with Monsieur Rinaldo, I will read it': Which she did, and finish'd with a Sigh. While she was reading, Charlot ran into the Garden, to see if they were not likely to be surpriz'd; and finding the Count and her Father set in an

Arbour, in deep Discourse, she brought Pen, Ink, and Paper to her Sister, and told her, she might write without the Fear of being disturbed: and urged her so long to what was enough her Inclination, that she at last obtained this Answer:

ATLANTE to RINALDO.

Charlot, your little importunate Advocate, has at last subdued me to a Consent of returning you This. She has put me on an Affair with which I am wholly unacquainted; and you ought to take this very kindly from me, since it is the very first time I ever writ to one of your Sex, tho' perhaps I might with less Danger have done it to any other Man. I tremble while I write, since I dread a Correspondence of this Nature, which may insensibly draw us into an Inconvenience, and engage me beyond the Limits of that Nicety I ought to preserve: For this Way we venture to say a thousand little kind Things, which in Conversation we dare not do: for now none can see us blush. I am sensible I shall this Way put my self too soon into your Power; and tho' you have abundance of Merit, I ought to be asham'd of confessing, I am but too sensible of it: But hold, I shall discover for your Repose (which I would preserve) too much of the Heart of Atlante.

She gave this Letter to Charlot; who immediately ran into the Balcony with it, where she still found Rinaldo in a melancholy Posture, leaning his Head on his Hand: She shewed him the Letter, but was afraid to toss it to him, for fear it might fall to the Ground; so he ran and fetched a long Cane, which he cleft at one End, and held it while she put the Letter into the Cleft, and staid not to hear what he said to it. But never was Man so transported with Joy, as he was at the reading of this Letter; it gives him new Wounds; for to the Generous, nothing obliges Love so much as Love: tho' it is now too much the Nature of that inconstant Sex, to cease to love as soon as they are sure of the Conquest. But it was far different with our Cavalier; he was the more inflamed, by imagining he had made some Impressions on the Heart of Atlante, and kindled some Sparks there, that in time might increase to something more; so that he now resolves to die hers: and considering all the Obstacles that may possibly hinder his Happiness, he found none but his Father's Obstinacy, perhaps occasioned by the Meanness of Atlante's Fortune. To this he urged again, that he was his only Son, and a Son whom he loved equal to his own Life; and that certainly, as soon as he should behold him dying for Atlante, which if he were forc'd to quit her he must be, he then believed the Tenderness of so fond a Parent would break forth into Pity, and plead within for his Consent. These were the Thoughts that flatter'd this young Lover all the Day; and whether he were riding the Great Horse, or at his Study of Philosophy, or Mathematicks, Singing, Dancing, or whatsoever other Exercise his Tutors ordered, his Thoughts were continually on Atlante. And now he profited no more, whatever he seem'd to do: every Day he fail'd not to write to her by the Hand of the kind Charlot; who, young as she was, had conceiv'd a great Friendship for Rinaldo, and fail'd not to fetch her Letters, and bring him Answers, such as he wish'd to receive. But all this did not satisfy our impatient Lover; Absence kill'd, and he was no longer able to support himself, without a sight of this adorable Maid; he therefore implores, she will give him that Satisfaction: And she at last grants it, with a better Will than he imagin'd. The next Day was the appointed Time, when she would, under Pretence of going to Church, give him an Assignation: And because all publick Places were dangerous, and might make a great Noise, and they had no private Place to trust to, Rinaldo, under Pretence of going up the River in his Pleasure-Boat, which he often did, sent to have it made ready by the next Day at Ten of the Clock. This was accordingly done, and he gave Atlante Notice of his Design of going an Hour or two on the River in his Boat, which lay near to such a Place, not far from the Church. She and Charlot came thither: and because they durst not come out without a Footman or two, they taking one, sent him with a How-do-ye to some young Ladies, and told him, he should find them at Church: So getting rid of their Spy, they hastened to the River-side, and found a Boat and Rinaldo, waiting to carry them on board his little

Vessel, which was richly adorn'd, and a very handsome Collation ready for them, of cold Meats, Sallads and Sweetmeats.

As soon as they were come into the Pleasure-Boat, unseen of any, he kneel'd at the Feet of Atlante, and there utter'd so many passionate and tender Things to her, with a Voice so trembling and soft, with Eyes so languishing, and a Fervency and a Fire so sincere, that her young Heart, wholly uncapable of Artifice, could no longer resist such Language, and such Looks of Love; she grows tender, and he perceives it in her fine Eyes, who could not dissemble; he reads her Heart in her Looks, and found it yielding apace; and therefore assaults it anew, with fresh Forces of Sighs and Tears: He implores she would assure him of her Heart, which she could no other way do, than by yielding to marry him: He would carry her to the next Village, there consummate that Happiness, without which he was able to live no longer; for he had a thousand Fears, that some other Lover was, or would suddenly be provided for her; and therefore he would make sure of her while he had this Opportunity: and to that End, he answer'd all the Objections she could make to the contrary. But ever, when he named Marriage, she trembled, with fear of doing something that she fancy'd she ought not to do without the Consent of her Father. She was sensible of the Advantage, but had been so us'd to a strict Obedience, that she could not without Horror think of violating it; and therefore besought him, as he valued her Repose, not to urge her to that: And told him further, That if he fear'd any Rival, she would give him what other Assurance and Satisfaction he pleas'd, but that of Marriage; which she could not consent to, till she knew such an Alliance would not be fatal to him: for she fear'd, as passionately as he lov'd her, when he should find she had occasion'd him the Loss of his Fortune, or his Father's Affection, he would grow to hate her. Tho' he answer'd to this all that a fond Lover could urge, yet she was resolv'd, and he forc'd to content himself with obliging her by his Prayers and Protestations, his Sighs and Tears, to a Contract, which they solemnly made each other, vowing on either Side, they would never marry any other. This being solemnly concluded, he assum'd a Look more gay and contented than before: He presented her a very rich Ring, which she durst not put on her Finger, but hid it in her Bosom. And beholding each other now as Man and Wife, she suffer'd him all the decent Freedoms he could wish to take; so that the Hours of this Voyage seem'd the most soft and charming of his Life: and doubtless they were so; every Touch of Atlante transported him, every Look pierced his Soul, and he was all Raptures of Joy, when he consider'd this charming lovely Maid was his own.

Charlot all this while was gazing above-deck, admiring the Motion of the little Vessel, and how easily the Wind and Tide bore her up the River. She had never been in any thing of this kind before, and was very well pleas'd and entertain'd, when Rinaldo call'd her down to eat; where they enjoy'd themselves, as well as was possible: and Charlot was wondring to see such a Content in their Eyes.

But now they thought it was high time for them to return; they fancy the Footman missing them at Church, would go home and alarm their Father, and the Knight of the Ill-favour'd Countenance, as Charlot call'd Count Vernole, whose Severity put their Father on a greater Restriction of them, than naturally he would do of himself. At the Name of this Count, Rinaldo chang'd Colour, fearing he might be some Rival; and ask'd Atlante, if this Vernole was a-kin to her? She answer'd no; but was a very great Friend to her Father, and one who from their Infancy had had a particular Concern for their Breeding, and was her Master for Philosophy. 'Ah! (reply'd Rinaldo, sighing) this Man's Concern must proceed from something more than Friendship for her Father'; and therefore conjur'd her to tell him, whether he was not a Lover: 'A Lover! (reply'd Atlante) I assure you, he is a perfect Antidote against that Passion': And tho' she suffer'd his ugly Presence now, she should loathe and hate him, should he but name Love to her.

She said, she believed she need not fear any such Persecution, since he was a Man who was not at all amorous; that he had too much of the Satire in his Humour, to harbour any Softness there: and Nature had form'd his Body to his Mind, wholly unfit for Love. And that he might set his Heart absolutely at rest, she assur'd him her Father had never yet propos'd any Marriage to her, tho' many advantageous ones were offer'd him every Day.

The Sails being turned to carry them back from whence they came; after having discoursed of a thousand Things, and all of Love, and Contrivance to carry on their mutual Design, they with Sighs parted; Rinaldo staying behind in the Pleasure-Boat, and they going a-shore in the Wherry that attended: after which he cast many an amorous and sad Look, and perhaps was answer'd by those of Atlante.

It was past Church-time two or three Hours, when they arrived at home, wholly unprepar'd with an Excuse, so absolutely was Atlante's Soul possest with softer Business. The first Person that they met was the Footman, who open'd the Door, and began to cry out how long he had waited in the Church, and how in vain; without giving them time to reply. De Pais came towards 'em, and with a frowning Look demanded where they had been? Atlante, who was not accustom'd to Excuses and Untruth, was a while at a stand; when Charlot with a Voice of Joy cry'd out, 'Oh Sir! we have been a-board of a fine little Ship': At this Atlante blush'd, fearing she would tell the Truth. But she proceeded on, and said, that they had not been above a Quarter of an Hour at Church, when the Lady ----, with some other Ladies and Cavaliers, were going out of the Church, and that spying them, they would needs have 'em go with 'em: My Sister, Sir, continu'd she, was very loth to go, for fear you should be angry; but my Lady ---- was so importunate with her on one side, and I on the other, because I never saw a little Ship in my Life, that at last we prevail'd with her: therefore, good Sir, be not angry. He promised them he was not. And when they came in, they found Count Vernole, who had been inspiring De Pais with Severity, and counselled him to chide the young Ladies, for being too long absent, under Pretence of going to their Devotion. Nor was it enough for him to set the Father on, but himself with a Gravity, where Concern and Malice were both apparent, reproached Atlante with Levity; and told her, He believed she had some other Motive than the Invitation of a Lady, to go on Ship-board; and that she had too many Lovers, not to make them doubt that this was a design'd thing; and that she had heard Love from some one, for whom it was design'd. To this she made but a short Reply, That if it was so, she had no reason to conceal it, since she had Sense enough to look after herself; and if any body had made love to her, he might be assur'd, it was some one whose Quality and Merit deserved to be heard: and with a Look of Scorn, she passed on to another Room, and left him silently raging within with Jealousy: Which, if before she tormented him, this Declaration increas'd it to a pitch not to be conceal'd. And this Day he said so much to the Father, that he resolv'd forthwith to send Charlot to a Nunnery: and accordingly the next day he bid her prepare to go. Charlot, who was not yet arrived to the Years of Distinction, did not much regret it; and having no Trouble but leaving her Sister, she prepared to go to a Nunnery, not many Streets from that where she dwelt. The Lady Abbess was her Father's Kinswoman, and had treated her very well, as often as she came to visit her: so that with Satisfaction enough, she was condemned to a Monastick Life, and was now going for her Probation-Year. Atlante was troubled at her Departure, because she had no body to bring and to carry Letters between Rinaldo and she: however, she took her leave of her, and promis'd to come and see her as often as she should be permitted to go abroad; for she fear'd now some Constraint extraordinary would be put upon her: and so it happened.

Atlante's Chamber was that to which the Balcony belong'd; and tho' she durst not appear there in the Daytime, she could in the Night, and that way give her Lover as many Hours of Conversation as she pleased, without being perceiv'd: But how to give Rinaldo notice of this, she could not tell; who not knowing Charlot was gone to a Monastery, waited many days at his Window to see her: at last, they neither of them knowing who to trust with any Message, one day, when he was, as usual upon his watch, he saw Atlante step into the Balcony, who having a Letter, in which she had put a piece of Lead, she tost it into his Window, whose Casement was open, and run in again unperceived by any but himself. The Paper contained only this:

My Chamber is that which looks into the Balcony; from whence, tho' I cannot converse with you in the Day, I can at Night, when I am retired to go to bed: therefore be at your Window. Farewel.

There needed no more to make him a diligent Watcher: and accordingly she was no sooner retired to her Chamber, but she would come into the Balcony, where she fail'd not to see him attending at his Window. This happy Contrivance was thus carry'd on for many Nights, where they entertain'd one another with all the Endearment that two Hearts could dictate, who were perfectly united and assur'd of each other; and this pleasing Conversation would often last till Day appear'd, and forced them to part.

But old Bellyaurd perceiving his Son frequent that Chamber more than usual, fancy'd something extraordinary must be the Cause of it; and one night asking for his Son, his Valet told him, he was gone into the great Chamber, so this was called: Bellyaurd asked the Valet what he did there; he told him he could not tell; for often he had lighted him thither, and that his Master would take the Candle from him at the Chamber-Door, and suffer him to go no farther. Tho' the old Gentleman could not imagine what Affairs he could have alone every Night in that Chamber, he had a Curiosity to see: and one unlucky Night, putting off his Shoes, he came to the Door of the Chamber, which was open; he enter'd softly, and saw the Candle set in the Chimney, and his Son at a great open Bay-Window: he stopt awhile to wait when he would turn, but finding him unmoveable, he advanced something farther, and at last heard the soft Dialogue of Love between him and Atlante, whom he knew to be she, by his often calling her by her Name in their Discourse. He heard enough to confirm him how Matters went; and unseen as he came, he returned, full of Indignation, and thought how to prevent so great an Evil, as this Passion of his Son might produce: at first he thought to round him severely in the Ear about it, and upbraid him for doing the only thing he had thought fit to forbid him; but then he thought that would but terrify him for awhile, and he would return again, where he had so great an Inclination, if he were near her; he therefore resolves to send him to Paris, that by Absence he might forget the young Beauty that had charm'd his Youth. Therefore, without letting Rinaldo know the Reason, and without taking Notice that he knew any thing of his Amour, he came to him one day, and told him, all the Masters he had for the improving him in noble Sciences were very dull, or very remiss: and that he resolved he should go for a Year or two to the Academy at Paris. To this the Son made a thousand Evasions; but the Father was positive, and not to be persuaded by all his Reasons: And finding he should absolutely displease him if he refus'd to go, and not daring to tell him the dear Cause of his Desire to remain at Orleans, he therefore, with a breaking Heart, consents to go, nay, resolves it, tho' it should be his Death. But alas! he considers that this Parting will not only prove the greatest Torment upon Earth to him, but that Atlante will share in his Misfortunes also: This Thought gives him a double Torment, and yet he finds no Way to evade it.

The Night that finished this fatal Day, he goes again to his wonted Station, the Window; where he had not sighed very long, but he saw Atlante enter the Balcony: He was not able a great while to speak to her, or to utter one Word. The Night was light enough to see him at the wonted Place; and she admires at his Silence, and demands the Reason in such obliging Terms as adds to his Grief; and he, with a deep Sigh, reply'd, 'Urge me not, my fair Atlante, to speak, lest by obeying you I give you more cause of Grief than my Silence is capable of doing': and then sighing again, he held his peace, and gave her leave to ask the Cause of these last Words. But when he made no Reply but by sighing, she imagin'd it much worse than indeed it was; and with a trembling and fainting Voice, she cried, 'Oh! Rinaldo, give me leave to divine that cruel News you are so unwilling to tell me: It is so,' added she, 'you are destin'd to some more fortunate Maid than Atlante.' At this Tears stopped her Speech, and she could utter no more. 'No, my dearest Charmer (reply'd Rinaldo, elevating his Voice) if that were all, you should see with what Fortitude I would die, rather than obey any such Commands. I am vow'd yours to the last Moment of my Life; and will be yours in spite of all the Opposition in the World: that Cruelty I could evade, but cannot this that threatens me.' 'Ah! (cried Atlante) let Fate do her worst, so she still continue Rinaldo mine, and keep that Faith he hath sworn to me entire: What can she do beside, that can afflict me?' 'She can separate me (cried he) for some time from Atlante.' 'Oh! (reply'd she) all Misfortunes fall so below that which I first imagin'd, that methinks I do not resent this, as I should otherwise have done: but I know, when I have a little more consider'd it, I shall even die with the Grief of it; Absence being so great an Enemy to Love, and making us soon forget the Object belov'd: This, tho' I never experienc'd, I have heard, and fear it may be my Fate.' He then convinc'd her Fears with a thousand new Vows, and a thousand Imprecations of Constancy. She then asked him, 'If their Loves were discover'd, that he was with such haste to depart?' He told her, 'Nothing of that was the Cause; and he could almost wish it were discover'd, since he could resolutely then refuse to go: but it was only to cultivate his Mind more effectually than he could do here; 'twas the Care of his Father to accomplish him the more; and therefore he could not contradict it. But (said he) I am not sent where Seas shall part us, nor vast Distances of Earth, but to Paris, from whence he might come in two Days to see her again; and that he would expect from that Balcony, that had given him so many happy Moments, many more when he should come to see her.' He besought her to send him away with all the Satisfaction she could, which she could no otherwise do, than by giving him new Assurances that she would never give away that Right he had in her to any other Lover: She vows this with innumerable Tears; and is almost angry with him for questioning her Faith. He tells her he has but one Night more to stay, and his Grief would be unspeakable, if he should not be able to take a better leave of her, than at a Window; and that, if she would give him leave, he would by a Rope or two, tied together, so as it may serve for Steps, ascend her Balcony; he not having time to provide a Ladder of Ropes. She tells him she has so great a Confidence in his Virtue and Love, that she will refuse him nothing, tho' it would be a very bold Venture for a Maid, to trust her self with a passionate young Man, in silence of Night: and tho' she did not extort a Vow from him to secure her, she expected he would have a care of her Honour. He swore to her, his Love was too religious for so base an Attempt. There needed not many Vows to confirm her Faith; and it was agreed on between them, that he should come the next Night into her Chamber.

It happen'd that Night, as it often did, that Count Vernole lay with Monsieur De Pais, which was in a Ground-Room, just under that of Atlante's. As soon as she knew all were in bed, she gave the word to Rinaldo, who was attending with the Impatience of a passionate Lover below, under the Window; and who no sooner heard the Balcony open, but he ascended with some difficulty, and enter'd the Chamber, where he found Atlante trembling with Joy and Fear: He throws himself at her Feet, as unable to speak as she; who nothing but blushed and bent down her Eyes, hardly daring to glance them towards the dear Object of her Desires, the Lord of all her Vows: She was asham'd to see a Man in her Chamber, where yet none had ever been alone, and by Night too. He saw her Fear, and felt her trembling; and after a thousand Sighs of Love had made way for Speech, he besought her to fear nothing from him, for his Flame was too sacred, and his Passion too holy to offer any thing but what Honour with Love might afford him. At last he brought her to some Courage, and the Roses of her fair Cheeks assum'd their wonted Colour, not blushing too red, nor languishing too pale. But when the Conversation began between them, it was the softest in the world: They said all that parting Lovers could say; all that Wit and Tenderness could express: They exchanged their Vows anew; and to confirm his, he tied a Bracelet of Diamonds about her Arm, and she returned him one of her Hair, which he had long begged, and she had on purpose made, which clasped together with Diamonds; this she put about his Arm, and he swore to carry it to his Grave. The Night was far spent in tender Vows, soft Sighs and Tears on both sides, and it was high time to part: but, as if Death had been to have arrived to them in that Minute, they both linger'd away the time, like Lovers who had forgot themselves; and the Day was near approaching when he bid farewel, which he repeated very often: for still he was interrupted by some commanding Softness from Atlante, and then lost all his Power of going; till she, more courageous and careful of his Interest and her own Fame, forc'd him from her: and it was happy she did, for he was no sooner got over the Balcony, and she had flung him down his Rope, and shut the Door, but Vernole, whom Love and Contrivance kept waking, fancy'd several times he heard a Noise in Atlante's Chamber. And whether in passing over the Balcony, Rinaldo made any Noise or not, or whether it were still his jealous Fancy, he came up in his Night-Gown, with a Pistol in his Hand. Atlante was not so much lost in Grief, tho' she were all in Tears, but she heard a Man come up, and imagin'd it had been her Father, she not knowing of Count Vernole's lying in the House that Night; if she had, she possibly had taken more care to have been silent; but whoever it was, she could not get to bed soon enough, and therefore turn'd her self to her Dressing-Table, where a Candle stood, and where lay a Book open of the Story of Ariadne and Theseus. The Count turning the Latch, enter'd halting into her Chamber in his Night-Gown clapped close about him, which betray'd an ill-favour'd Shape, his Night-Cap on, without a Perriwig, which discover'd all his lean wither'd Jaws, his pale Face, and his Eyes staring: and made altogether so dreadful a Figure, that Atlante, who no more dreamt of him than of a Devil, had possibly have rather seen the last. She gave a great Shriek, which frighted Vernole; so both stood for a while staring on each other, till both were recollected: He told her the Care of her Honour had brought him thither; and then rolling his small Eyes round the Chamber, to see if he could discover any body, he proceeded, and cry'd, 'Madam, if I had no other Motive than your being up at this time of Night, or rather of Day, I could easily guess how you have been entertain'd.' 'What Insolence is this (said she, all in a rage) when to cover your Boldness of approaching my Chamber at this Hour, you would question how I have been entertain'd! Either explain your self, or quit my Chamber; for I do not use to see such terrible Objects here.' 'Possibly those you do see (said the Count) are indeed more agreeable, but I am afraid have not that Regard to your Honour as I have': And at that word he stepped to the Balcony, open'd it, and look'd out; but seeing no body, he shut it to again. This enraged Atlante beyond all Patience; and snatching the Pistol out of his Hand, she told him, He deserved to have it aimed at his Head, for having the Impudence to question her Honour, or her Conduct; and commanded him to avoid her Chamber as he lov'd his Life, which she believ'd he was fonder of than of her Honour. She speaking this in a Tone wholly transported with Rage, and at the same time holding the Pistol towards him, made him tremble with Fear; and he now found, whether she were guilty or not, it was his turn to beg Pardon: For you must know, however it came to pass that his Jealousy made him come up in that fierce Posture, at other times Vernole was the most tame and passive Man in the World, and one who was afraid of his own Shadow in the Night: He had a natural Aversion for Danger, and thought it below a Man of Wit, or common Sense, to be guilty of that brutal thing, called Courage or Fighting; His Philosophy told him, It was safe sleeping in a whole Skin; and possibly he apprehended as much Danger from this Virago, as ever he did from his own Sex. He therefore fell on his Knees, and besought her to hold her fair Hand, and not to suffer that, which was the greatest Mark of his Respect, to be the Cause of her Hate or Indignation. The pitiful Faces he made, and the Signs of Mortal Fear in him, had almost made her laugh, at least it allay'd her Anger; and she bid him rise and play the fool hereafter somewhere else, and not in her Presence; yet for once she would deign to give him this Satisfaction, that she was got into a Book, which had many moving Stories very well writ; and that she found her self so well entertain'd, she had forgot how the Night passed. He most humbly thanked her for this Satisfaction, and retired, perhaps not so well satisfied as he pretended.

After this, he appear'd more submissive and respectful towards Atlante; and she carry'd herself more reserv'd and haughty towards him; which was one Reason, he would not yet discover his Passion.

Thus the Time run on at Orleans, while Rinaldo found himself daily languishing at Paris. He was indeed in the best Academy in the City, amongst a Number of brave and noble Youths, where all things that could accomplish them, were to be learn'd by those that had any Genius; but Rinaldo had other Thoughts, and other Business: his Time was wholly past in the most solitary Parts of the Garden, by the melancholy Fountains, and in the most gloomy Shades, where he could with most Liberty breathe out his Passion and his Griefs. He was past the Tutorage of a Boy; and his Masters could not upbraid him, but found he had some secret Cause of Grief, which made him not mind those Exercises, which were the Delight of the rest: so that nothing being able to divert his Melancholy, which daily increased upon him, he fear'd it would bring him into a Fever, if he did not give himself the Satisfaction of seeing Atlante. He had no sooner thought of this, but he was impatient to put it in execution; he resolved to go (having very good Horses) without acquainting any of his Servants with it. He got a very handsom and light Ladder of Ropes made, which he carry'd under his Coat, and away he rid for Orleans, stay'd at a little Village, till the Darkness of the Night might favour his Design: And then walking about Atlante's Lodgings, till he saw a Light in her Chamber, and then making that Noise on his Sword, as was agreed between them, he was heard by his adorable Atlante, and suffer'd to mount her Chamber, where he would stay till almost break of Day, and then return to the Village, and take Horse, and away for Paris again. This, once in a Month, was his Exercise, without which he could not live; so that his whole Year was past in riding between Orleans and Paris, between Excess of Grief, and Excess of Joy by turns.

It was now that Atlante, arrived to her fifteenth Year, shone out with a Lustre of Beauty greater than ever; and in this Year, in the Absence of Rinaldo, had carry'd herself with that Severity of Life, without the youthful Desire of going abroad, or desiring any Diversion, but what she found in her own retired Thoughts, that Vernole, wholly unable longer to conceal his Passion, resolv'd to make a Publication of it, first to the Father, and then to the lovely Daughter, of whom he had some Hope, because she had carry'd her self very well towards him for this Year past; which she would never have done, if she had imagin'd he would ever have been her Lover: She had seen no Signs of any such Misfortune towards her in these many Years he had conversed with her, and she had no Cause to fear him. When one Day her Father taking her into the Garden, told her what Honour and Happiness was in store for her; and that now the Glory of his fall'n Family would rise again, since she had a Lover of an illustrious Blood, ally'd to Monarchs; and one whose Fortune was newly encreased to a very considerable Degree, answerable to his Birth. She changed Colour at this Discourse, imagining but too well who this illustrious Lover was; when De Pais proceeded and told her, 'Indeed his Person was not the most agreeable that ever was seen: but he marry'd her to Glory and Fortune, not the Man: And a Woman (says he) ought to look no further.'

She needed not any more to inform her who this intended Husband was; and therefore, bursting forth into Tears, she throws herself at his Feet, imploring him not to use the Authority of a Father, to force her to a thing so contrary to her Inclination: assuring him, she could not consent to any such thing; and that she would rather die than yield. She urged many Arguments for this her Disobedience; but none would pass for current with the old Gentleman, whose Pride had flatter'd him with Hopes of so considerable a Son-in-law: He was very much surpriz'd at Atlante's refusing what he believ'd she would receive with Joy; and finding that no Arguments on his Side could draw hers to an obedient Consent, he grew to such a Rage, as very rarely possest him: vowing, if she did not conform her Will to his, he would abandon her to all the Cruelty of Contempt and Poverty: so that at last she was forced to return him this Answer, 'That she would strive all she could with her Heart; but she verily believed she should never bring it to consent to a Marriage with Monsieur the Count.' The Father continued threatning her, and gave her some Days to consider of it: So leaving her in Tears, he returned to his Chamber, to consider what Answer he should give Count Vernole, who he knew would be impatient to learn what Success he had, and what himself was to hope. De Pais, after some Consideration, resolved to tell him, she receiv'd the Offer very well, but that he must expect a little Maiden-Nicety in the Case: and accordingly did tell him so; and he was not at all doubtful of his good Fortune.

But Atlante, who resolved to die a thousand Deaths rather than break her solemn Vows to Rinaldo, or to marry the Count, cast about how she should avoid it with the least Hazard of her Father's Rage. She found Rinaldo the better and more advantageous Match of the two, could they but get his Father's Consent: He was beautiful and young; his Title was equal to that of Vernole, when his Father should die; and his Estate exceeded his: yet she dares not make a Discovery, for fear she should injure her Lover; who at this Time, though she knew it not, lay sick of a Fever, while she was wondering that he came not as he used to do. However she resolves to send him a Letter, and acquaint him with the Misfortune; which she did in these Terms:

ATLANTE to RINALDO.

My Father's Authority would force me to violate my sacred Vows to you, and give them to the Count Vernole, whom I mortally hate, yet could wish him the greatest Monarch in the World, that I might shew you I could even then despise him for your Sake. My Father is already too much enraged by my Denial, to hear Reason from me, if I should confess to him my Vows to you: So that I see nothing but a Prospect of Death before me; for assure your self, my Rinaldo, I will die rather than consent to marry any other: Therefore come my Rinaldo, and come quickly, to see my Funerals, instead of those Nuptials they vainly expect from

Your Faithful ATLANTE.

This Letter Rinaldo receiv'd; and there needed no more to make him fly to Orleans: This raised him soon from his Bed of Sickness, and getting immediately to horse, he arrived at his Father's House; who did not so much admire to see him, because he heard he was sick of a Fever, and gave him leave to return, if he pleas'd: He went directly to his Father's House, because he knew somewhat of the Business, he was resolv'd to make his Passion known, as soon as he had seen Atlante, from whom he was to take all his Measures: He therefore fail'd not, when all were in Bed, to rise and go from his Chamber into the Street; where finding a Light in Atlante's Chamber, for she every Night expected him, he made the usual Sign, and she went into the Balcony; and he having no Conveniency of mounting up into it, they discoursed, and said all they had to say. From thence she tells him of the Count's Passion, of her Father's Resolution, and that her own was rather to die his, than live any Body's else: And at last, as their Refuge, they resolv'd to discover the whole Matter; she to her Father, and he to his, to see what Accommodation they could make; if not, to die together. They parted at this Resolve, for she would permit him no longer to stay in the Street after such a Sickness; so he went home to bed, but not to sleep.

The next Day, at Dinner, Monsieur Bellyaud believing his Son absolutely cur'd, by Absence, of his Passion; and speaking of all the News in the Town, among the rest, told him he was come in good time to dance at the Wedding of Count Vernole with Atlante, the Match being agreed on: 'No, Sir (reply'd Rinaldo) I shall never dance at the Marriage of Count Vernole with Atlante; and you will see in Monsieur De Pais's House a Funeral sooner than a Wedding.' And thereupon he told his Father all his Passion for that lovely Maid; and assur'd him, if he would not see him laid in his Grave, he must consent to this

Match. Bellyaurd rose in a Fury, and told him, 'He had rather see him in his Grave, than in the Arms of Atlante: Not (continued he) so much for any Dislike I have to the young Lady, or the Smallness of her Fortune; but because I have so long warn'd you from such a Passion, and have with such Care endeavour'd by your Absence to prevent it.' He travers'd the Room very fast, still protesting against this Alliance: and was deaf to all Rinaldo could say. On the other side the Day being come, wherein Atlante was to give her final Answer to her Father concerning her Marriage with Count Vernole; she assum'd all the Courage and Resolution she could, to withstand the Storm that threatned a Denial. And her Father came to her, and demanding her Answer, she told him, 'She could not be the Wife of Vernole, since she was Wife to Rinaldo, only son to Bellyaurd.' If her Father storm'd before, he grew like a Man distracted at her Confession; and Vernole hearing them loud, ran to the Chamber to learn the Cause; where just as he enter'd he found De Pais's Sword drawn, and ready to kill his Daughter, who lay all in Tears at his Feet. He with-held his Hand; and asking the Cause of his Rage, he was told all that Atlante had confess'd; which put Vernole quite beside all his Gravity, and made him discover the Infirmity of Anger, which he used to say ought to be dissembled by all wise Men: So that De Pais forgot his own to appease his, but 'twas in vain, for he went out of the House, vowing Revenge to Rinaldo: And to that end, being not very well assur'd of his own Courage, as I said before, and being of the Opinion, that no Man ought to expose his Life to him who has injur'd him; he hired Swiss and Spanish Soldiers to attend him in the nature of Footmen; and watch'd several Nights about Bellyaurd's Door, and that of De Pais's, believing he should some time or other see him under the Window of Atlante, or perhaps mounting into it: for now he no longer doubted, but this happy Lover was he, whom he fancy'd he heard go from the Balcony that Night he came up with his Pistol; and being more a Spaniard than a Frenchman in his Nature, he resolv'd to take him any way unguarded or unarm'd, if he came in his Way.

Atlante, who heard his Threatnings when he went from her in a Rage, fear'd his Cowardice might put him on some base Action, to deprive Rinaldo of his Life; and therefore thought it not safe to suffer him to come to her by Night, as he had before done; but sent him word in a Note, that he should forbear her Window, for Vernole had sworn his Death. This Note came, unseen by his Father, to his Hands: but this could not hinder him from coming to her Window, which he did as soon as it was dark: he came thither, only attended with his Valet, and two Footmen; for now he car'd not who knew the Secret. He had no sooner made the Sign, but he found himself incompass'd with Vernole's Bravoes; and himself standing at a distance cry'd out, 'That is he': With that they all drew on both sides, and Rinaldo receiv'd a Wound in his Arm. Atlante heard this, and ran crying out, 'That Rinaldo, prest by Numbers, would be kill'd.' De Pais, who was reading in his Closet, took his Sword, and ran out; and, contrary to all Expectation, seeing Rinaldo fighting with his Back to the Door, pull'd him into the House, and fought himself with the Bravoes: who being very much wounded by Rinaldo, gave ground, and sheer'd off; and De Pais, putting up old Bilbo into the Scabbard, went into his House, where he found Rinaldo almost fainting with loss of Blood, and Atlante, with her Maids binding up his Wound; to whom De Pais said, 'This charity, Atlante, very well becomes you, and is what I can allow you; and I could wish you had no other Motive for this Action.' Rinaldo by degrees recover'd of his Fainting, and as well as his Weakness would permit him, he got up and made a low Reverence to De Pais, telling him, 'He had now a double Obligation to pay him all the Respect in the World; first, for his being the Father of Atlante; and secondly, for being the Preserver of his Life: two Tyes that should eternally oblige him to love and honour him, as his own Parent.' De Pais reply'd, 'He had done nothing but what common Humanity compell'd him to do: But if he would make good that Respect he profess'd towards him, it must be in quitting all Hopes of Atlante, whom he had destin'd to another, or an eternal Inclosure in a Monastery: He had another Daughter, whom if he would think worthy of his Regard, he should take his Alliance as a very great Honour; but his Word and Reputation, nay his Vows were past, to give Atlante to Count Vernole.' Rinaldo, who before he spoke took measure from Atlante's Eyes, which told him her Heart was his, return'd this Answer to De Pais,

'That he was infinitely glad to find by the Generosity of his Offer, that he had no Aversion against his being his Son-in-law; and that, next to Atlante, the greatest Happiness he could wish would be his receiving Charlot from his Hand; but that he could not think of quitting Atlante, how necessary soever it would be, for Glory, and his (the further) Repose.' De Pais would not let him at this time argue the matter further, seeing he was ill, and had need of looking after; he therefore begg'd he would for his Health's sake retire to his own House, whither he himself conducted him, and left him to the Care of his Men, who were escap'd the Fray; and returning to his own Chamber, he found Atlante retir'd, and so he went to bed full of Thoughts. This Night had increas'd his Esteem for Rinaldo, and lessen'd it for Count Vernole; but his Word and Honour being past, he could not break it, neither with Safety nor Honour: for he knew the haughty resenting Nature of the Count, and he fear'd some Danger might arrive to the brave Rinaldo, which troubled him very much. At last he resolv'd, that neither might take any thing ill at his Hands, to lose Atlante, and send her to the Monastery where her Sister was, and compel her to be a Nun. This he thought would prevent Mischiefs on both sides; and accordingly, the next Day, (having in the Morning sent Word to the Lady Abbess what he would have done) he carries Atlante, under pretence of visiting her Sister, (which they often did) to the Monastery, where she was no sooner come, but she was led into the Inclosure: Her Father had rather sacrifice her, than she should be the Cause of the Murder of two such noble Men as Vernole and Rinaldo.

The Noise of Atlante's being inclos'd, was soon spread all over the busy Town, and Rinaldo was not the last to whom the News arriv'd: He was for a few Days confin'd to his Chamber; where, when alone, he rav'd like a Man distracted; But his Wounds had so incens'd his Father against Atlante, that he swore he would see his Son die of them, rather than suffer him to marry Atlante; and was extremely overjoy'd to find she was condemn'd, for ever, to the Monastery. So that the Son thought it the wisest Course, and most for the advantage of his Love, to say nothing to contradict his Father; but being almost assur'd Atlante would never consent to be shut up in a Cloyster, and abandon him, he flatter'd himself with hope, that he should steal her from thence, and marry her in spite of all Opposition. This he was impatient to put in practice: He believ'd, if he were not permitted to see Atlante, he had still a kind Advocate in Charlot, who was now arriv'd to her Thirteenth Year, and infinitely advanc'd in Wit and Beauty. Rinaldo therefore often goes to the Monastery, surrounding it, to see what Possibility there was of accomplishing his Design; if he could get her Consent, he finds it not impossible, and goes to visit Charlot; who had command not to see him, or speak to him. This was a Cruelty he look'd not for, and which gave him an unspeakable Trouble, and without her Aid it was wholly impossible to give Atlante any account of his Design. In this Perplexity he remain'd many Days, in which he languish'd almost to Death; he was distracted with Thought, and continually hovering about the Nunnery-Walls, in hope, at some time or other, to see or hear from that lovely Maid, who alone could make his Happiness. In these Traverses he often met Vernole, who had Liberty to see her when he pleas'd: If it happen'd that they chanc'd to meet in the Daytime, tho' Vernole was attended with an Equipage of Ruffians, and Rinaldo but only with a couple of Footmen, he could perceive Vernole shun him, grow pale, and almost tremble with Fear sometimes, and get to the other Side of the Street; and if he did not, Rinaldo having a mortal Hate to him, would often bear up so close to him, that he would jostle him against the Wall, which Vernole would patiently put up, and pass on; so that he could never be provok'd to fight by Day-light, how solitary soever the Place was where they met: but if they chanc'd to meet at Night, they were certain of a Skirmish, in which he would have no part himself; so that Rinaldo was often like to be assassinated, but still came off with some slight Wound. This continu'd so long, and made so great a Noise in the Town, that the two old Gentlemen were mightily alarm'd by it; and Count Bellyaurd came to De Pais, one Day, to discourse with him of this Affair; and Bellyaurd, for the Preservation of his Son, was almost consenting, since there was no Remedy, that he should marry Atlante. De Pais confess'd the Honour he proffer'd him, and how troubled he was, that his Word was already past to his Friend, the

Count Vernole, whom he said she should marry, or remain for ever a Nun; but if Rinaldo could displace his Love from Atlante, and place it on Charlot, he should gladly consent to the Match. Bellyaurd, who would now do anything for the Repose of his Son, tho' he believ'd this Exchange would not pass, yet resolv'd to propose it, since by marrying him he took him out of the Danger of Vernole's Assassinates, who would never leave him till they had dispatch'd him, should he marry Atlante.

While Rinaldo was contriving a thousand ways to come to speak to, or send Billets to Atlante, none of which could succeed without the Aid of Charlot, his Father came and propos'd this Agreement between De Pais and himself, to his Son. At first Rinaldo receiv'd it with a chang'd Countenance, and a breaking Heart; but swiftly turning from Thought to Thought, he conceiv'd this the only way to come at Charlot, and so consequently at Atlante: he therefore, after some dissembled Regret, consents, with a sad put-on Look: And Charlot had Notice given her to see and entertain Rinaldo. As yet they had not told her the Reason; which her Father would tell her, when he came to visit her, he said. Rinaldo over-joy'd at this Contrivance, and his own Dissimulation, goes to the Monastery, and visits Charlot; where he ought to have said something of this Proposition: but wholly bent upon other Thoughts, he sollicits her to convey some Letters, and Presents to Atlante; which she readily did, to the unspeakable Joy of the poor Distrest. Sometimes he would talk to Charlot of her own Affairs; asking her, if she resolv'd to become a Nun? To which she would sigh, and say, If she must, it would be extremely against her Inclinations; and, if it pleas'd her Father, she had rather begin the World with any tolerable Match.

Things past thus for some Days, in which our Lovers were happy, and Vernole assur'd he should have Atlante. But at last De Pais came to visit Charlot, who ask'd her, if she had seen Rinaldo? She answer'd, 'She had.' 'And how does he entertain you? (reply'd De Pais) Have you receiv'd him as a Husband? and has he behav'd himself like one?' At this a sudden Joy seiz'd the Heart of Charlot; and both to confess what she had done for him to her Sister, she hung down her blushing Face to study for an Answer. De Pais continued, and told her the Agreement between Bellyaurd and him, for the saving of Bloodshed.

She, who blest the Cause, whatever it was, having always a great Friendship and Tenderness for Rinaldo, gave her Father a thousand Thanks for his Care; and assur'd him, since she was commanded by him, she would receive him as her Husband.

And the next Day, when Rinaldo came to visit her, as he us'd to do, and bringing a Letter with him, wherein he propos'd the flight of Atlante; he found a Coldness in Charlot, as soon as he told her his Design, and desir'd her to carry the Letter. He ask'd the Reason of this Change: She tells him she was inform'd of the Agreement between their two Fathers, and that she look'd upon herself as his Wife, and would act no more as a Confident; that she had ever a violent Inclination of Friendship for him, which she would soon improve into something more soft.

He could not deny the Agreement, nor his Promise; but it was in vain to tell her, he did it only to get a Correspondence with Atlante: She is obstinate, and he as pressing, with all the Tenderness of Persuasion: He vows he can never be any but Atlante's, and she may see him die, but never break his Vows. She urges her Claim in vain, so that at last she was overcome, and promised she would carry the Letter; which was to have her make her Escape that Night. He waits at the Gate for her Answer, and Charlot returns with one that pleased him very well; which was, that Night her Sister would make her Escape, and that he must stand in such a Place of the Nunnery-Wall, and she would come out to him.

After this she upbraids him with his false Promise to her, and of her Goodness to serve him after such a Disappointment. He receives her Reproaches with a thousand Sighs, and bemoans her Misfortune in not being capable of more than Friendship for her; and vows, that next Atlante, he esteems her of all Womankind. She seems to be obliged by this, and assured him, she would hasten the Flight of Atlante; and taking leave, he went home to order a Coach, and some Servants to assist him.

In the mean time Count Vernole came to visit Atlante; but she refused to be seen by him: And all he could do there that Afternoon, was entertaining Charlot at the Grate; to whom he spoke a great many fine Things, both of her improved Beauty and Wit; and how happy Rinaldo would be in so fair a Bride. She received this with all the Civility that was due to his Quality; and their Discourse being at an End, he took his Leave, being towards the Evening.

Rinaldo, wholly impatient, came betimes to the Corner of the dead Wall, where he was appointed to stand, having ordered his Footmen and Coach to come to him as soon it was dark. While he was there walking up and down, Vernole came by the End of the Wall to go home; and looking about, he saw, at the other End, Rinaldo walking, whose Back was towards him, but he knew him well; and tho' he feared and dreaded his Business there, he durst not encounter him, they being both attended but by one Footman a-piece. But Vernole's Jealousy and Indignation were so high, that he resolved to fetch his Bravoes to his Aid, and come and assault him: For he knew he waited there for some Message from Atlante.

In the mean Time it grew dark, and Rinaldo's Coach came with another Footman; which were hardly arrived, when Vernole, with his Assistants, came to the Corner of the Wall, and skreening themselves a little behind it, near to the Place where Rinaldo stood, who waited now close to a little Door, out of which the Gardeners used to throw the Weeds and Dirt, Vernole could perceive anon the Door to open, and a Woman come out of it, calling Rinaldo by his Name, who stept up to her, and caught her in his Arms with Signs of infinite Joy. Vernole being now all Rage, cry'd to his Assassinates, 'Fall on, and kill the Ravisher': And immediately they all fell on. Rinaldo, who had only his two Footmen on his Side, was forc'd to let go the Lady; who would have run into the Garden again, but the Door fell to and lock'd: so that while Rinaldo was fighting, and beaten back by the Bravoes, one of which he laid dead at his Feet, Vernole came to the frighted Lady, and taking her by the Hand, cry'd, 'Come, my fair Fugitive, you must go along with me.' She wholly scar'd out of her Senses, was willing to go any where out of the Terror she heard so near her, and without Reply, gave her self into his Hand, who carried her directly to her Father's House; where she was no sooner come, but he told her Father all that had past, and how she was running away with Rinaldo, but that his good Fortune brought him just in the lucky Minute. Her Father turning to reproach her, found by the Light of a Candle that this was Charlot, and not Atlante, whom Vernole had brought Home: At which Vernole was extremely astonish'd. Her Father demanded of her why she was running away with a Man, who was design'd her by Consent? 'Yes, (said Charlot) you had his Consent, Sir, and that of his Father; but I was far from getting it: I found he resolv'd to die rather than quit Atlante; and promising him my Assistance in his Amour, since he could never be mine, he got me to carry a Letter to Atlante; which was, to desire her to fly away with him. Instead of carrying her this Letter, I told her, he was design'd for me, and had cancell'd all his Vows to her: She swoon'd at this News; and being recover'd a little, I left her in the Hands of the Nuns, to persuade her to live; which she resolves not to do without Rinaldo. Tho' they press'd me, yet I resolv'd to pursue my Design, which was to tell Rinaldo she would obey his kind Summons. He waited for her; but I put my self into his Hands in lieu of Atlante; and had not the Count receiv'd me, we had been marry'd by this time, by some false Light that could not have discover'd me: But I am satisfied, if I had, he would never have liv'd with me longer than the Cheat had been undiscover'd; for I find them both resolved to die, rather than change. And for my part, Sir, I was not so much in Love with Rinaldo, as I was out of love with the Nunnery; and took any Opportunity to quit a Life absolutely contrary to my Humour.' She spoke this with a Gaiety so brisk, and an Air so agreeable, that Vernole found it touch'd his Heart; and the rather because he found Atlante would never be his; or if she were, he should be still in Danger from the Resentment of Rinaldo: he therefore bowing to Charlot, and taking her by the Hand, cry'd, 'Madam, since Fortune has dispos'd you thus luckily for me, in my Possession, I humbly implore you would consent she should make me entirely happy, and give me the Prize for which I fought, and have conquer'd with my Sword.' 'My Lord, (reply'd Charlot, with a modest Air) I am superstitious enough to believe, since Fortune, so contrary to all our Designs, has given me into your Hands, that she from the beginning destin'd me to the Honour, which, with my Father's Consent, I shall receive as becomes me.' De Pais transported with Joy, to find all Things would be so well brought about, it being all one to him, whether Charlot or Atlante gave him Count Vernole for his Son-in-law, readily consented; and immediately a Priest was sent for, and they were that Night marry'd. And it being now not above seven o'Clock, many of their Friends were invited, the Musick sent for, and as good a Supper as so short a Time would provide, was made ready.

All this was perform'd in as short a time as Rinaldo was fighting; and having kill'd one, and wounded the rest, they all fled before his conquering Sword, which was never drawn with so good a Will. When he came where his Coach stood, just against the Back-Garden-Door, he looked for his Mistress: But the Coachman told him, he was no sooner engaged, but a Man came, and with a thousand Reproaches on her Levity, bore her off.

This made our young Lover rave; and he is satisfied she is in the Hands of his Rival, and that he had been fighting, and shedding his Blood, only to secure her Flight with him. He lost all Patience, and it was with much ado his Servants persuaded him to return; telling him in their Opinion, she was more likely to get out of the Hands of his Rival, and come to him, than when she was in the Monastery.

He suffers himself to go into his Coach and be carry'd home; but he was no sooner alighted, than he heard Musick and Noise at De Pais's House. He saw Coaches surround his Door, and Pages and Footmen, with Flambeaux. The Sight and Noise of Joy made him ready to sink at the Door; and sending his Footmen to learn the Cause of this Triumph, the Pages that waited told him, That Count Vernole was this Night married to Monsieur De Pais's Daughter. He needed no more to deprive him of all Sense; and staggering against his Coach, he was caught by his Footmen and carried into his House, and to his Chamber, where they put him to Bed, all sensless as he was, and had much ado to recover him to Life. He ask'd for his Father, with a faint Voice, for he desir'd to see him before he died. It was told him he was gone to Count Vernole's Wedding, where there was a perfect Peace agreed on between them, and all their Animosities laid aside. At this News Rinaldo fainted again; and his Servants call'd his Father home, and told him in what Condition they had brought home their Master, recounting to him all that was past. He hasten'd to Rinaldo, whom he found just recover'd of his Swooning; who, putting his Hand out to his Father, all cold and trembling, cry'd, 'Well, Sir, now you are satisfied, since you have seen Atlante married to Count Vernole, I hope now you will give your unfortunate Son leave to die; as you wish'd he should, rather than give him to the Arms of Atlante.' Here his Speech fail'd, and he fell again into a Fit of Swooning; His Father ready to die with fear of his Son's Death, kneel'd down by his Bed-side; and after having recover'd a little, he said, 'My dear Son, I have been indeed at the Wedding of Count Vernole, but 'tis not Atlante to whom he is married, but Charlot; who was the Person you were bearing from the Monastery, instead of Atlante, who is still reserv'd for you, and she is dying till she hear you are reserv'd for her; Therefore, as you regard her Life, make much of your own, and make your self fit to receive her; for her Father and I have agreed the Marriage already.' And without giving him leave to think, he call'd to one of his Gentlemen, and sent him to the Monastery, with this News to Atlante. Rinaldo bowed himself as low as he could in his Bed, and kiss'd the Hand of his Father, with Tears of Joy:

But his Weakness continued all the next Day; and they were fain to bring Atlante to him, to confirm his Happiness.

It must only be guessed by Lovers, the perfect Joy these two receiv'd in the sight of each other. Bellyaurd received her as his Daughter; and the next Day made her so, with very great Solemnity, at which were Vernole and Charlot: Between Rinaldo and him was concluded a perfect Peace, and all thought themselves happy in this double Union.

NOTES: The Lucky Mistake.

This Dedication only appears in the first edition (12mo, 1689), 'for R. Bentley'. George Granville or Grenville, [1] Lord Lansdowne, the celebrated wit, dramatist and poet, was born in 1667. Having zealously offered in 1688 to defend James II, during the subsequent reign he perforce 'lived in literary retirement'. He then wrote The She Gallants (1696, and 4to, 1696), an excellent comedy full of jest and spirit. Offending, however, some ladies 'who set up for chastity' it made its exit. Granville afterwards revived it as Once a Lover and Always a Lover. Heroick Love, a tragedy (1698), had great success. The Jew of Venice (1701), is a piteously weak adaption of The Merchant of Venice. A short masque, Peleus and Thetis accompanies the play. The British Enchanters, an opera (1706), is a pleasing piece, and was very well received. At the accession of Queen Anne, Granville entered the political arena and attained considerable offices of state. Suspected of being an active Jacobite he was, under George I, imprisoned from 25 September, 1715, till 8 February, 1717. In 1722 he went abroad, and lived in Paris for ten years. In 1732 he returned and published a finely printed edition of his complete Works (2 Vols., 4to, 1732; and again, 3 Vols., 1736, 12mo). He died 30 January, 1735, and is buried in St. Clement Danes.

double Union. In a collection of Novels with running title: The Deceived Lovers (1696), we find No. V The Curtezan Deceived, 'An Addition to The Lucky Mistake, Written by Mrs. A. Behn.' This introduction of Mrs. Behn's name was a mere bookseller's trick to catch the unwary reader. The Curtezan Deceived is of no value. It has nothing to do with Aphra's work and is as commonplace a little novel as an hundred others of its day.

[**Footnote 1:** The spelling 'Greenvil' 'Greenviel' is incorrect.]

THE UNFORTUNATE BRIDE; OR, THE BLIND LADY A BEAUTY

TO RICHARD NORTON, OF SOUTHWICK IN HANTSHIRE, ESQUIRE.

Honour'd Sir,

Eminent Wit, Sir, no more than Eminent Beauty, can escape the Trouble and Presumption of Addresses; and that which can strike every body with Wonder, can never avoid the Praise which naturally flows from that Wonder: And Heaven is forc'd to hear the Addresses as well as praises of the Poor as Rich, of the Ignorant as Learned, and takes, nay rewards, the officious tho' perhaps impertinent Zeal of its least qualify'd Devotees. Wherefore, Sir, tho' your Merits meet with the Applause of the Learned and Witty, yet your Generosity will judge favourably of the untaught Zeal of an humbler Admirer, since what I do your eminent Vertues compel. The Beautiful will permit the most despicable of their Admirers to love them, tho' they never intend to make him happy, as unworthy their Love, but they will not be angry at the fatal Effect of their own Eyes.

But what I want in my self, Sir, to merit your Regard, I hope my Authoress will in some measure supply, so far at least to lessen my Presumption in prefixing your Name to a Posthumous Piece of hers, whom all the Men of Wit, that were her Contemporaries, look'd on as the Wonder of her Sex; and in none of her Performances has she shew'd so great a Mastery as in her Novels, where Nature always prevails; and if they are not true, they are so like it, that they do the business every jot as well.

This I hope, Sir, will induce you to pardon my Presumption in dedicating this Novel to you, and declaring my self, Sir,

Your most obedient and most humble Servant, S. Briscoe.

THE UNFORTUNATE BRIDE: or, The Blind Lady a Beauty

Frankwit and Wildvill, were two young Gentlemen of very considerable Fortunes, both born in Staffordshire, and, during their Minority, both educated together, by which Opportunity they contracted a very inviolable Friendship, a Friendship which grew up with them; and though it was remarkably known to every Body else, they knew it not themselves; they never made Profession of it in Words, but Actions; so true a Warmth their Fires could boast, as needed not the Effusion of their Breath to make it live. Wildvill was of the richest Family, but Frankwit of the noblest; Wildvill was admired for outward Qualifications, as Strength, and manly Proportions, Frankwit for a much softer Beauty, for his inward Endowments, Pleasing in his Conversation, of a free, and moving Air, humble in his Behaviour, and if he had any Pride, it was but just enough to shew that he did not affect Humility; his Mind bowed with a Motion as unconstrained as his Body, nor did he force this Vertue in the least, but he allowed it only. So aimable he was, that every Virgin that had Eyes, knew too she had a Heart, and knew as surely she should lose it. His Cupid could not be reputed blind, he never shot for him, but he was sure to wound. As every other Nymph admired him, so he was dear to all the Tuneful Sisters; the Muses were fired with him as much as their own radiant God Apollo; their loved Springs and Fountains were not so grateful to their Eyes as he, him they esteemed their Helicon and Parnassus too; in short, when ever he pleased, he could enjoy them all. Thus he enamour'd the whole Female Sex, but amongst all the sighing Captives of his Eyes, Belvira only boasted Charms to move him; her Parents lived near his, and even from their Childhood they felt mutual Love, as if their Eyes, at their first meeting, had struck out such Glances, as had kindled into amorous Flame. And now Belvira in her fourteenth Year, (when the fresh Spring of young Virginity began to cast more lively Bloomings in her Cheeks, and softer Longings in her Eyes) by her indulgent Father's Care was sent to London to a Friend, her Mother being lately dead: When, as if Fortune ordered it so, Frankwit's Father took a Journey to the other World, to let his Son the better enjoy the Pleasures and Delights of this: The young Lover now with all imaginable haste interred his Father, nor did he shed so many Tears for his Loss, as might in the least quench the Fire which he received from his Belvira's Eyes, but (Master of seventeen Hundred Pounds a Year, which his Father left him) with all the Wings of Love flies to London, and sollicits Belvira with such Fervency, that it might be thought he meant Death's Torch should kindle Hymen's; and now as soon as he arrives at his Journey's end, he goes to pay a Visit to the fair Mistress of his Soul, and assures her, That tho' he was absent from her, yet she was still with him; and that all the Road he travell'd, her beauteous Image danced before him, and like the ravished Prophet, he saw his Deity in every Bush; in short, he paid her constant Visits, the Sun ne'er rose or set, but still he saw it in her Company, and every Minute of the Day he counted by his Sighs. So incessantly he importuned her that she could no longer hold out, and was pleased in the surrender of her Heart, since it was he was Conqueror; and therefore felt a Triumph in her yielding. Their Flames now joyned, grew more and more, glowed in their Cheeks, and lightened in their Glances: Eager they looked, as if there were Pulses beating in their Eyes; and all endearing, at last she vowed, that Frankwit living she would ne'er be any other Man's. Thus they past on some time, while every Day rowl'd over fair; Heaven showed an Aspect all serene, and the Sun seemed to smile at what was done. He still caressed his Charmer, with an Innocence becoming his Sincerity; he lived upon her tender Breath, and basked in the bright Lustre of her Eyes, with Pride, and secret Joy.

He saw his Rivals languish for that Bliss, those Charms, those Raptures and extatick Transports, which he engrossed alone. But now some eighteen Months (some Ages in a Lover's Kalendar) winged with Delights, and fair Belvira now grown fit for riper Joys, knows hardly how she can deny her pressing Lover, and herself, to crown their Vows, and joyn their Hands as well as Hearts. All this while the young Gallant wash'd himself clean of that shining Dirt, his Gold; he fancied little of Heaven dwelt in his yellow Angels, but let them fly away, as it were on their own golden Wings; he only valued the smiling Babies in Belvira's Eyes. His Generosity was boundless, as his Love, for no Man ever truly loved, that was not generous. He thought his Estate, like his Passion, was a sort of a Pontick Ocean, it could never know an Ebb; But now he found it could be fathom'd, and that the Tide was turning, therefore he sollicits with more impatience the consummation of their Joys, that both might go like Martyrs from their Flames immediately to Heaven; and now at last it was agreed between them, that they should both be one, but not without some Reluctancy on the Female side; for 'tis the Humour of our Sex, to deny most eagerly those Grants to Lovers, for which most tenderly we sigh, so contradictory are we to our selves, as if the Deity had made us with a seeming Reluctancy to his own Designs; placing as much Discords in our Minds, as there is Harmony in our Faces. We are a sort of aiery Clouds, whose Lightning flash out one way, and the Thunder another. Our Words and Thoughts can ne'er agree. So this young charming Lady thought her Desires could live in their own longings, like Misers wealth-devouring Eyes; and e'er she consented to her Lover, prepared him first with speaking Looks, and then with a fore-running Sigh, applyed to the dear Charmer thus: 'Frankwit, I am afraid to venture the Matrimonial Bondage, it may make you think your self too much confined, in being only free to one.' 'Ah! my dear Belvira,' he replied, 'That one, like Manna, has the Taste of all, why should I be displeased to be confined to Paradice, when it was the Curse of our Forefathers to be set at large, tho' they had the whole World to roam in: You have, my love, ubiquitary Charms, and you are all in all, in every Part.' 'Ay, but,' reply'd Belvira, 'we are all like Perfumes, and too continual Smelling makes us seem to have lost our Sweets, I'll be judged by my Cousin Celesia here, if it be not better to live still in mutual Love, without the last Enjoyment.' (I had forgot to tell my Reader that Celesia was an Heiress, the only Child of a rich Turkey Merchant, who, when he dyed, left her Fifty thousand Pound in Money, and some Estate in Land; but, poor Creature, she was Blind to all these Riches, having been born without the use of Sight, though in all other Respects charming to a wonder.) 'Indeed,' says Celesia, (for she saw clearly in her Mind) 'I admire you should ask my Judgment in such a Case, where I have never had the least Experience; but I believe it is but a sickly Soul which cannot nourish its Offspring of Desires without preying upon the Body.' 'Believe me,' reply'd Frankwit, 'I bewail your want of Sight, and I could almost wish you my own Eyes for a Moment, to view your charming Cousin, where you would see such Beauties as are too dazling to be long beheld; and if too daringly you gazed, you would feel the Misfortune of the loss of Sight, much greater than the want of it: And you would acknowledge, that in too presumptuously seeing, you would be blinder then, than now unhappily you are.'

'Ah! I must confess,' reply'd Belvira, 'my poor, dear Cousin is Blind, for I fancy she bears too great an Esteem for Frankwit, and only longs for Sight to look on him.' 'Indeed,' reply'd Celesia, 'I would be glad to see Frankwit, for I fancy he's as dazling, as he but now describ'd his Mistress, and if I fancy I see him, sure I do see him, for Sight is Fancy, is it not? or do you feel my Cousin with your Eyes?' 'This is indeed, a charming Blindness,' reply'd Frankwit, 'and the fancy of your Sight excels the certainty of ours. Strange! that there should be such Glances even in blindness? You, fair Maid, require not Eyes to conquer, if your Night has such Stars, what Sunshine would your Day of Sight have, if ever you should see?' 'I fear those Stars you talk of,' said Belvira, 'have some Influence on you, and by the Compass you sail by now, I guess you are steering to my Cousin. She is indeed charming enough to have been another Offspring of bright Venus, Blind like her Brother Cupid.' 'That Cupid,' reply'd Celesia, 'I am afraid has shot me, for methinks I would not have you marry Frankwit, but rather live as you do without the last Enjoyment, for methinks if he were marry'd, he would be more out of Sight than he already is.' 'Ah, Madam,' return'd Frankwit, 'Love is no Camelion, it cannot feed on Air alone.' 'No but,' rejoyn'd Celesia, 'you Lovers that are not Blind like Love it self, have am'rous Looks to feed on.' 'Ah! believe it,' said Belvira, ''tis better, Frankwit, not to lose Paradise by too much Knowledge; Marriage Enjoyments does but wake you from your sweet golden Dreams: Pleasure is but a Dream, dear Frankwit, but a Dream, and to be waken'd.' 'Ah! Dearest, but unkind Belvira,' answer'd Frankwit, 'sure there's no waking from Delight, in being lull'd on those soft Breasts of thine.' 'Alas! (reply'd the Bride to be) it is that very lulling wakes you; Women enjoy'd, are like Romances read, or Raree-shows once seen, meer Tricks of the slight of Hand, which, when found out, you only wonder at your selves for wondering so before at them. 'Tis Expectation endears the Blessing; Heaven would not be Heaven, could we tell what 'tis. When the Plot's out you have done with the Play, and when the last Act's done, you see the Curtain drawn with great indifferency.' 'O my Belvira', answered Frankwit, 'that Expectation were indeed a Monster which Enjoyment could not satisfy: I should take no pleasure,' he rejoin'd, 'running from Hill to Hill, like Children chasing that Sun, which I could never catch.' 'O thou shalt have it then, that Sun of Love,' reply'd Belvira, fir'd by this Complaint, and gently rush'd into Arms, (rejoyn'd) so Phœbus rushes radiant and unsullied, into a gilded Cloud. 'Well then, my dear Belvira,' answered Frankwit, 'be assured I shall be ever yours, as you are mine; fear not you shall never draw Bills of Love upon me so fast, as I shall wait in readiness to pay them; but now I talk of Bills, I must retire into Cambridgeshire, where I have a small Concern as yet unmortgaged, I will return thence with a Brace of thousand Pounds within a Week at furthest, with which our Nuptials, by their Celebration, shall be worthy of our Love. And then, my Life, my Soul, we shall be join'd, never to part again.' This tender Expression mov'd Belvira to shed some few Tears, and poor Celesia thought herself most unhappy that she had not Eyes to weep with too; but if she had, such was the greatness of her Grief, that sure she would have soon grown Blind with weeping. In short, after a great many soft Vows, and Promises of an inviolable Faith, they parted with a pompous sort of pleasing Woe; their Concern was of such a mixture of Joy and Sadness, as the Weather seems, when it both rains and shines. And now the last, the very last Adieu's was over, for the Farewels of Lovers hardly ever end, and Frankwit (the Time being Summer) reach'd Cambridge that Night, about Nine a Clock; (Strange! that he should have made such Haste to fly from what so much he lov'd!) and now, tir'd with the fatigue of his Journey, he thought fit to refresh himself by writing some few Lines to his belov'd Belvira; for a little Verse after the dull Prose Company of his Servant, was as great an Ease to him, (from whom it flow'd as naturally and unartificially, as his Love or his Breath) as a Pace or Hand-gallop, after a hard, uncouth, and rugged Trot. He therefore, finding his Pegasus was no way tir'd with his Land-travel, takes a short Journey thro' the Air, and writes as follows:

My dearest dear Belvira,

You knew my Soul, you knew it yours before,

I told it all, and now can tell no more;
Your Presents never wants fresh Charms to move,
But now more strange, and unknown Pow'r you prove
For now your very Absence 'tis I love.
Something there is which strikes my wandring View,
And still before my Eyes I fancy you.
Charming you seem, all charming, heavenly fair,
Bright as a Goddess, does my Love appear,
You seem, Belvira, what indeed you are.
Like the Angelick Off-spring of the Skies,
With beatifick Glories in your Eyes:
Sparkling with radiant Lustre all Divine,
Angels, and Gods! oh Heavens! how bright they shine!
Are you Belvira? can I think you mine!
Beyond ev'n Thought, I do thy Beauties see,
Can such a Heaven of Heavens be kept for me!
Oh be assur'd, I shall be ever true, I must -
For if I would, I can't be false to you.
Oh! how I wish I might no longer stay,
Tho' I resolve I will no Time delay,
One Tedious Week, and then I'll fleet away.
Tho' Love be blind, he shall conduct my Road,
Wing'd with almighty Love, to your Abode,
I'll fly, and grow Immortal as a God.
Short is my stay, yet my impatience strong,
Short tho' it is, alas! I think it long.
I'll come, my Life, new Blessings to pursue,
Love then shall fly a Flight he never flew,
I'll stretch his balmy Wings; I'm yours, Adieu.

Frankwit.

This Letter Belvira receiv'd with unspeakable Joy, and laid it up safely in her Bosom; laid it, where the dear Author of it lay before, and wonderfully pleas'd with his Humour of writing Verse, resolv'd not to be at all behind-hand with him, and so writ as follows:

My dear Charmer,

You knew before what Power your Love could boast,
But now your constant Faith confirms me most.
Absent Sincerity the best assures,
Love may do much, but Faith much more allures
For now your Constancy has bound me yours.
I find, methinks, in Verse some Pleasure too,
I cannot want a Muse, who write to you.
Ah! soon return, return, my charming Dear,
Heav'n knows how much we Mourn your Absence here:
My poor Celesia now would Charm your Soul,

Her Eyes, once Blind, do now Divinely rowl.
An aged Matron has by Charms unknown,
Given her clear Sight as perfect as thy own.
And yet, beyond her Eyes, she values thee,
'Tis for thy Sake alone she's glad to see.
She begg'd me, pray remember her to you,
That is a Task which now I gladly do.
Gladly, since so I only recommend
A dear Relation, and a dearer Friend,
Ne're shall my Love--but here my Note must end.

Your ever true Belvira.

When this Letter was written, it was strait shown to Celesia, who look'd upon any Thing that belong'd to Frankwit, with rejoycing Glances; so eagerly she perus'd it, that her tender Eyes beginning to Water, she cry'd out, (fancying she saw the Words dance before her View) 'Ah! Cousin, Cousin, your Letter is running away, sure it can't go itself to Frankwit.' A great Deal of other pleasing innocent Things she said, but still her Eyes flow'd more bright with lustrous Beams, as if they were to shine out; now all that glancing Radiancy which had been so long kept secret, and, as if, as soon as the Cloud of Blindness once was broke, nothing but Lightnings were to flash for ever after. Thus in mutual Discourse they spent their Hours, while Frankwit was now ravished with the Receipt of this charming Answer of Belvira's, and blest his own Eyes which discovered to him the much welcome News of fair Celesia's. Often he read the Letters o're and o're, but there his Fate lay hid, for 'twas that very Fondness proved his Ruin. He lodg'd at a Cousin's House of his, and there, (it being a private Family) lodged likewise a Blackamoor Lady, then a Widower; a whimsical Knight had taken a Fancy to enjoy her: Enjoy her did I say? Enjoy the Devil in the Flesh at once! I know not how it was, but he would fain have been a Bed with her, but she not consenting on unlawful Terms, (but sure all Terms are with her unlawful) the Knight soon marry'd her, as if there were not hell enough in Matrimony, but he must wed the Devil too. The Knight a little after died, and left this Lady of his (whom I shall Moorea) an Estate of six thousand Pounds per Ann. Now this Moorea observed the joyous Frankwit with an eager Look, her Eyes seemed like Stars of the first Magnitude glaring in the Night; she greatly importuned him to discover the Occasion of his transport, but he denying it, (as 'tis the Humour of our Sex) made her the more Inquisitive; and being Jealous that it was from a Mistress, employ'd her Maid to steal it, and if she found it such, to bring it her: accordingly it succeeded, for Frankwit having drank hard with some of the Gentlemen of that Shire, found himself indisposed, and soon went to Bed, having put the Letter in his Pocket: The Maid therefore to Moorea contrived that all the other Servants should be out of the Way, that she might plausibly officiate in the Warming the Bed of the indisposed Lover, but likely, had it not been so, she had warmed it by his Intreaties in a more natural Manner; he being in Bed in an inner Room, she slips out the Letter from his Pocket, carries it to her Mistress to read, and so restores it whence she had it; in the Morning the poor Lover wakened in a violent Fever, burning with a Fire more hot than that of Love. In short, he continued Sick a considerable while, all which time the Lady Moorea constantly visited him, and he as unwillingly saw her (poor Gentleman) as he would have seen a Parson; for as the latter would have perswaded, so the former scared him to Repentance. In the mean while, during his sickness, several Letters were sent to him by his dear Belvira, and Celesia too, (then learning to write) had made a shift to give him a line or two in Postscript with her Cousin, but all was intercepted by the jealousy of the Black Moorea, black in her mind, and dark, as well as in her body. Frankwit too writ several Letters as he was able, complaining of her unkindness, those likewise were all stopt by the same Blackmoor Devil. At last, it happened that Wildvill, (who I told my Reader was Frankwit's friend) came to London, his Father likewise dead, and now Master of a very plentiful fortune, he resolves to marry, and paying a visit to Belvira, enquires of her concerning Frankwit, she all in mourning for the loss, told him his friend was dead. 'Ah! Wildvill, he is dead,' said she, 'and died not mine, a Blackmoor Lady had bewitched him from me; I received a Letter lately which informed me all; there was no name subscribed to it, but it intimated, that it was written at the request of dying Frankwit.' 'Oh! I am sorry at my Soul,' said Wildvill, 'for I loved him with the best, the dearest friendship; no doubt then,' rejoyned he, "tis Witchcaft indeed that could make him false to you; what delight could he take in a Blackmoor Lady, tho' she had received him at once with a Soul as open as her longing arms, and with her Petticoat put off her modesty. Gods! How could he change a whole Field Argent into downright Sables.' "Twas done,' returned Celesia, 'with no small blot, I fancy, to the Female 'Scutcheon.' In short, after some more discourse, but very sorrowful, Wildvill takes his leave, extreamly taken with the fair Belvira, more beauteous in her cloud of woe; he paid her afterwards frequent visits, and found her wonder for the odd inconstancy of Frankwit, greater than her sorrow, since he dy'd so unworthy of her. Wildvill attack'd her with all the force of vigorous love, and she (as she thought) fully convinc'd of Frankwit's death, urg'd by the fury and impatience of her new ardent Lover, soon surrender'd, and the day of their Nuptials now arriv'd, their hands were joyn'd. In the mean time Frankwit (for he still liv'd) knew nothing of the Injury the base Moorea practis'd, knew not that 'twas thro' her private order, that the fore-mention'd account of his falshood and his death was sent; but impatient to see his Dear Belvira, tho' yet extremely weak, rid post to London, and that very day arriv'd there, immediately after the Nuptials of his Mistress and his Friend were celebrated. I was at this time in Cambridge, and having some small acquaintance with this Blackmoor Lady, and sitting in her Room that evening, after Frankwit's departure thence, in Moorea's absence, saw inadvertently a bundle of Papers, which she had gathered up, as I suppose, to burn, since now they grew but useless, she having no farther Hopes of him: I fancy'd I knew the Hand, and thence my Curiosity only led me to see the Name and finding Belvira subscrib'd, I began to guess there was some foul play in Hand. Belvira being my particularly intimate Acquaintance, I read one of them, and finding the Contents, convey'd them all secretly out with me, as I thought, in Point of Justice I was bound, and sent them to Belvira by that Night's Post; so that they came to her Hands soon after the Minute of her Marriage, with an Account how, and by what Means I came to light on them. No doubt but they exceedingly surpriz'd her: But Oh! Much more she grew amaz'd immediately after, to see the Poor, and now unhappy Frankwit, who privately had enquir'd for her below, being received as a Stranger, who said he had some urgent Business with her, in a back Chamber below Stairs. What Tongue, what Pen can express the mournful Sorrow of this Scene! At first they both stood Dumb, and almost Senseless; she took him for the Ghost of Frankwit; he looked so pale, new risen from his Sickness, he (for he had heard at his Entrance in the House, that his Belvira marry'd Wildvill) stood in Amaze, and like a Ghost indeed, wanted the Power to speak, till spoken to the first. At last, he draws his Sword, designing there to fall upon it in her Presence; she then imagining it his Ghost too sure, and come to kill her, shrieks out and Swoons; he ran immediately to her, and catch'd her in his Arms, and while he strove to revive and bring her to herself, tho' that he thought could never now be done, since she was marry'd. Wildvill missing his Bride, and hearing the loud Shriek, came running down, and entring the Room, sees his Bride lie clasp'd in Frankwit's Arms. 'Ha! Traytor!' He cries out, drawing his Sword with an impatient Fury, 'have you kept that Strumpet all this while, curst Frankwit, and now think fit to put your damn'd cast Mistress upon me: could not you forbear her neither ev'n on my Wedding Day? abominable Wretch!' Thus saying, he made a full Pass at Frankwit, and run him thro' the left Arm, and quite thro' the Body of the poor Belvira; that thrust immediately made her start, tho' Frankwit's Endeavours all before were useless. Strange! that her Death reviv'd her! For ah! she felt, that now she only liv'd to die! Striving thro' wild Amazement to run from such a Scene of Horror, as her Apprehensions shew'd her; down she dropt, and Frankwit seeing her fall, (all Friendship disannull'd by such a Chain of Injuries) Draws, fights with, and stabs his own loved Wildvill. Ah! Who can express the Horror and Distraction of this fatal Misunderstanding! The House was alarm'd, and in came poor Celesia, running in Confusion just as Frankwit was off'ring to kill himself, to die with a false Friend, and perjur'd Mistress, for he suppos'd them such. Poor Celesia now bemoan'd her unhappiness of sight, and wish'd she again were blind. Wildvill dy'd immediately, and Belvira only surviv'd him long enough to unfold all their most unhappy fate, desiring Frankwit with her dying breath, if ever he lov'd her, (and now she said that she deserv'd his love, since she had convinced him that she was not false) to marry her poor dear Celesia, and love her tenderly for her Belvira's sake; leaving her, being her nearest Relation, all her fortune, and he, much dearer than it all, to be added to her own; so joyning his and Celesia's Hands, she poured her last breath upon his Lips, and said, 'Dear Frankwit, Frankwit, I die yours.' With tears and wondrous sorrow he promis'd to obey her Will, and in some months after her interrment, he perform'd his promise.

NOTES: The Unfortunate Bride.

To Richard Norton. This Epistle Dedicatory is only to be found in the first edition of The Unfortunate Bride; or, The Blind Lady a Beauty, 'Printed for Samuel Briscoe, in Charles-Street, Covent-Garden, 1698', and also dated, on title page facing the portrait of Mrs. Behn, 1700.

Southwick, Hants, is a parish and village some 1¾ miles from Portchester, 4½ from Fareham. Richard Norton was son and heir of Sir Daniel Norton, who died seised of the manor in 1636. Richard Norton married Anne, daughter of Sir William Earle, by whom he had one child, Sarah. He was, in his county at least, a figure of no little importance. Tuesday, 12 August, 1701, Luttrell records that 'an addresse from the grand jury of Hampshire . . . was delivered by Richard Norton and Anthony Henly, esqs. to the lords justices, to be laid before his majestie.' He aimed at being a patron of the fine arts, and under his superintendence Dryden's The Spanish Friar was performed in the frater of Southwick Priory,[1] the buildings of which had not been entirely destroyed at the suppression. Colley Cibber addresses the Dedicatory Epistle (January, 1695) of his first play, Love's Last Shift (4to, 1696), to Norton in a highly eulogistic strain. The plate of Southwick Church (S. James), consisting of a communion cup, a standing paten, two flagons, an alms-dish, and a rat-tail spoon, is silver-gilt, and was presented by Richard Norton in 1691. He died 10 December, 1732.

[**Footnote 1**: The house was one of Black (Austin) Canons.]

THE DUMB VIRGIN; OR, THE FORCE OF IMAGINATION

INTRODUCTION

Consanguinity and love which are treated in this novel so romantically and with such tragic catastrophe had already been dealt with in happier mood by Mrs. Behn in The Dutch Lover. Vide Note on the Source of that play, Vol. I, p. 218.

In classic lore the Œdipus Saga enthralled the imagination of antiquity and inspired dramas amongst the world's masterpieces. Later forms of the tale may be found in Suidas and Cedrenus.

The Legend of St. Gregory, based on a similar theme, the hero of which, however, is innocent throughout, was widely diffused through mediæval Europe. It forms No. 81 of the Gesta Romanorum.

There is an old English poem[1] on the subject, and it also received lyric treatment at the hands of the German meistersinger, Hartmann von Aue. An Italian story, Il Figliuolo di germani, the chronicle of St. Albinus, and the Servian romaunt of the Holy Foundling Simeon embody similar circumstances.

Matteo Bandello, Part II, has a famous[2] novel (35) with rubric, 'un gentiluomo navarrese sposa una, che era sua sorella e figliuola, non lo sapendo,' which is almost exactly the same as the thirtieth story of the Heptameron. As the good Bishop declares that it was related to him by a lady living in the district, it is probable that some current tradition furnished both him and the Queen of Navarre with these horrible incidents and that neither copied from the other.[3]

Bandello was imitated in Spanish by J. Perez de Montalvan, Sucesos y Prodigios de Amor, La Mayor confusion; in Latin by D. Otho Melander; and he also gave Desfontaines the subject of L'Inceste Innocent; Histoire Véritable (Paris, 1644). A similar tale is touched upon in Amadis de Gaule, and in a later century we find Le Criminel sans le Savoir, Roman Historique et Poëtique (Amsterdam and Paris, 1783). It is also found in Brevio's Rime e Prose; Volgari, novella iv; and in T. Grapulo (or Grappolino), Il Convito Borghesiano (Londra, 1800). A cognate legend is Le Dit du Buef and Le Dit de la Bourjosee de Rome. (ed. Jubinal, Nouveau Recueil; and Nouveau Recueil du Sénateur de Rome . . . ed. Méon.) Again: the Leggenda di Vergogna, etc. testi del buon secolo in prosa e in verso, edited by A. D'Ancona (Bologna, 1869) repeats the same catastrophe. It is also related in Byshop's Blossoms.

In Luther's Colloquia Mensalia, under the article 'Auricular Confession', the occurrence is said to have taken place at Erfurt in Germany. Julio de Medrano, a Spanish writer of the sixteenth century, says that a similar story was related to him when he was in the Bourbonnois, where the inhabitants pointed out the house which had been the scene of these morbid passions. France, indeed, seems to have been the home of the tradition, and Le Roux de Lincy in the notes to his excellent edition of the Heptameron quotes from Millin, Antiquités Nationales (t. iii. f. xxviii. p. 6.) who, speaking of the Collegiate Church of Ecouis, says that in the midst of the nave there was a prominent white marbel tablet with this epitaph:

Cy-gist la fille, cy-gist le père,
Cy-gist la soeur, cy-gist le frère;
Cy-gist la femme, et le mary,
Et si n'y a que deux corps icy.

The tradition ran that a son of 'Madame d'Ecouis avait eu de sa mère sans la connaître et sans en être reconnu une fille nommée Cécile. Il épousa ensuite en Lorraine cette même Cécile qui était auprès de la Duchesse de Bar . . . Il furent enterrés dans le même tombeau en 1512 à Ecouis.' An old sacristan used to supply curious visitors to the church with a leaflet detailing the narrative. The same story is attached to other parishes, and at Alincourt, a village between Amiens and Abbeville, the following lines are inscribed upon a grave:

Ci git le fils, ci git la mère,
Ci git la fille avec le père,
Ci git la soeur, ci git le frère,
Ci git la femme et le mari,
Et ne sont pas que trois corps ici.

When Walpole wrote his tragedy, The Mysterious Mother (1768), he states he had no knowledge of Bandello or the Heptameron, but he gives the following account of the origin of his theme. 'I had heard when very young, that a gentlewoman, under uncommon agonies of mind, had waited on Archbishop Tillotson and besought his counsel. A damsel that served her had, many years before, acquainted her that she was importuned by the gentlewoman's son to grant him a private meeting. The mother ordered the maiden to make the assignation, when she said she would discover herself and reprimand him for his criminal passion; but, being hurried away by a much more criminal passion herself, she kept the assignation without discovering herself. The fruit of this horrid artifice was a daughter, whom the gentlewoman caused to be educated very privately in the country; but proving very lovely and being accidentally met by her father-brother, who never had the slightest suspicion of the truth, he had fallen in love with and actually married her. The wretched guilty mother learning what had happened, and distracted with the consequence of her crime, had now resorted to the Archbishop to know in what manner she should act. The prelate charged her never to let her son and daughter know what had passed, as they were innocent of any criminal intention. For herself, he bad her almost despair.'

The same story occurs in the writings of the famous Calvinistic divine, William Perkins (1558-1602), sometime Rector of St. Andrew's, Cambridge. Thence it was extracted for The Spectator.

In Mat Lewis' ghoulish romance, The Monk (1796) it will be remembered that Ambrosio, after having enjoyed Antonia, to whose bedchamber he has gained admittance by demoniacal aid, discovers that she is his sister, and heaping crime upon crime to sorcery and rape he has added incest.

There is a tragic little novel, 'The Illegal Lovers; a True Secret History. Being an Amour Between A Person of Condition and his Sister. Written by One who did reside in the Family.' (8vo, 1728.) After the death of his wife, Bellario falls in love with his sister Lindamira. Various sentimental letters pass between the two, and eventually Bellario in despair pistols himself. The lady lives to wed another admirer. The tale was obviously suggested by the Love Letters between a Nobleman and his Sister.

[**Footnote 1**: There are three MSS. Vernon MS., Oxford, edited by Horstmann; MS. Cott, Cleop. D. ix, British Museum; Auchinleck MS., Advocates' Library, Edinburgh, edited with glossary by F. Schultz, 1876.]

[**Footnote 2**: cf. Masuccio. Il Novellino, No. 23.]

[**Footnote 3**: Bandello's novels first appeared at Lucca, 4to, 1554. Marguerite of Angoulême died 21 December, 1549. The Heptameron was composed 1544-8 and published 1558.]

THE DUMB VIRGIN: or, the Force of Imagination

Rinaldo, a Senator of the great City Venice, by a plentiful Inheritance, and industrious Acquisitions, was become Master of a very plentiful Estate; which, by the Countenance of his Family, sprung from the best Houses in Italy, had rendred him extreamly popular and honoured; he had risen to the greatest Dignities of that State, all which Offices he discharged with Wisdom and Conduct, befitting the Importance of his Charge, and Character of the Manager; but this great Person had some Accident in his Children, sufficient to damp all the Pleasure of his more smiling Fortunes; he married when young, a beautiful and virtuous Lady, who had rendred him the happy Father of a Son; but his Joys were soon disturbed by the following Occasion.

There stands an Island in the Adriatick Sea, about twenty Leagues from Venice, a Place wonderfully pleasant in the Summer, where Art and Nature seem to out-rival each other, or seem rather to combine in rendring it the most pleasant of their products; being placed under the most benign climate in the World, and situated exactly between Italy and Greece, it appears an entire Epitome of all the Pleasures in them both; the proper glories of the Island were not a little augmented by the confluence of Gentlemen and Ladies of the chiefest Rank in the City, insomuch that this was a greater mark for Beauty and Gallantry, than Venice for Trade. Among others Rinaldo's Lady begged her Husband's permission to view this so much celebrated place.

He was unwilling to trust his treasure to the treachery of the watry element; but repeating her request, he yielded to her desires, his love not permitting him the least shew of command, and so thro' its extent, conspiring its own destruction. His Lady with her young Son (whom she would not trust from her sight) and a splendid attendance in a Barge well fitted, sets out for the Island, Rinaldo being detained at home himself about some important affairs relating to the publick, committed the care of his dear Wife and Child to a faithful Servant call'd Gaspar; and for their greater security against Pyrates, had obtained his Brother, who commanded a Venetian Galley, to attend them as Convoy. In the evening they set out from Venice, with a prosperous gale, but a storm arising in the night, soon separated the Barge from her Convoy, and before morning drove her beyond the designed Port, when, instead of discovering the wish'd-for Island, they could see a Turkish Pyrate bearing towards them, with all her Sail; their late apprehensions of Shipwrack, were drowned in the greater danger of Captivity and lasting Slavery, their fears drove some into resolutions as extravagant as the terrors that caused them, but the confusion of all was so tumultuous, and the designs so various, that nothing could be put in execution for the publick safety; the greatest share of the passengers being Ladies, added strangely to the consternation; beauty always adds a pomp to woe, and by its splendid show, makes sorrow look greater and more moving. Some by their piteous plaints and wailings proclaimed their griefs aloud, whilst others bespoke their sorrows more emphatically by sitting mournfully silent; the fears of some animated them to extravagant actions, whilst the terrors of others were so mortifying, that they shewed no sign of Life, but by their trembling; some mourned the rigour of their proper fate, others conscious of the sorrows their Friends and Relations should sustain through their loss, made the griefs of them their own; but the heaviest load of misfortunes lay on Rinaldo's Lady, besides the loss of her liberty, the danger of her honour, the separation from her dear Husband, the care for her tender Infant wrought rueful distractions; she caught her Child in her Arms, and with Tears extorted thro' Fear and Affection, she deplor'd the Misfortune of her Babe, the pretty Innocent smiling in the Embraces of its Mother, shew'd that Innocence cou'd deride the Persecution of Fortune; at length she delivered the Infant into the Hand of Gasper, begging him to use all Endeavours in its Preservation, by owning it for his, when they fell into the Hands of the Enemy.

But Gasper, who amidst the universal Consternation, had a peculiar Regard to his own Safety, and Master's Interest, undertook a Design desperately brave. Two long Planks, which lay lengthwise in the Barge, as Seats, he had ty'd together with Ropes, and taking the Infant from the Mother, whilst the whole Vessel was in a distracted Confusion, he fast'ned it to the Planks, and shoving both over-board before him, plung'd into the Sea after, dragging the Planks that bore the Infant with one Hand, and swimming with t'other, making the next Land; he had swam about two hundred Paces from the Barge before his Exploit was discover'd, but then the Griefs of Rinaldo's Lady were doubly augmented, seeing her Infant expos'd to the Fury of the merciless Winds and Waves, which she then judged more rigorous than the Turks; for to a weak Mind, that Danger works still the strongest, that's most in View; but when the Pirate, who by this time had fetch'd them within Shot, began to Fire, she seem'd pleas'd that her Infant was out of that Hazard, tho' exposed to a greater. Upon their Sign of yielding, the Turk launching out her Boat, brought them all on board her; but she had no time to examine her Booty, being saluted by a Broadside, vigorously discharg'd from a Venetian Galley, which bore down upon them, whilst they were taking aboard their Spoil; this Galley was that commanded by Rinaldo's Brother, which cruising that Way in quest of the Barge, happily engag'd the Turk, before they had Leisure to offer any Violence to the Ladies, and plying her warmly the Space of two Hours, made her a Prize, to the inexpressible Joy of the poor Ladies, who all this time under Hatches, had sustain'd the Horrors of ten thousand Deaths by dreading one.

All the greater Dangers over, Rinaldo's Lady began to reflect on the strange Riddle of her Son's Fortune, who by shunning one Fate, had (in all Probability) fallen into a worse, for they were above ten Leagues from any Land, and the Sea still retain'd a Roughness, unsettled since the preceeding Storm; she therefore begg'd her Brother-in-Law to Sail with all Speed in Search of her Son and Gasper; but all in vain, for cruising that Day, and the succeeding Night along the Coasts, without making any Discovery of what they sought, he sent a Boat to be inform'd by the Peasants, of any such Landing upon their Coast; but they soon had a dismal Account, finding the Body of Gasper thrown dead on the Sand, and near to him the Planks, the unhappy Occasion of his Flight, and the Faithless Sustainers of the Infant. So thinking these mournful Objects Testimonies enough of the Infant's Loss, they return'd with the doleful Relation to their Captain and the Lady; her Grief at the recital of the Tragic Story, had almost transported her to Madness; what Account must she now make to the mournful Father, who esteem'd this Child the chief Treasure of his Life; she fear'd, that she might forfeit the Affection of a Husband, by being the unfortunate Cause of so great a Loss; but her Fears deceiv'd her, for altho' her Husband, receiv'd her with great Grief, 'twas nevertheless moderated by the Patience of a Christian, and the Joy for recovering his beloved Lady.

This Misfortune was soon lessen'd by the growing Hopes of another Off-spring, which made them divest their Mourning, to make Preparations for the joyful Reception of this new Guest into the World; and upon its Appearance their Sorrows were redoubled, 'twas a Daughter, its Limbs were distorted, its Back bent, and tho' the face was the freest from Deformity, yet had it no Beauty to Recompence the Dis-symetry of the other Parts; Physicians being consulted in this Affair, derived the Cause from the Frights and dismal Apprehensions of the Mother, at her being taken by the Pyrates; about which time they found by Computation, the Conception of the Child to be; the Mother grew very Melancholy, rarely speaking, and not to be comforted by any Diversion. She conceiv'd again, but no hopes of better Fortune cou'd decrease her Grief, which growing with her Burden, eased her of both at once, for she died in Child-birth, and left the most beautiful Daughter to the World that ever adorn'd Venice, but naturally and unfortunately Dumb, which defect the learn'd attributed to the Silence and Melancholy of the Mother, as the Deformity of the other was to the Extravagance of her Frights.

Rinaldo, waving all Intentions of a second Marriage, directs his Thoughts to the Care of his Children, their Defects not lessening his Inclination, but stirring up his Endeavours in supplying the Defaults of Nature by the Industry of Art; he accordingly makes the greatest Provision for their Breeding and Education, which prov'd so effectual in a little Time, that their Progress was a greater Prodigy than themselves.

The Eldest, called Belvideera, was indefatigably addicted to Study, which she had improv'd so far, that by the sixteenth Year of her Age, she understood all the European Languages, and cou'd speak most of'em, but was particularly pleas'd with the English, which gave me the Happiness of many Hours Conversation with her; and I may ingenuously declare, 'twas the most Pleasant I ever enjoy'd, for besides a piercing Wit, and depth of Understanding peculiar to herself, she delivered her Sentiments with that easiness and grace of Speech, that it charm'd all her Hearers.

The Beauties of the second Sister, nam'd Maria, grew with her Age, every twelve Months saluting her with a New-years Gift of some peculiar Charm; her Shapes were fine set off with a graceful and easy Carriage; the Majesty and Softness of her Face, at once wrought Love and Veneration; the Language of her Eyes sufficiently paid the Loss of her Tongue, and there was something so Commanding in her Look, that it struck every Beholder as dumb as herself; she was a great Proficient in Painting, which puts me in mind of a notable Story I can't omit; her Father had sent for the most Famous Painter in Italy to draw her Picture, she accordingly sat for it; he had drawn some of the Features of her Face; and coming to the Eye, desired her to give him as brisk and piercing a Glance as she cou'd; but the Vivacity of her Look so astonished the Painter, that thro' concern he let his Pencil drop and spoiled the Picture; he made a second Essay, but with no better Success, for rising in great Disorder, he swore it impossible to draw that which he cou'd not look upon; the Lady vexed at the Weakness of the Painter, took up his Pencils and the Picture, and sitting down to her Glass, finished it herself; she had improv'd her silent Conversation with her Sister so far, that she was understood by her, as if she had spoke, and I remember this Lady was the first I saw use the significative Way of Discourse by the Fingers; I dare not say 'twas she invented it (tho' it probably might have been an Invention of these ingenious Sisters) but I am positive none before her ever brought it to that Perfection.

In the seventeenth of Belvideera's, and sixteenth Year of Maria's Age, Francisco, Brother to Rinaldo, was made Admiral of the Venetian Fleet, and upon his first Entrance upon his Command, had obtained a signal Victory over the Turks; he returning to Venice with Triumph, applause and spoil, presented to the great Duke a young English Gentleman, who only as a Volunteer in the Action, had signalized himself very bravely in the Engagement, but particularly by first boarding the Turkish Admiral Galley, and killing her Commander hand to hand; the Fame of this Gentleman soon spread over all Venice, and the two Sisters sent presently for me, to give an Account of the Exploits of my Countryman, as their Unkle had recounted it to them; I was pleas'd to find so great an Example of English Bravery, so far from Home, and long'd extreamly to converse with him, vainly flattering myself, that he might have been of my Acquaintance. That very Night there was a grand Ball and Masquerade at the great Duke's Palace, for the most signal Joy of the late Success, thither Belvideera invited me to Accompany her and Maria, adding withal as a Motive, that we might there most probably meet, and Discourse with this young Hero; and equipping me with a Suit of Masquerade, they carried me in their Coach to the Ball, where we had pass'd half an Hour, when I saw enter a handsom Gentleman in a rich English Dress; I show'd him to Belvideera, who moving towards him, with a gallant Air, slaps him on the Shoulder with her Fan, he turning about, and viewing her Person, the Defaults of which were not altogether hidden by her Disguise; 'Sir, (said he) if you are a Man, know that I am one, and will not bear Impertinence; but, if you are a Lady, Madam, as I hope in Heavens you are not, I must inform you, that I am under a Vow, not to converse with any Female to Night;' 'Know then, Sir, (answered Belvideera very smartly) that I am a Female, and you have broke your Vow already; but methinks, Sir, the Ladies are very little oblig'd to your Vow, which wou'd rob them of the Conversation of so fine a Gentleman.'

'Madam, (said the Gentleman) the Sweetness of your Voice bespeaks you a Lady, and I hope the breaking my Vow will be so far from Damning me, that I shall thereby merit Heaven, if I may be blest in your Divine Conversation.' Belvideera made such ingenious and smart Repartees to the Gentleman, who was himself a great Courtier, that he was entirely captivated with her Wit, insomuch, that he cou'd not refrain making Protestations of his Passion; he talked about half an Hour in such pure Italian, that I began to mistrust my Englishman, wherefore taking some Occasion to jest upon his Habit, I found 'twas only a Masquerade to cloak a down-right Venetian; in the mean Time, we perceiv'd a Gentleman Gallantly attir'd with no Disguise but a Turkish Turbant on, the richliest beset with Jewels I ever saw; he addressed Maria with all the Mien and Air of the finest Courtier; he had talked to her a good while before we heard him, but then Belvideera, knowing her poor Sister uncapable of any Defence, 'Sir, (said she to the Venetian,) yonder is a Lady of my Acquaintance, who lies under a Vow of Silence as you were, I must therefore beg your Pardon, and fly to her Relief': 'She can never be conquer'd, who has such a Champion,' (reply'd the Gentleman) upon which Belvideera turning from him, interpos'd between the Gentleman and her Sister, saying, 'This Lady, Sir, is under an Obligation of Silence, as a Penance imposed by her Father-Confessor.' 'Madam, (reply'd the Gentleman) whoever impos'd Silence on these fair Lips, is guilty of a greater Offence than any, such a fair Creature cou'd commit.' 'Why, Sir, (said Belvideera) have you seen the Lady's Beauty': 'Yes, Madam, (answer'd he) for urging her to talk, which I found she declin'd, I promis'd to disengage her from any farther Impertinence, upon a Sight of her Face; she agreed by paying the Price of her Liberty, which was ransom enough for any Thing under Heavens, but her fair Company'; he spoke in an Accent that easily shew'd him a Stranger; which Belvideera laying hold of, as an Occasion of Railery, 'Sir, (said she,) your Tongue pronounces you a great Stranger in this Part of the World, I hope you are not what that Turbant represents; perhaps, Sir, you think your self in the Seraglio'; 'Madam, (reply'd he,) this Turbant might have been in the Turkish Seraglio, but never in so fair a one as this; and this Turbant (taking it off) is now to be laid at the Foot of some Christian Lady, for whose safety, and by whose protecting Influence, I had the Happiness to win it from the Captain of the Turkish Admiral Galley.' We were all surpriz'd, knowing him then the young English Gentleman, we were so curious of seeing; Belvideera presently talk'd English to him, and made him some very pretty Complements upon his Victory, which so charm'd the young Soldier, that her Tongue claim'd an equal Share in his Heart with Maria's Eyes; 'Madam, (said he to her) if you have the Beauty of that Lady, or if she has your Wit, I am the most happy, or the most unfortunate Man alive.' 'Sir,' said the Venetian coming up, 'pray give me leave to share in your Misfortunes.' 'Sir, (said Belvideera very smartly) you must share in his good Fortunes, and learn to conquer Men, before you have the Honour of being subdu'd by Ladies, we scorn mean Prizes, Sir.' 'Madam, (said the Venetian in some Choler) perhaps I can subdue a Rival.' 'Pray, Sir, (said the Stranger) don't be angry with the Lady, she's not your Rival I hope, Sir.' Said the Venetian, 'I can't be angry at the Lady, because I love her; but my Anger must be levell'd at him, who after this Declaration dare own a Passion for her.' 'Madam, (said the English Gentleman turning from the Venetian) Honour now must extort a Confession from me, which the Awfulness of my Passion durst never have own'd: And I must declare,' added he in a louder Voice, 'to all the World, that I love you, lest this Gentleman shou'd think his Threats forc'd me to disown it.' 'O! then (said Belvideera) you're his Rival in Honour, not in Love.' 'In honourable Love I am, Madam,' answer'd the Stranger. 'I'll try,' (said the Venetian, going off in Choler,) he Whisper'd a little to a Gentleman, that stood at some Distance, and immediately went out; this was Gonzago, a Gentleman of good Reputation in Venice, his Principles were Honour and Gallantry, but the Former often sway'd by Passions, rais'd by the Latter. All this while, Maria and I were admiring the Stranger, whose Person was indeed wonderfully Amiable; his Motions were exact, yet free and unconstrain'd; the Tone of his Voice carried a sweet Air of Modesty in it, yet were all his Expressions manly; and to summ up all, he was as fine an English Gentleman, as I ever saw Step in the Mall.

Poor Maria never before envied her Sister the Advantage of Speech, or never deplor'd the Loss of her own with more Regret, she found something so Sweet in the Mien, Person, and Discourse of this Stranger, that her Eyes felt a dazling Pleasure in beholding him, and like flattering Mirrours represented every Action and Feature, with some heightning Advantage to her Imagination: Belvideera also had some secret Impulses of Spirit, which drew her insensibly into a great Esteem of the Gentleman; she ask'd him, by what good Genius, propitious to Venice, he was induced to Live so remote from his

Country; he said, that he cou'd not imploy his Sword better than against the common Foe of Christianity; and besides, there was a peculiar Reason, which prompted him to serve there, which Time cou'd only make known. I made bold to ask him some peculiar Questions, about Affairs at Court, to most of which he gave Answers, that shew'd his Education liberal, and himself no Stranger to Quality; he call'd himself Dangerfield, which was a Name that so pleas'd me, that being since satisfied it was a Counterfeit, I us'd it in a Comedy of mine: We had talk'd 'till the greater Part of the Company being dispers'd, Dangerfield begg'd Leave to attend us to our Coach, and waiting us to the Door, the Gentleman, whom Gonzago whisper'd, advanc'd and offer'd his Service to hand Maria; she declin'd it, and upon his urging, she turn'd to the other Side of Dangerfield, who, by this Action of the Ladies finding himself intitled to her Protection, 'Sir, (said he) Favours from great Beauties, as from great Monarchs, must flow Voluntarily, not by Constraint, and whosoever wou'd extort from either, are liable to the great Severity of Punishment.' 'Oh! Sir, (reply'd the Venetian very arrogantly,) I understand not your Monarchy, we live here under a free State; besides, Sir, where there is no Punishment to be dreaded, the Law will prove of little Force; and so, Sir, by your Leave,' offering to push him aside, and lay hold on the Lady. Dangerfield returned the Justle so vigorously, that the Venetian fell down the Descent of some Stairs at the Door, and broke his Sword: Dangerfield leap'd down after him, to prosecute his Chastizement, but seeing his Sword broken, only whisper'd him, that if he wou'd meet him next Morning at Six, at the Back-part of St. Mark's Church, he wou'd satisfie him for the Loss of his Sword; upon which, the Venetian immediately went off, cursing his ill Fate, that prevented his quarrelling with Dangerfield, to whom he had born a grudging Envy ever since his Success in the late Engagement, and of whom, and his Lodgings, he had given Gonzago an Account, when he whisper'd him at the Ball. Dangerfield left us full of his Praises, and went home to his Lodgings, where he found a Note directed to him to this Effect:

SIR,

You declared Publickly at the Ball, you were my Rival in Love and Honour: If you dare prove it by Maintaining it, I shall be to morrow Morning at Six, at the Back-part of St. Mark's Church, where I shall be ready to fall a Sacrifice to both.

Gonzago.

Dangerfield, on the Perusal of this Challenge, began to reflect on the Strangeness of that Evening's Adventure, which had engag'd him in a Passion for two Mistresses, and involv'd him in two Duels; and whether the Extravagance of his Passion, or the Oddness of his Fighting-Appointments, were most remarkable, he found hard to Determine; his Love was divided between the Beauty of one Lady, and Wit of another, either of which he loved passionately, yet nothing cou'd satisfy him, but the Possibility of enjoying both. He had appointed the Gentleman at the Ball to meet him at the same Time and Place, which Gonzago's Challenge to him imported; this Disturbance employed his Thought till Morning, when rising and dressing himself very richly, he walked to the appointed Place. Erizo, who was the Gentleman whose Sword he had broke, was in the Place before him; and Gonzago entered at the same Time with him. Erizo, was surprized to see Gonzago, as much as he was to find Erizo there. 'I don't remember, Friend (said Gonzago) that I desired your Company here this Morning.' 'As much as I expected yours,' answered Erizo. 'Come, Gentlemen, (said Dangerfield, interrupting them) I must fight you both, it seems: which shall I dispatch first?' 'Sir, (said Erizo) you challeng'd me, and therefore I claim your Promise.' 'Sir, (reply'd Gonzago) he must require the same of me first, as I challenged him.' Said Erizo, 'the Affront I received was unpardonable, and therefore I must fight him first, lest if he fall by your Hands, I be depriv'd of my Satisfaction.' 'Nay (reply'd Gonzago) my Love and Honour being laid at Stake, first claims his Blood; and therefore, Sir, (continued he to Dangerfield) defend yourself.' 'Hold (said Erizo interposing,) if you thrust home, you injure me, your Friend.' 'You have forfeited that title, (said Gonzago all in Choler,) and therefore if you stand not aside, I'll push at you.' 'Thrust home then, (said Erizo) and take what follows.' They immediately assaulted each other vigorously. 'Hold, Gentlemen, (said Dangerfield striking down their Swords) by righting your selves you injure me, robbing me of that Satisfaction, which you both owe me, and therefore, Gentlemen, you shall fight me, before any private Quarrel among your selves defraud me of my Revenge, and so one or both of you,' thrusting first at Erizo. 'I'm your Man,' (said Gonzago) parrying the Thrust made at Erizo. The Clashing of so many Swords alarm'd some Gentlemen at their Mattins in the Church, among whom was Rinaldo, who since the Death of his Wife, had constantly attended Morning-Service at the Church, wherein she was buried. He with Two or Three more, upon the Noise ran out, and parting the three Combatants, desired to know the Occasion of their Promiscuous Quarrel. Gonzago and Erizo knowing Rinaldo, gave him an Account of the Matter, as also who the Stranger was. Rinaldo was overjoy'd to find the brave Britain, whom he had received so great a Character of, from his Brother the Admiral, and accosting him very Courteously, 'Sir, (said he) I am sorry our Countrymen shou'd be so Ungrateful as to Injure any Person, who has been so Serviceable to the State; and pray, Gentlemen, (added he, addressing the other two) be intreated to suspend your Animosities, and come Dine with me at my House, where I hope to prevail with you to end your Resentments.' Gonzago and Erizo hearing him Compliment the Stranger at their Expence, told him in a Rage, they wou'd chuse some other Place than his House, to end their Resentments in, and walk'd off. Dangerfield, on Rinaldo's farther Request, accompanied him to his House.

Maria had newly risen, and with her Night-gown only thrown loose about her, had look'd out of the Window, just as her Father and Dangerfield were approaching the Gate, at the same Instant she cast her Eyes upon Dangerfield, and he accidentally look'd up to the Window where she stood, their Surprize was mutual, but that of Dangerfield the greater; he saw such an amazing Sight of Beauty, as made him doubt the Reality of the Object, or distrust the Perfection of his Sight; he saw his dear Lady, who had so captivated him the preceeding Day, he saw her in all the heightning Circumstances of her Charms, he saw her in all her native Beauties, free from the Incumbrance of Dress, her Hair as black as Ebony, hung flowing in careless Curls over her Shoulders, it hung link'd in amorous Twinings, as if in Love with its own Beauties; her Eyes not yet freed from the Dullness of the late Sleep, cast a languishing Pleasure in their Aspect, which heaviness of Sight added the greatest Beauties to those Suns, because under the Shade of such a Cloud, their Lustre cou'd only be view'd; the lambent Drowsiness that play'd upon her Face, seem'd like a thin Veil not to hide, but to heighten the Beauty which it cover'd; her Night-gown hanging loose, discover'd her charming Bosom, which cou'd bear no Name, but Transport, Wonder and Extasy, all which struck his Soul, as soon as the Object hit his Eye; her Breasts with an easy Heaving, show'd the Smoothness of her Soul and of her Skin; their Motions were so languishingly soft, that they cou'd not be said to rise and fall, but rather to swell up towards Love, the Heat of which seem'd to melt them down again; some scatter'd jetty Hairs, which hung confus'dly over her Breasts, made her Bosom show like Venus caught in Vulcan's Net, but 'twas the Spectator, not she, was captivated. This Dangerfield saw, and all this at once, and with Eyes that were adapted by a preparatory Potion; what must then his Condition be? He was stricken with such Amazement, that he was forced to Support himself, by leaning on Rinaldo's Arm, who started at his sudden Indisposition. 'I'm afraid, Sir, (said he) you have received some Wound in the Duel.' 'Oh! Sir, (said he) I am mortally wounded'; but recollecting himself after a little Pause, 'now I am better.' Rinaldo wou'd have sent for a Surgeon to have it searched. 'Your pardon, Sir, (said Dangerfield) my Indisposition proceeds from an inward Malady, not by a Sword, but like those made by Achilles's Spear, nothing can cure, but what gave the Wound.' Rinaldo guessing at the Distemper, but not the Cause of it, out of good Manners declined any further enquiry, but conducting him in, entertained him with all the Courtesy imaginable; but in half a Hour, a Messenger came from the Senate, requiring his immediate Attendance; he lying under an indispensable Necessity of making his personal Appearance, begg'd Dangerfield's Pardon, intreating him to stay, and command his House till his return, and conducting him to a fine Library, said he might there find Entertainment, if he were addicted to Study; adding withal, as a farther Engagement of his Patience, that he should meet the Admiral at the Senate, whom he wou'd bring home as an Addition to their Company at Dinner. Dangerfield needed none of these Motives to stay, being detained by a secret Inclination to the Place; walking therefore into the Library, Rinaldo went to the Senate. Dangerfield when alone, fell into deep Ruminating on his strange Condition, he knew himself in the House, with one of his dear Charmers, but durst not hope to see her, which added to his Torment; like Tantalus remov'd the farther from Happiness, by being nearer to it, contemplated so far on the Beauties of that dear Creature, that he concluded, if her Wit were like that of his t'other Mistress, he wou'd endeavour to confine his Passion wholly to that Object.

In the mean Time, Maria was no less confounded, she knew herself in Love with a Stranger, whose Residence was uncertain, she knew her own Modesty in concealing it; and alas! she knew her Dumbness uncapable of ever revealing it, at least, it must never expect any Return; she had gather'd from her Sister's Discourse, that she was her Rival; a Rival, who had the Precedency in Age, as the Advantage in Wit, and Intreague, which want of Speech render'd her uncapable of; these Reflections, as they drew her farther from the dear Object, brought her nearer Despair; her Sister was gone that Morning with her Unkle, the Admiral, about two Miles from Venice, to drink some Mineral Waters, and Maria finding nothing to divert her, goes down to her Father's Library, to ease her Melancholy by reading. She was in the same loose Habit in which she appeared at the Window, her Distraction of Thought not permitting her any Care in dressing herself; she enter'd whilst Dangerfield's Thoughts were bent by a full Contemplation of her Idea, insomuch that his Surprize represented her as a Phantom only, created by the Strength of his Fancy; her depth of Thought had cast down her Eyes in a fix'd Posture so low, that she discover'd not Dangerfield, till she stood close where he sat, but then so sudden an Appearance of what she so lov'd, struck so violently on her Spirits, that she fell in a Swoon, and fell directly into Dangerfield's Arms; this soon wakened him from his Dream of Happiness, to a Reality of Bliss, he found his Phantom turn'd into the most charming Piece of Flesh and Blood that ever was, he found her, whom just now he despair'd of seeing; he found her with all her Beauties flowing loose in his Arms, the Greatness of the Pleasure rais'd by the two heightning Circumstances of Unexpectancy and Surprize, was too large for the Capacity of his Soul, he found himself beyond Expression happy, but could not digest the Surfeit; he had no sooner Leisure to consider on his Joy, but he must reflect on the Danger of her that caus'd it, which forced him to suspend his Happiness to administer some Relief to her expiring Senses: He had a Bottle of excellent Spirits in his Pocket, which holding to her Nose, soon recover'd her; she finding herself in the Arms of a Man, and in so loose a Dress, blush'd now more red, than she look'd lately pale; and disengaging herself in a Confusion, wou'd have flung from him; but he gently detaining her by a precarious Hold, threw himself on his Knees, and with the greatest Fervency of Passion cry'd out: 'For Heavens sake, dearest Creature, be not offended at the accidental Blessing which Fortune, not Design, hath cast upon me; (She wou'd have rais'd him up,) No Madam, (continu'd he) never will I remove from this Posture, 'till you have pronounc'd my Pardon; I love you, Madam, to that Degree, that if you leave me in a distrust of your Anger, I cannot survive it; I beg, intreat, conjure you to speak, your Silence torments me worse than your Reproaches cou'd; am I so much disdain'd, that you will not afford me one Word?' The lamentable Plight of the wretched Lady every one may guess, but no Body can comprehend; she saw the dearest of Mankind prostrate at her Feet, and imploring what she wou'd as readily grant as he desire, yet herself under a Necessity of denying his Prayers, and her own easy Inclinations. The Motions of her Soul, wanting the freedom of Utterance, were like to tear her Heart asunder by so narrow a Confinement, like the force of Fire pent up, working more impetuously; 'till at last he redoubling his Importunity, her Thoughts wanting Conveyance by the Lips, burst out at her Eyes in a Flood of Tears; then moving towards a Writing-Desk, he following her still on his Knees, amidst her Sighs and Groans she took Pen and Paper, writ two Lines, which she gave him folded up, then flinging from him, ran up to her Chamber: He strangely surpriz'd at this odd manner of Proceeding, opening the Paper, read the following Words:

You can't my Pardon, nor my Anger move.
For know, alas! I'm dumb, alas! I love.

He was wonderfully Amaz'd reading these Words. 'Dumb, (cried he out) naturally Dumb? O ye niggard Powers, why was such a wond'rous Piece of Art left imperfect?' He had many other wild Reasonings upon the lamentable Subject, but falling from these to more calm Reflections, he examined her Note again, and finding by the last Words that she loved him, he might presently imagine, that if he found not some Means of declaring the Continuance of his Love, the innocent Lady might conjecture herself slighted, upon the Discovery of her Affection and Infirmity: Prompted, by which Thought, and animated by the Emotions of his Passion, he ventured to knock at her Door; she having by this Time dressed herself, ventured to let him in: Dangerfield ran towards her, and catching her with an eager Embrace, gave her a thousand Kisses; 'Madam, (said he) you find that pardoning Offences only prepares more, by emboldning the Offender; but, I hope, Madam,' shewing her the Note, 'this is a general Pardon for all Offences of this sort, by which I am so encouraged to Transgress, that I shall never cease Crimes of this Nature'; Kissing her again. His Happiness was interrupted by Belvideera's coming Home, who running up Stairs, called, 'Sister, Sister, I have News to tell you': Her Voice alarms Maria, who fearing the Jealousy of Belvideera, shou'd she find Dangerfield in her Bed-Chamber, made Signs that he shou'd run into the Closet, which she had just lock'd as Belvideera came in: 'Oh, Sister! (said Belvideera) in a lucky Hour went I abroad this Morning.' In a more lucky Hour stay'd I at home this Morning, thought Maria. 'I have, (continued she,) been Instrumental in parting two Gentlemen fighting this Morning, and what is more, my Father had parted them before, when engag'd with the fine English Gentleman we saw at the Ball yesterday; but the greatest News of all is, that this fine English Gentleman is now in the House, and must Dine here to Day; but you must not appear, Sister, because 'twere a Shame to let Strangers know that you are Dumb.' Maria perceived her Jealousy, pointed to her Limbs, intimating thereby, that it was as great a Shame for her to be seen by Strangers; but she made farther Signs, that since it was her Pleasure, she wou'd keep her Chamber all that Day, and not appear abroad. Belvideera was extreamly glad of her Resolution, hoping that she shou'd enjoy Dangerfield's Conversation without any Interruption. The Consternation of the Spark in the Closet all this while was not little, he heard the Voice of the Charmer, that had so captivated him, he found that she was Sister to that Lady, whom he just now was making so many Protestations to, but he cou'd not imagine how she was Instrumental in parting the two Gentlemen, that shou'd have fought him; the Occasion was this:

Gonzago and Erizo, parting from Rinaldo and Dangerfield, had walk'd towards the Rialto, and both exasperated that they had missed their intended Revenge against Dangerfield, turned their Fury upon each other, first raising their Anger by incensed Expostulations, then drawing their Swords, engaged in a desperate Combat, when a Voice very loud calling, (Erizo, hold) stopt their Fury to see whence it proceeded; when a Coach driving at full Flight stopt close by them, and Francisco the Venetian Admiral leaped out with his Sword drawn, saying, 'Gentlemen, pray let me be an Instrument of Pacification: As for your part, Erizo, this Proceeding suits not well with the Business I am to move in Favour of you in the Senate to Day; the Post you sue for claims your Blood to be spilt against the common Foe, not in private Resentment, to the Destruction of a Citizen; and therefore I intreat you as my Friend, or I command you as your Officer, to put up.' Erizo, unwilling to disoblige his Admiral, upon whose Favour his Advancement depended, told Gonzago, that he must find another time to talk with him. 'No, no, Gentlemen, (said the

Admiral) you shall not part 'till I have reconciled you, and therefore let me know your Cause of Quarrel.' Erizo therefore related to him the whole Affair, and mentioning that Dangerfield was gone Home to Dine with Rinaldo; 'With Rinaldo my Father?' said Belvideera from the Coach, overjoy'd with Hopes of seeing Dangerfield at Home. 'Yes, (reply'd Gonzago surpriz'd) if Rinaldo the Senator be your Father, Madam.' 'Yes, he is,' reply'd Belvideera. Gonzago then knew her to be the Lady he was enamour'd of, and for whom he wou'd have fought Dangerfield; and now cursed his ill Fate, that he had deny'd Rinaldo's Invitation, which lost him the Conversation of his Mistress, which his Rival wou'd be sure of. 'Come, come, Gentlemen, (said the Admiral) you shall accompany me to see this Stranger at Rinaldo's House, I bear a great Esteem for him, and so it behoves every loyal Venetian, for whose Service he hath been so signal.' Erizo, unwilling to deny the Admiral, and Gonzago glad of an Opportunity of his Mistress's Company, which he just now thought lost, consented to the Proposal, and mounting all into the Coach, the three Gentlemen were set down at the Senate, and the Lady drove Home as above-mentioned.

Rinaldo in the mean Time was not idle in the Senate, there being a Motion made for Election of a Captain to the Rialto Galleon, made void by the Death of its former Commander in the late Fight, and which was the Post designed by the Admiral for Erizo. Rinaldo catching an Opportunity of obliging Dangerfield, for whom he entertain'd a great Love and Respect, proposed him as a Candidate for the Command, urging his late brave Performance against the Turks, and how much it concerned the Interest of the State to encourage Foreigners. He being the Admiral's Brother, and being so fervent in the Affair, had by an unanimous Consent his Commission sign'd just as his Brother came into the Senate, who fearing how Things were carried, comforted Erizo by future Preferment; but Erizo, however he stifled his Resentment, was struck with Envy, that a Stranger, and his Enemy shou'd be preferred to him, and resolved Revenge on the first Opportunity. They all went home with Rinaldo, and arrived whilst Belvideera was talking above Stairs with her Sister. Rinaldo, impatient to communicate his Success to Dangerfield, ran into the Study, where he left him; but missing him there, went into the Garden, and searching all about, returned to the Company, telling them he believ'd Dangerfield had fallen asleep in some private Arbor in the Garden, where he cou'd not find him, or else impatient of his long stay, had departed; but he was sure, if he had gone, he wou'd soon return: However they went to Dinner, and Belvideera came down, making an Apology for her Sister's Absence, thro' an Indisposition that had seized her. Gonzago had his wished for Opportunity of entertaining his Mistress, whilst she always expecting some News of Dangerfield, sat very uneasie in his Company; whilst Dangerfield in the Closet, was as impatient to see her. The short Discourse she had with her Sister, gave him assurance that his Love wou'd not be unacceptable. Maria durst not open the Closet, afraid that her Sister shou'd come up every Minute, besides, 'twas impossible to convey him out of the Chamber undiscovered, untill 'twas dark, which made him Wonder what occasioned his long Confinement; and being tired with sitting, got up to the Window, and softly opening the Casement, looked out to take the Air; his Footman walking accidentally in the Court, and casting up his Eye that way, spy'd him, which confirm'd his Patience in attending for him at the Gate; at length it grew Dark, and Maria knowing that her Sister was engag'd in a Match at Cards with her Father, Gonzago and Erizo, the Admiral being gone, she came softly to the Closet, and innocently took Dangerfield by the Hand, to lead him out, he clapt the dear soft Hand to his Mouth, and kissing it eagerly, it fired his Blood, and the unhappy Opportunity adding to the Temptation, raised him to the highest Pitch of Passion; he found himself with the most beautiful Creature in the World, one who loved him, he knew they were alone in the Dark, in a Bed-chamber, he knew the Lady young and melting, he knew besides she cou'd not tell, and he was conscious of his Power in moving; all these wicked Thoughts concurring, establish'd him in the Opinion, that this was the critical Minute of his Happiness, resolving therefore not to lose it, he fell down on his Knees, devouring her tender Hand, sighing out his Passion, begging her to Crown it with her Love, making Ten thousand Vows and Protestations of his Secrecy and Constancy, urging all the Arguments that the Subtilty of the Devil or

Man could suggest. She held out against all his Assaults above two Hours, and often endeavoured to Struggle from him, but durst make no great Disturbance, thro' fear of Alarming the Company below, at last he redoubling his Passion with Sighs, Tears, and all the rest of Love's Artillery, he at last gain'd the Fort, and the poor conquered Lady, all panting, soft, and trembling every Joynt, melted by his Embraces, he there fatally enjoy'd the greatest Extasy of Bliss, heightned by the Circumstances of Stealth, and Difficulty in obtaining. The ruin'd Lady now too late deplored the Loss of her Honour; but he endeavour'd to Comfort her by making Vows of Secrecy, and promising to salve her Reputation by a speedy Marriage, which he certainly intended, had not the unhappy Crisis of his Fate been so near. The Company by this Time had gone off, and Belvideera had retir'd to her Chamber, melancholy that she had missed her Hopes of seeing Dangerfield. Gonzago and Erizo going out of the Gate, saw Dangerfield's Footman, whom they knew, since they saw him with his Master in the Morning. Gonzago asked him why he waited there? 'For my Master, Sir,' reply'd the Footman. 'Your Master is not here sure,' said Gonzago. 'Yes, but he is, Sir,' said the Servant, 'for I attended him hither this Morning with Rinaldo, and saw him in the Afternoon look out of a Window above Stairs.' 'Ha!' said Gonzago, calling Erizo aside, 'by Heavens, he lies here to Night then, and perhaps with my Mistress; I perceiv'd she was not pressing for our Stay, but rather urging our Departure. Erizo, Erizo, this Block must be remov'd, he has stepped between you and a Command to Day, and perhaps may lye between me and my Mistress to Night.' 'By Hell (answered Erizo) thou hast raised a Fury in me, that will not be lulled asleep, but by a Potion of his Blood; let's dispatch this Blockhead first': And running at the Footman, with one Thrust killed him. Dangerfield by this time had been let out, and hearing the Noise, ran to the Place; they presently assaulted him; he defended himself very bravely the space of some Minutes, having wounded Gonzago in the Breast; when Rinaldo hearing the Noise, came out; but too late for Dangerfield's Relief, and too soon for his own Fate; for Gonzago, exasperated by his Wound, ran treacherously behind Dangerfield, and thrust him quite thro' the Body. He finding the mortal Wound, and wild with Rage, thrust desperately forward at Erizo, when at the instant Rinaldo striking in between to part them, received Dangerfield's Sword in his Body, which pierced him quite thro'. He no sooner fell, than Dangerfield perceived his fatal Error, and the other Two fled. Dangerfield curs'd his Fate, and begg'd with all the Prayers and Earnestness of a dying Man, that Rinaldo wou'd forgive him. 'Oh!' said Rinaldo, 'you have ill rewarded me for my Care in your Concerns in the Senate to Day.' The Servants coming out, took up Rinaldo, and Dangerfield leaning upon his Sword, they led him in. Belvideera first heard the Noise, and running down first met the horrid Spectacle, her dear Father breathing out his last, and her Lover, whom she had all that Day flattered her self with Hopes of seeing, she now beheld in Streams of his Blood; but what must poor Maria's Case be? besides the Grief for her Father's Fate, she must view that dear Man, lately Happy in her Embraces, now folded in the Arms of Death, she finds herself bereft of a Parent, her Love, her Honour, and the Defender of it, all at once; and the greatest Torment is, that she must bear all this Anguish, and cannot Ease her Soul by expressing it. Belvideera sat wiping the Blood from her Father's Wound, whilst mournful Maria sat by Dangerfield, administring all the Help she cou'd to his fainting Spirits; whilst he viewed her with greater Excess of Grief, than he had heretofore with Pleasure; being sensible what was the Force of her silent Grief, and the Wrong he had done her, which now he cou'd never Redress: He had accidentally dropt his Wig in the Engagement, and inclining his Head over the Couch where he lay, Rinaldo casting his Eye upon him, perceiv'd the Mark of a bloody Dagger on his Neck, under his left Ear: 'Sir, (said Rinaldo, raising himself up) I conjure you answer me directly, were you born with the Mark of that Dagger, or have you received it since by Accident.' 'I was certainly born with it,' answer'd he. 'Just such a Mark had my Son Cosmo, who was lost in the Adriatick.' 'How! (reply'd Dangerfield, starting up with a wild Confusion) Lost! say'st thou in the Adriatick? Your Son lost in the Adriatick?' 'Yes, yes,' said Rinaldo, 'too surely lost in the Adriatick.' 'O ye impartial Powers (said Dangerfield), why did you not reveal this before? Or why not always conceal it? How happy had been the Discovery some few Hours ago, and how Tragical is it now? For know,' continued he, addressing himself to Rinaldo, 'know that my suppos'd Father, who was a Turky Merchant, upon his Death-bed call'd me to him, and told me 'twas time to undeceive me, I was not his Son, he found me in the Adriatick Sea, ty'd to two Planks in his Voyage from Smyrna to London; having no Children, he educated me as his own, and finding me worth his Care, left me all his Inheritance with this dying Command, that I shou'd seek my Parents at Venice.' Belvideera hearkning all this while to the lamentable Story, then conjectured whence proceeded the natural Affection the whole Family bore him, and embracing him, cry'd out, 'Oh my unhappy Brother.' Maria all the while had strong and wild Convulsions of Sorrow within her, 'till the working Force of her Anguish racking at once all the Passages of her Breast, by a violent Impulse, broke the Ligament that doubled in her Tongue, and she burst out with this Exclamation; 'Oh! Incest, Incest.' Dangerfield eccho'd that Outcry with this, 'O! Horror, Horror, I have enjoy'd my Sister, and murder'd my Father.' Maria running distracted about the Chamber, at last spy'd Dangerfield's Sword, by which he had supported himself into the House, and catching it up, reeking with the Blood of her Father, plung'd it into her Heart, and throwing herself into Dangerfield's Arms, calls out, 'O my Brother, O my Love,' and expir'd. All the Neighbourhood was soon alarm'd by the Out-cries of the Family. I lodged within three Doors of Rinaldo's House, and running presently thither, saw a more bloody Tragedy in Reality, than what the most moving Scene ever presented; the Father and Daughter were both dead, the unfortunate Son was gasping out his last, and the surviving Sister most miserable, because she must survive such Misfortunes, cry'd to me; 'O! behold the Fate of your wretched Countryman.' I cou'd make no Answer, being struck dumb by the Horror of such woeful Objects; but Dangerfield hearing her name his Country, turning towards me, with a languishing and weak Tone, 'Madam,' said he, 'I was your Countryman, and wou'd to Heavens I were so still; if you hear my Story mention'd, on your Return to England, pray give these strange Turns of my Fate not the Name of Crimes, but favour them with the Epithet of Misfortunes; my Name is not Dangerfield, but Cla -' His Voice there fail'd him, and he presently dy'd; Death seeming more favourable than himself, concealing the fatal Author of so many Misfortunes, for I cou'd never since learn out his Name; but have done him the justice, I hope, to make him be pity'd for his Misfortunes, not hated for his Crimes. Francisco being sent for, had Gonzago and Erizo apprehended, condemn'd, and executed. Belvideera consign'd all her Father's Estate over to her Uncle, reserving only a Competency to maintain her a Recluse all the rest of her Life.

NOTES: The Dumb Virgin.

Dangerfield. This name is not to be found in any one of Mrs. Behn's plays, but as it does occur in Sedley's Bellamira; or, The Mistress (1687), one can only conclude that Aphra gave it to Sir Charles and altered her own character's nomenclature. Mrs. Behn, it may be remembered, was more than once extraordinarily careless with regard to the names of the Dramatis Personæ in her comedies. A striking example occurs in Sir Patient Fancy, where the 'precise clerk' is called both Abel and Bartholomew. In The Feign'd Curtezans Silvio and Sabina are persistently confused, and again, in The Town Fop (Vol. III, p. 15 and p. 20), the name Dresswell is retained for Friendlove. Sedley's Bellamira is derived from Terence's Eunuchus, and Dangerfield is Thraso; the Pyrgopolinices, Miles Gloriosus, of Plautus.

THE WANDERING BEAUTY

I was not above twelve Years old, as near as I can remember, when a Lady of my Acquaintance, who was particularly concern'd in many of the Passages, very pleasantly entertain'd me with the Relation of the young Lady Arabella's Adventures, who was eldest Daughter to Sir Francis Fairname, a Gentleman of a noble Family, and of a very large Estate in the West of England, a true Church-Man, a great Loyalist, and a most discreetly-indulgent Parent; nor was his Lady any Way inferiour to him in every Circumstance of Virtue. They had only two Children more, and those were of the soft, unhappy Sex too; all very beautiful, especially Arabella, and all very much alike; piously educated, and courtly too, of naturally-virtuous Principles and Inclinations.

'Twas about the sixteenth Year of her Age, that Sir Robert Richland, her Father's great Friend and inseparable Companion, but superiour to him in Estate as well as Years, felt the resistless Beauty of this young Lady raging and burning in his aged Veins, which had like to have been as fatal to him, as a Consumption, or his Climacterical Year of Sixty Three, in which he dy'd, as I am told, though he was then hardly Sixty. However, the Winter Medlar would fain have been inoculated in the Summer's Nacturine. His unseasonable Appetite grew so strong and inordinate, that he was oblig'd to discover it to Sir Francis; who, though he lov'd him very sincerely, had yet a Regard to his Daughter's Youth, and Satisfaction in the Choice of a Husband; especially, when he consider'd the great Disproportion in their Age, which he rightly imagin'd would be very disagreeable to Arabella's Inclinations: This made him at first use all the most powerful and perswading Arguments in his Capacity, to convince Sir Robert of the Inequality of such a Match, but all to no Purpose; for his Passion increasing each Day more violently, the more assiduously, and with the greater Vehemence, he press'd his Friend to use his Interest and Authority with his Lady and Daughter, to consent to his almost unnatural Proposition; offering this as the most weighty and prevailing Argument, (which undoubtedly it was,) That since he was a Batchelor, he would settle his whole Estate upon her, if she surviv'd him, on the Day of Marriage, not desiring one Penny as a Portion with her. This Discourse wrought so powerfully with her Mother, that she promis'd the old Lover all the Assistance he could hope or expect from her: In order to which, the next Day she acquainted her fair Daughter with the Golden Advantage she was like to have, if she would but consent to lye by the Parchment that convey'd them to her. The dear, fair Creature, was so surpriz'd at this Overture made by her Mother, that her Roses turn'd all into Lillies, and she had like to have swoon'd away; but having a greater Command of her Passions than usually our Sex have, and chiefly Persons of her Age, she, after some little Disorder, which by no Means she could dissemble, she made as dutiful a Return to her Mother's Proposition, as her Aversion to it would permit; and, for that Time, got Liberty to retreat, and lament in private the Misfortune which she partly fore-saw was impending. But her Grief (alas) was no Cure of her Malady; for the next Day she was again doubly attack'd by her Father and Mother, with all the Reasons that Interest and Duty could urge, which she endeavour'd to obviate by all the Arguments that Nature and Inclination could offer; but she found them all in vain, since they continu'd their ungrateful Solicitations for several Days together, at the End of which, they both absolutely commanded her to prepare her self for her Nuptials with Sir Robert; so that finding her self under a Necessity of complying, or at least of seeming so, she made 'em hope, that her Duty had overcome her Aversion; upon which she had a whole Week's Liberty to walk where she would, unattended, or with what Company she pleas'd, and to make Visits to whom she had a Mind, either of her Relations or Acquaintance thereabouts; tho' for three or four Days before, she was strictly confin'd to her Chamber.

After Dinner, on the third Day of her Enlargement, being Summer Time, she propos'd to her Mother that she would take a Walk to a Cousin of hers, who liv'd about four Miles thence, to intreat her to be one of her Bride-Maids, being then in a careless plain Dress, and having before discours'd very pleasantly and freely of her Wedding-Day, of what Friends she would have invited to that Solemnity, and what Hospitality Sir Robert should keep when she was marry'd to him: All which was highly agreeable to her Parents, who then could not forbear thanking and kissing her for it, which she return'd to 'em both with a Shower of Tears. This did not a little surprize 'em at first, but asking her what could cause such Signs of Sorrow, after so chearful a Discourse on the late Subject? She answer'd, 'That the Thoughts of her going now suddenly to live from so dear and tender a Father and Mother, were the sole Occasion of such Expressions of Grief.' This affectionate Reply did amply satisfy their Doubts; and she presently took Leave of 'em, after having desir'd that they would not be uneasy if she should not return 'till a little before 'twas dark, or if her Cousin should oblige her to stay all Night with her; which they took for a discreet Caution in her, considering that young Maidens love dearly to talk of Marriage Affairs, especially when so near at Hand: And thus easily parted with her, when they had walk'd with her about a Mile, over a Field or two of their own.

Never before that Time was the dear Creature glad that her Father and Mother had left her, unless when they had press'd her to a Marriage with the old Knight. They were therefore no sooner got out of Sight, e're she took another Path, that led cross the Country, which she persu'd 'till past eight at Night, having walk'd ten Miles since two a Clock, when Sir Francis and her Mother left her: She was just now got to a little Cottage, the poor, but cleanly Habitation of a Husbandman and his Wife, who had one only Child, a Daughter, about the Lady Arabella's Age and Stature. 'Twas happy for her she got thither before they were a Bed; for her soft and beautiful Limbs began now to be tir'd, and her tender Feet to be gall'd. To the good Woman of the House she applies her self, desiring Entertainment for that Night, offering her any reasonable Satisfaction. The good Wife, at first Sight of her, had Compassion of her, and immediately bid her walk in, telling her, that she might lye with her Daughter, if she pleas'd, who was very cleanly, tho' not very vine. The good Man of the House came in soon after, was very well pleas'd with his new Guest; so to Supper they went very seasonably; for the poor young Lady, who was e'en ready to faint with Thirst, and not overcharg'd with what she had eaten the Day before. After Supper they ask'd her whence she came, and how she durst venture to travel alone, and a Foot? To which she reply'd, That she came from a Relation who liv'd at Exeter, with whom she had stay'd 'till she found she was burthensome: That she was of Welsh Parents, and of a good Family; but her Father dying, left a cruel Mother-in-Law, with whom she could by no Means continue, especially since she would have forc'd her to marry an old Man, whom it was impossible she should love, tho' he was very rich: That she was now going to seek her Fortune in London, where she hop'd, at least, to get her a good Service. They all seem'd to pity her very heartily; and, in a little Time after, they went to their two several Apartments, in one of which Arabella and the Damsel of the House went to Bed, where the young Lady slept soundly, notwithstanding the Hardness of her Lodging. In the Morning, about Four, according to her laudable Custom, the young hardy Maiden got up to her daily Employment; which waken'd Arabella, who presently bethought her self of an Expedient for her more secure and easy Escape from her Parents Pursuit and Knowledge, proposing to her Bedfellow an Exchange of their Wearing-Apparel. The Heiress and Hope of that little Family was extreamly fond of the Proposal, and ran immediately to acquaint her Mother with it, who was so well pleas'd, that she could hardly believe it, when the young Lady confirm'd it, and especially, when she understood the Exchange was to be made on even Hands. 'If you be in earnest, Forsooth, (said the Mother) you shall e'en have her Sunday-Cloaths.' 'Agreed (return'd Arabella) but we must change Shifts too; I have now a Couple about me, new and clean, I do assure you: For my Hoods and Head-dress you shall give me two Pinners, and her best Straw-Hat; and for my Shoes, which I have not worn above a Week, I will have her Holliday Shoes.' 'A Match, indeed, young Mistress,' cry'd the good Wife. So without more Ceremony, the young unhappy Lady was attir'd in her Bedfellow's Country Weeds, by Help of the Mother and Daughter. Then, after she had taken her Leave of the good old Man too, she put a broad round Shilling into his Wife's Hand, as a Reward for her Supper and Lodging, which she would fain have return'd, but t'other would not receive it. 'Nay, then, by the Mackins, (said her Hostess) you shall take a Breakfast e're you go, and a Dinner along with you, for Fear you should be sick by the Way.' Arabella stay'd to eat a Mess of warm Milk, and took some of their

Yesterday's Provision with her in a little course Linnen Bag. Then asking for the direct Road to London, and begging a few green Wall-nuts, she took her last Farewel of them.

Near Twelve at Noon she came to a pleasant Meadow, through which there ran a little Rivulet of clear Water, about nine miles from her last Lodging, but quite out of the Way to London. Here she sate down, and after drinking some of the Water out of the Hollow of her Hand, she open'd her Bag, and made as good a Meal as the Courseness of the Fare, and the Niceness of her Appetite would permit: After which, she bruis'd the outward green Shells of a Wall-nut or two, and smear'd her lovely Face, Hands, and Part of her Arms, with the Juice; then looking into the little purling Stream, that seem'd to murmur at the Injury she did to so much Beauty, she sigh'd and wept, to think to what base Extremities she was now likely to be reduc'd! That she should be forc'd to stain that Skin which Heaven had made so pure and white! 'But ah! (cry'd she to her self) if my Disobedience to my Parents had not stain'd my Conscience worse, this needed not to have been done.' Here she wept abundantly again; then, drying her Eyes, she wash'd her Feet to refresh 'em, and thence continu'd her Journey for ten Miles more, which she compass'd by seven a Clock; when she came to a Village, where she got Entertainment for that Night, paying for it, and the next Morning, before Six, as soon as she had fill'd her little Bag with what good Chear the Place afforded, she wander'd on 'till Twelve again, still crossing the Country, and taking her Course to the Northern Parts of England, which doubtless was the Reason her Father and his Servants miss'd of her in their Pursuit; for he imagin'd that for certain she had taken her nearest Way to London. After she had refresh'd her self for an Hour's Time by the Side of a Wood, she arose and wander'd again near twelve Miles by eight a Clock, and lodg'd at a good substantial Farmer's.

Thus she continu'd her Errantry for above a Fortnight, having no more Money than just thirty Shillings, half of which brought her to Sir Christian Kindly's House in Lancashire. 'Twas near five a Clock in the Afternoon when she reach'd that happy Port, when, coming to the Hall Door, she enquir'd for the Lady of the House, who happily was just coming into the Hall with a little Miss in her Arms, of about four Years old, very much troubled with weak and sore Eyes: The fair Wanderer, addressing her self to the Lady with all the Humility and Modesty imaginable, begg'd to know if her Ladyship had any Place in her Family vacant, in which she might do her Service? To which the Lady return'd, (by Way of Question) Alas! poor Creature! what canst thou do? Any thing, may it please your Ladyship, (reply'd the disguis'd Beauty) any thing within my Strength and my Knowledge, I mean, Madam. Thou say'st well, (said the Lady) and I'm sorry I have not any vacant for thee. I beseech your Ladyship then (said Arabella) let me lodge in your Barn to-Night; for I am told it is a great Way hence to any Town, and I have but little Money. In my Barn, poor Girl! (cry'd the Lady, looking very earnestly on her) ay, God forbid else, unless we can find a better Lodging for thee. Art thou hungry or thirsty? Yes, Madam (reply'd the wandering Fair One) I could both eat and drink, if it please your Ladyship. The Lady commanded Victuals and Drink to be brought, and could not forbear staying in the Hall 'till she had done; when she ask'd her several Questions, as of what Country she was? To which she answer'd truly, of Somersetshire. What her Parents were, and if living? To which she return'd, They were good, honest, and religious People, and she hop'd they were alive, and in as good Health as when she left 'em. After the Lady had done catechising her, Arabella, looking on the little Child in her Ladyship's Arms, said, Pardon me, Madam, I beseech you, if I am too bold in asking your Ladyship how that pretty Creature's Eyes came to be so bad? By an extream Cold which she took, (reply'd the Lady.) I had not presum'd (return'd t'other) to have ask'd your Ladyship this Question, were I not assur'd that I have an infallible Cure for the Infirmity; and if, Madam, you will be pleas'd to let me apply it, I will tell your Ladyship the Remedy in private. The Lady was much surpriz'd to hear a young Creature, so meanly habited, talk so genteelly; and after surveying her very strictly, said the Lady, Have you ever experienc'd it before? Yes, Madam (reply'd the fair Physician) and never without happy Success: I dare engage, Madam, (added she) that I will make 'em as well as my own, by God's Blessing, or else I will be content to lose mine, which Heaven forbid. Amen, (cry'd the good Lady) for they are very fine ones, on my Word. Stay, Child, I will desire Sir Christian to hear it with me; and if he approves it, you shall about it; and if it take good Effect, we will endeavour to requite the Care and Pains it shall cost you. Saying thus, she immediately left her, and return'd very speedily with Sir Christian, who having discours'd Arabella for some time, with great Satisfaction and Pleasure, took her into the Parlour with his Lady, where she communicated her Secret to 'em both; which they found so innocent and reasonable, that they desir'd her to prepare it as soon as possible, and to make her Application of it with all convenient Speed; which she could not do 'till the next Morning. In the mean Time she was order'd a Lodging with the House-Maid, who reported to her Lady, That she found her a very sweet and cleanly Bed-fellow; (adding) That she never saw nor felt so white, so smooth, and soft a Skin. Arabella continu'd her Remedy with such good Success, that in a Fortnight's Time little Miss's Eyes were as lively and strong as ever. This so endear'd her to the Knight and his Lady, that they created a new Office in their Family, purposely for her, which was, Attendant on their eldest Daughter Eleanora, a Lady much about her Years and Stature; who was so charm'd with her Conversation, that she could not stir Abroad, nor eat, nor sleep, without Peregrina Goodhouse (for those were the Names she borrow'd:) Nor was her Modesty, Humility, and Sweetness of Temper, less engaging to her Fellow-Servants, who all strove which should best express their Love to her. On Festival-Days, and for the Entertainment of Strangers, she would lend her helping Hand to the Cook, and make the Sauce for every Dish, though her own Province was only to attend the young Lady, and prepare the Quidlings, and other Sweet-Meats, for the Reception of Sir Christian's Friends; all which she did to Admiration. In this State of easy Servitude she liv'd there for near three Years, very well contented at all Times, but when she bethought her self of her Father, Mother, and Sisters, courted by all the principal Men-Servants, whom she refus'd in so obliging a Manner, and with such sweet, obliging Words, that they could not think themselves injur'd, though they found their Addresses were in vain. Mr. Prayfast, the Chaplain himself, could not hold out against her Charms. For her Skin had long since recover'd its native Whiteness; nor did she need Ornaments of Cloaths to set her Beauty off, if any Thing could adorn her, since she was dress'd altogether as costly, though not so richly (perhaps) as Eleanora. Prayfast therefore found that the Spirit was too weak for the Flesh, and gave her very broad Signs of his Kindness in Sonnets, Anagrams, and Acrosticks, which she receiv'd very obligingly of him, taking a more convenient Time to laugh at 'em with her young Lady.

Her kind Reception of them encourag'd him to that Degree, that within a few Days after, supposing himself secure on her Side, he apply'd himself to the good old Knight, his Patron, for his Consent to a Marriage with her, who very readily comply'd with his Demands, esteeming it a very advantagious Match for Peregrina, and withal told him, That he would give him three hundred Pounds with her, besides the first Benefit that should fall in his Gift. But (said he) as I doubt not that you are sufficiently acquainted with her Virtues and other excellent Qualifications, 'tis necessary that you should know the worst that I can tell you of her, which is, that she came to us a meer Stranger, in a very mean, tho' cleanly Habit; and therefore, as she confesseth, we may conclude, of very humble, yet honest Parentage. A! (possibly) her Father might have been, or is, some Husbandman, or somewhat inferiour to that; for we took her up at the Door, begging one Night's Entertainment in the Barn. How, Sir! (cry'd Prayfast, starting) have you no better Knowledge of her Birth, than what you are pleas'd to discover now? No better, nor more (reply'd the Knight.) Alas! Sir, then (return'd the proud canonical Sort of a Farmer) she is no Wife for me; I shall dishonour my Family by marrying so basely. Were you never told any Thing of this before? (ask'd the Knight.) You know, Sir, (answer'd the Prelate that would be) that I have not had the Honour to officiate, as your Chaplain, much more than half a Year; in which Time, 'tis true, I have heard that she was receiv'd as a Stranger; but that she came in so low a Capacity I never learn'd 'till now. I find then, Parson, (said the Knight) that you do not like the Author of your Happiness, at least, who might be so, because she comes to you in such an humble Manner; I tell you the Jews are miserable for the same Reason. She cannot be such perfectly to me (return'd t'other) without the Advantage of good Birth. With that I'm sure she would not, return'd his Patron, and left him to go to Peregrina, whom he happily found alone. Child, (said he to her) have you any Obligation to Mr. Prayfast? As how, Sir? She ask'd. Do you love him? Have you made him any Promise of Marriage? Or has he any Way engag'd himself to you? Neither, Sir, (she answer'd.) 'Tis true, I love him as my Fellow-Servant, no otherwise. He has indeed been somewhat lavish of his Wit and Rhimes to me, which serv'd well enough to divert my young Lady and me. But of all Mankind, perhaps, he should be the last I would choose for a Husband. I thought (said the good-humour'd old Knight) that he had already obtain'd a Promise from you, since he came but just now to ask my Consent, which I freely gave him at first, upon that Thought; but he is doubtful of your Birth, and fears it may dishonour his Family, if he should marry you. On my Word, Sir, (return'd Peregrina, blushing with Disdain, no doubt) our Families are by no Means equal. What thy Family is, I know not; (said Sir Christian) but I am sure thou art infinitely superiour to him in all the natural Embelishments both of Body and Mind. Be just to thy self, and be not hasty to wed: Thou hast more Merit than Wealth alone can purchase. O! dear Sir, (she return'd) you ruin me with Obligations never to be re-paid, but in Acknowledgment, and that imperfectly too. Here they were interrupted by the young Lady, to whom she repeated the Conference betwixt Sir Christian and Prayfast, as soon as ever Sir Christian left the Room.

About a Week after, Sir Lucius Lovewell, (a young Gentleman, of a good Presence, Wit, and Learning enough, whose Father, dying near a Twelve-month before, had left him upwards of 3000l. a Year, which, too, was an excellent Accomplishment, tho' not the best; for he was admirably good-humour'd) came to visit Sir Christian Kindly; and, as some of the Family imagin'd, 'twas with Design to make his Addresses to the young Lady, Sir Christian's Daughter. Whatever his Thoughts were, his Treatment, there, was very generous and kind. He saw the Lady, and lik'd her very well; nay, doubtless, would have admitted a Passion for her, had not his Destiny at the same Time shewn him Peregrina. She was very beautiful, and he as sensible; and 'tis not to be doubted, but that he immediately took Fire. However, his Application and Courtship, free and unaffected, were chiefly directed to Sir Christian's Daughter: Some little Respects he paid to Peregrina, who could not choose but look on him as a very fine, good-humour'd, and well-accomplish'd Gentleman. When the Hour came that he thought fit to retreat, Sir Christian ask'd him, When he would make 'em happy again in his Conversation? To which he return'd, That since he was not above seven or eight Miles from him, and that there were Charms so attractive at Sir Christian's, he should take the Liberty to visit him sooner and oftener than he either expected or desir'd. T'other reply'd, That was impossible; and so, without much more Ceremony, he took his Leave of that delightful Company for two or three Days; at the End of which he return'd, with Thoughts much different from those at his first Coming thither, being strongly agitated by his Passion for Peregrina. He took and made all the Opportunities and Occasions that Chance and his own Fancy could offer and present to talk to her, both before, at, and after Dinner; and his Eyes were so constantly fix'd on her, that he seem'd to observe nothing else; which was so visible to Sir Christian, his Lady, and Daughter, that they were convinc'd of their Error, in believing, that he came to make his Court to the young Lady. This late Discovery of the young Knight's Inclinations, was no Way unpleasant to Sir Christian and his Lady; and to the young Lady it was most agreeable and obliging, since her Heart was already pre-engag'd elsewhere; and since she did equally desire the good fortune of her beautiful Attendant with her own.

The Table was no sooner clear'd, and a loyal Health or two gone round, e're Sir Christian ask'd his young amorous Guest to take a Walk with him in the Gardens: To which Sir Lucius readily consented, designing to disclose that to him for a Secret, which was but too apparent to all that were present at Table: When therefore he thought he had sufficiently admir'd and commended the Neatness of the Walks and Beauty of the Flowers, he began, to this Effect:

Possibly, Sir Christian, I shall surprize you with the Discourse I'm going to make you; but 'tis certain no Man can avoid the Necessity of the Fate which he lies under; at least I have now found it so. I came at first, Sir, with the Hopes of prevailing on you to honour and make me happy in a Marriage with Madam Eleanora your Daughter; but at the same Instant I was seiz'd with so irresistable a Passion for the charming Peregrina, that I find no Empire, Fame, nor Wit, can make me perfectly bless'd here below, without the Enjoyment of that beautiful Creature. Do not mistake me, Sir, (I beseech you, continu'd he) I mean an honourable Enjoyment. I will make her my Wife, Sir, if you will be generously pleas'd to use your Interest with her on my Part.

To which the good old Knight reply'd, What you think (Sir) you have now imparted as a Secret, has been the general Observation of all my Family, e're since you gave us the Happiness of your Company to Day: Your Passion is too great to be disguis'd; and I am extremely pleas'd, that you can think any Thing in my House worthy the Honour you intend Peregrina. Indeed, had you made any particular and publick Address to my Daughter, I should have believ'd it want of Merit in her, or in us, her Parents, that you should, after that, quit your Pretensions to her, without any willing or known Offence committed on our Side. I therefore (Sir) approve your Choice, and promise you my utmost Assistance afar. She is really virtuous in all the Latitude of Virtue; her Beauty is too visible to be disputed ev'n by Envy it self: As for her Birth, she best can inform you of it; I must only let you know, that, as her Name imports, she was utterly a Stranger, and entertain'd by us in pure Charity. But the Antiquity and Honour of your Family can receive no Diminution by a Match with a beautiful and virtuous Creature, for whom, you say, and I believe, you have so true a Passion. I have now told you the worst (Sir) that I know of her; but your Wealth and Love may make you both eternally happy on Earth. And so they shall, by her dear self, (return'd the amorous Knight) if both of 'em may recommend me to her, with your Perswasions added, which still I beg. Say, rather you command; and with those three hundred Pounds which I promis'd her, if she marry'd with my Consent to Mr. Prayfast.

To this, the other smiling, reply'd, Her Person and Love is all I court or expect, Sir: But since you have thought her worthy of so great an Expression of your Favour and Kindness, I will receive it with all Humility as is from a Father, which I shall ever esteem you. But see, Sir, (cry'd he in an Extasy) how she comes, led by Madam Eleanora, your Daughter. The young Lady coming to him, began thus: I know (Sir) 'tis my Father and Mother's Desire and Ambition to shew you the heartiest Welcome in their Power, which can by no Means be made appear so particularly and undisputably, as by presenting you with what you like best in the Family: In Assurance therefore that I shall merit their Favour by this Act, I have brought your dear Peregrina to you, not without Advice, and some Instructions of mine, that may concern her Happiness with you, if discreetly observ'd and persu'd by her. In short, (Sir) I have told her, that a Gentleman of so good a Figure, such excellent Parts, and generous Education, of so ancient and honourable a Family, together with so plentiful an Estate as you at present possess, is capable of bringing Happiness to any, the fairest Lady in this Country at least. O Madam! (return'd Sir Lucius) your Obligation is so great, that I want Sense to receive it as I ought; much more Words to return you any proportionable Acknowledgment of it. But give me Leave to say thus much, Madam; that my Thoughts of making my Court to your Ladiship, first invited me to give Sir Christian, your Father, the Trouble of a Visit, since the Death of mine. However, the over-ruling Powers have thought to divert my Purpose, and the offering of my Heart, which can never rest, but with this dear charming Creature. Your Merits, Madam, are sufficient for the Gentleman on whom I entirely fix'd my Affections, before you did me the Honour and your self the Trouble of your first Visit (interrupted Sir Christian's Daughter.) And now, Sir, (added she to her Father) if you please, let us leave 'em to make an End of this Business between themselves. No, Madam, (cry'd Sir Lucius) your Father has promis'd me to make Use of his Interest with her for my Sake. This I now expect, Sir. Then (said the old Knight) thou dear beautiful and virtuous Stranger! if I have any Power to perswade thee, take my Advice, and this honourable Gentleman to thy loving Husband; I'm sure he'll prove so to thee. If I could command thee I would. Ah Sir! (said she, kneeling, with Tears falling from her charming Eyes) I know none living that has greater Right and Power. But (alas Sir!) this honourable Person knows not the Meanness of my Birth, at least, he cannot think it any Way proportionable or suitable to his. O thou dear Creature, (cry'd her Lover, setting one Knee to the Ground, and taking her up) Sir Christian has already discours'd all thy Circumstances to me: Rise and bless me with thy Consent. I must ask my Lady's, Sir, (she reply'd.) See, here my Mother comes (said the young Lady) and entreated her good Word for Sir Lucius. The good ancient Lady began then to use all the Arguments to incline her to yield to her Happiness; and, in fine, she was prevail'd on to say, I do consent, and will endeavour to deserve the honourable Title of your dutiful Wife, Sir. 'Twas with no common Joy and Transport that he receiv'd her Hand, and kiss'd those dear Lips that gave him an Assurance of his Happiness; which he resolv'd should begin about a Month or two afterwards; in which Time he might send Orders to London for the making their Wedding Cloaths. Into the House then they all went, Sir Lucius leading Peregrina, and the first they met of the Family was Prayfast, who was not a little surpriz'd nor discompos'd at that Sight; and more especially when Sir Christian told him, That tho' he did not think that beautiful sweet Stranger worthy the Title of his Wife, yet now he should be oblig'd to join her to that honourable Person. The Slave bow'd, and look'd very pale.

All Things were at last got ready for the Consummation of their Bliss, and Prayfast did their Business effectually, tho' much against his Will; however he receiv'd the Reward of twenty Broad Pieces. The Wedding was kept for a Week at Sir Christian's House; after which they adjourn'd to the Bridegroom's, where it lasted as long as Sir Christian, his Lady, Daughter, and the rest of that Family would stay. As they were leaving him, Sir Lucius dispos'd of two hundred Pounds amongst Sir Christian's Servants, and the rest of the three hundred he distributed among the Poor of both Parishes.

When they were gone, the affectionate tender Bridegroom could by no Means be perswaded by any Gentlemen, his Neighbours, to hunt with 'em, or to take any Divertisement, tho' but for half a Day; esteeming it the highest Unkindness imaginable to leave his Lady: Not that she could be alone neither in his Absence; for she never wanted the Visits of all the Ladies round about, and those of the best Quality; who were equally charm'd with her Sweetness of Temper, as the Men were with her outward Beauties. But in a Month's time, or thereabout, observing that he was continually solicited and courted to some Sport or Pastime with those Gentlemen of his Neighbourhood, she was forc'd to do her self the Violence to beg of him that he would divert himself with 'em, as before their Marriage he us'd: And she had so good Success, that he did allow himself two Days in the Week to hunt: In one of which, coming Home about five a Clock, and not finding his Lady below Stairs, he went directly up to her Chamber, where he saw her leaning her Head on her Hand, and her Handkerchief all bath'd in Tears. At this Sight he was strangely amaz'd and concern'd. Madam, (cry'd he in an unusual Tone) what means such Postures as these? Tell me! For I must know the Occasion. Surpriz'd, and trembling at this his unwonted Manner of saluting her, she started up, and then, falling on her Knees, she wept out, O thou dear Author and Lord of all my Joys on Earth! Look not, I beseech you, so wildly, nor speak terribly to me! Thou Center of all my Happiness below, (return'd he) rise, and make me acquainted with the dreadful Occasion of this afflicting and tormenting Sight! All you shall know, (she reply'd) dearest of human Blessings! But sit, and change your Looks; then I can speak. Speak then, my Life, (said he) but tell me all; all I must know. Is there a Thought about my Soul that you shall not partake? I'm sure there is not; (he reply'd) say on then. You know, Sir, (she return'd) that I have left my Parents now three Years, or thereabouts, and know not whether they are living or dead: I was reflecting, therefore, on the Troubles which my undutiful and long Absence may have caus'd them; for poor and mean as they may be, they well instructed me in all good Things; and I would once more, by your dear Permission, see them, and beg their Pardon for my Fault; for they are my Parents still, if living, Sir, though (unhappily) not worth your Regard. How! (cry'd he) can that Pair who gave my Dearest Birth, want my Regard, or ought I can do for them? No! thou shalt see them, and so will I: But tell me, Peregrina, is this the only Cause of your Discomposure? So may I still be bless'd in your dear Love, (she reply'd) as this is Truth, and all the Cause. When shall we see them, then? (he ask'd). We see them, (cry'd she) O! your Goodness descends too much; and you confound me with your unmerited and unexpected Kindness. 'Tis I alone that have offended, and I alone am fit to see them. That must not be; (return'd her affectionate Husband) no, we'll both go together; and if they want, either provide for them there, or take them hither with us. Your Education shews their Principles, and 'tis no Shame to own virtuous Relations. Come, dry thy dear lamenting Eyes; the Beginning of the next Week we'll set forwards. Was ever Disobedience so rewarded with such a Husband? (said she) those Tears have wash'd that childish Guilt away; and there is no Reward above thy Virtue.

In a few Days, Monday began the Date of their Journey to the West of England; and in five or six Days more, by the Help of a Coach and Six, they got to Cornwall; where, in a little Town, of little Accommodation, they were oblig'd to take up their Lodgings the first Night. In the Morning (said his Lady to him) My Dear, about a Mile and a half hence lives one Sir Francis Fairname and his Lady, if yet they be living, who have a very fine House, and worth your seeing; I beg of you therefore, that you will be so kind to your self as to walk thither, and dine with the old Gentleman; for that you must, if you see him; whilst I stay here, and send to my Father and Mother, if to be found, and prepare them to receive you at your Return. I must not have no Denial; (added she) for if you refuse this Favour, all my Designs are lost. Make Haste, my Life; 'tis now eleven a Clock; In your Absence I'll dress, to try if Change of Cloaths can hide me from them. This was so small a Request, that he did not stay to reply to't, but presently left her, and got thither in less than half an Hour, attended only by one Footman. He was very kindly and respectfully receiv'd by the old Gentleman, who had certainly been a very beautiful Person in his Youth; and Sir Lucius, fixing his Eyes upon his Face, could hardly remove 'em, being very pleasantly and surprisingly entertain'd with some Lines that he observ'd in it. But immediately recollecting himself, he told him, that having heard how fine a Seat that was, his Curiosity led him to beg the Favour that he might see it. The worthy old Knight return'd, that his House and all the Accommodations in it were at his Service: So inviting him in, he satisfy'd his pretended Curiosity; and after he had shewn all that was worthy the Sight of a Stranger, in the House, he led him into his Gardens, which furnish'd Sir Lucius with new Matter of Admiration; whence the old Knight brought him into the Parlour, telling him, that 'twas his Custom to suffer no Stranger to return, till he had either din'd or supp'd with him, according as the Hour of the Day or Night presented.

'Twas here the affectionate Husband was strangely surpriz'd at the Sight of a Picture, which so nearly counterfeited the Beauties of his dear-lov'd Lady, that he stood like an Image himself, gazing and varying; the Colours of his Face agitating by the Diversity of his Thoughts; which Sir Francis perceiving, ask'd him, What it was that so visibly concern'd him? To which he reply'd, That indeed he was concern'd, but with great Satisfaction and Pleasure, since he had never seen any Thing more beautiful than that Picture, unless it were a Lady for whom he had the most sincere Affection imaginable, and whom it did very nearly represent; and then enquir'd for whom that was drawn? Sir Francis answer'd him, 'Twas design'd for one who was, I dare not say who is, my Daughter; and the other two were drawn for her younger Sisters. And see, Sir, (persu'd he) here they come, following their Mother: At which Words Sir Lucius was oblig'd to divorce his Eyes from the charming Shadow, and make his Compliments to them; which were no sooner over than Dinner was serv'd in, where the young Knight eat as heartily as he could, considering he sate just opposite to it, and in Sight of the two Ladies, who were now exactly like his own Wife, though not so very beautiful.

The Table being uncover'd, Sir Lucius desir'd to know why Sir Francis said, He doubted whether the Original of that Picture were yet his Daughter? To which the Mother return'd (big with Sorrow, which was seen in her Tears) That her Husband had spoken but too rightly: For (added she) 'tis now three Years since we have either seen her or heard from her. How, Madam! three Years, (cry'd Sir Lucius) I believe I can shew your Ladiship a dear Acquaintance of mine, so wonderfully like that Picture, that I am almost perswaded she is the very Original; only (pardon me, Madam) she tells me her Parents are of mean Birth and Fortune. Dear Sir, (cry'd the tender Mother) Is she in this Country? She is not two Miles hence, reply'd Sir Lucius. By all Things most dear to you, Sir, (said the Lady) let us be so happy as to see her, and that with all convenient Expedition! for it will be a Happiness to see any Creature, the only Like my dearest Arabella. Arabella, Madam! alas! No, Madam, her Name is Peregrina. No Matter for Names, Sir, (cry'd the Lady) I want the Sight of the dear Creature. Sir, (added the worthy old Knight) I can assure you it will be an eternal Obligation to us; or, if you please, we will wait on you to her. By no Means, Sir, (return'd Sir Lucius) I will repeat my Trouble to you with her, in an Hour at farthest. We shall desire the Continuance of such Trouble as long as we live, reply'd Sir Francis. So, without farther Ceremony, Sir Lucius left 'em and return'd to his Lady, whom he found ready dress'd, as he wish'd he might. Madam, (said he) where are your Father and Mother? I know not, yet, my Dear, she reply'd. Well, (return'd he) we will expect 'em, or send for 'em hither at Night; in the mean Time I have engag'd to bring you with me to Sir Francis Fairname and his Lady, with all imaginable Expedition. So immediately, as soon as Coach and Six and Equipage was ready, he hurry'd her away with him to Sir Francis, whom they found walking with his Lady and two Daughters in the outward Court, impatiently expecting their Coming. The Boot of the Coach (for that was the Fashion in those Days) was presently let down, and Sir Lucius led his Lady forwards to them; who coming within three or four Paces of the good old Knight, his Lady fell on her Knees, and begg'd their Pardon and Blessing. Her affectionate Father answer'd 'em with Tears from his Eyes; but the good ancient Lady was so overcome with Joy, that she fell into a Swoon, and had like to have been accompany'd by her Daughter, who fell upon her Knees by her, and with her Shrieks recall'd her, when she strait cry'd out, My Daughter, my Daughter's come again! my Arabella alive! Ay, my dear offended Mother! with all the Duty and Penitence that Humanity is capable of, return'd the Lady Lovewell. Her Sisters then express'd their Love in Tears, Embraces, and Kisses, while her dear Husband begg'd a Blessing of her Parents, who were very pleasantly surpriz'd, to know that their Daughter was so happily marry'd, and to a Gentleman of such an Estate and Quality as Sir Lucius seem'd to be: 'Twas late that Night e'er they went to Bed at Sir Francis's. The next Day, after they had all pretty well eas'd themselves of their Passions, Sir Francis told his Son-in-Law, that as he had three Daughters, so he had 3000l. a Year, and he would divide it equally among 'em; but for Joy of the Recovery of his eldest Daughter, and her fortunate Match with so worthy a Gentleman as Sir Lucius, who had given him an Account of his Estate and Quality, he promis'd him ten thousand Pounds in ready Money besides; whereas the other young Ladies were to have but five thousand a Piece, besides their Dividend of the Estate. And now, (said he) Daughter, the Cause of your Retreat from us, old Sir Robert Richland, has been dead these three Months, on such a Day. How, Sir, (cry'd she) on such a Day! that was the very Day on which I was so happy as to be marry'd to my dear Sir Lucius.

She then gave her Father, and Mother, and Sisters, a Relation of all that had happen'd to her since her Absence from her dear Parents, who were extremely pleas'd with the Account of Sir Christian and his Lady's Hospitality and Kindness to her; and in less than a Fortnight after, they took a Journey to Sir Lucius's, carrying the two other young Ladies along with 'em; and, by the Way, they call'd at Sir

Christian's, where they arriv'd Time enough to be present the next Day at Sir Christian's Daughter's Wedding, which they kept there for a whole Fortnight.

two Pinners. A pinner is 'a coif with two long flaps one on each side pinned on and hanging down, and sometimes fastened at the breast . . . sometimes applied to the flaps as an adjunct of the coif.' N.E.D. cf. Pepys, 18 April, 1664: 'To Hyde Park . . . and my Lady Castlemaine in a coach by herself, in yellow satin and a pinner on.'

THE UNHAPPY MISTAKE; OR, THE IMPIOUS VOW PUNISH'D

The Effects of Jealousy have ever been most fatal; and it is certainly one of the most tormenting Passions that an human Soul can be capable of, tho' it be created by the least Appearances of Reason: The Truth of which this following Story will evince.

Sir Henry Hardyman was a Gentleman of a very large Estate in Somersetshire, of a very generous Temper, hospitable almost to Extravagancy; a plain down-right Dealer, wonderfully good-natur'd, but very passionate: Whose Lady dying, left him only a Son and a Daughter; between whom there were about six Years Difference in their Age. Miles Hardyman (for so the Son was call'd) being the eldest; both of naturally virtuous Inclinations, which were carefully improv'd by a generous and pious Education. Miles was a very tall, large, and well-proportion'd Person at Two and Twenty; brave and active, and seem'd to be born for War, tho' he had a Heart as tender and capable of receiving the Impressions of Love as any of our Sex. He had been bred for some Years at the University; where, among other Things, he learn'd to fence; in which, however, he was mightily improv'd in a Twelvemonth's Time that he stay'd here in Town. Lucretia, his Sister, was beautiful enough, her Father designing to give ten thousand Pounds with her on Marriage; but (which is above all) she was incomparably good-humour'd.

At his Return to his Father in the Country, young Hardyman found Madam Diana Constance, a most beautiful Lady, with his Sister, at that Time about 16 Years old; somewhat tall of her Age, of happy and virtuous Education, of an indifferent Fortune, not exceeding two thousand Pounds, which was no Way answerable to the Expectations he had after his Father's Death; but it was impossible he should not love her, she was so prodigiously charming both in her inward and outward Excellencies; especially since he had the Opportunity of conversing with her at his Father's for above a Month. 'Tis true, he had seen her before, but it was then five Years since. Love her he did then, and that most passionately; nor was she insensible or ungrateful. But our young Lovers had not Discretion enough to conceal the Symptoms of their Passion, which too visibly and frequently sally'd out at their Eyes before the old Gentleman; which made him prudently, as he thought, and timely enough, offer his Daughter Lucretia the Liberty of taking a small Journey with Diana to her House, which was not above 20 Miles thence, where that young Lady's Aunt govern'd in her Absence; for Diana had no other Relation, so near as she was, living in England, her only Brother Lewis having been in Italy and France ever since her Father dy'd, which was then near five Years past.

Lucretia, over-joy'd at her Father's pretended Kindness, propos'd it to the young Lady, her Friend, who was very fond of the Proposal, hoping that Lucretia's Brother might bear 'em Company there for some little Time; but old Sir Henry had quite different Thoughts of the Matter. The third Day, from the first Discourse of it, was assign'd for their Departure. In the mean Time young Hardyman knew not what to think of the Divorce he was going to suffer; for he began to have some Apprehensions that the old Knight was sensible, and displeas'd, that they lov'd each other: Not but that the Family of the Constances was as ancient and honourable as that of Hardymans, and was once endow'd with as plentiful an Estate, tho' now young Lewis Constance had not above 1200l. a Year. (O the unkind Distance that Money makes, even between Friends!)

Old 'Squire Constance was a very worthy Gentleman, and Sir Henry had a particular Friendship for him; but (perhaps) that dy'd with him, and only a neighbourly Kindness, or something more than an ordinary Respect, surviv'd to his Posterity. The Day came that was to carry 'em to the young Lady Constance's, and her Lover was preparing to attend 'em, when the old Gentleman ask'd him, What he meant by that Preparation? And whether he design'd to leave him alone? Or if he could think 'twere dutifully or decently done? To which the Son reply'd, That his Care of his Sister, and his Respect to a young Lady, in a Manner a Stranger to him, had misled his Thoughts from that Duty and Regard he ought to have pay'd to his Father, which he hop'd and begg'd he would pardon, tho' he design'd only just to have seen her safe there, and to have return'd at Night. With this the old Gentleman seem'd pacify'd for the present; and he bid him go take Leave of the Lady; which he did with a great deal of Concern, telling her, that he should be most miserable 'till he had the Happiness of seeing her again; however, he begg'd she would converse with him by Letters, which might (happily) a little palliate his Misfortune in her Absence: Adding, that he would be eternally hers, and none but hers. To which she made as kind a Return as he could wish; letting him know, that she desired to live no longer than she was assur'd that she was belov'd by him. Then taking as solemn a Farewel of her as if he had never been to see her more, after he had given his Sister a parting Kiss or two, he led 'em down to his Father, who saw 'em mounted, and attended by two of his Servants. After which he walked with 'em about a Mile from the House, where he and young Hardyman left 'em to persue their Journey.

In their Return to the House, said Sir Henry, I find, Son, I have hitherto mistaken your Inclinations: I thought they had altogether prompted you to great and manly Actions and Attempts; but, to my Sorrow, I now find my Error. How, I beseech you, Sir? (ask'd the Son.) You are guilty of a foolish lazy Passion, (reply'd the Father) you are in Love, Miles; in Love with one who can no Way advance your Fortune, Family, nor Fame. 'Tis true, she has Beauty, and o'my Conscience she is virtuous too; but will Beauty and Virtue, with a small Portion of 2000l. answer to the Estate of near 4000l. a Year, which you must inherit if you survive me? Beauty and Virtue, Sir, (return'd young Hardyman) with the Addition of good Humour and Education, is a Dowry that may merit a Crown. Notion! Stuff! All Stuff (cry'd the old Knight) Money is Beauty, Virtue, good Humour, Education, Reputation, and high Birth. Thank Heaven, Sir, (said Miles) you don't live as if you believ'd your own Doctrine; you part with your Money very freely in your House-keeping, and I am happy to see it. 'Tis that I value it for; (reply'd the Father) I would therefore have thee, my Son, add to what in all Likelihood will be thine, so considerably, by Marriage, that thou mayst better deserve the Character of Hospitable Hardyman than thy Father Sir Henry. Come, Miles, (return'd he) thou shalt think no more on her. I can't avoid it, Sir, (said t'other.) Well, well, think of her you may, (said Sir Henry) but not as for a Wife; no, if you mean to continue in your Father's Love, be not in Love with Madam Diana, nor with any of her Nymphs, tho' never so fair or so chast, unless they have got Store of Money, Store of Money, Miles. Come, come in, we'll take a Game at Chess before Dinner, if we can. I obey you, Sir, (return'd the Son) but if I win, I shall have the Liberty to love the Lady, I hope. I made no such Promise, (said the Knight) no, no Love without my Leave; but if you give me Checque-Mate, you shall have my Bay Gelding, and I would not take 50 Broad Pieces for him. I'll do my best, Sir, to deserve him, (said the young Gentleman.) 'Tis a mettl'd and fiery Beast (said Sir Henry.) They began their Game then, and had made about six Moves apiece before Dinner, which was serv'd up near four Hours after they sate down to play. It happen'd they had no Company din'd with 'em that Day; so they made a hasty Meal, and fell again to their former Dispute, which held 'em near six Hours longer; when, either the Knight's Inadvertency, or the young Gentleman's Skill and Application, gave him the Victory and Reward.

The next Day they hunted; the Day following, the House was fill'd with Friends, and Strangers; who came with 'em; all which were certain of a hearty Welcome e'er they return'd. Other Days other Company came in, as Neighbours; and none of all that made their Visits, could be dismiss'd under three or four Days at soonest.

Thus they past the Hours away for about six Weeks; in all which Time our Lover could get but one Opportunity of writing to his adorable, and that was by the Means of a Servant, who came with a Letter from his Sister Lucretia to Sir Henry, and another to him, that held one inclos'd to him from the beautiful Diana; the Words, as perfectly as I can remember 'em, were these, or to this Effect:

My Hardyman,

Too Dear! No, too much lov'd! That's impossible too. How have I enjoy'd my self with your Letters since my Absence from you! In the first, how movingly you lament the unkind Distances of Time and   Place that thus divorces you from me! In another, in what tender and prevailing Words your Passion is express'd! In a Third, what   invincible Arguments are urg'd to prove the Presence of your Soul to me in the Absence of your Body! A Fourth, how fill'd with just Complaints of a rigorous Father! What Assurances does the Fifth give me of your speedy Journey hither! And the Sixth, (for no less methought I should have receiv'd from you) confirms what you last said to me, That you will ever be mine, and none but mine. O boundless Blessing! These (my Life) are the Dreams, which, for six several Nights, have mock'd the real Passion of

Your forgotten Diana.

He read it, smil'd, and kiss'd it, and then proceeded to examine his Sisters, which held a great many Expressions of a tender Affection, and withal gave him Notice, that there was a mighty Spark lately come from Town into those Parts, that made his Court to the young Lady Constance; desiring him therefore to be as sudden in his Visit, if he intended any, as Possibility would permit. This startled and stung him: Wherefore, taking the Opportunity of his Father's Retirement, to write to the young Lady and his Sister; he dispatch'd a Letter to Lucretia, wherein he thank'd her for her Intelligence and Caution, and promis'd to be with her the next Night at farthest, if alive; and, at the same Time, writ to this Purpose to Diana:

Thou only Blessing for which I wish to live,

How delightfully do you punish my seeming Neglect! I acknowledge I have not sent to you 'till now, but it was because it was utterly impossible, my Father continually keeping so strict a Guard over me himself, that not even Mercury could evade or illude his Vigilance. Alas! my Soul, he is now no Stranger to my Passion for you, which he pretends, at least, is highly offensive to him, for what Reasons I blush to think. But what signifies an Offence to him of so generous a Nature as my Love! I am assured I was born for you, or none other of your fair Sex, though attended with all the Advantages of Birth and Fortune. I will therefore proceed in this Affair, as if we were already united by the outward Ceremonies of the

Church, and forsake him and all the World for you, my better Part! Be certain, therefore, that to-Morrow Night, e'er you sleep, you shall see (my Life, my Soul, my All)

Your most sincere, and Most passionate Lover, Hardyman.

This, with the Letter to his Sister, he convey'd into the Servant's Hand that came from 'em, undiscover'd of his Father; who likewise dismiss'd the Messenger with his grave Epistle, full of musty Morals, to the two young gay Ladies. But he had an unlucky Thought, that he was overseen in giving his Son the Opportunity of retiring from him, whilst he was writing to his Daughter and t'other fair Creature, having a Jealousy that young Hardyman might have made Use of that very Article of Time to the same End. This made him very uneasy and restless. On t'other Side, the young Gentleman though he was extreamly satisfy'd with those endearing Expressions of Love which he found in Diana's Letter, yet he was all on Fire with the Apprehension of a Rival, and the Desire to see him, that he might dispute with him for the glorious Prize.

The next Day, at Four in the Afternoon, they went to Bowls about a Mile off; where, after several Ends, the Knight and his Party lay all nearest about the Jack for the Game, 'till young Hardyman put in a bold Cast, that beat all his Adversaries from the Block, and carry'd two of his Seconds close to it, his own Bowl lying partly upon it, which made them up. Ha! (cry'd a young Gentleman of his Side) bravely done, Miles, thou hast carry'd the Day, and kiss'd the Mistress. I hope I shall before 'tis dark yet, (return'd he.) Sir Henry overhearing him, said, (his Face all glowing red with Passion) How dare you, Sir, express your self so freely in my Hearing? There, (persu'd he, and struck him a Blow on the Ear) I first salute you thus: Do you know where you are, and who I am? Yes, you are my Father, Sir, (reply'd young Hardyman, bowing.) If you see her to Night, (said the passionate Father) resolve to see me no more. By Heaven, and all my Hopes, no more I will, after this Minute, (return'd the Son, being retreated some Distance from him, out of his Hearing.) So taking his Leave of the Company, with the usual Ceremony, he went directly Home, where immediately he order'd his Servant Goodlad to saddle their Horses, whilst he himself went up to his Chamber, and took all the Rings and Jewels that his Mother had left him, and the Money that he had then in his Possession, which altogether amounted to near twelve hundred Pounds; and packing up some Linnen in his Portmanteau, he quickly mounted with his Servant, and made his Way towards the Lady Constance's.

'Twas near seven a Clock e'er they got within Sight of his Mistress's, when our Lover perceiv'd a Gentleman and his Servant mounted at some Distance on t'other Side of the House, as coming from London: This unfortunately happen'd to be Lewis Constance, just return'd from his Travels, whom young Hardyman had never seen before, and therefore could not know him at that Time: Observing therefore that they made to the same Place for which he was design'd, he halted a little, taking Covert under a large Elm-Tree, within a hundred Paces of the House, where he had the unlucky Opportunity to see his Mistress and Sister come out; whom Lewis perceiving at the same Time, alighted, and ran eagerly to embrace her, who receiv'd him with Arms expanded, crying, O my Dear, dearest Brother; but that last Word was stifled with Kisses. Do I once more hold thee in my Arms! O come in, and let me give my Joys a Loose! I am surpriz'd, and rave with extream Hapiness! O! thou art all to me that is valuable on Earth! (return'd he.) At these Words she, in a Manner, hal'd him in. This Sight was certainly the greatest Mortification to her Lover that ever Man surviv'd! He presently and positively concluded it could be none but that Rival, of whom his Sister had given him Advice in her Letter. What to do he could by no Means determine; sometimes he was for going in, and affronting him before his Mistress; a second Thought advis'd him to expect his coming out near that Place; upon another Consideration he was going to send him a Challenge, but by whom he knew not, for his Servant was as well known there as himself.

At last he resolv'd to ride farther out of the Road, to see for some convenient Retreat that Night, where he might be undiscover'd: Such a Place he found about two Miles thence, at a good substantial Farmer's, who made him heartily welcome that Night, with the best Beer he had in his Cellar, so that he slept much better than he could have expected his Jealousy would have permitted: But the Morning renew'd and redoubled his Torture: But this jolly Landlord, hugely pleas'd with his good Company the Night past, visited him as he got out of his Bed, which was near two Hours after he wak'd; in which Time he had laid his Design how to proceed, in order to take Satisfaction of this Rival. He suffer'd himself, therefore, to be manag'd by the good Man of the House, who wou'd fain have made a Conquest of him; but he found that the young Gentleman could bear as much in his Head as he could on his Shoulders, which gave Hardyman the Opportunity of keeping a Stowage yet for a good Dinner: After which they fell to bumping it about, 'till the Farmer fell asleep; when young Hardyman retir'd into his Chamber, where, after a Turn or two, he writ as follows to his Mistress's Brother, whose Name he knew not; and therefore the Billet is not superscrib'd.

SIR,

You have done me an unpardonable Injury; and if you are a Gentleman, as you seem, you will give me Satisfaction within this Hour at the Place whither this Messenger shall lead you. Bring nothing with you but your Sword and your Servant, as I with mine, to take Care of him that falls. 'Till I see you, I am your Servant, &c.

An Hour before Supper, his kind Host wak'd, and they eat heartily together that Night, but did not drink so plentifully as they had since their first Meeting; young Hardyman telling him, that he was oblig'd to be mounted at the fore-mention'd Morning, in order to persue his Journey; and that, in the mean Time, he desir'd the Favour of him to let one of his Servants carry a Letter from him, to one that was then at the young Lady Constance's: To which t'other readily agreed. The young Gentleman then made him a Present of a Tobacco-Box, with the Head of King Charles the First on the Lid, and his Arms on the Bottom in Silver; which was very acceptable to him, for he was a great Loyalist, tho' it was in the Height of Oliver's Usurpation. About four a-Clock in the Morning, as our jealous Lover had order'd him, one of the Servants came to him for the Letter; with which he receiv'd these Instructions, that he should deliver that Note into the Gentleman's own Hand, who came to the Lady Constance's the Night before the last. That he should shew that Gentleman to the Field where young Hardyman, should deliver the Note to the Servant, which was just a Mile from either House; or that he should bring an Answer to the Note from that Gentleman. The Fellow was a good Scholar, tho' he could neither read nor write. For he learn'd his Lesson perfectly well, and repeated it punctually to Lewis Constance; who was strangely surpriz'd at what he found in the Billet. He ask'd the Messenger if he knew his Name that sent it; or if he were a Gentleman? Nay (Mass, quoth the Fellow) I warrant he's a Gentleman; for he has given me nine good Shillings here, for coming but hither to you; but for his Name, you may e'en name it as well as I. He has got one to wait a top of him almost as fine as himself, zure. The surpriz'd Traveller jump'd out of his Bed, slipt on his Gown, and call'd up his Servant: Thence he went to his Sister's Chamber, with whom Lucretia lay: They both happen'd to be awake, and talking, as he came to the Door, which his Sister permitted him to unlock, and ask'd him the Reason of his so early Rising? Who reply'd, That since he could not sleep, he would take the Air a little. But first, Sister (continu'd he) I will refresh my self at your Lips: And now, Madam, (added he to Lucretia) I would beg a Cordial from you. For that (said his Sister) you shall be oblig'd to me this once; saying so, she gently turn'd Lucretia's Face towards him, and he had his Wish. Ten to one, but he had rather continu'd with Lucretia, than have gone to her Brother, had he known him; for he lov'd her truly and passionately: But being a Man of true Courage and Honour, he took his Leave of 'em, presently dress'd, and tripp'd away with the Messenger, who made more than ordinary Haste, because of his Success, which was rewarded with another piece of Money; and he danc'd Home to the Sound of the Money in his Pocket.

No sooner was the Fellow out of Hearing, than Lewis, coming up to his Adversary, shew'd him the Billet, and said, Sent you this to me, Sir? I did, Sir, reply'd Hardyman: I never saw you 'till now, return'd Lewis; how then could I injure you? 'Tis enough that I know it, answer'd Miles. But to satisfy you, you shall know that I am sensible that you pretend to a fair Lady, to whom I have an elder Title. In short, you entrench on my Prerogative. I own no Subjection to you, (return'd Constance) and my Title is as good as your Prerogative, which I will maintain as I can hold this, (continu'd he, and drew his Sword) Hah! Nobly done! (cry'd Hardyman drawing) I could almost wish thou wert my Friend: You speak generously, return'd Lewis, I find I have to do with a Gentleman. Retire to a convenient Distance, said Hardyman to Goodlad. If you come near while we are disputing, my Sword shall thank you for't; and you, Sir, retire! said Constance to his Servant. And if you will keep your Life, keep your Distance! O my brave Enemy! (cry'd Miles) Give me thy Hand! Here they shook Hands, and gave one another the Compliment of the Hat, and then (said Hardyman) Come on, Sir! I am with you, Sir, (reply'd Lewis standing on his Guard) they were both equally knowing in the Use of their Swords; so that they fought for some few Minutes without any Wound receiv'd on either Side. But, at last, Miles being taller and much stronger than his Adversary, resolv'd to close with him; which he did, putting by a Pass that Lewis made at him with his left Hand, and at the same Time he run him quite thro' the Body, threw him, and disarm'd him. Rise if thou can'st! (cry'd Hardyman) thou art really brave. I will not put thee to the Shame of asking thy Life. Alas! I cannot rise, (reply'd Lewis, endeavouring to get up) so short a Life as mine were not worth the Breath of a Coward. Make Haste! Fly hence! For thou are lost if thou stay'st. My Friends are many and great; they will murther thee by Law. Fly! Fly in Time! Heaven forgive us both! Amen! (Cry'd Miles) I hope thou may'st recover! 'Tis Pity so much Bravery and Honour should be lost so early. Farewel. And now Adieu to the fair and faithless Diana! Ha! (Cry'd Constance) O bloody Mistake! But could speak no more for Loss of Blood. Hardyman heard not those last Words, being spoken with a fainting Voice, but in Haste mounted, and rode with all Speed for London, attended by Goodlad; whilst Constance's Servant came up to him, and having all along travell'd with him, had two or three Times the Occasion of making Use of that Skill in Surgery which he had learn'd Abroad in France and Italy, which he now again practis'd on his Master, with such Success, that in less than half an Hour, he put his Master in a Capacity of leaning on him; and so walking Home with him, tho' very gently and slowly. By the Way, Lewis charg'd his Servant not to say which Way Hardyman took, unless he design'd to quit his Service for ever. But pardon me, Sir! (return'd t'other) your Wound is very dangerous, and I am not sure that it is not mortal: And if so, give me Leave to say, I shall persue him over all England, for Vengeance of your Death. 'Twas a Mistake on both Sides, I find; (said Lewis) therefore think not of Revenge: I was as hot and as much to blame as he. They were near an Hour getting to the House, after his Blood was stopp'd. As he was led in, designing to be carry'd to his Chamber, and to take his Bed as sick of an Ague, his Sister and Lucretia met him, and both swoon'd away at the Sight of him; but in a little Time they were recover'd, as if to torment him with their Tears, Sighs, and Lamentations. They ask'd him a thousand impertinent Questions, which he defer'd to answer, 'till he was laid in Bed; when he told his Sister, that the Gentleman who had thus treated him, bid her Adieu, by the Epithet of Fair and Faithless. For Heaven's Sake, (cry'd Diana) what Manner of Man was he? Very tall and well set, (reply'd her Brother) of an austere Aspect, but a well-favour'd Face, and prodigiously strong. Had he a Servant with him, Sir? (ask'd Lucretia) Yes, Madam (answer'd her Lover) and describ'd her Servant. Ah! my Prophetic Fears (cry'd she) It was my Brother, attended by Goodlad. Your Brother! Dearest and Fairest of your Sex, (said Lewis) Heaven send him safely out of England then! Nay, be he who he may, I wish the same; for he is truly brave. Alas, my dear, my cruel Hardyman! (cry'd Diana) Your Hardyman, Sister! (said Lewis) Ah! would he had been so! You might then have had Hopes of an affectionate Brother's Life; which yet I will endeavour to preserve, that by the Enjoyment of your dear and nearest Conversation, Madam, (persu'd he to Lucretia) I may be prepar'd to endure the only greater Joys of Heaven. But O! My Words prey on my Spirits. And all the World, like a huge Ship at Anchor, turn round with the ebbing Tide. I can no more. At these Words both the Ladies shriek'd aloud, which made him sigh, and move his Hand as well as he could toward the Door; his Attendant perceiv'd it, and told 'em he sign'd to them to quit the Room; as indeed it was necessary they should, that he might repose a while if possible, at least that he might not be oblig'd to talk, nor look much about him. They obey'd the Necessity, but with some Reluctancy, and went into their own Chamber, where they sigh'd, wept, and lamented their Misfortunes for near two Hours together: When all on a suddain, the Aunt, who had her Share of Sorrow too in this ugly Business, came running up to 'em, to let 'em know that old Sir Harry Hardyman was below, and came to carry his Daughter Madam Lucretia Home with him. This both surpriz'd and troubled the young Ladies, who were yet more disturb'd, when the Aunt told them, that he enquir'd for his Son, and would not be convinc'd by any Argument whatever; no, nor Protestation in her Capacity, that young Hardyman was not in the House, nor that he had not been entertain'd there ever since he left his Father. But come, Cousin and Madam, (said she to the young Ladies) go down to him immediately, or I fear he'll come up to you. Lucretia knew she must, and t'other would not be there alone: So down they came to the Old testy Gentleman. Your Servant, Lady, (said he to Diana) Lucretia then kneel'd for his Blessing. Very well, very well, (cry'd he hastily) God bless you! Where's your Brother? Ha! Where's your Brother? I know not, Sir, (she answer'd) I have not seen him since I have been here. No, (said he) not since you have been in this Parlour last, you mean. I mean, Sir, (she return'd) upon my Hopes of yours and Heaven's Blessing, I have not seen him since I saw you, Sir, within a Mile of our own House. Ha! Lucretia, Ha! (cry'd the old Infidel) have a Care you pull not mine and Heaven's Curse on your Head! Believe me, Sir, (said Diana) to my Knowledge, she has not. Why, Lady, (ask'd the passionate Knight) are you so curious and fond of him your self, that you will allow no Body else the Sight of him? Not so much as his own Sister? I don't understand you, Sir, (she reply'd) for, by my Hopes of Heaven, I have not seen him neither since that Day I left you. Hey! pass and repass, (cry'd the old suspicious Father) presto, be gone! This is all Conjuration. 'Tis diabolical, dealing with the Devil! In Lies, I mean, on one Side or other; for he told me to my Teeth, at least, he said in my Hearing, on the Bowling-Green, but two Nights since, that he hop'd to see your Ladyship (for I suppose you are his Mistress) that Night e're 'twas dark: Upon which I gave him only a kind and fatherly Memorandum of his Duty, and he immediately left the Company and me, who have not set Eye on him, nor heard one Syllable of him since. Now, judge you, Lady, if I have not Reason to conclude that he has been and is above still! No, (said the Aunt) you have no Reason to conclude so, when they both have told you solemnly the contrary; and when I can add, that I will take a formal Oath, if requir'd, that he has not been in this House since my Cousin Lewis went to travel, nor before, to the best of my Memory; and I am confident, neither my Cousin Diana, nor the Lady your Daughter, have seen him since they left him with you, Sir, I wish, indeed, my dear Cousin Lewis had not seen him since. How! What's that you say, good Lady? (ask'd the Knight) Is Mr. Lewis Constance then in England? And do you think that he has seen him so lately? for your Discourse seems to imply as much. Sir Henry, (reply'd the Aunt) you are very big with Questions, but I will endeavour to satisfy you in all of 'em. My Cousin Lewis Constance is in England; nay, more, he is now in his Chamber a-Bed, and dangerously, if not mortally, wounded, by 'Squire Miles Hardyman, your Son. Heaven forbid, (cry'd the Father) sure 'tis impossible. All Things are so to the Incredulous. Look you, Sir, (continu'd she, seeing Lewis's Servant come in) do you remember his French Servant Albert, whom he took some Months before he left England? There he is. Humh! (said the old Sceptic) I think verily 'tis the same. Ay, Sir, (said the Servant) I am the same, at your Service. How does your Master? (ask'd Sir Henry) Almost as bad as when the 'Squire your Son left him, (reply'd Albert) only I have stopp'd the Bleeding, and he is now dozing a little; to say the Truth, I have only Hopes of his Life because I wish it. When was this done? (the Knight inquir'd) Not three Hours since, (return'd t'other.) What was the Occasion? (said Sir Henry) An ugly Mistake on both Sides; your Son, as I understand, not knowing my Master, took him for his Rival, and bad him quit his Pretensions to the fair Lady, for whom he had a Passion: My Master thought he meant the Lady Lucretia, your Daughter, Sir, with whom I find he is passionately in Love, and - Very well - so - go on! (interrupted the Knight with a Sigh) and was resolv'd to dispute his Title with him; which he did; but the 'Squire is as strong as the Horse he rides on! And! 'tis a desperate Wound! Which Way is he gone, canst thou tell? (ask'd the Father) Yes, I can; but I must not, 'tis as much as my Place is worth. My Master would not have him taken for all the World; nay, I must needs own he is a very brave Person. But you may let me know; (said the Father) you may be confident I will not expose him to the Law: Besides, if it please Heaven that your Master recovers, there will be no Necessity of a Prosecution. Prithee let me know! You'll pardon me, Sir, (said Lewis's trusty Servant) my Master, perhaps, may give you that Satisfaction; and I'll give you Notice, Sir, when you may conveniently discourse him. Your humble Servant, Sir, (he added, bowing, and went out.) The old Gentleman was strangely mortify'd at this News of his Son; and his Absence perplex'd him more than any thing besides in the Relation. He walk'd wildly up and down the Room, sighing, foaming, and rolling his Eyes in a dreadful Manner; and at the Noise of any Horse on the Road, out he would start as nimbly as if he were as youthful as his Son, whom he sought in vain among those Passengers. Then returning, he cry'd out to her, O Lucretia! Your Brother! Where's your Brother? O my Son! the Delight, Comfort, and Pride of my Old Age! Why dost thou fly me? Then answering as for young Hardyman, (said he) you struck me publickly before much Company, in the Face of my Companions. Come, (reply'd he for himself) 'Twas Passion, Miles, 'twas Passion; Youth is guilty of many Errors, and shall not Age be allow'd their Infirmities? Miles, thou know'st I love thee. Love thee above Riches or long Life. O! Come to my Arms, dear Fugitive, and make Haste to preserve his, who gave thee thy Life! Thus he went raving about the Room, whilst the sorrowful, compassionate Ladies express'd their Grief in Tears. After this loving Fit was over with him, he would start out in a contrary Madness, and threaten his Son with the greatest and the heaviest Punishment he could imagine; insomuch, that the young Ladies, who had Thoughts before of perswading Lewis to inform Sir Harry which Way his Son rode, were now afraid of proposing any such Thing to him. Dinner was at last serv'd in, to which Diana with much Difficulty prevail'd with him to sit. Indeed, neither he, nor any there present, had any great Appetite to eat; their Grief had more than satiated 'em. About five a-Clock, Albert signify'd to the Knight, that he might then most conveniently speak with his Master; but he begg'd that he would not disturb him beyond half a Quarter of an Hour: He went up therefore to him, follow'd by the young Lady and the Aunt: Lewis was the first that spoke, who, putting his Hand a little out of the Bed, said with a Sigh, Sir Henry, I hope you will pity a great Misfortune, and endeavour to pardon me, who was the greatest Occasion of it; which has doubly punish'd me in these Wounds, and in the Loss of that Gentleman's Conversation, whose only Friendship I would have courted. Heaven pardon you both the Injuries done to one another; (return'd the Knight) I grieve to see you thus, and the more, when I remember my self that 'twas done by my Son's unlucky Hand. Would he were here. So would not I (said Lewis) 'till I am assur'd my Wound is not mortal, which I have some Reasons to believe it is not. Let me beg one Favour of you, Sir, (said Sir Henry) I beseech you do not deny me. It must be a very difficult Matter that you, Sir, shall not command of me, (reply'd Constance.) It can't be difficult to you to tell me, or to command your Servant to let me know what Road my Son took. He may be at Bristol long e're this, (return'd Lewis.) That was the Road they took (added the Servant.) I thank you, my worthy, my kind Friend! (said the afflicted Father) I will study to deserve this Kindness of you. How do you find your self now? that I may send him an Account by my Servant, if he is to be found in that City? Pretty hearty, (return'd Lewis) if the Wounds your adorable Daughter here has given me, do not prove more fatal than my Friend's your Son's. She blush'd, and he persu'd, My Servant has sent for the best Physician and Surgeon in all these Parts; I expect them every Minute, and then I shall be rightly inform'd in the State of my Body. I will defer my Messenger 'till then (said Sir Henry.) I will leave that to your Discretion, Sir, (return'd Constance.) As they were discoursing of 'em, in came the learned Sons of Art: The Surgeon prob'd his Wound afresh, which he found very large, but not mortal, his Loss of Blood being the most dangerous of all his Circumstances. The Country-Æsculapius approv'd of his first Intention, and of his Application; so dressing it once himself, he left the Cure of Health to the Physician, who prescrib'd some particular Remedy against Fevers, and a Cordial or two; took his Fee without any Scruples, as the Surgeon had done before, and then took both their Leaves. Sir Henry was as joyful as Lewis's Sister, or as his own Daughter Lucretia, who lov'd him perfectly, to hear the Wound was not mortal; and immediately dispatch'd a Man and Horse to Bristol, in Search of his Son: The Messenger return'd in a short Time with this Account only, that such a kind of a Gentleman and his Servant took Shipping the Day before, as 'twas suppos'd, for London. This put the old Gentleman into a perfect Frenzy. He ask'd the Fellow, Why the Devil he did not give his Son the Letter he sent to him? Why he did not tell him, that his poor old forsaken Father would receive him with all the Tenderness of an indulgent Parent? And why he did not assure his Son, from him, that on his Return, he should be bless'd with the Lady Diana? And a thousand other extravagant Questions, which no body could reply to any better than the Messenger, who told him, trembling; First, That he could not deliver the Letter to his Son, because he could not find him: And Secondly and Lastly, being an Answer in full to all his Demands, That he could not, nor durst tell the young Gentleman any of those kind Things, since he had no Order to do so; nor could he enter into his Worship's Heart, to know his Thoughts: Which Return, tho' it was reasonable enough, and might have been satisfactory to any other Man in better Circumstances of Mind; so enrag'd Sir Henry, that he had certainly kill'd the poor Slave, had not the Fellow sav'd his Life by jumping down almost half the Stairs, and continuing his Flight, Sir Henry still persuing him, 'till he came to the Stables, where finding the Door open, Sir Henry ran in and saddl'd his Horse his own self, without staying for any Attendant, or so much as taking his Leave of the Wounded Gentleman, or Ladies, or giving Orders to his Daughter when she should follow him Home, whither he was posting alone; but the Servant who came out with him, accidentally seeing him as he rode out at the farthest Gate, so timely persu'd him, that he overtook him about a Mile and half off the House. Home they got then in less than three Hours Time, without one Word or Syllable all the Way on either Side, unless now and then a hearty Sigh or Groan from the afflicted Father, whose Passion was so violent, and had so disorder'd him, that he was constrain'd immediately to go to Bed, where he was seiz'd with a dangerous Fever, which was attended with a strange Delirium, or rather with an absolute Madness, of which the Lady Lucretia had Advice that same Night, tho' very late. This News so surpriz'd and afflicted her, as well for the Danger of her Lover as of her Father, that it threw her into a Swoon; out of which, when, with some Difficulty she was recover'd, with great Perplexity and Anguish of Mind she took a sad Farewel of the Lady Diana, but durst not be seen by her Brother on such an Occasion, as of taking Leave, lest it should retard his Recovery: To her Father's then she was convey'd with all convenient Expedition: The old Gentleman was so assiduously and lawfully attended by his fair affectionate Daughter, that in less than ten Days Time his Fever was much abated, and his Delirium had quite left him, and he knew every Body about him perfectly; only the Thoughts of his Son, by Fits, would choak and discompose him: However, he was very sensible of his Daughter's Piety in her Care of him, which was no little Comfort to him: Nor, indeed, could he be otherwise than sensible of it by her Looks, which were then pale and thin, by over-watching; which occasion'd her Sickness, as it caus'd her Father's Health: For no sooner could Sir Henry walk about the Room, than she was forc'd to keep her Bed; being afflicted with the same Distemper from which her Father was yet but hardly freed: Her Fever was high, but the Delirium was not so great: In which, yet, she should often discover her Passion for Lewis Constance, her wounded Lover; lamenting the great Danger his Life had been in, as if she had not receiv'd daily Letters of his Amendment. Then again, she would complain of her Brother's Absence, but more frequently of her Lover's; which her Father hearing, sent to invite him to come to her, with his Sister, as soon as young Constance was able to undertake the Journey; which he did the very next Day; and he and Diana gave the languishing Lady a Visit in her Chamber, just in the happy Time of an Interval, which, 'tis suppos'd, was the sole Cause of her Recovery; for the Sight of her Lover and Friend was better than the richest

Cordial in her Distemper. In a very short Time she left her Bed, when Sir Henry, to give her perfect Health, himself join'd the two Lovers Hands; and not many Weeks after, when her Beauty and Strength return'd in their wonted Vigour, he gave her 10000l. and his Blessing, which was a double Portion, on their Wedding-Day, which he celebrated with all the Cost and Mirth that his Estate and Sorrow would permit: Sorrow for the Loss of his Son, I mean, which still hung upon him, and still hover'd and croak'd over and about him, as Ravens, and other Birds of Prey, about Camps and dying People. His Melancholy, in few Months, increas'd to that Degree, that all Company and Conversation was odious to him, but that of Bats, Owls, Night-Ravens, &c. Nay, even his Daughter, his dear and only Child, as he imagin'd, was industriously avoided by him. In short, it got so intire a Mastery of him, that he would not nor did receive any Sustenance for many Days together; and at last it confin'd him to his Bed; where he lay wilfully speechless for two Days and Nights; his Son-in-Law, or his own Daughter, still attending a-Nights by Turns; when on the third Night, his Lucretia sitting close by him in Tears, he fetch'd a deep Sigh, which ended in a pitious Groan, and call'd faintly, Lucretia! Lucretia! The Lady being then almost as melancholy as her Father, did not hear him 'till the third Call; when falling on her Knees, and embracing his Hand, which he held out to her, she return'd with Tears then gushing out, Yes, Sir, it is I, your Lucretia, your dutiful, obedient, and affectionate Lucretia, and most sorrowfully-afflicted Daughter. Bless her, Heaven! (said the Father) I'm going now, (continu'd he weakly) O Miles! yet come and take thy last Farewel of thy dear Father! Art thou for ever gone from me? Wilt thou not come and take thy dying Father's Blessing? Then I will send it after thee. Bless him! O Heaven! Bless him! Sweet Heaven bless my Son! My Miles! Here he began to faulter in his Speech, when the Lady gave a great Shriek, which wak'd and alarm'd her Husband, who ran down to 'em in his Night-Gown, and, kneeling by the Bed-side with his Lady, begg'd their departing Father's Blessing on them. The Shriek had (it seems) recall'd the dying Gentleman's fleeting Spirits, who moving his Hand as well as he could, with Eyes lifted up, as it were, whisper'd, Heaven bless you both! Bless me! Bless my, O Miles! Then dy'd. His Death (no Doubt) was attended with the Sighs, Tears, and unfeign'd Lamentations of the Lady and her Husband; for, bating his sudden Passion, he was certainly as good a Father, Friend, and Neighbour, as England could boast. His Funeral was celebrated then with all the Ceremonies due to his Quality and Estate: And the young happy Couple felt their dying Parent's Blessing in their mutual Love and uninterrupted Tranquillity: Whilst (alas) it yet far'd otherwise with their Brother; of whose Fortune it is fit I should now give you an Account.

From Bristol he arriv'd to London with his Servant Goodlad; to whom he propos'd, either that he should return to Sir Henry, or share in his Fortunes Abroad: The faithful Servant told him, he would rather be unhappy in his Service, than quit it for a large Estate. To which his kind Master return'd, (embracing him) No more my Servant now, but my Friend! No more Goodlad, but Truelove! And I am - Lostall! 'Tis a very proper Name, suitable to my wretched Circumstances. So after some farther Discourse on their Design, they sold their Horses, took Shipping, and went for Germany, where then was the Seat of War.

Miles's Person and Address soon recommended him to the chief Officers in the Army; and his Friend Truelove was very well accepted with 'em. They both then mounted in the same Regiment and Company, as Volunteers; and in the first Battel behav'd themselves like brave English-men; especially Miles, whom now we must call Mr. Lostall, who signaliz'd himself that Day so much, that his Captain and Lieutenant being kill'd, he succeeded to the former in the Command of the Company, and Truelove was made his Lieutenant. The next Field-Fight Truelove was kill'd, and Lostall much wounded, after he had sufficiently reveng'd his Friend's Death by the Slaughter of many of the Enemies. Here it was that his Bravery was so particular, that he was courted by the Lieutenant-General to accept of the Command of a Troop of Horse; which gave him fresh and continu'd Occasions of manifesting his Courage and Conduct. All this while he liv'd too generously for his Pay; so that in the three or four Years Time, the

War ceasing, he was oblig'd to make use of what Jewels and Money he had left of his own, for his Pay was quite spent. But at last his whole Fund being exhausted to about fifty or threescore Pounds, he began to have Thoughts of returning to his native Country, England; which in a few Weeks he did, and appear'd at the Tower to some of his Majesty's (King Charles the Second's) Officers, in a very plain and coarse, but clean and decent Habit: To one of these Officers he address'd himself, and desir'd to mount his Guards under his Command, and in his Company; who very readily receiv'd him into Pay. (The Royal Family had not then been restor'd much above a Twelve-Month.) In this Post, his Behaviour was such, that he was generally belov'd both by the Officers and private Soldiers, most punctually and exactly doing his Duty; and when he was off the Guard, he would employ himself in any laborious Way whatsoever to get a little Money. And it happen'd, that one Afternoon, as he was helping to clean the Tower Ditch, (for he refus'd not to do the meanest Office, in Hopes to expiate his Crime by such voluntary Penances) a Gentleman, very richly dress'd, coming that Way, saw him at Work; and taking particular Notice of him, thought he should know that Face of his, though some of the Lines had been struck out by a Scar or two: And regarding him more earnestly, he was at last fully confirm'd, that he was the Man he thought him; which made him say to the Soldier, Prithee, Friend, What art thou doing there? The unhappy Gentleman return'd, in his Country Dialect, Why, Master, Cham helping to clear the Tower Ditch, zure, an't please you. 'Tis very hot, (said t'other) Art thou not a dry? Could'st thou not drink? Ay, Master, reply'd the Soldier, with all my Heart. Well, (said the Gentleman) I'll give thee a Flaggon or two; Where is the best Drink? At yonder House, Master, (answer'd the Soldier) where you see yon Soldier at the Door, there be the best Drink and the best Measure, zure: Chil woit a top o your Worship az Zoon as you be got thare. I'll take thy Word, said t'other, and went directly to the Place; where he had hardly sate down, and call'd for some Drink, e'er the Soldier came in, to whom the Gentleman gave one Pot, and drank to him out of another. Lostall, that was the Soldier, whipp'd off his Flaggon, and said, bowing, Well, Master, God bless your Worship! Ich can but love and thank you, and was going; but the Gentleman, who had farther Business with him, with some Difficulty prevail'd on him to sit down, for a Minute or two, after the Soldier had urg'd that he must mind his Business, for he had yet half a Day's Work almost to complete, and he would not wrong any Body of a Quarter of an Hour's Labour for all the World. Th'art a very honest Fellow, I believe, said his Friend; but prithee what does thy whole Day's Work come to? Eighteen-pence, reply'd Lostall: Look, there 'tis for thee, said the Gentleman. Ay; but an't like your Worship, who must make an End of my Day's Business? (the Soldier ask'd.) Get any Body else to do it for thee, and I'll pay him. Can'st prevail with one of thy Fellow-Soldiers to be so kind? Yes, Master, thank God, cham not so ill belov'd nother. Here's honest Frank will do so much vor me, Zure: Wilt not, Frank? (withal my Heart, Tom, reply'd his Comrade.) Here, Friend, (said Lostall's new Acquaintance) here's Eighteen-pence for thee too. I thank your Honour, return'd the Soldier, but should have but Nine-pence. No Matter what thou should'st have, I'll give thee no less, said the strange Gentleman. Heavens bless your Honour! (cry'd the Soldier) and after he had swigg'd off a Pot of good Drink, took Lostall's Pick-ax and Spade, and went about his Business. Now (said the Stranger) let us go and take a Glass of Wine, if there be any that is good hereabouts, for I fancy thou'rt a mighty honest Fellow; and I like thy Company mainly. Cham very much bound to behold you, Master, (return'd Lostall) and chave a Fancy that you be and a West-Country-Man, zure; (added he) you do a take zo like en; vor Mainly be our Country Word, zure. We'll talk more of that by and by, said t'other: Mean while I'll discharge the House, and walk whither thou wilt lead me. That shan't be var, zure; (return'd Lostall) vor the Gun upon the Hill there, has the best Report for Wine and Zeck Ale hereabouts. There they arriv'd then in a little Time, got a Room to themselves, and had better Wine than the Gentleman expected. After a Glass or two a-piece, his unknown Friend ask'd Lostall what Country-Man he was? To whom the Soldier reply'd, That he was a Zomerzetshire Man, zure. Did'st thou never hear then of one Sir Henry Hardyman? (the Stranger ask'd.) Hier of'n! (cry'd t'other) yes, zure; chave a zeen 'en often. Ah! Zure my Mother and I have had many a zwindging Pitcher of good Drink, and many a good

Piece of Meat at his House. Humh! (cry'd the Gentleman) It seems your Mother and you knew him, then? Ay, zure, mainly well; ich mean, by zight, mainly well, by zight. They had a great deal of farther Discourse, which lasted near two Hours; in which Time the Gentleman had the Opportunity to be fully assur'd, that this was Miles Hardyman, for whom he took him at first. At that first Conference, Miles told him his Name was honest Tom Lostall; and that he had been a Souldier about five Years; having first obtain'd the Dignity of a Serjeant, and afterward had the Honour to be a Trooper, which was the greatest Post of Honour that he could boast of. At last, his new Friend ask'd Miles, if he should see him there at Three in the Afternoon the next Day? Miles return'd, That he should be at his Post upon Duty then; and that without Leave from his Lieutenant, who then would command the Guards at the Tower, he could not stir a Foot with him. His Friend return'd, That he would endeavour to get Leave for him for an Hour or two: After which they drank off their Wine; the Gentleman pay'd the Reckoning, and gave Miles a Broad piece to drink more Wine 'till he came, if he pleas'd, and then parted 'till the next Day. When his Friend was gone, Miles had the Opportunity of reflecting on that Day's Adventure. He thought he had seen the Gentleman's Face, and heard his Voice, but where, and upon what Occasion, he could not imagine; but he was in Hopes, that on a second Interview, he might recollect himself where it was he had seen him. 'Twas exactly Three a-Clock the next Afternoon, when his Friend came in his own Mourning-Coach, accompany'd by another, who look'd like a Gentleman, though he wore no Sword. His Friend was attended by two of his own Foot-men in black Liveries. Miles was at his Post, when his Friend ask'd where the Officer of the Guard was? The Soldier reply'd, That he was at the Gun. The Gentleman went directly to the Lieutenant, and desir'd the Liberty of an Hour or two for Miles, then Tom Lostall, to take a Glass of Wine with him: The Lieutenant return'd, That he might keep him a Week or two, if he pleas'd, and he would excuse him; for (added he) there is not a more obedient nor better Soldier than Tom was in the whole Regiment; and that he believ'd he was as brave as obedient. The Gentleman reply'd, That he was very happy to hear so good a Character of him; and having obtain'd Leave for his Friend, made his Compliment, and return'd, to take Miles along with him: When he came to the trusty Centinel, he commanded the Boot to be let down, and desir'd Miles to come into the Coach, telling him, That the Officer had given him Leave. Ah! Sir, (return'd Miles) altho' he has, I cannot, nor will quit my Post, 'till I am reliev'd by a Corporal; on which, without any more Words, the Gentleman once more went to the Lieutenant, and told him what the Soldier's Answer was. The Officer smil'd, and reply'd, That he had forgot to send a Corporal with him, e'er he was got out o' Sight, and begg'd the Gentleman's Pardon that he had given him a second Trouble. Then immediately calling for a Corporal, he dispatch'd him with the Gentleman to relieve Miles, who then, with some little Difficulty, was prevail'd on to step into the Coach, which carry'd 'em into some Tavern or other in Leadenhall-street; where, after a Bottle or two, his Friend told Miles, that the Gentleman who came with him in the Coach, had some Business with him in another Room. Miles was surpriz'd at that, and look'd earnestly on his Friend's Companion; and seeing he had no Sword, pull'd off his own, and walk'd with him into the next Room; where he ask'd the Stranger, What Business he had with him? To which the other reply'd, That he must take Measure of him. How! (cry'd Miles) take Measure of me? That need not be; for I can tell how tall I am. I am (continu'd he) six Foot and two Inches high. I believe as much (said t'other.) But, Sir, I am a Taylor, and must take Measure of you to make a Suit of Cloaths or two for you; or half a Dozen, if you please. Pray, good Mr. Taylor (said Miles) don't mock me; for tho' cham a poor Fellow, yet cham no Vool zure. I don't, indeed, Sir, reply'd t'other. Why, who shall pay for 'em? Your Friend, the Gentleman in the next Room: I'll take his Word for a thousand Pounds, and more; and he has already promis'd to be my Pay-Master for as many Suits as you shall bespeak, and of what Price you please. Ah! mary, (cry'd Miles) he is a Right Worshipful Gentleman; and ich caunt but love 'n and thank 'n. The Taylor then took Measure of him, and they return'd to the Gentleman; who, after a Bottle or two a-piece, ask'd Miles when he should mount the Guard next? Miles told him four Days thence, and he should be posted in the same Place, and that his Captain would then command the Guard, who was a very noble Captain, and a good Officer. His Friend, who then had no farther Business with Miles at that Time, once more parted with him, 'till Three a-Clock the next Saturday; when he return'd, and ask'd if the Captain were at the Gun, or no? Miles assur'd him he was. His Friend then went down directly to the Tavern, where he found the Captain, the Lieutenant, and Ensign; upon his Address the Captain most readily gave his Consent that Miles might stay with him a Month, if he would; and added many Things in Praise of his trusty and dutiful Soldier. The Gentleman then farther entreated, that he might have the Liberty to give him and the other Officers a Supper that Night; and that they would permit their poor Soldier, Tom Lostall, the Honour to eat with 'em there. To the first, the Captain and the rest seem'd something averse; but to the last they all readily agreed; and at length the Gentleman's Importunity prevail'd on 'em to accept his Kindness, he urging that it was in Acknowledgment of all those Favours they had plac'd on his Friend Tom. With his pleasing Success he came to Miles, not forgetting then to take a Corporal with him. At this second Invitation into the Coach, Miles did not use much Ceremony, but stepp'd in, and would have sate over against the Gentleman, by the Gentleman-Taylor; but his Friend oblig'd him to sit on the same Seat with him. They came then again to their old Tavern in Leadenhall-street, and were shew'd into a large Room; where they had not been above six Minutes, e'er the Gentleman's Servants, and another, who belong'd to Monsieur Taylor, brought two or three large Bags; out of one they took Shirts, half Shirts, Bands, and Stockings; out of another, a Mourning-Suit; out of a third, a Mourning Cloak, Hat, and a large Hatband, with black Cloth-Shoes; and one of the Gentleman's Servants laid down a Mourning Sword and Belt on the Table: Miles was amaz'd at the Sight of all these Things, and kept his Eyes fix'd on 'em, 'till his Friend cry'd, Come, Tom! Put on your Linnen first! Here! (continu'd he to his Servant) Bid 'em light some Faggots here! For, tho' 'tis Summer, the Linnen may want Airing, and there may be some ugly cold Vapours about the Room, which a good Fire will draw away. Miles was still in a Maze! But the Fire being well kindled, the Gentleman himself took a Shirt, and air'd it; commanding one of his Servants to help Tom to undress. Miles was strangely out o' Countenance at this, and told his Friend, that he was of Age and Ability to pull off his own Cloaths; that he never us'd to have any Valets de Chambre; (as they call'd 'em) and for his Part, he was asham'd, and sorry that so worshipful a Gentleman should take the Trouble to warm a Shirt for him. Besides (added he) chave Heat enough (zure) to warm my Shirt. In short, he put on his Shirt, half Shirt, his Cloaths and all Appurtenances, as modishly as the best Valet de Chambre in Paris could. When Miles was dress'd, his Friend told him, That he believ'd he look'd then more like himself than ever he had done since his Return to England. Ah! Noble Sir! said Miles. Vine Feathers make vine Birds. But pray, Sir, Why must I wear Mourning? Because there is a particular Friend of mine dead, for whose Loss I can never sufficiently mourn my self; and therefore I desire that all whom I love should mourn with me for him, return'd the Gentleman; not but that there are three other Suits in Hand for you at this Time. Miles began then to suspect something of his Father's Death, which had like to have made him betray his Grief at his Eyes; which his Friend perceiving, took him by the Hand, and said, Here, my dear Friend! To the Memory of my departed Friend! You are so very like what he was, considering your Difference in Years, that I can't choose but love you next to my Wife and my own Sister. Ah! Sir! (said he, and lapping his Handkerchief to his Eyes) How can I deserve this of you? I have told you (reply'd t'other.) But - Come! Take your Glass, and about with it! He did so; and they were indifferently pleasant, the Subject of Discourse being chang'd, 'till about a quarter after Five; when the Gentleman call'd to pay, and took Coach with Miles only, for the Gun-Tavern; where he order'd a very noble Supper to be got ready with all Expedition; mean while they entertain'd one another, in a Room as distant from the Officers as the House would permit: Miles relating to his new Friend all his Misfortunes Abroad, but still disguising the true Occasion of his leaving England. Something more than an Hour after, one of the Drawers came to let 'em know, that Supper was just going to be serv'd up. They went then directly to the Officers, whom they found all together, with two or three Gentlemen more of their Acquaintance: They all saluted the Gentleman who had invited 'em first, and then complimented Miles, whom they mistook for another Friend of the Gentleman's that gave 'em the Invitation; not in the least imagining that it was Tom Lostall. When they were all sat, the Captain ask'd, Where is our trusty and well-beloved Friend Mr. Thomas Lostall? Most honoured Captain! (reply'd Miles) I am here, most humbly at your Honour's Service, and all my other noble Officers. Ha! Tom! (cry'd the Lieutenant) I thought indeed when thou first cam'st in, that I should have seen that hardy Face of thine before. Face, Hands, Body, and Heart and all, are at your, all your Honours Service, as long as I live. We doubt it not, dear Tom! (return'd his Officers, unanimously.) Come, noble Gentlemen! (interrupted Miles's Friend) Supper is here, let us fall to: I doubt not that after Supper I shall surprise you farther. They then fell to eating heartily; and after the Table was clear'd they drank merrily: At last, after the King's, Queen's, Duke's, and all the Royal Family's, and the Officers Healths, his Friend begg'd that he might begin a Health to Tom Lostall; which was carry'd about very heartily; every one had a good Word for him, one commending his Bravery, another, his ready Obedience; and a third, his Knowledge in material Discipline, &c. 'till at length it grew late, their Stomachs grew heavy, and their Heads light; when the Gentleman, Miles's Friend, calling for a Bill, he found it amounted to seven Pounds ten Shillings, odd Pence, which he whisper'd Tom Lostall to pay; who was in a Manner Thunder-struck at so strange a Sound; but, recollecting himself, he return'd, That if his Friend pleas'd, he would leave his Cloak, and any Thing else, 'till the House were farther satisfy'd: T'other said, He was sure Miles had Money enough about him to discharge two such Bills: To which Miles reply'd, That if he had any Money about him, 'twas none of his own, and that 'twas certainly conjur'd into his Pockets. No Matter how it came there (said t'other;) but you have above twenty Pounds about you of your own Money: Pray feel. Miles then felt, and pull'd out as much Silver as he could grasp, and laid it down on the Table. Hang this white Pelf; (cry'd his Friend) pay it in Gold, like your self, Come, apply your Hand to another Pocket: He did so, and brought out as many Broad-Pieces as Hand could hold. Now (continu'd his Friend) give the Waiter eight of 'em, and let him take the Overplus for his Attendance. Miles readily obey'd, and they were Very Welcome, Gentlemen.

Now, honoured Captain, (said his Friend) and you, Gentlemen, his other worthy Officers, be pleas'd to receive your Soldier, as Sir Miles Hardyman, Bar., Son to the late Sir Henry Hardyman of Somersetshire, my dear and honoured Brother-in-Law: Who is certainly, the most unhappy Wretch crawling on Earth! (interrupted Miles) O just Heaven! (persu'd he) How have I been rack'd in my Soul ever since the Impious Vow I made, that I never would see my dearest Father more! This is neither a Time nor Place to vent your Sorrows, my dearest Brother! (said his Friend, tenderly embracing him.) I have something now more material than your Expressions of Grief can be here, since your honoured Father has been dead these five Years almost: Which is to let you know, that you are now Master of four thousand Pounds a Year; and if you will forgive me two Years Revenue, I will refund the rest, and put you into immediate and quiet Possession; which I promise before all this worthy and honourable Company. To which Miles return'd, That he did not deserve to inherit one Foot of his Father's Lands, tho' they were entail'd on him, since he had been so strangely undutiful; and that he rather thought his Friend ought to enjoy it all in Right of his Sister, who never offended his Father in the whole Course of her Life: But, I beseech you, Sir, (continu'd he to his Friend) how long is it since I have been so happy in so good and generous a Brother-in-Law? Some Months before Sir Henry our Father dy'd, who gave us his latest Blessing, except that which his last Breath bequeath'd and sigh'd after you. O undutiful and ungrateful Villain that I am, to so kind, and so indulgent, and so merciful a Father: (cry'd Miles) But Heaven, I fear, has farther Punishments in Store for so profligate a Wretch and so disobedient a Son. But your Name, Sir, if you please? (persu'd he to his Brother) I am Lewis Constance, whom once you unhappily mistook for your Rival. Unhappily, indeed: (return'd Miles) I thought I had seen you before. Ay, Sir, (return'd Constance) but you could never think to have seen me again, when you wounded and left me for dead, within a Mile of my House. O! thou art brave, (cry'd his Brother, embracing him affectionately) 'tis too much Happiness, for such a Reprobate to find so true a Friend and so just a Brother. This, this does in some

Measure compensate for the Loss of so dear a Father. Take, take all, my Brother! (persu'd he, kissing Lewis's Cheek) Take all thou hast receiv'd of what is call'd mine, and share my whole Estate with me: But pardon me, I beseech you my most honour'd Officers, and all you Gentlemen here present, (continu'd he to the whole Company, who sate silent and gazing at one another, on the Occasion of so unusual an Adventure) pardon the Effects of Grief and Joy in a distracted Creature! O, Sir Miles, (cry'd his Captain) we grieve for your Misfortune, and rejoice at your Happiness in so noble a Friend and so just a Brother. Miles then went on, and gave the Company a full but short Account of the Occasion of all his Troubles, and of all his Accidents he met with both Abroad and at Home, to the first Day that Constance saw him digging in the Tower-Ditch. About one that Morning, which preceded that Afternoon (persu'd he) whereon I saw my dear Brother here, then a Stranger to me, I dream'd I saw my Father at a Distance, and heard him calling to me to quit my honourable Employment in his Majesty's Service: This (my Thought) he repeated seven or nine Times, I know not which; but I was so disturb'd at it, that I began to wake, and with my Eyes but half open was preparing to rise; when I fancy'd I felt a cold Hand take me by the Hand, and force me on my hard Bolster again, with these Words, take thy Rest, Miles! This I confess did somewhat surprize me; but I concluded, 'twas the Effect of my Melancholy, which, indeed, has held me ever since I last left England: I therefore resolutely started up, and jump'd out of Bed, designing to leave you, and sit up with my Fellow-Soldiers on the Guard; but just then I heard the Watchman cry, Past one a Clock and a Star-light Morning; when, considering that I was to be at Work in the Ditch by four a Clock, I went to Bed again, and slumber'd, doz'd, and dream'd, 'til Four; ever when I turn'd me, still hearing, as I foolishly imagin'd, my Father crying to me, Miles! Sleep, my Miles! Go not to that nasty Place, nor do such servile Offices! tho' thou dost, I'll have thee out this Day, nay, I will pull thee out: And then I foolishly imagin'd, that the same cold Hand pull'd me out of the Ditch; and being in less than a Minute's Time perfectly awake, I found my self on my Feet in the Middle of the Room; I soon put on my Cloaths then, and went to my Labour. Were you thus disturb'd when you were Abroad? (the Captain ask'd) O worse, Sir, (answer'd Miles) especially on a Tuesday Night, a little after One, being the Twelfth of November, New Style, I was wak'd by a Voice, which (methought) cry'd, Miles, Miles, Miles! Get hence, go Home, go to England! I was startled at it, but regarded it only as proceeding from my going to Sleep with a full Stomach, and so endeavour'd to sleep again, which I did, till a second Time it rouz'd me, with Miles twice repeated, hazard not thy Life here in a foreign Service! Home! to England! to England! to England! This disturb'd me much more than at first; but, after I had lay'n awake near half an Hour, and heard nothing of it all that Time, I assur'd my self 'twas nothing but a Dream, and so once more address'd my self to Sleep, which I enjoy'd without Interruption for above two Hours; when I was the third Time alarm'd, and that with a louder Voice, which cry'd, as twice before, Miles! Miles! Miles! Miles! Go Home! Go to England! Hazard not thy Soul here! At which I started up, and with a faultering Speech, and Eyes half sear'd together, I cry'd, In the Name of Heaven, who calls? Thy Father, Miles: Go Home! Go Home! Go Home! (it said.) O then I knew, I mean, I thought I knew it was my Father's Voice; and turning to the Bed-Side, from whence the Sound proceeded, I saw, these Eyes then open, these very Eyes, at least, my Soul saw my Father, my own dear Father, lifting up his joined Hands, as if he begg'd me to return to England. I saw him beg it of me. O Heaven! The Father begs it of the Son! O obstinate, rebellious, cruel, unnatural, barbarous, inhuman Son! Why did not I go Home then! Why did I not from that Moment begin my Journey to England? But I hope, e'er long, I shall begin a better. Here his o'ercharg'd Heart found some little Relief at his Eyes, and they confess'd his Mother: But he soon resum'd the Man, and then Constance said, Did you ne'er dream of your Sister, Sir? Yes, often, Brother, (return'd Miles) but then most particularly, before e'er I heard the first Call of the Voice; when (my Thought) I saw her in Tears by my Bed Side, kneeling with a Gentleman, whom I thought I had once seen; but knew him not then, tho', now I recal my Dream, the Face was exactly yours. 'Twas I, indeed, Sir, (return'd Lewis) who bore her Company, with Tears, at your Father's Bed-Side; and at twelve a Clock at Night your Father dy'd. But come, Sir, (persu'd he) 'tis now near twelve a Clock, and there is Company waits for you at Home, at my House here in Town; I humbly beg the Captain's Leave, that I may rob 'em of so dutiful a Soldier for a Week or two. Sir, (return'd the Captain) Sir Miles knows how to command himself, and may command us when he pleases. Captain, Lieutenant, and Ensign, (reply'd Sir Miles) I am, and ever will continue, during Life, your most dutiful Soldier, and your most obedient and humble Servant. Thus they parted.

As soon as Constance was got within Doors, his Lady and Sir Miles's Sister, who both did expect him that Night, came running into the Hall to welcome him? his Sister embrac'd and kiss'd him twenty and twenty Times again, dropping Tears of Joy and Grief, whilst his Mistress stood a little Distance, weeping sincerely for Joy to see her Love return'd: But long he did not suffer her in that Posture; for, breaking from his Sister's tender Embraces, with a seasonable Compliment he ran to his Mistress, and kneeling, kiss'd her Hand, when she was going to kneel to him; which he perceiving, started up and took her in his Arms, and there, it may be presum'd, they kiss'd and talk'd prettily; 'till her Brother perswaded 'em to retire into the Parlour, where he propos'd to 'em that they should marry on the very next morning; and accordingly they were, after Lewis had deliver'd all Sir Henry's Estate to Sir Miles, and given him Bills on his Banker for the Payment of ten thousand Pounds, being the Moiety of Sir Miles's Revenue for five Years. Before they went to Church, Sir Miles, who then had on a rich bridal Suit, borrow'd his Brother's best Coach, and both he and Lewis went and fetch'd the Captain, Lieutenant, and Ensign, to be Witnesses of their Marriage. The Captain gave the Bride, and afterwards they feasted and laugh'd heartily, 'till Twelve at Night, when the Bride was put to Bed; and there was not a Officer of 'em all, who would not have been glad to have gone to Bed to her; but Sir Miles better supply'd their Places.

NOTES: The Unhappy Mistake.

The Jack. The small bowl placed as a mark for the players to aim at. cf. Cymbeline II, i: 'Was there ever man had such luck! when I kissed the jack upon an up-cast to be hit away!'

The Block. cf. Florio (1598). 'Buttino, a maister or mistres of boules or coites whereat the plaiers cast or playe; some call it the blocke.'

Vor Mainly be our Country Word, zure. Wright, English Dialect Dictionary, gives apposite quotations for 'mainly' from Gloucester, Wilts and Devon. He also has two quotations, Somerset and West Somerset for 'main' used adverbially. But 'mainly' is also quite common in that county.

The Gun. A well-known house of call. 2 June, 1668, Pepys 'stopped and drank at the Gun'.

A Broad piece. This very common name was 'applied after the introduction of the guinea in 1663 to the "Unite" or 20 shilling pieces (Jacobus and Carolus) of the preceeding reigns, which were much broader and thinner than the new milled coinage.'

APHRA BEHN – A SHORT BIOGRAPHY

Aphra Behn was baptised on December 14th in 1640.

Although she was a prolific and well established writer in her own lifetime facts about her remain scant and difficult to confirm. What can safely be said though is that Aphra Behn is now regarded as a key English playwright and a major figure in Restoration theatre

In fact even where and to whom she was born are subject to discussion.

According to which account you read – and there are many – Aphra was born in Harbledown, near Canterbury. Another that she was born to a barber, John Amis and his wife Amy. Or again she was born to a couple named Cooper.

In the "The Histories And Novels of the Late Ingenious Mrs. Behn" (1696) it is written that Aphra was born to Bartholomew Johnson, a barber, and Elizabeth Denham, a wet-nurse. However a claim by Colonel Thomas Colepeper, who states he knew her as a child, wrote in Adversaria that she was born at "Sturry or Canterbury" to a Mr Johnson and that she had a sister named Frances. Anne Kingsmill Finch, Countess of Winchilsea, a poetic contemporary, says that Aphra was born in Wye in Kent, and was the 'Daughter to a Barber.'

None of these accounts can be relied upon and it follows that with so few facts the early part of her life cannot be clearly illustrated.

However what can be accurately suggested is that Aphra was born in the rising tensions to the English Civil War. Obviously a time of much division and difficulty as the King and Parliament, and their respective forces, came ever closer to conflict.

But still facts do not reveal themselves in any quantity. As a young woman a version exists of Aphra's journeying to Surinam with Bartholomew Johnson. He was said to have died on the journey, leaving his wife and children spending some months in the country. It is during this trip that Aphra claims to have met an African slave leader. These experiences formed the basis for one of her most famous works, "Oroonoko". In "Oroonoko" Behn Aphra gifts herself the position of narrator and her first biographer accepted the proposition that Aphra was indeed the daughter of the lieutenant general of Surinam, as in the story. There is little evidence to support this case, and none of her contemporaries acknowledge this, or any, aristocratic status. There is also no evidence that Oroonoko existed as an actual person or that any such slave revolt, is anything but an invention.

However it is possible that she acted a spy in the colony. Possibilities exist. Perhaps Aphra re-wrote her own history as and when it suited her needs at the time.

The common method of gathering information in these times was Church records and for a few, tax records. Aphra Behn is mentioned in neither. As well as Aphra Behn or Mrs Behn she was, at times, also known as Ann Behn, Mrs Bean, agent 160 and Astrea.

Shortly after her supposed return to England from Surinam in 1664, Aphra may have married Johan Behn (also written as Johann and John Behn). He could have been a merchant of German or Dutch extraction, possibly from Hamburg. He died or the couple separated that same year, however from this point we can be sure Aphra used the title "Mrs Behn" as her professional name.

There is some suggestion that Aphra may have been a Catholic or at least leaned towards this school of faith. She once commented that she was "designed for a nun." Many of those around her were Catholic, such as Henry Neville who was later arrested for his Catholicism, and this would have aroused suspicions during the anti-Catholic fervour of the 1680s. She was a monarchist, and her sympathy for the Stuarts, and particularly for the Catholic Duke of York may be demonstrated by her dedication of her play "The Rover, Part II" to him after he had been exiled for the second time. Aphra was dedicated to the restored King Charles II. As political parties emerged during this time, Aphra became a Tory supporter.

By 1666 Aphra had become attached to the court. Domestically the Plague was sweeping the Nation and the Great Fire was about to erupt through London. In foreign affairs England and the Netherlands had engaged in The Second Anglo-Dutch War from 1665. Aphra was recruited as a political spy in Antwerp on behalf of King Charles II, possibly in league with Thomas Killigrew.

This is probably the beginning of more accurate records on Aphra's life. Her code name is said to have been Astrea (though there are others), a name under which she later published many of her writings. Her chief duty was to establish a relationship with William Scot, son of Thomas Scot, a regicide who had been executed in 1660. Scot was believed to be ready to become a spy in the English service and to report on the activities of the English exiles who were thought to be plotting against the King. Aphra arrived in Bruges in July 1666 with a mission to secure Scot into a double agent, but there is evidence that Scot would betray her to the Dutch.

Aphra however found life as a spy not quite the romantic interlude that many assume would be the case. She arrived unprepared; the cost of living shocked her, and after a month, she had to pawn her jewellery. King Charles was slow in paying, either for her services or for her expenses whilst abroad. She had to borrow money so she could return to London, where she spent a year petitioning King Charles for payment unsuccessfully. A short while later a warrant was issued for her arrest, but little to suggest it was actually served or that she went to prison for her debt.

The death of her husband and her debts seemed to push her towards a more sustainable and substantial career. Aphra began work for the King's Company and the Duke's Company players as a scribe. These were, in fact, the only two licensed theatre groups in London. The theatres had been closed under Cromwell and were now re-opening under Charles II and a more liberal atmosphere. Theatre technology was being imported from Europe and being integrated into the staging of some plays. It was a great moment on which to embark upon a career in theatre.

Aphra who had previously only written poetry now embarked on such a career. Her first, "The Forc'd Marriage", was staged in 1670, followed by "The Amorous Prince" (1671). After her third play, "The Dutch Lover", fails to please Aphra had a three year lull in her writing career. Again it is speculated that she went travelling again, possibly once again as a spy.

After this sojourn her writing moves towards comic works, which prove commercially more successful. Her most popular works included "The Rover" and "Love-Letters Between a Nobleman and His Sister" (1684–87).

With her growing reputation Aphra became friends with many of the most notable writers of the day. This is The Age of Dryden and his literary dominance. As well as his friendship she includes also those of Elizabeth Barry, John Hoyle, Thomas Otway and Edward Ravenscroft, and was also attached to the circle of the Earl of Rochester.

Aphra often used her plays to attack the parliamentary Whigs claiming, "In public spirits call'd, good o' th' Commonwealth... So tho' by different ways the fever seize...in all 'tis one and the same mad disease." This was Aphra's criticism to parliament which had denied the king funds.

From the mid 1680's Aphra's health began to decline. This was exacerbated by her continual state of debt and descent into poverty.

In 1687 she published A Discovery of New Worlds, a translation of a French popularisation of astronomy, Entretiens sur la pluralité des mondes, by Bernard le Bovier de Fontenelle, written as a novel in a form similar to her own work, but with her new, religiously oriented preface.

As her end approached in 1689 it became increasingly hard for her to even hold a pen though her desire to continue to write was unquenchable. In her final days, she wrote the translation of the final book of Abraham Cowley's Six Books of Plants.

Aphra Behn died on April 16th 1689, and is buried in the East Cloister of Westminster Abbey. The inscription on her tombstone reads: "Here lies a Proof that Wit can never be Defence enough against Mortality." She was quoted as stating that she had led a "life dedicated to pleasure and poetry."

Her legacy is broad. Firstly as a woman she broke down many of the barriers which regarded only men as writers, especially in the commercial arena. In all she would write and have performed 19 plays, contribute to more, and become one of the first prolific, high-profile female dramatists in these Isles.

In her own golden age of the 1670s and 1680s she was one of the most productive playwrights in Britain, second only to the immense talents of the Poet Laureate John Dryden.

Much of her work has been criticised for its bawdy tone as well as its masculine form but needs must and she was working to live, to survive, and to widen her spread as an author.

She received widespread support from many other successful writers including Thomas Otway, Nahum Tate (also a Poet Laureate), Jacob Tonson, Nathaniel Lee and Thomas Creech.

Aphra is now rightly seen as a key dramatist of the seventeenth-century theatre. Her prose vitally important to the on-going development of the English novel.

Following Aphra's death new female dramatists such as 'Ariadne', Delarivier Manley, Mary Fix, Susanna Centlivre and Catherine Trotter acknowledged Behn as an inspiration who opened up the public space for women writers to be accepted.

In succeeding centuries her appreciation has been volatile. For instance in the morally reserved Victorian clime both the writer and her works were ignored or dismissed as indecent. The Victorian novelist and critic Julia Kavanagh wrote, "the disgrace of Aphra Behn is that, instead of raising man to woman's moral standard, she sank woman to the level of man's coarseness".

However by the 20th century, however, Aphra's fame was back in fashion. Since then her works have been well appreciated and her place in our literary pantheon assured.

APHRA BEHN – A CONCISE BIBLIOGRAPHY

Plays
The Forced Marriage (1670)
The Amorous Prince (1671)
The Dutch Lover (1673)
Abdelazer (1676)
The Town Fop (1676)
The Rover, Part I (1677)
Sir Patient Fancy (1678)
The Feigned Courtesans (1679)
The Young King (1679)
The False Count (1681)
The Rover, Part II (1681)
The Roundheads (1681)
The City Heiress (1682)
Like Father, Like Son (1682)
Prologue and Epilogue to Romulus and Hersilia, or The Sabine War (November 1682)
The Lucky Chance (1686) with composer John Blow
The Emperor of the Moon (1687)
The Widow Ranter (1689)
The Younger Brother (1696)

Novels
The Fair Jilt
Agnes de Castro
Love-Letters Between a Nobleman and His Sister (1684)
Oroonoko (1688)

Short Stories
The Fair Jilt (1688)
The History of the Nun: or, the Fair Vow-Breaker (1688)
The History of the Servant
The Lover-Boy of Germany
The Girl Who Loved the German Lover-Boy

Poetry Collections
Poems upon Several Occasions, with A Voyage to the Island of Love (1684)
Lycidus; or, The Lover in Fashion (1688)